PENGUI

THE CONCERT TICKET

Olga Grushin was born in Moscow in 1971. Her novel *The Dream Life of Sukhanov* was shortlisted for the Orange Award for New Writers 2006 and the *LA Times* Seidenbaum Award for First Fiction 2006. Grushin was selected as one of *Granta*'s Best Young American Novelists 2007. Her writing has appeared in the *Guardian*, *Granta* and the *Partisan Review*. She lives in Washington, D.C. with her husband and two children.

The Concert Ticket

OLGA GRUSHIN

PENGUIN BOOKS

PENGUIN BOOKS

Published by the Penguin Group
Penguin Books Ltd, 80 Strand, London WC2R ORL, England
Penguin Group (USA) Inc., 375 Hudson Street, New York, New York 10014, USA
Penguin Group (Canada), 90 Eglinton Avenue East, Suite 700, Toronto, Ontario, Canada M4P 2Y3
(a division of Pearson Penguin Canada Inc.)
Penguin Ireland, 25 St Stephen's Green, Dublin 2, Ireland (a division of Penguin Books Ltd)
Penguin Group (Australia), 250 Camberwell Road, Camberwell, Victoria 3124, Australia
(a division of Pearson Australia Group Pty Ltd)
Penguin Books India Pvt Ltd, 11 Community Centre, Panchsheel Park, New Delhi – 110 017, India
Penguin Group (NZ), 67 Apollo Drive, Rosedale, North Shore 0632, New Zealand
(a division of Pearson New Zealand Ltd)
Penguin Books (South Africa) (Pty) Ltd, 24 Sturdee Avenue, Rosebank, Johannesburg 2196, South Africa

Penguin Books Ltd, Registered Offices: 80 Strand, London WC2R ORL, England

www.penguin.com

First published as *The Line* in the USA by G. P. Putnam's Sons,
a member of Penguin Group (USA) Inc. 2010
First published as *The Concert Ticket* in Great Britain by Viking 2010
Published in Penguin Books 2011

1

Printed in England by Clays Ltd, St Ives plc

ISBN: 978-0-141-04482-8

www.greenpenguin.co.uk

IN MEMORIAM
BORIS GRUSHIN, MY FATHER

I WISH THERE HAD BEEN MORE TIME.

For we are saved by hope: but hope that is seen is not hope:
for what a man seeth, why doth he yet hope for?
But if we hope for that we see not, then do we with patience wait for it.

—ROMANS 8:24–25

PART ONE

WINTER

1

"WHO'S LAST IN LINE? Are you last in line? What are they selling?"

"No idea, but I'm hoping for something good. Maybe some gloves, my hands are cold."

"Imported scarves, I've heard."

"Oh, are they silk? And what color? Blue would be nice. Or green."

"You don't want much, do you, woman? Silk scarves, indeed! It's toothpaste, someone told me."

"Toothpaste? Toothpaste?! You idiot, would all these people wait here for toothpaste?"

"What's wrong with toothpaste? I could use some."

"By the looks of your teeth, it would be the first time."

"Oh, shut up!"

"Shut up yourself!"

"Both of you shut up, it's not toothpaste. A man up front was saying they just received a shipment of women's boots, genuine leather."

"Ooh, I'd love some of those! Where is that man, I'll ask him myself."

"He got tired of waiting and left half an hour ago."

"Nah, a full hour at least."

"Two hours, more like it. I could still feel my fingers back then."

"Well, can't be boots, or he wouldn't have left."

"But what if he wasn't married, now? What would he need with a pair of women's boots if he wasn't married?"

"Maybe he has a lady friend."

"A lady friend! Do you hear that, a lady friend, and him with a mug like that—worse than that fellow over there!"

"Hey, what—did he just call me ugly? . . . You there, yes, you, did you just call me ugly?"

"And what if I did, what are you going to do about it?"

"I'll show you who's ugly, let me just get a hold of you, move there, people, move—"

"Hey, watch your elbows, there's an old man back here, don't push!"

"And who are *you* to tell me what to do?"

"No, no, I wouldn't . . . Wait, I wasn't—you misunderstood—I—"

"Good, good, knock some of his teeth out, help him save on the toothpaste!"

"Oh God, there she goes again with the toothpaste! It's not toothpaste, it's not toothpaste, you stupid cow, how many times must you be told, it's not toothpaste!"

"Oh, bother, looks like no one knows what they're selling. Could be something really good, though . . . Well, I have some time on my hands, might as well join in for a while. Are you last in line?"

2

ONE DAY IN NOVEMBER, returning home from work, Anna walked a different way. Her usual street was flooded with a spontaneous citizens' parade celebrating the thirty-seventh anniversary of the Change. Ordinarily she enjoyed such diversions, but today she felt too tired to shuffle for hours in a press of other passersby, even though she knew her husband was likely to be marching, his tuba propped up on his shoulder, in the midst of the volunteer neighborhood band whose dull brass snails were even now crawling up behind her, devouring the city in an explosion of triumphant sound.

It was only three o'clock in the afternoon, but the air hung heavy with the nearing of the night, the swelling of the snow. The world smelled of heated copper and wilting carnations. In a few blocks, the streets grew deserted; everyone had left for the demonstration, and the neighborhood, on the outskirts of the city, lay bare, damp, and gray, like the bottom of some northern sea with its dregs exposed by a receding tide. Anna's flat-heeled shoes fell to the pavements with loud thumps. Striding quickly as if trying to escape the echoes of her passage, she turned into an alley, crossed a courtyard, its sky elimi-

nated by gloomy, drooping buildings, rounded a corner—and slowed
her steps.

A small crowd of fifteen or twenty people stood lining the sidewalk before her; autumn's last brown leaves twirled above the dark
curves of their backs. Another parade preparing to set off, Anna decided after a moment, and walked faster now, clutching her bag to
her chest.

As she drew even with them, an old man turned toward her.

"Join us," he said.

She wanted to move past, then stopped, afraid that her refusal to
take part in the communal merriment might appear unpatriotic—
but already she noticed that the people on the sidewalk did not
resemble a joyful gathering of neighbors. Hushed and oddly solitary, they waved no homemade banners, chanted no slogans; she
saw an aged woman leaning on a cane, a youth with the sharpened
cheekbones of someone recently ill. Uncertain, she looked back at
the man who had spoken. He was dressed in a threadbare, earth-
colored coat; the stealthily creeping shadows had eaten away most
of his face, becoming tangled in his untidy beard, gouging deep lines
in the parchment of his skin, pooling his eyes with darkness. His un-
blinking, sorrowful gaze unsettled Anna, and she glanced away—
and it was then that she saw the kiosk.

She had been wrong, she realized, relaxing her grip on the bag.
This was not a parade—merely a line. The little kiosk before her was
nondescript, with no sign above it. Its single window was boarded
shut, a handwritten notice tacked onto it; she was too far away to
read the words. She could not recall seeing any kiosk here before, but
then, it had been so long since she had last found herself deviating
from her daily route—months, maybe even a couple of years, possibly longer; time had all run together for quite a while, merging into
a solid, hard, flat essence, a bit like concrete, she thought unexpectedly, yes, like a vat of frozen concrete, undistinguished save for a
succession of doled-out State festivities, a smattering of red and yel-

low candy wrappers sucked here and there into the concrete's mono-lithic mass.

Not that she was complaining, of course. She had a good life, such a good life.

They all did.

"So what are they selling here?" she asked.

The old man smiled, and as his wrinkles multiplied, a deeper darkness suffused them.

"What would you like?" he said softly.

"I'm sorry?"

"They are selling," he said, "whatever you'd most like to have. What would you like?"

She stared at him. A leaf slowly sailed through the congealed air. The people around them were quiet, their faces hazy, averted. The old man is mad, she understood with a precipitate chill, and stepped away abruptly. The sign in the window, she saw as she hastened past, announced in a scrawl: *Gone to the parade*. There were more words scribbled below, but she did not stop to decipher them, keeping her eyes focused on some invisible, faraway destination instead, sensing all the while the weight of the old man's gaze upon her, sliding the length of her, from her hair, along her back, to the scuffed-up soles of her shoes.

That night, she waited for her husband to return from his march before calling the family to supper. It was, perhaps, the uncustom-ary lateness of the hour that made the kitchen seem somehow smaller, darker than usual; the black-and-white clock up on the wall, big, round, and bare-faced just like a clock at a train station, had presided indifferently over the departure of the last fleeting light, the arrival of the slow, ponderous shadows. From her corner at the stove, pretending to spoon a second serving into her bowl, Anna watched her mother mince a morsel of meat, watched her son listlessly construct a potato fortification all along the rim of his plate, lumpy towers rising, then mash it into dust. When, having finished their silent meal, her mother and son departed, she poured two cups of tea, added a cube of sugar to hers, and for another minute watched her husband blow at the scalding liquid, his mouth set in sullen lines, his jaws moving in some internal rhythm she could not follow.

At last, suppressing a sigh, she turned away, looked out the window. Through the gap in the curtains, which rippled faintly with the insidious autumnal drafts, the night gazed back at her with a gentle face molded by light, obscured by shadow, reshaped by darkness into a hazy semblance of a once familiar, soft, youthful beauty.

"Something strange happened to me this afternoon," she said quietly, as if to herself. "I was walking down this empty street, and—"

He glanced up sharply. "You didn't go to the parade?"

Anna's eyes met the eyes of the woman floating outside, and the night seemed to fill those eyes to the brim. She turned back to her husband.

"No, no," she said. "I went. Of course I went, to hear you play. It was very good, I mean wonderful as always, of course."

"Of course," he said, but his voice had deflated, and he resumed sloshing the weak tea in his cup. She waited, then dropped another sugar cube into her water, listened to it fall with a small plop, took a sip. Her husband asked nothing else, and after a while she stood up, crossed to the sink, and carefully poured out her nearly full cup.

The next few weeks at school were very busy, and Anna soon forgot about the gathering of people at the kiosk, until one day in December, between classes, she came upon two teachers whispering in the corridor. As she paused at a bulletin board to pin the announcement of the annual composition contest ("The Revolutionary Hero I Would Most Like to Meet" was this year's topic), she overheard

Tatyana Alekseyevna say in an agitated undertone, "It appeared out of nowhere not long ago, and no one, no one at all, knows what they're selling!"

"But doesn't it have a sign?" Emilia Khristianovna asked.

Anna lingered with the thumbtack in the hollow of her hand, pretending to skim the other notices, her back suddenly tense.

"No, there's no sign, nothing at all. But I heard this wild rumor—"

The bell thrashed shrilly above their heads. She looked back just in time to see the math teacher bend to shout the end of the sentence into the physics teacher's ear and the physics teacher ripple like dough in inaudible astonishment. She was tempted to intrude, but Tatyana Alekseyevna had already tied her lips into a prim little bow and pranced off down the hall, trailing a mawkish vanilla scent in her wake, while Emilia Khristianovna had been rolled away in the opposite direction by a stampede of children late for class.

With a sigh, Anna pushed the thumbtack into the board.

That afternoon, on her way home, she found herself halting for a moment at a turn in the road, then, feeling vaguely embarrassed, continued straight; but in the soggy predawn hours of that night, with the wind rattling the windowpanes on their sixth floor and the world the shade of lead, she dreamed of turning left, and reaching the street with the kiosk. The dream street did not resemble the actual street, that graying afterthought of a shortcut with an abandoned old church at one end, a fence meandering like a sparsely toothed grin at the other, a row of dour six-story buildings in between. It was a slice of some outlandish town instead, like nothing she had ever seen, with a ruined clock tower rising like an accusing finger where the church should have been, eggshells and potato scum running down the gutters, and bald, faceless mannequins contorted in flooded shop windows—yet as she rushed past, her hair flying in a honey-smelling, sun-colored halo about her head, her arms heaped with flowers, she knew the street to be the same. The people were there still, waiting, but she had no desire to stop. She kept glancing at her hands—the delicate, smooth hands, with pearly pink petals of perfect fingernails and a lovely ring on one finger. And then that mad old man lifted his face to her, and his eyes were two round black mirrors, with clouds and branches and her own self reflected in them; but in his eyes she saw no honey mane of hair and no flowers, only an aging, badly combed woman in a shapeless brown skirt.

Anna disliked dreams. Dreams had an unpredictable, shimmering quality to them, seemed to her to be cut from the same illusory, wavering, precarious essence as life before the Change, the way she imagined it from history lessons, at least; she had been too young to remember much herself. Hers was a good life, a stable life. None of them ever went hungry, their apartment was warm in winter, they had their fair share of comforts and, too, more than a few accomplishments; last spring, for instance, she had been named District Teacher of the Year and received a roll of red silk—not real silk, but very smooth and gleaming all the same—from which she had made two pretty pillows for the bed. Not everything was perfect, of course, but if she could change one thing, any one thing, about her life, she was not sure what that thing would be, because her life was good, she said to herself once again as she sat behind her desk in class later that day. But as she thought it, her lips must have moved, or perhaps she even whispered it half audibly, for a few children stopped writing and were now staring at her with flat, incurious eyes resembling buttons and beetles. Looking down quickly, she found herself studying her hands, the weathered, naked hands of a woman no longer young, with blunt nails and fingers that were too short, their tips crumbling with pale chalk—and then she knew where she would go as soon as she was set free into the glittering white stretch of the afternoon.

When she turned into the street, she let out a gasp. More than fifty people stood before the kiosk, back after back, taking over the width of the sidewalk. The kiosk was closed as before, another sheet of paper pasted to its shuttered window.

She approached, squinted at the almost illegible scribble.

Gone to dinner, said the notice. *Back after three.*

She consulted her watch—it was two-thirty—then looked back at the line.

"So, what are they selling?" she asked.

A wide-faced woman in a fur hat, her mouth painted the color of ripe cherries, shrugged.

"I'm hoping for imported leather boots," she said.

"Children's coats, I heard," a man behind her offered shyly.

"You imbecile, they don't sell children's coats in kiosks," hissed a massive old woman next to him. "Cakes is my guess. Layered cakes with coconut shavings on top." She smacked her lips. "The kiosk by the tram stop had them last week, but they ran out before my turn."

"No one knows, then," Anna said thoughtfully, and checked her watch again. She had half an hour to spare. Of course, on any other day, she would hardly consider wasting her time waiting for God knew what. Today, though—today was different; today, she realized suddenly, she wanted to be surprised; felt entitled to a surprise, in truth. Making up her mind, she hurried down the line, blinking at the snow; the descending sun made things bright and hazy, breaking the city into blinding triangles of chill and brilliance. She took her place at the end. A cake would be lucky, she mused—she loved the anticipation of a sweet mouthful traveling down her tongue, narrowing the whole universe to a pinpoint of one flaking, sugar-sprinkled moment—but of course, she would like any number of nice things: a pair of sheer stockings with their faintly chemical smell, for instance, or a ruby-red drop of nail polish in a square glass bottle, or a smooth pebble of jasmine soap. Once, on a winter afternoon just like this, she had chanced upon a kiosk selling oranges; true, the oranges had turned out to be sour and riddled with hard, bitter seeds, but their smell had been beautiful, beautiful, making her remember something she had not known she remembered, something from the dimmest reaches of childhood: the twilight deepening in a great, silk-lined, velvet-cushioned space, the majestic swaying of crimson and gold as the curtain rose, the rush of sound and motion and color, the stiffness of the lacy collar scratching her chin, the porous spiraling of the aromatic rind under her clumsy fingers as she leaned over the padded edge of the balcony, struggling to peel an orange, her eyes on the stage, now on the fruit, now on the stage again, and the disembodied voice, her father's voice, breathing into her ear, "There—there she is, in white, do you see her—"

"What are you waiting for?" someone asked.

The question startled her out of her reverie into a world that was being swiftly drained of color. Gray hollows were already stretching by her feet like shadowy, somnolent beasts wearied by the passing of another day. Lazy snowflakes wandered through the air.

She frowned at the pale, skinny boy before her; she did not recognize him from school. He could not be more than ten; she was reminded of her own son when he had been that age, though the boy looked nothing like him.

"I don't think anyone knows," she said.

"But if you don't know what it is," said the boy, "how do you know you need it?"

He wore no mittens, was cradling one hand in the other.

"I'm sure it will be something good," Anna replied patiently. "Otherwise all these people wouldn't be here."

The boy appeared puzzled. His eyes were two tiny pieces of a wintry sky; she could see herself in them, just like in her dream— two dark little figures drowning in a swirling of clouds, then gone in a blink, erased by a sweep of eyelashes wet with snow.

"And in any case," she said impulsively, "it's better this way, not knowing. It might be something you don't *need* but really like. Like a present. Like flowers—"

She stopped, embarrassed. The boy breathed pensively on his fingers.

She watched the curling of his breath.

"I wonder if Mama would like it," he said. "Whatever it is."

"It might be perfume," suggested a girl a few steps back.

The line had continued to grow all the while.

Anna glanced at her watch and was astonished to see that it was after four. "Would you like to take my place?" she asked. "I have to go, they'll be worried about me at home."

"Let him wait his turn like everyone else," spat out someone behind her.

"That's right, he isn't with you, woman!" another voice shouted.

"He's just a boy," said Anna reproachfully, but the boy had already slunk away. "Shame," she sighed, not certain what she meant precisely. Then, having cast one last glance at the boarded window, she ran through the disappearing city.

She burst into their apartment all out of breath, rehearsing some plausible explanation for being late—for some reason, she felt reluctant to confess to her futile two-hour wait in the waning light of the year—but no one asked her. She busied herself at the stove. At seven o'clock, they sat down to supper; her husband had been granted an evening off for the occasion. When she began to pour hot water over damp, odorless tea leaves saved from the previous teatime, her mother rose and, as always, wordlessly departed for her room. Anna set three cups on the table, looked from her husband to her son across the shadows of the dim, stuffy kitchen.

"I was hoping to buy a cake for tonight," she announced brightly.

"A cake's always good," her son rejoined without enthusiasm.

In a small hush, she could hear the clock's hand rustling toward the next minute, the gulp of liquid traveling down her husband's throat. "Do you remember," he said without raising his head, "in the old days, they put those skinny candles into birthday cakes, as many candles as you had years, and then you'd make a wish and blow them out?"

She laughed and protested in a flirtatious, insincere voice: "No, no, there wouldn't have been space enough!"—yet already imagining the swoosh of the air escaping her lungs, the flickering dance of forty-three candles casting warm spells of golden-red light upon the convexity of the teacups, the concavity of the spoons, before rearing up and dying all at once—already wondering what she would have wished for, what special, unexpected, lovely thing . . .

Her husband did not contradict her but stared into his cup instead, and her son said, "Well, anyway, happy birthday!"

The boy's face wore a startled expression, as if he'd only now remembered.

That night, tiptoeing along the unlit corridor, Anna collided with her mother, and her mother wound her thin arms about Anna and stood clinging to her for a moment, light as a bird, then, releasing her, flitted away, as before, in silence.

Anna gazed after her, not moving. In the darkness ahead, the door shut softly.

The next morning, she chanced to leave the house early, so she had time to walk the longer way; it was, after all, not that much of a detour, only a few extra blocks. The sun had not yet risen, and the kiosk was still closed—most places did not open until nine—but people were already starting to come by, drifting down sidewalks like pockets and patches of the departing night in the limpid green twilight of the last predawn hour. Noticing the bright-mouthed woman in the fur hat at the end of the line, Anna approached with hesitant steps.

"Good day. You may remember me—I was here yesterday, but I had to go—"

The woman regarded her blankly, her eyelids gleaming with lavender sleekness.

"Please, what did they end up selling?"

"A big fat nothing," the woman said, flicking her flimsy scarf over her shoulder. "The cursed kiosk never reopened. Today's the day, though, I can feel it. Whatever it is, it'll go fast."

"Oh." Anna fiddled with her glove to keep from staring at the mesmerizing rotation of the woman's earrings. "If you don't mind . . . I have to go to work for a few hours—a school just around the corner—I'm a literature teacher . . . Would you be so kind as to hold the place for me, I'll come as soon as I can—"

"The nerve," said the woman indifferently. "The nerve of it. You think just because you're educated, you don't have to wait like everyone else?"

"Oh no, it's not . . . I didn't . . . I'll be happy to replace you as soon as I . . . I mean, we could take turns—"

A few shadows around them tsked and shook their heads, and the woman turned away with a liquid toss of her earrings. Mortified, Anna pulled her gloves back on and stumbled off without looking up; but all day in school she felt stabs of acute shame at the memory of her audacity, mixed with a profound impatience that made her yearn to rush out in the middle of class, not waiting for the pupil to finish reciting "Ode to the Industrial Accomplishments of the Eastern Region," and fly down the white streets, her unbuttoned coat flapping behind her. She felt like crying when the vice-principal, dropping by during her last hour, moved his pale fishlike lips and gleefully informed her that she must stay a while longer, to supervise a boy in detention. It was after five o'clock when she finally gathered her papers, struggled into the tight confinement of her sleeves. The night had already drawn its shutters over the city; windows were glowing with dull, steady lights, and the sky waved back and forth in a skeletal dance of black branches. She arrived just in time to see the line dispersing, to see the woman in the fur hat disappearing into the darkness with furious strides. The kiosk was boarded once again.

Slowly she came closer, and stopped. There was a new notice pasted to the window.

She strained to read it in the wavering light of the streetlamp, the branches' shadows constantly tossed over the words, and at last made it out.

Closed for accounting. Back on Monday.

Footsteps shuffled behind her. A man was plodding away, his face blotted out by a raised collar, his shoulders hunched against the wind, muttering, "They think they can do anything, do they? Some joker comes by, puts up this garbage, then just saunters off—"

Her heart started to beat. "Excuse me," she called out, "but— could you tell me—did they say what they would be selling? On Monday?"

She discovered that she was afraid of the answer—afraid that the night would throw back at her: "Laundry powder!" or "Socks!" She no longer wanted it to be a mundane, a trivial, thing. It was as if, unreasonable as she knew it to be, she had really begun to think of— of whatever it was—as some sort of a mystery birthday present meant for her.

The man was half a block away now, almost invisible, a denser darkness in the dark, but his words sliced sharp and angry through the empty street: "Nobody knows, woman! Why don't you wait in line yourself if you're so curious?"

Exhaling, Anna gathered up her bags and walked through the snow, raising small sparkling flurries with each step. At the corner, the mad old man from her dream sat on the curb, drawing some glowing symbol in the air with the burning tip of his cigarette; she smiled absently as she passed him, was smiling still as she unlocked her door.

She spent the next few days distracted, moving mindlessly

through her chores and routines. On Sunday night, the night before
the kiosk was set to open, she lay in bed unable to sleep, watching
rare headlights stumble over the lump of her slumbering husband,
thinking of the day, five, no, not five, seven years ago now (they
had been celebrating Three Glorious Decades since the Change, and
the city had shaken with garlands of festive flags mauled by the
November wind)—the day when she had brought home the square
tin box.

There had been a picture on the lid—an elephant under some
exotic-looking, richly embroidered cloth in vibrant red and yellow
patterns. She had hesitated to open it for the longest time, sitting
alone at the kitchen table, cradling the box in her hands under the
feeble glare of the lightbulb. At last she carefully slid the edge of a
knife around the lid to loosen it, then prodded it free, releasing that
dry, dense, delicious fragrance that did not smell of anything exactly
and yet, she found, seemed to contain within it a wealth of other
smells. They tumbled one after another into the cramped kitchen—
the bright watermelon aroma of a chilly sunrise in the country in
May, the intoxicating daffodil sweetness of a full-mooned June
evening, the grassy ripeness of July on the veranda of a light-walled
house tipping into the blue well of the night on a wave of laughter.
    Funny, she thought, how her memory kept the smells, kept them
perfectly, collected them like precious, rare specimens laid out on the
black velvet lining of its few secret drawers, ready to spill its darkly
glittering secrets whenever a long-forgotten smell sprang its lid
open. Her mother had rented that house the last summer before the
Change. There had been other children there, neighbors, friends. In
an immediate, breathless rush, she recalled spoons clicking against
cups, and the charmed, weightless leaps of the sad melody her mother
had played so much on that funny rickety piano as their guests gathered for tea. Anna had never had an ear for music—indeed, she did

not even like music all that much, she preferred the quiet—but this melody was special, it was sad and simple and special, and every time she had heard it, it had been as if someone's cold, agile, silver-tipped fingers had slid swiftly up and down the clavichord of her spine.

She tried to hum it as she bent over the tin box with the elephant on its cover, but the tune proved elusive. Then the floor creaked, and her mother was looking at her, her eyes quiet, her long, painfully thin fingers pulling the purple velvet of her old robe tight at her throat. Anna struggled to empty her face of all traces of happiness— and then her mother spoke.

"Real eastern tea, how nice, shall we have a cup together?" she said in a casual, even voice, quite as if she spoke to Anna all the time, quite as if she had not maintained an aloof, maddening silence for so many years—and Anna felt that she had been granted permission to keep the happiness on her face just a while longer, and had to turn away and stare at the impossibly straight silhouette of her mother in their kitchen window, to hide the sudden welling in her eyes.

She had saved the box after the tea was gone, of course. Every so often, when sure that no one was watching, she would open it and press her nose against its cold metallic insides and breathe, and breathe, and try to remember; but no new memories came, the music did not distill into a clearer melody, and after some time, her mother reverted to her habitual thin-lipped silence. In another year or two Anna filled the box with an assortment of mismatched buttons. Her son had impatient fingers and was always pulling buttons off his clothes.

On Monday morning, she did the unthinkable: she rang her school and sneezed into the phone. "Oh yes, there's a flu going around," said the secretary sympathetically. "Emilia Khristianovna's sick also. Squeeze a lemon into hot water."

"I will," Anna lied, and dressed quickly, then extracted the family's savings from inside a sock in the bureau's bottom drawer (just in case, one never knew, it might be something pricey), and walked out, pressing her handbag to her chest.

It was early, but some thirty or forty people already stood before the kiosk. One of them, a stocky woman in felt boots, rather resembled the physics teacher, but a garish knit scarf obscured her face, and Anna was not sure. She pulled her own scarf closer to her eyes all the same; then, opening the book she had brought along—the latest collection by the country's most honored poet, whose work she frequently assigned to her pupils for memorization—she began to read, forming the words half volubly, a teacher's habit:

> *The works of cruel gods*
> *In ruins lie.*
> *Above the crumbs of columns*
> *Swallows fly.*
> *And men are joyful*
> *Slavery to avoid.*
> *Where mighty temples stood*
> *Now lies—*

"Ah," said a voice behind her, "here already? Mind if I join?"

Today her lipstick was an unbecoming shade of orange, Anna noted with spite.

"You shouldn't be cutting in front of anyone," she said. "The end's over there."

The line was swelling rapidly.

"Fine, I wasn't asking you for a favor anyway," the woman announced airily, and walked off with a haughty click of her elegant earrings.

"I hope they run out of it just before your turn!" Anna cried, and, just as the squat woman who might or might not have been Emilia Khristianovna appeared to twitch in her direction, hastily hid behind her volume, embarrassed already by her unlikely outburst.

For an hour or two she tried to read, but found the poems difficult to like, whether because she could not concentrate or for some other reason. As the morning condensed into a dreary afternoon and the strengthening wind started to throw heavy hours back and forth like smudged, icy snowballs, she shut the book decisively and stood still, listening to conversations rise and collide and fade around her. People argued about the unknown merchandise at the end of their wait; every so often someone abandoned the line after much complaining; others joined. Anna soon gathered that over the past two months the kiosk had become a neighborhood obsession. It had appeared in the fall, but, unlike other local kiosks, which, regularly and with no secrecy, dispensed cheap cigarettes and vegetables or, on thrilling and brief occasions, chocolates and cosmetics, this kiosk had never sold anything at all, not even on those rare days when a fake blonde with a pasty face made surly appearances in the kiosk window. The woman would answer no questions, thereby deepening the general suspicion of some momentous mystery. As weeks went by, speculation and agitation only mounted. Rumors had spread; people whispered of imported crystal or ingenious toys or exclusive book subscriptions, or tickets for a new State lottery in which one could win an automobile or a vacation by the sea. An enterprising man had recently begun to take bets on the day of the week and the time of day when the nebulous something would finally go on sale. There were, of course, a few nonbelievers—"cynical, dried-out souls," a man behind Anna grumbled—who predicted it would turn out to be something pathetic, say canned soup or matches, and who often came by the line to mock the trusting fools freezing off varied pieces of their anatomy; but many of those who lived nearby made it a habit to spend at least a couple of weekly hours at the kiosk, just in case. A handful even arrived by tram from farther out, and there were not a few, among housewives and pensioners, who waited daily. And the more Anna heard, the more filled she was with a sure presentiment of a change, whether small or boundless she did not know—but in any case, something, she thought, to make her and her family happier, or lend some simple beauty to her everyday life, or perhaps even infuse her entire existence, working into its minute cracks and voids, knitting it into a tighter, brighter, fuller fabric.

Shortly after four, the line surged forward. She felt someone's chin prodding her back, and, looking up, saw a uniformed man unlocking the kiosk door. In the next moment her nose was driven into the back before her, her face flattened against a damp coat, her body trapped in a crush of other bodies.

"What's happening, I can't see," she pleaded, her words muffled.

An exhalation brushed her ear: "The shutter's been lifted!"

The world closed in on her, brown and hushed, warm with collectively held breath. The next minute stretched on, slowly, inexorably, spreading outward like a dense, viscous spill. A sharp heel grazed her foot; something hard and angular smashed painfully against her hip. She closed her eyes, let her whole being go still, settled into the faintly sour, furtive scents of wet wool and steaming whispers and anticipation.

The line sagged in a moan.

"Not another *scribble!*" a woman's wail rose.

"A notice? What does it say?"

Someone read aloud: *Out with flu. Will reopen in January.*

The crowd slackened. Anna fought her way clear of coats, knees, and elbows just in time to see the shutter chomping down. The uniformed man emerged, manipulated the lock on the door. In the dejected silence, she could hear the muted screech of metal resisting metal, could smell the rust. As the man strolled away, she wanted terribly to follow, to ask, to demand, but she did not move.

No one did.

Then a polite voice called out: "Pardon me, but what might they be selling here, exactly?"

The uniformed man continued to walk away as if he had not heard.

"I don't know about you," said the bright-lipped woman, flying past in a blur of silk and fur, "but I've just about had enough of this!" People muttered, dispersing. Anna lingered for a while longer, even though it was clear to her that no one else was going to appear, nothing else was going to happen. At last she too turned toward home. She had, of course, resolved to be here on the first day of the new year. Surprisingly, she did not seem to mind all that much.

She felt purposeful and light, and strangely hopeful, as she moved along the darkening streets, chased by the dull rhythm of her flat heels slapping the frozen pavements.

3

A FEW DAYS LATER, Sergei woke up in a mood of suppressed anticipation. He tried to steel himself against disappointment, convinced that fate would do its best to cheat him yet again at the last possible moment: the director telephoning to inform him that his services for the evening were no longer required, or else his slipping in the street on the way and breaking an arm, or—or any number of scenarios on which he preferred not to dwell. He moved through his day with deliberation, pretending that nothing out of the ordinary awaited him. He ate an unhurried breakfast, perused the front page of a newspaper, then spent his customary two or three hours behind the closed bedroom door playing what his wife called his "songs."

He knew, of course, that such rigorous practicing was excessive, since the music he was routinely called upon to perform was of a crude, simple nature—brass exclamations punctuating anthems and marches, not worth his time, not worth his breath, not worth the very air he sent vibrating. He despised it, in fact; despised, too, those of his fellow citizens who, uncoerced, attended his band's performances or, year after year, meekly followed its hollow booming as the parades rolled through the streets. Despising it, he indulged in it daily all the same. The mere act of fleshing out a series of notes on his tuba always filled his chest with an expansive, cresting excitement, until, closing his eyes, he could imagine other instruments weaving into the phrase, swelling with a full orchestral glory, the melody in his mind moving farther and farther away from the threadbare score before him, sounding more and more like the brilliant, complex, unique symphony he had dreamed of hearing, and playing, for so long.

Tonight, he thought, he would get his chance at last.

He had not told his wife for fear of jinxing it.

At three o'clock, setting his tuba aside, he meticulously polished his special-occasion shoes, removed a few invisible dust motes from the lapels of his best suit, and started to get dressed; he chose not to notice that the jacket had grown somewhat tight in the armpits. At three-thirty, fully attired, he looked at his watch, picked up the tuba, and practiced some more. As the low, furry-clawed sounds resumed shuffling up and down invisible stairs like clumsy circus bears, the musically challenged downstairs neighbor again began to bang her broom against her ceiling; he did his best to ignore her. At four he laid the tuba down, looked at his watch, found a remnant of the morning newspaper, read an editorial. At three minutes past four, he sighed. At five minutes past, he looked at his watch. At seven minutes, he crumpled the newspaper, grabbed his tuba, threw the bedroom door open, and plunged into the corridor.

The corridor was hazy with smoke. He fought his way into the kitchen, coughing. Soft blue dusk was already rising in the solitary kitchen window like water poured slowly into a glass; beneath it, a splayed chicken corpse lay decomposing on the plastic tablecloth in a pool of oily lamplight. His wife stood at the stove, wagging a ladle in a pot.

"I'm afraid the onions will be a bit crisp," she said with an apologetic smile, and glanced up, and paused in her stirring. "Oh, Serezha, you didn't have to, it's just the four of us, nothing fancy—but you do look really—"

He bent his head to adjust the knot of his tie.

"Yes, that," he mumbled. "I meant to tell you, we have an important engagement in the city, sort of last-minute. Ivan Anatolievich asked me in person. I won't be staying for supper."

Emitting a little gasp, she splashed her hands. The ladle clunked onto the floor, and drops flew everywhere; a murky tear of some viscous substance trickled down the wall.

He stepped back hastily, brushing at his sleeve.

"But Serezha," she said, "I've borrowed a piece of cheese and a tomato from downstairs. I was planning a soufflé for the second course. It is, after all—"

Her mother glided into the kitchen, straight and small and royal, without a word, without a noise. They watched her float gracefully between the disorder of pots and pans, pour tea into a porcelain cup with a thin gilded edge, reserved for her use alone, and glide away, her earlobes flashing with those precious earrings she always wore.

He heard a pointedly tactful click of the door closing, and breathed out.

"I must be off." He would not meet her eyes. "I'm late already."

She followed him into the hallway, stood there as he tightened his shoelaces.

"Don't forget your tuba now," she said, and added, a pitiful smile struggling on her lips, her voice flaking ever so slightly about the edges, "See you next year!"

He remembered the sound of her laughter, light and girlish, curling up at its ends into delighted little half-squeaks—in the beginning, so many years ago . . . His heart contracted. Giving his laces one final tug, he rose, opened the door with a jerk.

"Happy New Year," he said from the threshold.

She might have said something in reply, but he had already descended a flight of stairs.

The streets stretched deserted, the haloes of recently lit streetlamps turning blue with the cold. He chanced upon a miraculous trolley, boarded it with all the haste his unwieldy instrument allowed him, and from inside the jaundiced, loosely jangling, drafty box watched the frozen apartment blocks slip on ice and tumble backward into the night. Monolithic and shabby at first, the city grew brighter, less geometrical, as he approached its heart, sprouting frivolous little balconies and plump caryatids along the façades of pastel-colored palaces from distant, sleepy centuries. At last he was disgorged onto a sidewalk before an imposing yellow mansion caged behind a stern row of columns; its gates, he saw, were already letting in a timid trickle of middle-aged men in baggy coats bent all out of shape beneath their bulky burdens.

He handed his documents to the guard in a booth, shifted from foot to foot, listened to the snow moaning under his shoes. The shoes, more than a decade old, pinched.

"Proceed," the guard said.

"But my papers—"

"Proceed. You'll receive them upon departing."

The guard's stare was a lengthy coda.

He hesitated for an instant, then walked in.

There was the briefest glowing, astonishing glimpse of marble and crystal set aflame and multiplied in a great mirrored chamber visible through a succession of doorways just ahead; but already he was being ushered into a small windowless room, no different from any of the rooms in which his life customarily took place. The security search was thorough and humiliating. When it was over, he was swept along a blind corridor and down a service staircase to another windowless room, where a few of them already waited, standing awkwardly along the walls, bleak brasses gleaming, strings lifeless in their black coffins; he noticed Sviatoslav in the corner, looking oddly deflated behind the bloated barrels of his drums.

There was only one chair in the room, next to a desk piled high with folders; in the chair sprawled a sleek-haired man in a much nicer suit than his own. The man was talking. Too anxious to follow the speech—something about the honor to have been selected as the State's representatives in this bastion of foreign power, the trust that had been accorded them by the country—Sergei looked around the room, nodded to a couple of acquaintances, shifted his hold on the tuba. As his wedding ring grazed it, the metal emitted a loud, hollow clang, and he found the man's lead-colored eyes boring into his. "And do not, I repeat, do not, address or make eye contact or communicate in *any* way with *any* of them," the man said, holding Sergei with his flat, lusterless gaze. "Naturally, there is no need to remind you of the scrutiny to which each and every one of you will be subjected during and after this evening."

He smiled a thin, ominous smile and, leaning forward slowly, tapped the stack of folders on the desk. The dry sound of his knuckles scratching cardboard made Sergei's skin grow clammy, as if a nail had been deliberately dragged along a windowpane.

For a moment there was absolute stillness in the room.

"Dismissed," the man said, and, looking thoroughly bored, reached for a drawer.

Already across the threshold, Sergei cast a glance back.

The man was clipping his fingernails.

A different corridor filled with the disconcerting echoes of invisible sentries' footsteps, always seemingly marching toward them yet never arriving, led them farther down, to the basement, where the rest of the orchestra, some twenty of them altogether, had by now gathered. Another man, this one in a resplendent tuxedo, strode past them, briskly distributing sheets of music. Breathlessly, Sergei watched the tuxedo's officious progress across the room. At last his

fingers closed over his own set of pages, and a swift, chilled, delicious gust of anticipation blew through his chest, cleansing it of
fear. Anyone chosen for these events signed an oath not to disclose
anything witnessed or performed, but he had heard rumors, whispered half-confidences amidst deafening cacophonies of wearying
parades, semi-voiced intimations of flight, of daring—enough to
convince him that music from Over There was nothing like the
turgid State-sanctioned drivel that drowned his lungs every day—
enough to make him believe that tonight he would finally have
something real, something special, to play, something to justify all
the hours, the years, of practices, his neighbor stabbing the floor beneath his feet with her broom, his son slamming his door shut, his
wife tiptoeing past him, massaging away her headache, careful not
to lift toward him her dull, tortured gaze . . .

"We'll be coming for you around nine. We trust that is suffi-
cient," the man in the tuxedo said from the doorway, and, stepping
outside, closed the metal-bound door behind him.

Sergei barely registered the key forcing the lock. Impatiently,
clumsily, he tore at the score, skimmed the first page, and the second,
then brought the notes closer to his eyes; the lamps in the basement
burned low. A stretch of time passed. As the hum of blood receded
from his temples, he could suddenly hear pipes gurgling softly in
the bowels of the place, a steady rhythm of water dripping somewhere from a forgotten faucet, the wheezing of an overweight
trombone player behind him. He turned a page, frowning, scanned
another song, felt his insides yawn with a premonition of emptiness,
condensing already into bitter disbelief.

Someone issued a cough, someone else set his score down on
a chair.

"Shall we try this, then?" inquired a hearty voice. "Has everyone
familiarized themselves with the spirit of the thing?"

They cocked their instruments at the ready, began to play; and as one trite little ditty replaced another, their sounds floated about the basement, weightless as soap bubbles.

At seven o'clock, trays of food and drinks were brought in. There were tiny round flaky pastries and tiny elongated crispy pastries, delicacies stuffed with melted cheese and bits of olives, sprinkled with caviar, speckled with strange, strong-flavored meats and spices, tall glasses of emerald-green and azure-blue liquids stitched through with strings of bubbles yet not inebriating in the least. They took a break, and many started to laugh, grew flushed with excitement; Sergei alone remained seated, staring into space, the score still crucified on the note stand before him. Sviatoslav lumbered over, nudged him with a shiny elbow of his worn suit.

"What do you think this is? And have you tasted that?" he shouted, crumbs mingling with beads of sweat in his quivering mustache. "Smell it, smell it, isn't it heavenly?"

Sergei nodded vaguely, though he could smell nothing; he had been born without a sense of smell—a minor nasal deviation, he had been told as a child. "I'm not hungry," he said.

"Go on, go on, try this, you'll thank me later. What's with you, are you sick?"

He scraped something many-layered and brittle off the drummer's palm, ate it without noticing its taste.

"Out of this world, isn't it?" Sviatoslav sighed, spraying him with spittle.

"It sure is," Sergei replied, and looked away.

At a quarter to nine the door opened again, and they were each handed a spotless white shirt with a tight collar, and a tuxedo jacket with a moist white bud in a buttonhole. "No one will be able to see your pants, the way the stage is set up," they were told as they dressed. Afterward, they were led upstairs, into the chamber Sergei had glimpsed hours before, and there installed amidst the marble and the crystal in all their above-the-waist black-and-white splendor. The double doors swung outward, the ball began. Pausing between tunes, Sergei caught glimpses of glasses touching with expensively muted peals, pale green-and-silver sofas diminishing endlessly in the misty distance of the mirrors like waves of an elegant, silk-textured sea, the low notes of men's placid chins pushing forward from beneath black masks, the high notes of women's sharp chins peeking out from underneath rose-tinted masks, and lights, lights, lights, in candelabra, in chandeliers, flitting like a flock of dizzy moths under a ceiling so grand it hurt one's neck to look up.

Sergei did not look up.

At midnight the clocks started to chime in the corners, the tall windows were thrown open, and the guests cheered and kissed and tossed their masks in the air. A sliver of a silvery streamer spiraled wildly onto Sergei's sleeve. The orchestra banged and trilled. Then, gradually, the exuberant gestures wound themselves down. At a signal, the musicians ceased making noise, the chiming came to an end, the last masks descended, and all at once Sergei became aware of the silent northern night crashing through the windows in immense, hard, dark chunks of stillness and cold—and aware of everyone else in the room becoming aware of it at the same time.

There was a hush, complete, uncanny, as if an invisible hand had pressed itself against the guests' mouths. "In our city," a child's voice sounded plaintively in the hush, speaking with an exaggerated foreign accent, "if you open the windows on New Year's Eve, you hear bells ringing, crowds in the streets, singing everywhere—"

The invisible hand lifted just as suddenly, and laughter bubbled back up throughout the room. Sergei picked the streamer off his borrowed jacket, dropped it onto the floor, played another song. He had expected something else, but it was just another year—hardly worth the torment of a guard's beefy hands running up his legs.

An hour or two later, he asked for permission to visit the facilities.

The man from before, the one in the resplendent tuxedo, trained a
double-barrel gaze on his face, then motioned to a guard whose head
looked disturbingly small atop the massive expanse of his shoulders,
like a lightbulb propped up on a shelf. They moved across the ballroom in a short grim procession, the tuxedo in front, the shoulders in
the rearguard, another, upside-down procession at their feet, reflected
in the shining floors. Sergei turned to face them by the door.

"Are you going to follow me in?" he asked without expression.

The lightbulb looked at the tuxedo. The tuxedo shook his head.

"Wait for him here," he said. "And you, hurry up."

Beyond, there were more mirrors, more flowers, more marble. A
row of doors ran along the wall. Averting his eyes from the hordes
of tall, middle-aged, morose tuba players in ill-fitting jackets who
dogged his steps from mirror to mirror, he tried one of the inner
doors, was blinded by porcelain, spent some time fighting the odd
springing mechanism of the lock. After a while he heard a swelling
of noise outside his stall, a snippet of jaunty music; then, with a soft
percussive clap, the noise cut off, and two sets of steps walked across
the marble, one crisp and assured, the other shuffling, old.

Water splashed. Sergei negotiated his zipper.

"—thirty-six years ago, as I recall," said a low voice. "He left
just after the closing of the borders. Escaped across the sea. Our loss,
your gain. But are you sure?"

"Oh, quite," replied the other. "It's in all our newspapers."

The second voice had a crack running down the middle, a crack
of age—the shuffling steps, then—but what gave Sergei a start was
the accent. The speaker was a foreigner.

He checked his hand on his belt, afraid now to give away his
presence.

"Yes, imagine that, how time flies," the accented voice said,
"after all these years—" The words drowned as a cascade of water
fell into the sink, and for two or three endless minutes, frozen in
mid-movement, he heard nothing but splashing. Then the splashing

slowed to a steady trickle, and the foreigner's voice dove in and out:
". . . so they are finally allowing him . . . one concert in his home-
town . . . a new symphony he's written . . . the concert will take
place a year from now, on New Year's Eve . . . only three hundred
seats, so the tickets will be rather—"

Sergei found himself straining to hear with such intensity that
the insides of his ears were starting to ache. More water gurgled, then
the native voice swam up, speaking urgently: "—his music is so un-
orthodox, so unusual—aren't they afraid that people might—"

In the next instant, a thundering waterfall erupted under Sergei's
elbow: he had accidentally rested it on some handle that had given
way. A shocked silence rang outside, followed by the hasty retreat of
the shuffling steps, the tide of the party coming in, then rolling back.
Cursing under his breath, he tore at the lock, clambered out of the
stall—and nearly collided with a tall gray-haired man in a tuxedo,
his face concealed by a mask.

Got the steps wrong, Sergei thought mechanically.

The foreigner's hands were bleeding soap onto the marble floor,
the foaming pink suds touching down with the faintest of sighs.
Water dripped from a bright faucet, drip-drip, drip-drip-drip, a
melody lost there somewhere. Giving a small shrug, the man turned
toward the sink, and fleetingly Sergei saw the distorted, fattened reflections of his fingers slide across the faucet's silver surface—the unmistakable, immaculate fingers of a musician . . .

He took an unthinking step forward.

"The man you were talking about just now," he said in a voice
that was nothing like his own, high and pinched, "the musician
who's coming here, who is he? I too am a musician. I heard you
speak. I—"

The door yawned open, and the massive shoulders filled the
frame. The guard leveled a low-voltage stare at Sergei's face.

"Is this person bothering you, *sir*?" he asked, his voice sagging
with menace.

Sergei's heart thudded, then stopped, then fell somewhere, and he fell after it, through a trapdoor he had not known was there— into a blinding light of danger, of madness, of sheer unreality, the water dripping, the pompous lavatory, the foreign embassy, oh what have I done, what reckless, irretrievable, criminal thing have I done—

"I not understand," the foreigner said dismissively.

Frozen with mute horror, Sergei watched him dry his hands on a towel. As the guard strode along the stalls, peeking under the doors, the foreigner raised his eyes to the mirror; they glittered through the slits of the mask, calm and unreadable, but it seemed to Sergei that somewhere in the uncertain, multiplying world of reflections, a gray eye closed in a nearly imperceptible, knowing wink. Then the man was gone.

"This incident will be recorded in your dossier," the guard hissed.

Recovering his speech, Sergei began to stammer. He was one of the most reliable members of his orchestra, ask anyone, ask the drummer, he has known me all my life, he will vouch for me, ask the director, just don't put this stain on my blameless record, a simple misunderstanding, two men obeying the call of nature, could happen to anyone, I would never, I'm forty-seven years old and in all this time I never—

The heavy stare was pawing, pawing at his face.

"We will be watching you *closely*," the guard said at last. "Resume your duties."

The dim lightbulb of the guard's stare went out. He was free to return to the ballroom stage, to continue breathing a bouncy beat into his tuba.

It was close to four in the morning when they were finally divested of their tuxedos. The festivities had long since unraveled, the rooms lay empty and echoing; a solitary woman in a low-cut satin dress sat on a sofa in a corner, her mask askew, absently dropping green grapes into her gaping, drunken mouth. Sergei made his way to the exit, a trembling tightness in his stomach, praying that his documents would be returned to him without trouble. He was crossing the vestibule when, through the open front door, he saw two men smoking on the steps outside, conversing loudly in a foreign tongue. He halted. Their faces were bare now. One of them said something, and they both laughed, and tossed away their half-finished cigarettes.

"Wasteful bastards," Sviatoslav grumbled, overtaking him. "Coming?"

Recollecting himself, Sergei hurried across the threshold after the drummer, nearly slipping on the sleek polished floors; but already the two foreigners had turned to go in, and he had to step aside to let them pass. In the doorway, the taller of the two, a gray-haired man with clear gray eyes and a thin aristocratic nose, glanced at Sergei with a small yet significant smile, and a footfall later Sergei heard the soft sound of something light hitting the stones.

A flat blue box lay on the steps where the men had just stood.

He cast a panicked look around him. No one was watching. The last members of the orchestra were receiving their papers at the booth ahead, the tuxedoed backs were retreating into the mansion behind him. He bent down, grabbed the tiny box, which threw a golden flash in his eyes, nearly dropped it at the unexpected dry rattle it emitted—there was something inside—stuffed it into his pocket, and, his upper lip glistening with sweat, his heart wobbling, caught up with the other musicians.

His documents bore no mark of the evening's events.

In another two or three minutes, he was through the gates.

The embassy's façade was still ablaze, and as the light welled through the bright silk draperies, the snow along the wrought-iron fence glimmered in pale squares of crimson and green and blue. A few steps beyond, they were cast into the darkness, the chill, the si-

lence. Horns, trombones, and a timid, bug-eyed violin exchanged
dispirited farewells and trudged off in different directions; snow
crunched for some minutes, then all was quiet again.

"Well, that was some party," Sviatoslav said, his massive jowls
shuddering with a flattened yawn. "Sure, their music's fluff, but they
know how to have a good time, you have to give them that." He
brought his face close to Sergei's. "Don't tell anyone, this is risky, but
I smuggled something out for my better half, look—"

Blindly Sergei nodded at the confusion of crumbs wrapped in
a greasy napkin.

"Hey, want to drop by my place, have a drink? I tell you, the
women we saw tonight, all trotting about like giraffes in those heels!
Too skinny, though, if you ask me—"

"Listen, I'm worn out," Sergei said. "See you at the theater,
all right?"

The last of the trolleys had ceased running hours earlier, in the
previous year; the first day of January pressed heavily onto the
ground. As he strode through the deserted city, he thought of
the New Years of his childhood, before he was ten, before the
Change, when the city had still glowed with the soft, deep
enchantment of sugared angels spreading their sparkling wings in
bakery windows, and bells whose limpid sounds rose like the sea at
a moonlit tide, and glass ornaments turning slowly this way and that
on dark tree branches, gathering in their reflections the whole wondrous, promise-filled world.

His fingers were tightly curled around the mysterious object in
his pocket—his own, private communication from a different life.

He was not far from his building when he stopped. The street
did not look familiar. There was a dilapidated church at one end, a
squat little kiosk with a boarded window at the other. The solitary
streetlamp was lavender in tint, low and sickly. He withdrew his

hand, unlocked his cramping fingers, looked at the small sky-blue box on his palm. It was made of cardboard; one side was blank, the other had two words engraved on it. He deciphered the foreign script, which he had learned as a boy. *Café Apollo*, the letters spelled out in curly gold. With a careful finger, he pushed at the inside of the box, ready to receive the final mystery.

The inner compartment slipped out.

There were matches in it. Sturdy white matches with generous red and yellow tips.

Sergei gazed at the matches for a long minute, until his fingers began to burn with cold, then gave a laugh so short and harsh it sounded like a bark, and threw the foreign matchbox into the night—and the night seemed to solidify, to lunge toward him in a flowing, shifting shape. He felt a stab of indistinct yet acute fear, then, blinking, saw it was only an old man in an odd baggy cape, of the kind gnarled hermits wore in the lavish illustrated books he had found as a child underneath the glittering tree.

The old man brushed the snow off his knees, stepped forward into the light.

"Matches falling from the sky into my lap, must be my lucky day," he said, smiling. "Now, if only I could get some cigarettes. You don't smoke, do you?"

Sergei shook his head, already moving off.

"Didn't think so, or you wouldn't be throwing good matches away," the old man observed to himself. "Curious, what's this, something written on it, let me see if I can make it out, my eyes aren't what they used to be . . . 'I-gor Se-lin-sky,' yes, that's it, Igor Selinsky—"

He was back in one leap, snatching the matchbox from the old man's grasp, turning it in the streetlamp's scanty light, forgetting to breathe, yes, indeed, he had missed it somehow—the golden engraving *Café Apollo* on one side, and on the other, scribbled in a hasty, almost indecipherable hand across the matchbox's glossy underbelly: *Igor Selinsky*. He laughed and would have embraced the old man but did not, crying instead, "Keep it, keep it!"—pushing the matchbox into the man's hands, hard and twisted like ancient tree bark, and running down the streets, and up the stairs, humming, no, singing, exuberantly singing the melody that had burst with such immediate triumph into his mind, that melody he had learned to play in his tenth year—the melody that, he had once believed, would change his whole life—a deceptively simple tune, simple and sad, one of Selinsky's early pieces, yet already containing within it a promise, a dazzling promise of things that were to come but that never came, not for him, not for them, not here, not in this dark, cold place oppressed by winter—but somewhere else perhaps, yes, somewhere else for sure, somewhere luminous and bright and full of music, where life was like art and art like life, and soon to be his, theirs, here, because times were changing, because life was changing at last.

When he finally managed to control the shaking in his hands long enough to fit the key in the lock and push the door open and stumble inside, he was blinded by the light springing into life and his wife rising from the kitchen table.

"What's that you're singing?" she said, with a strange lapsing in her voice.

"Oh, Anya, you wouldn't believe what just—"

"But you're traipsing snow everywhere!" she exclaimed, and, surging toward him, fussed about, shaking him out of his wet coat. "Did you have far to walk? Your shoes must be soaked through. Here, I'll hang that . . . Do you think you've caught a cold? You'd better have a cup of tea, I'll make it for you, sit down, sit down—"

He looked at the pots in the sink, their insides clotted with grayish lumps, and the pile of thick stockings in a basket on the windowsill, waiting their turn to be mended, and his wife's broad back bending over the teakettle.

Silent now, he lowered himself onto a chair, began to pry his frozen shoelaces loose.

"Here," she said, "nice and hot, with lemon . . . So what was that song, then?"

"Just something I heard on the radio the other day," he said shortly.

He finished his cup, then walked off, leaving her at the table, and in the graying predawn bedroom fell into a humming, gleaming well, which overflowed with barely audible melodies he strove to hear through the rush of waters, and satin women playing cheerful little songs with silver spoons on ripened grapes, and, toward mid-morning, when the light outside the window had grown broad and white, the old man with the scraggly beard and deep dark eyes standing under the streetlamp before the boarded-up kiosk, smiling a cunning smile.

4

THE FIRST TWO WEEKS of January there was no school. This fact made little difference to Alexander. As always, he left the apartment in the morning, and as always, he did not go to school. The second Friday of the new year found him sitting on a bench in a small park some blocks from home, watching pigeons root through the garbage that spilled out of trash cans. He was not all that curious about pigeons—indeed, he found them revolting, the way they appeared so puffy and glossy, so cozily substantial, but would, he knew, be skinny and tremulous to the touch, tiny, mousy bodies palpitating inside a ball of feathers. All the same, sitting here, in the cold, empty park, watching the birds, whiled away the time.

When the pigeons had stuffed their bellies with trash and waddled off, he rested his head against the bench's back and did not move for many long minutes, staring upward at the flat gray sky that was sliding past him, unceasingly, quickly, spreading its wind-filled clouds like powerful sails and departing somewhere—perhaps toward another, brighter, deeper sky far, far away—leaving behind the pathetic park, the immobile city, the paralyzed day. At last he stirred as if awakening, sat up, groped for a splinter of a broken bottle under the bench, then proceeded to scratch his initials into its frozen wood; there was a bare patch amidst all the clumsy hearts, anatomical schematics, and equations that would never add up, all these adolescent confessions, $O + N = LOVE$.

"There," he said aloud when he was done. "My contribution to humanity, my immortality." He considered adding a short yet expressive word, but the glass felt brittle and icy in his gloveless fingers, and in any case, there was no room. He tossed the jagged piece into the snow and rose, and drifted through the city.

A few streets away, men were unloading large crates from a truck, slapping their padded gloves together with halfhearted grunts; he stopped and looked until one of them shooed him away. The movie theater was just around the corner, so he walked there next. The deserted foyer smelled of damp shoes and stale cigarettes growing in spittoons. He read the announcements on the wall, though without much interest: they had been running the same two features since November—a documentary called *The Anvil of Righteousness* and a historical epic, whose poster depicted three fierce-eyed, bare-chested slaves trampling into marbled dust an effeminate degenerate in a jeweled toga. He had seen neither film; he never had the money. He was just tilting his head sideways, studying a potentially promising toppled statue in the poster's lurid background, when the double doors groaned open, and there dribbled out a few people who had attended the matinee. He peered hopefully into their faces as they stumbled past him one by one; sometimes, if he caught them at the precise instant when they stepped squinting into the pale wintry light from the theater's shadows, just before they adjusted their expressions, buttoned their coats, and trudged off toward the rest of their day, he was able to see their faces naked, split open like ripened fruit—and in their eyes, raw and urgent, unhappiness, or loneliness, or yearning. Catching such glimpses gave him brief comfort—he felt less alone. Today, though, the six or seven women who emerged into the foyer looked merely tired. One of them dragged a reluctant little boy by the hand; another yawned, and paused, and glared.

"What are you gawking at?" she snarled.

Alexander moved off.

The pet shop across the road, another one of his haunts, turned out to be locked, a sign on the door stating, tersely and indefinitely: *Closed for accounting*. He pressed his nose to the dim window, trying to discern, in the gloom beyond, the enormous, dusty aquarium in which, he knew, lethargic, bleary-eyed fish were pushing through the faintly illuminated water as through thick jelly; but it was rather like peering inside a bottle of dense brown glass. He gave the door a cursory kick, then cut through an alley, crossed a courtyard, swung into a street with a kiosk at one end. He had passed here before; the kiosk never seemed to be open, yet it always had a line before it. Lines depressed him, and he strode past with quick, determined steps, debating whether to make a trip to his favorite place of all before evening fell—a place that was breathing, throbbing, heaving on the other side of the city, a private place he had sworn never to share with anyone—when someone called his name. The name was common, so he took a few more resolute steps, and heard his name again. Looking up, he saw an aging woman in a lopsided coat, with a round face and unevenly drawn eyebrows, waving at him from the thick of the line.

It took him a second to recognize her as his mother.

He wondered whether he could just keep walking, but it was obvious that she had seen that he had seen her. "Ah, Sasha, how good that you happened by!" she exclaimed, even before he approached. Her tone was unnatural, too cheerful, too loud; as she spoke, she half turned to someone behind her, though not addressing anyone exactly. Out of the corner of his eye, he saw fur and glitter, but did not care to look closer.

"What are they selling?" he said sullenly. "Tablecloths? Curtains?"

"No, not—I don't actually . . ." Her voice dipped lower. "Why? Do you think we need new curtains? In the bedroom, maybe? Have you noticed that hole? I mended it, but maybe it's—"

"Our curtains are fine," he said.

"Well, anyway, it's lucky you came by, I just remembered I haven't yet ironed your father's shirt for his *important performance tonight*"—she pronounced the words in that same unnecessarily loud voice, her head turned to the side—"so I must run home, but you won't have to wait long, no more than an hour, perhaps only forty—"

"I'm busy," he said.

"Oh, I'll be right back, half an hour, no longer. Here, take this, just in case. I don't want to lose my place, I've been here two weeks, it's supposed to reopen any day now, but of course not in the next twenty minutes. Just wait for me to get back, a quarter of an hour, all right?"

He looked at the wallet she had pressed into his hand.

"Fine," he said. "Fine. Don't rush."

Not that he was going to take any of their money, of course, despite the fact that they never gave him anything and surely owed him by now—no, he wouldn't even check how much there was, not until she rounded the corner—and not then either. He stuffed the wallet in his pocket and stood staring into space. After a while, the air abruptly grew a shade grayer, as if some giant fish in the cloudy waters over which the skies were sailing had flipped belly up, turning toward him its darker back. Snowflakes began to scratch his exposed face, hands, neck with tiny needles of wetness. "About time!" a voice shrieked ahead.

Emerging from his trance, Alexander peered into the drifting snow.

The kiosk shutter had been lifted, its insides lit. He saw the top of a woman's head bent in the window. Oh great, he thought, and I don't even know how many napkins Mother wants or whatever;

but, since the circumstances seemed to call for it, he pulled the wallet out anyway, and glanced inside—and was startled to find a handful of large bills, more than he had ever seen at once, two months' salary at least, he estimated, holding his breath now.

"Can anyone tell me what the devil they're selling?" a man's gruff voice asked in his ear.

His face hot, Alexander snapped the wallet shut. "No clue," he muttered, turning.

The man was his father's age, dressed in an oversized torn jacket, his chin unevenly sketched out with stubble, his right cheekbone slapped with the shadow of an old bruise.

"Hold my place, will you," he said happily, sending an exhalation of mingled drink and sweat toward Alexander, and ambled off.

"Thinks he's smarter than everyone else, that one," someone threw after him with disapproval. "Better men have tried and failed."

The line was already contracting, gathering itself, rearing up like a caterpillar about to creep forth. Alexander waited, clutching the wallet tightly. People shuffled forward one by one; he could now make out, in the glare of the lightbulb, the darkening roots of the kiosk woman's bright hair. The afternoon was just beginning to vibrate with the aftershocks of some heated altercation at the kiosk window when the man in the torn jacket returned.

"Concert tickets," he declared, and spat richly on the ground. "Can you believe it? All these fools have waited days for *concert tickets!*"

The announcement dropped into the crowd, and a heavy, open-mouthed silence settled on it. Then a chorus of troubled voices rippled through, widening like circles on the water.

"Concert?"

"Did someone say 'concert'?"

"What kind of concert, did you hear?"

The man choked on a curt laugh. "Folk dancing, boot-slapping, waltzing, violin-trilling, it's all the same to me, I'm not hanging around for some symphony. It's freezing, my throat's dry, I'm off to get myself something to warm up and cheer the soul. How about it, my friend?"

"Me? Sure, whatever," Alexander said with a nonchalant shrug, and abandoned his place in the line.

They moved through the frozen black-and-white city in silence.

"So, do your tastes run to simple or refined?" the man asked after a few blocks.

Alexander looked at him blankly.

"Vodka or cognac?" the man elaborated.

Alexander thought of the time when he and two classmates had met after school, emptied their pockets of ice cream money, bus money, absentminded neighbors' money, sent in the tallest of the three, whose upper lip was already shaded with the premonition of a mustache, and afterward sat for some hours on a bench in the park, waiting for the darkness to dim their eager conspiratorial faces. Later they passed the bottle one to another until the world grew bright and angry before turning muddled, which was when the third classmate, the one without a mustache, claimed that this stuff wasn't real vodka anyway but some horrible cheap concoction corroding their innards, even as he took another, unfairly generous swill, and that it probably wouldn't burn if they set a match to it. Alexander left to accost frightened passersby for matches, and by the time he came back his two classmates had quarreled terribly and the shorter of the two had a cracked lip, though in the end he turned out to have been right, for a poisonous purplish, or maybe bluish, flame flickered briefly, then went out, and Alexander was spectacularly sick in the bushes.

"I'm a cognac man," he said.

"Excellent, I know just the thing, then," said the man merrily.

They strode through the streets, diving into alleys, cutting across passageways, walking in the shadow of a drunken fence for a spell. Alexander prided himself on knowing his neighborhood down to every boil of graffiti on its concrete expanses, but he was beginning to feel disoriented by the time the man stopped to pull open the door of an old apartment building. Pale spills of the January daylight dimly fleshed out an unclean staircase descending into nether regions, its top steps gleaming with the slush of many snow-coated footsteps.

Alexander hesitated on the threshold. He had no idea where he was.

"Care to join me, then?" the man's voice boomed from the bottom of the stairs. "Don't worry, you'll be all right if you stick with me." And when Alexander caught up, the slippery steps he had run down resounding like deep, rapid beats in his heart, he guessed at a quick brightening of the man's teeth in the underground murk. "Of course, if you tell anyone about this little place, well—" Smiling still, the man drew a finger across his throat.

With a cold kind of thrill, Alexander realized he did not know whether the man was joking.

They traveled through low, faintly lit corridors at a brisk pace, pipes erupting moistly beside them, pockets of sudden hot air gushing into their faces with the concentrated smells of fried onions and detergent from the floors above. Then the man veered off, threw his shoulder against a wall. Invisible hinges moaned, and unexpectedly they were outside, stepping into a large courtyard closed off by low buildings.

Alexander halted. A derelict church slumped among the snowdrifts in the middle of the yard, gilt still streaking down its domes, shallow lakes of paint splashed on the peeling plaster. Of course, there were dozens like it in the city, tucked away in many forgotten, decaying corners, some with laundry drying between the twisted columns of their porches, others echoing shelters for colonies of crows or packs of homeless dogs; yet what surprised him about this one was the restless, purposeful activity he seemed to detect underneath its sagging arches.

He squinted to see better.

Strikingly stylish fellows were darting in and out of the gaping doorway.

"Hey there, you awake?" the man tossed over his shoulder as he too disappeared inside the ruin. Alexander ran.

When the church's shadow fell over him, the brisk, frosty air of the midwinter day seemed to alter, growing somehow looser, damper; unsettling smells of urine, dust, and dissolution reached him through the slits of the empty windows above. Again he hesitated, then, with a small shudder, followed the echoes of the man's assured steps inside. The sun had not yet set, but it was almost night within; the chill deepened here, and the cavernous dimness hung heavy on the crossing beams of many lanterns. Their flares of cold white light called into transient existence the hands, boots, faces of men loitering among a bewildering profusion of objects piled on invisible crates along the walls or revealed in brief flashes from under the sleek lining of the men's leather jackets. As Alexander hurried across the ancient stones, trying not to wonder about the unpleasant sound of something bone-dry crunching underfoot, he glimpsed a bouquet of silver spoons with intricate handles; a pitcher with a pointy stopper that broke a flashlight's ray into pieces and threw one jagged bright edge into his eyes; a fanned-out pack of curious-looking pictures, which appeared tantalizingly as so many pale curves in the shifting twilight and at which he wouldn't have minded taking a closer peek; a magnificent, hefty knife, right next to the cracked icon of an old saint whose stark gaze condensed out of the darkness and pursued him uncomfortably for a few steps before melting back into the darkness; a small army of bottles glinting in a pool of light from a kerosene lamp hanging on a hook overhead—

"Just what we need," said the man, braking so precipitately that Alexander nearly smashed into him. "You can always count on Stepan to deliver the goods. This one, I think."

The fellow he addressed bent to pick up a plump bottle with a swelling of wax on its long throat; as his face passed in and out of a strip of light, Alexander saw a youth who looked to be only two or three years older than himself, with a short, angry scar under his left eye.

Straightening, the youth held up the bottle, named the price in a voice at once contemptuous and uneasy. Alexander swallowed.

"Could have just bought a fiver from a State store, sure," said the man, "but I figured you'd appreciate the best there is. It's from Over There, you know." He paused; in the dimness, Alexander could hear him patting his jacket, rustling inside his pockets. "Bad luck, it appears I've left my funds at home. Well, next time, perhaps—"

"My treat," said Alexander, stepping forward into the lamplight. "I'm flush today."

Producing his wallet with a casual flourish, he leafed through the bills, then cast the smallest of glances at his companion.

"Good of you," said the man. "Anything else your heart desires? Look around, go on."

It might have been only the treacherous flickering of the shadows, but he did not appear overly impressed, or indeed all that surprised—and almost immediately Alexander felt his shaky surge of elation grow hollow, flutter into his stomach like the queasiness of indigestion.

"That knife over there," he said tersely, as if arguing with someone.

The man nodded, already turning to go.

Back in the sickly light of the basement, the man beat the snow off his shoes, then expertly sliced through the bottle's wax with the knife's edge, pulled out the sweet-smelling cork, and took a slow swig. Alexander stared at his bobbing Adam's apple, bristling with rough, graying hairs. Lowering the bottle, the man wiped his lips and looked back at him.

Alexander stretched out his hand.

The man went on looking at him in silence—and all at once, Alexander became aware of the echoing isolation of the stairwell and the man's burly bulk and the tumorous growth of his mother's wallet in his pocket. His hand wavered, but he did not withdraw it.

"My turn," he said harshly.

The hush crept on, for one instant, and two, and three. Then, abruptly baring his large, bright teeth, the man slapped Alexander on the back and passed him the knife and the bottle. "I see you're worried about your better half missing the money," he said, "so here's what you do—spin her a tale that you were mugged, gets you loads of sympathy. Me and the boys had a bit too much fun the other day, but it worked like a charm, always does."

Alexander's throat, clenched only moments before, was swept open in a vast gulp of relief, and he spluttered at the shock of the scalding yet somehow smooth taste sliding downward, slicing through his innards as through butter. "My better half, yeah!" Laughing now, he wiped his mouth with his sleeve, just as the man had done, and laughed again, flushed with pleasure.

"Don't hoard it, you must share with your fellow citizens," said the man. "By the way, name's Nikolai, no need to stand on ceremony here . . . So, where to now, my friend?"

Alexander took another deep gulp before handing over the bottle. His expansive feeling had returned. "Well, Nikolai," he said, "there is this one place I happen to know—"

Two hours later they were sitting shoulder to shoulder on the steps leading down to the platforms, watching the trains below labori-

ously peel themselves off the tracks and edge out of the station—
rickety, drafty little trains with broken windows, shuttling back and
forth between the city and nearby provincial towns, disgorging from
their jerking, smoky interiors drab streams of people, baskets, bags,
dogs, buckets, cages, dust; and the other, rarer kind, whose softly
lit windows stayed blank with drawn curtains the shade of warm
cream, whose doors slid open soundlessly to allow in small knots
of orderly passengers with bulky suitcases, whose carriages displayed neat little plaques with the names of their long-distance
destinations.

Alexander was talking. He might have been talking for quite some
time, because his throat ached; he was not sure. He was telling a story.
He had taken an overnight train once, on a class excursion. "Back
when I was still in school," he added for clarity. The teacher had
brought a whole roasted chicken, and they ate it cold, in the dark
compartment; the light had burned out, but they liked it better that
way. There was a full moon, and he pushed down the window and
the moon ran along the train for hours, for hours, and the wind came
gusting into his face, and it smelled of all sorts of strange, wonderful, wild things, like the sea and wet grass and great, mossy woods.
One time they were passing this black plain, and he saw three or four
pale horses running. He hadn't known there were still horses out
there. He sang too, everyone sang. The conductor came by with a
clinking tray, and the glasses were set in these beautiful filigree holders, and they drank tea, snug in a hollow of some small hour after
midnight. No one slept. In the morning, when they arrived, the city
was much like this one—ugly new buildings on the outskirts,
neglected old buildings in the center, fences and kiosks and ruined
churches everywhere—but the train, the train had been different.

He had never told this to anyone, and it felt liberating and frightening at once to tell it now. To be honest, he was not certain he was
speaking all that clearly, because some of his words, quite a few of
his words perhaps, while flowing with perfect ease, even eloquence,

in his mind, tended to stumble and fall into pits that kept opening
with an alarming regularity in the middle of his sentences. But
Nikolai listened, and nodded, and drank, and he drank too, and the
trains kept pulling in and out of the station, their windows burning
brighter and brighter as the night moved in, until the trains themselves became barely visible and the clatter of wheels seemed to rush
ribbons of fiery squares out into the darkness, toward strange, secret
destinations, toward unknown cities far, far away.

They sat in companionable silence for a long while. The snow
had stopped falling. Alexander felt very warm inside. The crowds
thinned, then grew dense, then began to thin again.

"This is good," he said at last. "Right now I don't even mind
about all that time stuff."

"What time stuff?"

"You know how, when you're growing up, your father tells you
life is short and you need to set your goals and work hard and all
that drivel, or you'll wake up one day and realize your time has run
out or something? . . . Hey, give me that, my turn . . . Anyway, I
used to believe him when I was, you know, young. As if time were
some real thing you can lose or save or spill or break or put on a shelf.
You must hoard it grain by grain, I remember he told me once."

"Like sand in an hourglass," Nikolai said, nodding thoughtfully.
"An hourglass compartment of your soul. So to speak."

Alexander stared at him.

"Kind of like that, yeah," he said then, and tipped the bottle into
his mouth.

"Your father's wise."

"No, he isn't. He works in this pathetic little place with a bunch
of losers. He doesn't know anything. See, the way I figure it, life
isn't short. It's long. Too long. I don't want to save time, see, I want
to kill it. I mean, look at all this useless time we have—days and
hours and months and years and . . . and whatever comes after

that . . . but nothing ever changes, no matter what we do with it, do you understand? Not here, anyway . . . I guess, though, it could be different in other places . . . It probably is, don't you think?"

"Well, some things change." Nikolai wrested the bottle away from him, held it up to the light, shook it roughly. "See, almost gone now."

He guffawed, or else hiccuped.

Alexander did not take his eyes off the tracks. "I come here a lot," he said sternly. "Just to watch. But one day I'll save enough money, and board one of these trains, and go—go far away." He touched the wallet, still in his pocket, then frowned into the night, which dipped and shimmered in thrilling but disorienting ways before his eyes.

"East or West?" Nikolai asked.

"What?"

"You want to go East or West?"

Alexander giggled at the joke. No one ever went West anymore, except for diplomats and other important persons on special State missions; the borders had been closed for decades. Of course, not that many people went East, either: one needed work permits, residency registration, relocation documents, security clearance . . . Or at least he thought that one did; he had seen the conductors study passengers' papers before letting them board.

"Yeah, I used to think about it myself," Nikolai said. "Hey, watch where you're stepping, people sitting here! . . . Goes down smooth, doesn't it? Mind if I . . . ? The gold mines in the East, the forests, the lakes—they say the water out there is bright blue, so blue you wouldn't believe it, and the trees so green, I dreamed of seeing it all when I was your age."

"I'm color-blind," Alexander announced.

Nikolai opened his mouth, threw his head back, and there was his Adam's apple again, wobbling up and down while he laughed.

Watching it move, Alexander was unexpectedly seized with a vague worry. An enormous clock was hovering over the platform, but the numbers glowed with an unpleasant neon haze, melting into one another, making it impossible to see what time it was. He supposed he was feeling a bit . . . yes, just a little bit . . .

"Color-blind? Isn't that like a family disease or something? Your parents have it too?"

"No, they see colors fine. Mother's tone-deaf, though, and—" He was going to say something witty, something witty about his family, but instead blurted out, "She wouldn't want tickets to any concert, so that was all right, leaving the line like that . . . I mean, she wouldn't want to go, anyway."

Nikolai stopped laughing, was quiet for a minute.

"My daughter loves music," he said then. "Violins, symphonies, pretty melodies . . . She doesn't get out much, though. And the symphonies, when they sell the tickets, they're never for today or to-morrow. It's stupid to throw money away on things like that. I mean, who knows if next November or December we're even going to be—well, you know."

"My parents believe I'll enroll in the university in the fall," said Alexander. "After I finish with school. But I won't. There's no point. I'll just—"

A guttural voice, interrupting, rumbled a long, incoherent an-nouncement from a speaker.

"Hey, listen, did you hear that?" Nikolai said, grabbing Alexan-der's arm.

"What language was it in?" said Alexander, and chuckled. "Get it? What language—"

"No, listen, that's the weekly eastern, crosses the whole coun-try. Leaves in two hours. Go. You have the money. Go. You'll be dipping your toes in the eastern sea come next week."

"Very funny. You need all kinds of papers and stuff—"

"All you need is your passport and a ticket. You're sixteen, right, old enough to have a passport? Two hours is plenty of time for you to go home, grab your things, get back here. Go."

And suddenly Alexander feels a chill of coherence, a draft at the back of his head as if a window has opened there, and everything that has happened to him this day, that has ever happened to him, begins to make sense, the way he knew it would when he was given that wallet in that street, that remote street somewhere—the fence, the kiosk, the elderly men and women waiting, waiting for nothing—but not him, no, not him, because for him, he believes now, he has always believed, yes, for him there will be a splash of cold waves on a remote, desolate, beautiful shore, and strange birds dipping and rising overhead, and whispers of tall silver trees, and horses running, and the sea, the sea, rippling paths of invisible whales and fishing boats and sunrises so majestic he will see their flaming, golden colors at last . . .

He stumbles to his feet, and his legs buckle, but it's all right, he can stand all right if he just leans against something, someone, if he just . . .

"Easy, easy there," says his best friend, laughing. "I'll wait for you right here, on the steps . . . And tell you what, why don't I buy your ticket for you, just give me the—"

Perfect, perfect idea, he replies, or maybe he only thinks it, but in any case, here's some, is this enough, well, just a couple more, then, yes, that should do it, I don't have much left, anyway, just enough for a tram home and back, I'll see you in just a bit . . . Some steps to navigate here, must be careful, very slippery, oh and look, a tram, there's a tram, but they don't want him to board for some reason, which is fine with him, he'll just walk, it's a wonderful frozen night full of snow, full of hush, the roofs sparkle, the trees are still, and maybe he'll even miss all this a little, but only a little, when he is out there, with the sea, with the birds, with the horses. And as he walks, he imagines the train dissolving on the red sunburst horizon, and a wide, rolling freedom of space, the grasses waving, his chest filled to the point of bursting with bracing air, a rhythmic, pulsating alteration of dark and light, sunrises over new towns, sunsets in dazzling blue lakes, and the women, the women with red hair—a life, a real life!—and then his building runs into him before he expects it. He tiptoes up the stairs very quietly, and unlocks the door with no noise so he can steal into his room, pick up his bag, his documents, a sweater or two—but the whole place is flooded with lights, and his mother is pacing up and down the corridor, her hands at an unnatural angle.

Oh my God, she moans, oh my God—I thought you were—oh my God; and his father says, You have a lot of explaining to do, young man. Things do get a bit squashed together after that, one minute running into another running into another, all stuck together, and the floor keeps moving as if he were on a ship, or at least he thinks that's what a ship would be like, because he has never been on a ship. And suddenly he knows that he will not see the sunrise over the eastern sea next week, or ever, and because his heart feels like it's breaking, he grows angry and tells them he has been mugged, and that he left their stupid line because it was only for concert tickets, some stupid symphony, someone said, and not until next December, anyway.

And then there is another stretch of confusion, but they are all in the kitchen now, and the sink's enamel is comforting, cool against his forehead, and his father is talking with much excitement, though not to him, saying something about some composer. Igor Selinsky, he keeps repeating, this must be the symphony, I've been trying for days to find out where they'll sell the tickets, no one knows, but this must be it, it would be in December, so I heard, the genius forced to leave the country, Igor Selinsky, and his mother, who seems distracted and somehow concerned about the sink, keeps asking, Who is that, who is that? And then he knows that he must tell them the truth, so he straightens up and explains to them that being color-blind is really not as bad as it sounds, it's not like you see everything in black-and-white, unless, of course, it's very dark or it's winter, which, now that he thinks about it, it always is in this goddamned place. His mother tries to stop him, something about the neighbors who might be listening, but he doesn't care about any neighbors, in fact, it might enlighten them to know, it's not like you can't see any colors, you just get a few of them mixed up, the reds and the greens mostly, but on the plus side, and this is kind of funny, all the banners are green in his world, and all those idiotic garlands they put up on their idiotic holidays, and the portraits, and not even a nice green, but a dirty, brown, unappetizing sort of green, the color of vomit, though as he says that, he feels he should have used a different word, because his mother is looking distressed again.

Why don't you go sleep it off now, she says in a tired voice. He wants to shout at her, but after thinking a minute, or not thinking, exactly, just kind of swaying a bit, he turns and stumbles to the door instead—which is when he realizes, when they all realize, that this horrible, horrible woman is standing there on the kitchen threshold, has been standing there for who knows how long, in that horrible decaying robe of hers, in those painfully bright earrings, bursting, bursting with explosions of unbearable light into his eyes. She opens her thin, white lips, but she can't possibly be saying anything, he thinks, she has not spoken to anyone for years, she is his grand-mother, she is insane, and then indeed she is speaking, and everyone gasps, and her words are drowned, so she opens her lips again, and re-peats it.

And what she says is, "I would very much like to go to this con-cert, please."

5

THE NEXT MORNING, Sergei rose well before sunrise and groped for his clothes without switching on the lamp. His socks proved elusive, but at last he cornered two—one under the bed, the other still balled up inside his shoe. His wife did not wake up. He dressed, tiptoed outside, and strode through the darkness torn here and there by the stab of misty streetlight. As he drew closer, he found himself walking faster and faster, until he was running, winter surging in and out of his lungs in chilly fits, the excitement billowing inside him like a sail full of wind. When his ears started to burn, he realized he had forgotten his hat, but he did not slow down.

The night was just beginning to be diluted by a thin blue haze when he arrived at the kiosk. He approached panting, feeling somehow years younger after his wild, bare-headed sprint through the empty predawn streets. A few lone figures were already shuffling about, hanging streamers of steamy breaths in the frozen air; a piece of cardboard was propped in the shuttered window. *Will reopen upon restocking,* read the handwritten notice, and underneath, in smaller, printed letters: REGULAR WINTER HOURS 10 TO 5.

"It will be today for sure, though, right?" he said, looking up with a smile. Shadows shifted between scarves and hats where faces should have been; no one replied. His smile faded.

"So, who's last here?" he asked after a moment, raising his collar.

He waited until early afternoon, but the window remained blind. All the same, the elated certainty that had gripped him the night before—a certainty not unlike a sense of fate, reaffirmed by the immensity of the coincidence that placed the concert with such neatness within his reach, constructing the tickets kiosk so obligingly in his own corner of the city—the certainty, then, that this was the very place he had sought, did not waver in the slightest, though, oddly, no one in the growing line appeared to have heard about the symphony. Some concert tickets had, indeed, been sold the day before, "only it wasn't any what-do-you-call-it," he was told by an elderly man whose voice kept getting lost amidst layers of wool, "it was a visiting song-and-dance group. A good one, I'm hoping they haven't run out. Who's this Selyodsky, anyway?"

Shortly before three o'clock, Sergei left for work. For some blocks he kept glancing over his shoulder, tensing his legs for a dash back, until the kiosk vanished from sight behind the drifting snow. After the clear white stretches of a day so vast with possibility, the dim cavern of the People's Theater, its walls the color of dried blood, its stage decorations a claustrophobic cardboard forest of smokestacks and assembly plants, struck him as unusually oppressive. He spat his thawing breaths into the tuba with increasing impatience, attempting to catch Sviatoslav's eye through the monotonous seesawing of the trombones. During the intermission, when most of the orchestra crowded smoking and chatting around the spittoon in the stairwell, he pulled his friend aside.

"Listen," he said in an urgent undertone, "I have some amazing news."

"I've got some for you too," the drummer whispered. "I overheard—"

"Later, later! . . . It's about Selinsky, you know, the concert rumors I told you about, well, I think they're actually selling the tickets just around—"

Sviatoslav pushed his walruslike mustache into Sergei's face. "Forget Selinsky, you have troubles enough. I overheard our director on the phone, talking about you, making excuses. He sounded almost frightened. Something about the embassy. What the hell happened?"

A heartbeat of silence welled between them.

"No idea," Sergei said in a flattened voice.

"Come on, you can tell me."

He saw again the marble lavatory, the dripping water, the gray eye winking in the lustrous mirrors . . . Sharp little hammers beat at his temples. "It's nothing."

"Fine," Sviatoslav said dryly, releasing him. "By the way, your socks don't match."

Through the rest of the performance, he kept searching other faces for secret signs of his disfavor, repeatedly missing his cues, recalling himself only upon discovering the monumental elbow of a fellow tuba player embedded painfully in his side. Well, let the bastards fire me, this concert changes everything, he thought as snowdrifts settled on his shoulders while he waited at the kiosk the next day. So I'll become a tram conductor, a truck driver, I'll even sweep the streets—but at least I won't have to spend evening after evening playing their thumping songs, wasting my life away in that hellhole. And maybe, maybe, as I sweep the streets through the year, the melodies I once dreamed of composing will come to me at last— and notes will alight on my staffs like scores of migrant birds returned home. At the end of the year I will gather the pages, I will go to the concert, I will at last see the man I should have seen on that day thirty-seven years ago. In the stunned hush that will descend after he lowers his baton, just before the world explodes with applause, I will make my way to the stage, and our eyes will meet briefly, and—and—and here the vision blurred a little, for Sergei could not remember Selinsky's features, which he must have glimpsed as a boy in those pre-revolutionary photographs where tuxedoed men in unnaturally exalted poses swam in the oily glow of hazy backgrounds; but he quickly filled the blank with a genius's expansive forehead, an aristocratic thin nose, an attentive gray gaze—and I will toss him a bouquet wrapped in my secret score, my address concealed in a corner. That night, well after midnight, there will be a knock on my door. He will be alone. Grasping my hand in his own, he will say, "This dazzling masterpiece you showed me—this divine music—could it be that here, in this place, in this time, there still live such giants"—and he will ask me—and I will reply—and then—and afterward—

And afterward, that evening, in fact, standing mute and diminished amidst the expanses of the director's office, he tried to hold his future conversation with Selinsky intact in his mind, brilliant and hard like a diamond, turning it to this or that facet, this or that phrase, to keep his dread at bay; but as the heavy silence continued, Selinsky's noble features quivered, reverted to the sepia fog of a forgotten snapshot, then dissipated altogether. He shifted from foot to foot, bumped against his tuba, which lay curled up on the floor like a beaten dog, stared at the artificial plants on the windowsill, the monstrous ashtray shaped like a dying swan, the director's fat neck piled in loose folds on the maroon silk of his collar.

The director would not look at him. The director was drumming his sausagelike fingers against a nondescript folder open on the desk before him.

"Please, Ivan Anatolievich," he said hoarsely. "Please."

He was conscious of steps thumping in the stairwell just outside the door; the last actors were leaving the theater, going home to their safe, uneventful lives.

The director said nothing.

"Please. I have a son, a wife, a mother-in-law to support. I won't disappoint you again. I . . . Ivan Anatolievich, I'll be most grateful. On Friday."

Friday was the next payday. The unspoken knowledge hovered in the air for a tense minute. Then the director's body heaved with an immense sigh.

"How long have you worked here, Sergei?"

"Twenty-four years."

"Twenty-four years, is that right? Astonishing how time flies . . . I remember when you first came, such a dashing fellow, practically a boy, bushes of curly hair, milk on your lips . . . Well, tell you what. I'm willing to close my eyes to this unpleasant incident. Of course, some disciplinary action seems called for, especially given your, shall we say, questionable origins." His fat finger slithered along the folder's spine. "You'll be transferred to matinees, with a corresponding decrease in pay. Morning rehearsals are at ten. You'll be teaching an afternoon workshop as well, three to five. That's on a strictly volunteer basis, you understand—one must do one's best to give back to the community. In truth, though, I'm doing you a favor: you'll be home in time for supper, restored, so to speak, to the bosom of your loving family, eh?"

His relief leaked away with an almost audible hiss.

"But," he said in a wooden voice, "but that means I'll have to be here from ten till five. That's . . . I'm afraid it's not very . . . I mean, there is somewhere else . . . that is, I would prefer . . ."

He wanted to shout at the odious man before him, to bang his fists against the desk, to grab his dossier and rip it in half. Instead, his words sputtered and fizzled out; he felt his limbs fill with lead, and his throat with dead, dusty insects. He stood without moving, without speaking, staring with pure, fierce hatred at the marble swan expiring on the obese man's desk.

"I confess I expected a little more enthusiasm," said Ivan Anatolievich frostily. "You start your new schedule on Thursday. And remember, I'll be watching you."

Sergei backed out of the office.

The kiosk's hours were ten to five.

Unless the tickets went on sale in the next three days, it was unlikely he would go to the concert.

That night he barely slept, and at dawn the next morning he was the first to arrive in the quiet street; but the kiosk remained closed, as before. Neither did it open on Tuesday, though by then, at least, he had the satisfaction of being publicly confirmed in his belief: the line was swelling with an excited buzz of the Selinsky symphony. On Wednesday, the temperature dropped. People stomped their boots, puffed on their gloves; many left early, mumbling that no concert was worth freezing to death for. Sergei waited stubbornly, though he had lost all feeling in the toes of his left foot and though his breath, escaping in steaming bursts, had caused a whole beard of miniature icicles to grow on his scarf; but in mid-afternoon he too was forced to give up his place at the head of the line—as it was, he risked being late for work.

He was already at the next intersection when a small beat-up van labored past him. His heart quickening, he turned, followed it with his eyes. The van pulled up to the curb by the kiosk.

He swallowed an incoherent, thwarted gasp, and, just as the dented door of the van began to jerk open, dashed back, and instantly tripped over his shoelaces and started to fall, but somehow righted himself and, vaulting forward, slipped on the ice and fell again, and this time kept falling, skidding, sliding in a flurry of snow, closing his eyes against the dazzling, wet confusion, fully sprawled on his back now, coming at last to a blind, whirling stop.

For a moment he did not move. Then, deciding that nothing was broken, he opened his eyes, and was just attempting to scramble up when he saw the sky.

The sky was pale and empty and vast, and it appeared to float ever higher in transparent layers gradually bleached of all blue tints and shadows, until, at some vertiginous, unimaginable height, it seemed to him bled of all color, of all confusion, intense and pure like the essence of one sustained, crystal note.

He lay still and looked at it.

The van door slammed shut, and two pairs of legs crossed his upended horizon at odd angles. The first pair, ending with black shoes, possibly imported, stepped over him; the second, clumsy in felt boots, circled around, encumbered by a ladder. Sergei looked at the sky. From somewhere above drifted a scraping of wood against metal, a peremptory voice issuing commands, "Move to the left!" "Make sure it's not crooked!" and, after a minute, the blows of a hammer. Winter muffled each harsh burst in cold, snowy pockets before the sounds could quite take their jagged, crowlike flight skyward; the sky did not reverberate, for it was immensely distant— and filled to the brim with its own clear, silent, infinite music. When the banging stopped, the two pairs of legs swerved back around him, the door moaned in opening and barked in closing, the motor sneezed and coughed and spat going past. Then all was quiet.

A couple of people from the line helped him up. There was now a large sign nailed above the kiosk. It announced, in bleached blue letters: CONCERT TICKETS.

"Too faded to have been freshly painted," a man in a fedora noted with disapproval. "They must have taken it from some old kiosk no longer in operation."

Sergei gazed at it blankly, then, recalling the time, hurried to the theater. He arrived nearly half an hour late, his coat caked with sleet and missing two buttons. Ivan Anatolievich, whom he encountered in a corridor on the way in, gave him a dirty look.

"Ten o'clock sharp tomorrow!" he boomed as Sergei was squeezing past. "And oh, I'll be in on Friday if you feel the urge to drop by."

The brittle January days, all sunshine and chunks of ice, soon darkened and shrank, passing into February in a sinking, gray procession. Every evening, the instant he was allowed to leave, Sergei flung his coat over his back and, too rushed to thread his arms through the sleeves, ran across the city, his coat leaping after him. The kiosk was always boarded up by the time he arrived, the purple streetlamp illuminating the deserted street. Wheezing, he would hobble up to the window, circle the kiosk once or twice, try to peer inside in an attempt to discern whether any tickets had been sold that day. He would gauge the length of the day's line by looking at the sidewalk: at some distance, the pavement would be hard and white with ice, then, as he got closer, would turn black and naked, its snow having melted in the shuffling of dozens of feet. The ground bristled with a stubble of cigarette butts; over the next week or two, he watched them steadily encroach upon the surrounding snowdrifts.

By the time the butts were dotting the sidewalk all the way down the block and around the corner, he had given up hope of ever buying the ticket, and was taking a direct route home. One evening, as he was trudging along, giving cautious berth to dog feces, feeling an unaccustomed ache in his back, he glimpsed a portly woman moving with slow, laden steps in the snow-whirled darkness ahead, a bulging bag in each hand.

Briefly he hesitated, then caught up. "Here," he said, "let me."

"Oh." A small laugh escaped her. "Thank you, Serezha. Lots of homework today."

For some time they walked in silence. Damp snow slapped at his eyes, flew into his mouth. "It must be tedious for you," he said at last. "Waiting in that line day after day."

"It's not too bad. I come in the afternoons, as soon as my classes are done. I'm worried, of course, that they'll deliver the tickets in the morning, but starting in March, two of my mornings will open up. Of course, it will be before then for sure—who's ever heard of a line lasting two months, you know—but just in case. Emilia Khristianovna is in line also, we've been talking about working something out between us, covering for each other—"

"Sure, that sounds reasonable," he said, not listening. "Look, Anya, I've been meaning to talk to you about something for a while, but I haven't had a chance at home—"

She smiled uncertainly. "We eat supper together every night."

"Yes, well," he mumbled. "It just keeps slipping my mind, I guess. Anyway, you know I was hoping to get a ticket myself, to go to the concert, that is, but with my new schedule, I can never get to the kiosk on time, and, well"—she was descending a short flight of steps now; he followed—"I was thinking, since you're in line anyway, you might be able to, you know—"

She reached the door at the bottom of the stairs, turned toward him. Shadows gathered here, the streetlamp above leaking in blotchy dribbles; he could see only her hands, pressed against her rough gray coat as if in prayer, and, in the twilight of her face, her eyebrows, glistening with tiny droplets of melting snow, lifting like the wings of a nervous bird.

"But Serezha," she said quietly, "they'll sell only one ticket per person, you know that. I promised mine to Mama."

"Of course," he said, "but it's obvious that she—"

"I'm sorry, I must buy some bread . . . See you at home?"

"I'll come with you," he offered quickly. "Anyway, it's obvious that she doesn't—"

She pushed the door open. It was suffocating inside; in the bakery's hot yellow light, a throng of middle-aged women milled about, prodding loaves with pairs of bright tongs, calling to one another. He hurried after her, sweeping away cobwebs of conver-

sations, blinded by the lamps, disoriented by the heat, by the hub-
bub, still talking rapidly into her neck, "Look, we both know your
mother doesn't really need this ticket, she doesn't—"

"Black or white?" she asked, glancing back at him.

"What? . . . Oh, I don't care, whichever kind you like . . . She
doesn't intend to go, she never even leaves the house, she—"

She had already moved away, not having heard, repeating, "Ah,
it smells so good in here."

He tried to stay close but got tangled in a gaggle of noisy school-
girls rushing toward the cashier; when he caught up at last, she was
greeting an acquaintance. All at once he felt frantic, for it had to be
now; the walls in their apartment were paper-thin, and with her
mother always hovering a breath away, he would never dare to ask
her again.

"Anya," he said, placing his hand on her sleeve. "Do you think,
maybe, this ticket—"

The acquaintance had meandered off.

His wife stood looking at him now, pressing the white loaf
tightly to her chest, her fingers crushing its crust, her face oddly
still—and he knew that she had heard him all along.

"Serezha," she said. Her voice was pleading. "I can't. Mama
asked me."

And for one moment, suspended in this warm, well-lit, close
place, amidst the bustle of women, amidst the buns of bread, amidst
all the hot, moist, rich smells of domesticity from which he felt eternally cut off, he wondered, in a kind of desperation, what he could
possibly say to make her understand the immensity of his longing.
He could tell her, perhaps, about that piece he had played as a child
thirty-seven years ago—or else his trouble at work—or how, even
though he had so wastefully squandered his best decades, he saw in
Selinsky's music his chance to start living at last, to become something more than he was, to try summoning into existence the notes
he could almost imagine flowing from the tips of his fingers—

"Oh, don't be upset," she said gently. "There will be other nice concerts."

He stared at her; then, without speaking, turned and walked out into the frozen darkness. Minutes later she came running behind him, gathering up the hems of her coat. She kept saying things, apologizing, promising something. He was silent on the way home, silent in the elevator, silent in the kitchen. "Please, don't worry about it," he said as he switched off the light on his nightstand. "Sleep well."

He said little else in the coming days, practicing away his evenings, flooding the hush of their bedroom with his instrument's hoarse respirations. One afternoon in mid-February, his two sole workshop students quarreled, and the older one smashed his tuba over the younger one's head. The boys were sent home, and, finding himself with some daylight hours to spare, he came to the familiar street, took his place at the end of the line, and, his eyes closed, stood still for a while, listening to the voices that trudged, muffled and weary, through the day's early shadows.

"Pardon me, if I may disturb you for a moment, what might they be selling here?"

"Concert tickets."

"And would you be so obliging as to tell me what kind of concert, please?"

"The do-re-mi kind."

"Indeed, but—"

"Listen, intelligentsia, do you want me to break your glasses for you? What are you bothering me for? Beat it."

"For God's sake, can't you just answer the poor man, don't you see how old he is?"

"Fine, then, it's the Northern Nightingales. Happy now?"

"I'm sorry, I'm not quite familiar with—"

"See what I mean? He doesn't know the Nightingales! There's education for you."

"Don't mind him, grandpa, maybe his wife ran off with the plumber. It's a group from the North. They wear beautiful costumes and sing about the friendship of the peoples and the happy tomorrow. It's very soulful."

"Oh, I see, thank you for your kindness, I suppose I'd better be—"

"Well, go on, woman, tell him about the symphony too, that will be more up his alley!"

"Pardon, did you say 'symphony'?"

"Yeah, I forgot, there's some symphony, but it won't be until next New Year's Eve, they haven't sold any tickets for it yet. It's some fancy composer, Vselensky, I think—"

"The name's Solyonsky, you illiterate!"

"Not Solyonsky, Selyodsky!"

"Terribly sorry to interrupt, but . . . Not Selinsky, certainly? Not Igor Selinsky?"

"That's just what I'm saying, or are you deaf? Selinsky, Selyodsky, whatever—"

"Wait a minute, Selinsky, Selinsky, I remember something . . . That's right, wasn't he the turncoat who traded his country for a life of ease Over There? I'll tell you what I think, no decent person would want to watch some dusty aristocrat in a bow tie prance about with a baton!"

"And I'll tell you what *I* think, such traitors to our Motherland should be shot. Just like that, with no trial. Bam, and that's the end of it. What say you, Professor?"

"What, old man, swallowed your tongue? The fellow's talking to you!"

"Oh, just leave him alone, all of you! Poor thing, his hands are shaking . . . Stop shouting now, he's trying to say something. Don't mind them, grandpa, speak up, speak up!"

"Thank you for your kindness. The tickets to the Selinsky symphony, would you happen to know when they might be on sale?"

"The kiosk woman says any day now. Oh, and it's only three hundred seats, so they'll go fast."

"Oh dear, in that case . . . Excuse me, if I may trouble you, are you last in line?"

"Yes," Sergei said, opening his eyes, "but you can take my place, I'm leaving now."

The darkness under his eyelids had become, almost without his noticing, the darkness outside; evening had fallen. A street away, men in enormous gloves tottered on ladders affixing slogans to dim streetlamps in preparation for Army Day. Blindly he trudged in and out of the strips of ailing light, vowing to waste no more time on this hopeless, heart-wrenching wait, not noticing his wife, who trailed a block behind him all the way home.

6

My PARENTS TOOK ME there when I was seven, to study ballet with the most celebrated teacher of the day. It was winter when we arrived in the city. Winter there was not like winter here—not dark but translucent. Maybe it's still like that, maybe not. Probably not. This century has trodden heavy, and nothing is the same, not even the seasons. But back then, the sky was like milky glass, the roofs like wet bark, the trees like cobwebs in the air. My father rented an apartment in an old, stately building on one of the boulevards. I went to my classes in the morning, and in the early afternoon I returned to our place. For hours I sat on the windowsill, watching lamplighters light the gas lamps, watching chimney sweeps tiptoe on invisible ropes across the evening, listening to the bells as they floated over the river.

One February day my mother came home accompanied by two small liveried men carrying an enormous gray roll on their shoulders. They set the rug down on the living room floor and began to unroll it. The inside was soft and crimson, abundant with flowers, and I got down on my knees to see it better. And it was then that I noticed the first one.

This is how I always imagine telling the story. I imagine someone sitting before me, leaning forward, listening eagerly, and at this point he always asks: The first what? But there is no one to hear my stories. So now, I close my door, cover my lamp with an old green shawl—I like the soft light, the shifting sea-green shadows—and wait until everyone in the house is asleep. Then I talk to myself.

So it was then that I noticed the first bead. There was a bead, a vivid blue speck of light, wedged in one of the cracks in the hardwood floor. When I saw it, I felt the same kind of stillness I used to feel playing a game I had invented as a very young child. I would dig in the snow, searching for what I called a "secret," which I myself would have buried under a shard of glass some days before—a candy wrapper, a shred of silk cloth, any other small treasure I had mined from my winters in the countryside. Sitting on the floor as the two men with fluttering hands unrolled the carpet, I was brushed by the same kind of happiness I had felt when my stiff fingers would scratch away a hard layer of snow to reveal the bright burst of miraculous color.

One bead was all it took before I saw another one, and another, and another—before I realized that all the cracks in the living room floor were filled with beads.

They put the carpet down, but every afternoon when I returned home, I would lie on the floor, still in my damp dancing clothes, peel a corner of the carpet away, and labor at the cracks with the tip of a pin. After a while, my eyes would grow tired, and I would begin to imagine the whole world as one dark, flat, unclean expanse through which flowed threadlike lines of melted glass, of molten gold. Whenever I caught one bead stream with the sharp prick of the pin and liberated it from its confinement, its droplets would turn into jeweled grains and leap all over the floors. There were hundreds of them—cones striped red and white like circus hats, glowing glass balls, tiny cubes with silver splotches on their sides. In the end, all of them fit into a small caviar jar. I kept it for a long time. It was lost in the revolution.

Now, if I had a listener, he would ask, of course, where the beads came from. He would not know me well enough to distrust my answers. I would be glad to tell him. The beads were the last, forgotten fragments of a special, enchanted world, like petrified coral and shells left embedded in rocks centuries after the sea has retreated from its black depths to a shoreline with beach umbrellas and plastic buckets. I used to imagine it, this world. It had once been filled with joyful, mischievous creatures who flew on the backs of dragonflies, sewed curly clouds onto the skies, pretended to be mossy weathervanes on the spires of ancient castles, tossed sunbeams at one another. When the sunbeams fell to the floor, they crystallized into tiny pieces of glass.

Pardon me? Oh, is it really that important? Fine, then, they were probably spilled by a couple of children whose parents had rented the apartment before us. They might have left the city in a hurry—perhaps there'd been a violent upheaval in their country. Or maybe a weak-eyed seamstress had spent years in a cozy armchair by the window, doing handiwork for sale. Or else—or else a girl working on an embroidered wallet for her beloved had received sudden news of his death, and let it all fall from her hands.

So now you wish you hadn't asked.

The real explanations are usually the simplest, and often the saddest.

7

ON A DREARY DAY toward the end of February, when tempers had worn raw, a particularly ugly brawl broke out in the line, complete with the usual threats to polish someone's glasses clean and dust off someone else's hat with a brick. People were scrambling to get out of the way of the impending fracas when a short man with a jet-black beard was seen stepping forth and addressing the warring factions. Inevitably, voices rose in doubt—"Who the hell is he?" "One of those stuck-up university folks, I bet." "Nah, he looks like a pirate." "All the same, why should we listen to *him*?"—but eventually the line agreed to hear him out. The man, it transpired, had a radical reorganization to propose, beginning with the separation of those waiting for the Northern Nightingales tickets from those hoping to attend the symphony, and ending with numbers, from 1 to 300, being assigned to everyone in the symphony camp. This line, he said, was unprecedented in its nature; they needed to devise a few basic rules, make a list, check off the names; life would become immeasurably more civilized for all involved.

He talked rather at length. Some were able to understand him.

There followed the times of chaos, the times of confusion, the times of arguments. For days snow fell without cease, in big flakes, which flared up, theatrical, brilliant, as they passed under the street-lamp. The arguments died down slowly. On the fourth day, when the snow had dwindled away at long last, a middle-aged woman with a tired face, dressed in an ill-fitting coat and wet low-heeled shoes, stood clutching a square bit of paper in her chilled, reddened fingers. Her number was 137. In front of her was a woman in her thirties, with a bright mouth and a fur hat low on her forehead, and behind, a small boy with fragments of a cloudy sky for eyes.

The woman with the tired face turned from the one to the other.

"I've seen you both many times, but I don't know your names," she said. "I'm Anna."

PART TWO

SPRING

1

THE DAYS WERE LENGTHENING, turning pale and deep. Under skies the shade of northern porcelain, the snow had begun to melt, and the glittering, leaking, rushing unrest of waters filled the city with a noise like that of a constant twittering of birds. Their home, though, lay quiet and still, as if under a snowdrift. His mother spent her afternoons waiting in line, and his father moved through the rooms in a sulking, taciturn mood, slamming doors and spitefully banging his tuba against corners. Alexander himself felt depressed and, to make matters worse, was having trouble sleeping: since the beginning of March, their building appeared to have sprung numerous leaks, through which the outside world seeped in unsettlingly—little drafts of a springtime hum and bright, breezy smells, which wafted through the lifeless air of their apartment, keeping him awake.

In the middle of the month, he had a particularly restless night. Some neighbors were talking, and snippets of strange conversations kept invading his dreams. "Pardon me?" someone was saying somewhere, quietly but distinctly. "No, I'm afraid that was not exactly true, the jar wasn't lost in the revolution. Many things were, some tangible, some rather less so—but not the beads. It just makes the story more dramatic, don't you find?" There was a pause, and he had just begun to fall asleep when the same old voice embarked on a long, pointless story about two men in workmen's overalls carrying a gigantic crystal chandelier through crooked medieval streets. The chandelier was all trussed up like a felled beast on a stick, and the crystals clicked softly, and wisps of the light watercolor skies became entangled like silk petals amidst the pieces of radiant glass, and some little girl stopped openmouthed and stared, then followed after them as if charmed, and it went on and on, and he thought, half awake, The walls in this damn building are absurdly thin, is this coming from above or below, and who spouts such inane nonsense at three in the morning anyway; and he even considered banging on the floor or the ceiling, though he was not sure which—and though a part of him rather wanted to hear how the tale ended—when suddenly there was silence.

He was starting to drift off once more, or had perhaps drifted off already, when the voice—his grandmother's voice, he knew all at once—said coyly, "Oh, so you've noticed at last. Yes, I did stop wearing them. Why? Because they are diamonds, and diamonds, my dear, are worn only in winter. Spring has come."

Awaking with a start, he realized that his grandmother's terrible earrings, which she never took off, had somehow slipped into his dream brewed from the neighbors' idiotic conversation. He lay in bed for some time after that, populating the mounds and hollows of his ceiling with shadowy profiles and downy limbs, then, giving up, rose. His parents' door was cracked open; the dark silence inside seemed denser than in the hallway. He slipped past. On the kitchen threshold, he shut his eyes against the unexpected glare.

"Mother?" he said, moving his head blindly from side to side.

"I can't sleep," her voice replied. "I keep hearing things—a radio somewhere, I guess—"

Unclenching his eyelids, he watched her emerge from the aching nothingness into a white haze, then, shedding the halo, slowly acquire untidy hair flattened by hours of insomniac tossing, a thick flannel gown the color of boiled milk, a piece of paper held in her fingers swollen from a recent wash. "What's that you're reading?" he asked, squinting.

They had barely spoken since the night he had lost the money; yet now, with his temples humming from the exhaustion of dammed dreams begging to be let out, he felt startled, or else released, into talking.

"It's nothing, just a recipe," she said. She sounded wistful. "For a date tart. It's been making the rounds in the . . . that is, your physics teacher copied it for me."

He bent over her shoulder, read aloud: *"Cream the butter and sugar until light, next stir in the ground almonds and the orange flower water—"*

"Better than poetry, no?" She folded the page carefully, smoothed its creases. "Some poetry, anyway. Of course, I'll never be able to make it, dates are impossible to find. There is this woman who keeps saying she can get anything, she eats dates every week, so she says, but I don't suppose it's true. She's always saying things."

"A woman. What woman?"

"Oh, just someone I've met in the line. You might have seen her yourself the time you—"

She stopped.

He shifted uncomfortably from foot to foot, suddenly aware of the cold linoleum beneath his bare toes. The hour floated around them, weightless and unreal; the train-station clock on the wall had slid into a deep crevice of shadows, and the whole kitchen had ceased to exist beyond their circle of undiluted, naked lamplight, beyond the two of them blinking owlishly at each other. And as the silence swelled, then brimmed over with a quiet click of the invisible clock's hand leaping from one notch to the next, Anna looked at her sixteen-year-old son standing before her in his touchingly childish pajamas, with a border of little sailboats along the cuffs too high on his wrists, and felt, for the first time since that night, that she had forgiven him, and was seized with an urge to tell him about the people in the line, about all the small, trivial encounters, conversations, nudges that made up her unrecorded, unshared days. That insufferable woman at 136, for instance, never tired of repeating that she was there only as a favor to her husband, who was a *man of importance* and intended to use the ticket to clench some deal with a *highly cultured* colleague. Anna did not like her. The boy at 138, now—him she liked very much. She had learned that he came from a family of musicians and was hoping to get the ticket for his grandfather, who would turn seventy-eight in December; she kept trying to talk to him, but he was always looking away, gnawing on his fingernails. Not that she had no one to talk to, of course: she often chatted with Emilia Khristianovna; they now worked around their schedules, spotting each other on alternate mornings. Emilia Khristianovna, it turned out, had a son only a couple of years older than Alexander, she wanted to tell him—did you know that, did you meet him in school perhaps? She's knitting a scarf for her boy, fretting that the colors don't go well together; orange and pink is all the wool she has left—

"My feet are frozen," Alexander mumbled. "I better get back to bed."

"Oh," Anna said. "Of course. Have a good night."

In the doorway he turned.

"Why do you do it?" he asked.

"Do what?"

"Stand in that line for hours."

"Because your grandmother asked me to," she replied wearily.

"But why does she want to go to some random concert? She never goes anywhere. Do you even know? Has she spoken to you at all since—I mean, has she even thanked you?"

She considered him in stony silence. He waited on the threshold for another minute, and still she said nothing. He nodded, and walked away, and, back in bed, fell into sleep as into still, dark water.

In the morning, when he tried to disentangle sleep from wakeful-
ness, the chandelier jolted by the two men striding through ancient
streets hung vivid and bright in his mind, and the predawn conversation with his mother swayed like a shadowy, vaguely shameful,
half-forgotten dream.

The following Monday, reopening after the midday break, the
kiosk seller shook her dyed curls and announced that a batch of tickets was expected shortly.

"Finally!" said the wife of the important man, and tossed a bag
at Anna. "Here, catch."

Anna made a grab for it, missed, bent to retrieve it from the
ground, from someone's watery footprint. The smell reached her
before she even saw what was inside: the dark, rich smell of southern earth, of unfamiliar trees with glossy leaves, of the measured
roll of some distant sea. She exhaled in astonishment. "For me?" she
whispered. "All this? Liubov Dmitriyevna, but that's so . . . so
unexpected. How can I—that is, how much do I—"

"Oh, I'm not taking any of *your* money." The woman's voice was
muffled, her chin tucked under as she struggled to free an earring
from the peacock swirls of a scarf. "Just think of it as a little char-
ity. Teachers aren't raking it in these days, I'm sure."

Anna slowly set the bag on the ground and, straightening, looked
at the woman.

"Now, me, I don't have to worry, my husband gets me everything
my little heart desires. See this hat? His Women's Day present. The
scarf too, pure silk, here, feel it . . . Fine, suit yourself . . . Wait, you've
forgotten the dates! . . . Where are you—just where do you think
you're—"

No longer listening, Anna was walking away. She walked past
middle-aged women copying the date tart recipe, past young women
bending over the tired fashion magazine that had been traveling down

the line these last few days, past boys scraping the remnants of the
winter into sickly snowmen. She walked not noticing the little
waterfalls erupting over her head, the wounding of shrunken snowdrifts by collapsed icicles, the world splashing about, wet and shining. Their building, when she reached at last its dim, concrete
hollows, was filled with infants' cries echoing in the stairwells and an
assortment of midday smells, mostly shoe polish and soapsuds.
When she stepped out of the elevator, her landing trembled with
laboring sighs of the tuba; it was, she recalled, her husband's afternoon off. She could feel the unpleasantly soft vibrations in the soles
of her feet as she wrestled for a long minute with the lock before
discovering she had the wrong key.

Once inside, she let her coat sink to the foyer floor, then moved
down the hallway, entered her mother's room without knocking.
On the rare occasions when she came in here, to bring a cup of tea
or quickly dust the shelves, empty save for a few thin, molting volumes, she was always visited by an uncomfortable feeling that she
had accidentally stepped over the threshold into another house, another time, where everything, even the dust, had its precise place
that she had no right to disturb. She stopped on the threshold now.
In the solitary, narrow window, daylight floundered weakly, and
died in the faded curtains the color of old tea roses; the small,
casketlike space lay in the shadows of its own private, rose-tinted,
faintly perfumed dusk. Her mother sat perched on the edge of her
only chair, prim and straight-backed, an old tasseled lampshade
billowing with soft brown light at the table before her, a fan of postcards spread in her lavender lap. When she looked up, her small,
birdlike eyes, dark as velvet, held no reflections.

"Mama," Anna said. "Mama, why do you need this ticket?"

The old woman made a tiny startled movement, and the postcards fell to the floor. She seemed about to speak, but did not. Anna
waited; then, after a lapse of silence, turned and left, shutting the

door behind her, careful to step over a sepia boulevard stained with horse-drawn carriages, which had fluttered out into the corridor.

The tuba sighs still ebbed and rose in the narrow veins of the apartment. She went into her son's empty room, sat on his unmade bed, and stared unseeingly at the naked walls before her, indifferent to the sour effluvia of unwashed socks and furtive smoke and adolescence, her hands lifeless on her knees. She thought of the time, seemingly not that long ago, when she had expected something thrilling from her days in the line—a surprise, a present for herself, an escape from stifling routine—the time when she had felt richer, fuller, nestled deep within her vast anticipation as within a warm, secret cave. Now her life was laid bare once again, the anticipation gone, wrung dry by the tedium of the everyday bureaucracy of lists and shifts; and the waiting itself was for someone else now—not for her, never for her. She felt a sharp pang of loss, of impoverishment, which made her want to cry; but her eyes were dry when, some minutes later, her husband nudged the door open and peeked inside, muttering, "I thought I heard . . . What's the matter?"

"Nothing, really," she said, not lifting her eyes from her hands. "Only that I waste my life standing before that pointless kiosk, not to mention being insulted by some really tactless, uncivilized people, and no one will even tell me why—and you, you . . . you never . . . while other women's husbands . . . you and I don't even . . . you—"

Her voice, though not loud, had wound up and up, tight, tighter yet, until she stopped abruptly, as if the winding mechanism had sprained a spring.

"What?" he said stiffly. "You and I don't even what?"

She studied her hands. Her nails were always breaking.

"Is this about Women's Day again?" he said. "Look, I've told you already, I meant to get some flowers, but I just . . . The matinee schedule is really . . . All the kiosks were closed by the time . . . Just what do you want me to do?"

"We'll lose our place," she said distantly, "unless someone is there this afternoon. They do a check at the end of the day, just before five."

"*Our* place?" he said. "You don't mean——"

She met his eyes at last.

"I made her a promise," she said, "but I'm very, very tired."

"You can't possibly expect *me* . . . Do you not realize how much——"

"Sergei," she said, "I don't need any flowers from you. But after all this time, I think I deserve something."

He forced himself to continue looking at her—at her face widened by age, at the thickened folds of her eyelids, at the row of beetle-black buttons crawling down her sagging beige cardigan, at the stolid shape of her legs in the brown woolen hose she wore every winter, at her flat-heeled, square-nosed shoes, which she always took off upon entering their home, lining them meticulously alongside his own pair by the doormat, but which now rested, slightly apart, on their son's bare floor in two darkening pools of melted mud . . .

He looked away.

"Fine," he said. His voice scratched itself fighting to get out between his teeth.

"Our number is one hundred thirty-seven," she called out after him. "There are some rules, I must explain, and you'll need this, here——"

"Fine," he said from the hallway, already punching his arms into his coat. "Fine, fine!"

He narrowly avoided crashing into his son, who had emerged, out of breath, from around the bend of the stairs, jerking his gaze away from his father's face as if caught doing something illicit. While Sergei stood waiting for the elevator's arrival, he heard the beginning of a quarrel inside the apartment, and, abandoning his wait, thumped

down the steps instead, past a rasping of small angry dogs, past pha-
lanxes of empty bottles behind the trash chute, past landing after
landing freshly defaced by some savage—a few primitively expressed
sentiments etched into the plaster with furious, knife-sharp slashes,
which, by the time he threw his weight against the front door and was
issued outside with a complaint of the hinges, reflected his own feelings with succinctness.

Seething, he strode down the street wet with puddles. He thought
he might spend the hours walking, or catch a matinee, or buy a
newspaper, find some dry place to read it. He paid no attention to
where he was going; when he rounded a random corner and plowed
into a crowd, he was momentarily disoriented, as if he had been
transported to some unfamiliar, unlikely landscape in an alien city.
He gazed at the orderly commas of bent backs marking the sidewalk
in a depressingly long sentence—and an instant later, as understanding came, was assaulted by a vehement desire to register his
protest, to say or do something offensive.

He approached the closed kiosk, read the handwritten sign in its
window.

Pending delivery. Back after restocking.

"Restocking again, huh?" he said, breathing harshly. "In no rush,
are they?"

The short, fierce-looking bearded man at the head of the line remained impassive.

"Are you on the list?" he asked, thrusting a sheet of paper at
Sergei.

Sergei glared into the man's face, noting the stray black hairs curling in the generous nostrils, the mole on the right cheek, the com-
manding intensity of the pinprick eyes. Oh, I can see right through
you, he thought with something quickly approaching hatred, you
self-appointed Saint Peter brandishing a list instead of a key, decid-

ing whom to admit into paradise and whom to turn away, while these—these sheep—all meekly serve their time in purgatories of their own devising; yet when they are at last allowed through the heavenly gates, admission stubs in their sweaty hands, not one of them, no, not one among these bored housewives and batty old women, will understand a single note—not one of them will even *hear* the music—while I, I who have waited for Selinsky all my life, I who belong here by right, I must be excluded, kept away, thwarted by a conspiracy of faceless embassy spies and obese men and boys eager to carry their tubas in future parades, and oh-so-dutiful daughters—

"It will likely be today or tomorrow," Saint Peter informed him matter-of-factly, holding out his pen. "Thursday at the latest. Possibly late in the evening, so be prepared to stay awhile this week, till ten maybe. The tickets will go fast once they've come in."

Sergei's hand froze in the mechanical act of accepting the pen.

"The tickets," he said. "Today or tomorrow. The actual *tickets*."

The man's beard bristled with impatience.

"You're here for Igor Selinsky, yes? Because if you want the Northern Nightingales, they were relocated to another kiosk two weeks ago. Do you have your number on you?"

"My . . . Yes, of course." Sergei ravaged his pockets. His mouth had gone dry and porous, and as he peeled his lips open, he could hear a small, crackling pat of a noise. "Number one thirty-eight, got it . . . Or no, sorry, one thirty-seven, under 'Anna,' see here, that's my wife."

He hastened down the line in a heated, incredulous haze. Near the kiosk, a vaguely familiar old man was drawing on a cigarette, his eyes filling with distance; a few steps away, a student in a group of other students had just finished telling a joke and collapsed laughing amidst the applause. On the corner, a man of thirty-some years, with a long, agile, tanned face, was talking to a woman behind him, pressing a bag into her hands, exclaiming, "But you never know, you might, you might someday—"

"I believe this is my place," Sergei mumbled, inserting himself between them.

He was panting as though he had just run an obstacle course; his blood throbbed in his ears. Today or tomorrow, today or tomorrow, today or tomorrow . . . The immensity of the chance that had been offered him so generously, so unexpectedly, seemingly by divine intercession, made some dark, still, deep place inside him well up with a trembling, long-suppressed, fluid feeling—

"Any use for them, then?"

"What?"

The tanned man had turned to face him.

"Any use for the dates?" the man repeated.

Sergei blinked, brushed at his eyes, forced himself to attend to the minute workings of the world around him. There would be time, he knew, there would be so much time later—the monotonous days in the burial pit of his orchestra, the sleepless nights next to his wife— oh yes, time enough for the joy, for the guilt, for the anticipation—

"Dates? What dates?"

"One can make a delightful tart with them, or so I hear. I've already offered them to Sofia Mikhailovna here, but she claims she doesn't cook."

Sergei glanced at the woman behind him—she was not old, no more than thirty—then turned back to the man. "This kind of thing should not be tolerated," he said. "If you want to fleece someone, there are designated places for that, go to the—"

The man's teeth split his face open. "I'm not selling anything," he said. "I just have a bag full of dates I don't need. Any cooks in your house?"

He cast another glance at the young woman. The streetlamp had just come on, with a long electric sigh, and in its tremulous, uneven light her skin appeared pale as the rice paper that had been used for printing books in the first years after the Change, and her eyelids so delicate, almost transparent, that he thought he could discern an intricate etching of tiny blue veins on their surface. She met his eyes with a quiet, reproachful gaze that reminded him of a medieval painting he had once seen in some folio of art reproductions—a tranquil green garden in cool, luminous colors, a floating petal-edged cloud, an orchestra of rainbow-winged angels with sharp, childlike faces and great, transparent insect eyes, fondling shiny musical instruments with their impossibly tiny hands . . .

Afraid to be caught staring, he looked away, started to decline the offer of the dates, then changed his mind mid-word, muttered awkwardly, "All right, then, I'll take them"—and, flustered, nearly made a little joke about his wife's arson attempts in the kitchen, but at the last minute did not, saying instead as he accepted the sticky load, "So, then, are you a musician?"

"Me? No, no," said the tanned man, and laughed again. "I sing a bit, though. Used to sing in a choir when I was young."

The young woman behind Sergei leaned forward. "Oh, Pavel, did you really? What kind of choir?"

"Folk songs mainly, nothing too terribly—"

"But I think folk songs can be lovely. Not the ones they usually—I mean—" She pressed her lips together, fell silent.

"Selinsky has some very original interpretations of northern folk songs in his early music," Sergei interjected quickly. "I'm a musician, myself. I played a few of his pieces before he—when I was a child."

"Did you really? I've never heard anything by him. They say he's amazing. I wonder what he'll be performing here."

"If I may be so bold as to intrude, I'm told it will be his latest symphony. His ninth. A kind of overview of civilization, from wild dances around a totem pole to the present day, told in an utterly groundbreaking musical language. Indeed, most of his instruments will have been designed specially for him, I hear."

"How interesting, where did you hear that? I've actually heard it will be a kind of tribute to the traditional musical modes, a celebration of the past. I work at the Museum of Musical History, Instruments Division, and there has been this rumor that Selinsky's orchestra will be borrowing some of our oldest pieces."

"No, no, it's a choral composition, they tell me. They'll be doing most of it a cappella, and the costumes will be quite elaborate. Blue and silver silk. And their voices are heavenly."

"Oh, I'd love to hear it."

"Well, you'll get your chance soon."

"Do you think they'll really have the tickets today? It's growing dark already."

"Maybe today, maybe tomorrow, I'll be here."

"Yes, me too . . . And by the way, thanks for the dates, most kind of you."

"Don't mention it, I hate dates myself, they get wedged in your teeth, my sister pressed these on me . . . Hey, since we're stuck here anyway, want to hear me sing?"

2

B Y EIGHT O'CLOCK, Anna had become somewhat unsettled by Sergei's absence. She had grown angry by nine. By ten, she was worried. After finishing with the dishes, she opened the window and, leaning on the windowsill, looked out. The spring night smelled young and raw, of gasoline, damp, and anxiety; the street jangled with the passage of rare trolleys, clicked with the determined retreats of couples on their way home. For some time she stood collecting splinters of quarrels, sorting through squeals of tires. Occasional headlights flashed by in a whirl of song, an unrecognizable fragment of merriment, which made her imagine a close, perfumed dimness, the city breezing past in a black square of smudged illumination, a head thrown back in laughter, a hand lightly grazing a hand . . . After a while, she moved to the bedroom.

She opened the window there as well, but as the room faced the building's inner courtyard, there were no cars, no steps, no voices, no music—no sounds at all. In the diffused, scant light from the hallway, Sergei's tuba lay coiled on the floor like a slumbering dragon, its skin glistening; she felt briefly calmer in its presence, better able to reassure herself that nothing was amiss, that her husband would be arriving at any moment. She had asked him a favor she should not have asked, perhaps, but even so, he would be arriving shortly. She waited, and after a while knew that the night was just as filled with sounds and smells on this darker, private side. They were different here, the sounds and the smells, furtive, hidden, subterranean almost—a whisper instead of a laugh, the wet dip and rise of a tiptoe instead of the click-clack of a heel, a sharp waft of cigarette smoke on the wing of a nocturnal wind, a teakettle singing softly in someone's flat across a span of sky, a bird stirring in precariously balanced sleep or else a girl sighing—a hushed, secret welling of invisible, joyous things within a tight bud of darkness. As she listened, trapped inside her own walled-in allotment of blind space, her breath stilled, her face grew hot, and her blood beat a solitary rhythm in her throat.

It was well past eleven—twenty-three minutes past—when she heard the key in the lock. She stayed where she was; she wanted him—willed him—to enter the shadows of the bedroom, to find her here, quiet and flushed, waiting at the heart of all the unspoken, barely remembered little moments of their nearly twenty years together. The apartment brimmed with the clutter of remote noises—shoes shed, keys tossed, coins dropped, an odd collection of unidentifiable rustles—but the noises failed to come closer, moving into the kitchen instead, expanding there into the clanging of dishes, the shutting of windows, the mechanics of a meal.

Unclenching her hands, she walked out of the bedroom.

Sergei was sitting at the table, a piece of bread on a plate before him.

"Where have you been?" she asked, her voice sharpened by disappointment.

"Standing in line," he said flatly, picking up a slice of butter on his knife.

"Oh," she said. His face was closed as before, but something in it, some thought, some emotion, seemed to have shifted, laying new perspectives open to internal illumination, giving rise to new shadows; it was lighter and darker at the same time. Suddenly uncertain, she tried to catch his eyes. He looked down at the knife; she imagined she glimpsed the reflection of his oblique gray gaze sliding down the stained blade like another sliver of butter.

"You forgot to shut the window," he said as he smeared the bread.

"Sorry, I just thought . . . It's almost April."

"Well, it's still cold at night . . . So they're extending the line hours for the next week or so. Until ten or eleven, they told us."

"Oh," she said again. She felt her whole body sinking, spoke as if drowning. "I suppose I should go to bed, so I'm better rested tomorrow evening, if that's—"

"I don't mind waiting in the evenings for you," he said. "Instead of you."

She went quiet inside, sat down. He studied his buttered bread, then rose, took the knife to the sink, turned on the water. She watched his back mutely.

"I could come by after work, around five," said his back. "To replace you, I mean."

"Serezha." She spoke slowly. "Serezha. I would never ask that of you."

"I don't mind," he repeated, still without turning; through the water's continuous splashing she strained to discern some meaning in his voice devoid of expression. It did not take this long to wash one knife, she thought. "Oh yes, I forgot—I brought you some dates, someone in line was selling them. They are in the bag on the windowsill. I hear you can make a nice cake with them or something . . . Well, my feet are sore, I better go lie down . . ." The water stopped running at last. He moved across the kitchen swiftly, a blur of gray. "Good night."

"Serezha, wait! You haven't yet eaten your bread. I'll sit with you—"

"I'm very tired. Have it if you like. Well, good night."

He left. She listened to his steps accompanied by the flipping of light switches. Then, compelled by a sudden desire to move, to make some gesture, to respond to some obscure feeling already rising inside her, threatening to overwhelm her, she stood abruptly, grabbed the bag with the dates off the windowsill, tied its handles together to prevent the smell from escaping, and walked to the front door, and onto the landing.

Her mouth set, she put the bag on the floor by the trash chute.

Back in the kitchen, she ate the piece of bread she did not want. A neighbor's radio chimed midnight. She thought of a cuckoo clock they had when she was little—a lacquered gingerbread house from whose balcony a crimson-beaked, brightly painted bird took eager, lopsided bows. She used to watch it for hours, she remembered, happily anticipating the passage of time, in some shadowy room of a shadowy house she could no longer trust her memory to furnish; though now the clock, too, had an unreal, dusty quality to it, as if it had been merely an illustration to some fairy tale, glimpsed through a milky, semitransparent sheet used to cover pictures in old books, or a stanza from a poem that now alighted on her lips, a few stray lines she repeated, not knowing where she had heard them.

She fell asleep with the words still moving through her mind— *I live like a cuckoo in a clock, I don't envy birds in forests, They wind me, and I sing*—and their deceptively lighthearted nursery-rhyme rhythm bounced in her barefoot steps when, at three or four in the morning, she rose and traversed the unlit treachery of cluttered hallways, gathering bruises on her naked shins. On the way back from the bathroom she paused, for a strange green light, wavering like seaweed, seemed to seep from under her mother's door. She pressed her temple against the doorjamb and, barely awake, thought she heard a voice, quivering like sunlight under the water, weaving in and out of sleep, then falling silent. Lowering herself onto the floor, she leaned against the wall and drifted into an uneasy doze; and in her slumber, the voice was speaking again, and her dream was spin-

ning, spinning it out like a thread of fine silk, and the thread gently
wound round and round, and round, enclosing her in a warm co-
coon, and the voice asked:

Have you ever seen a chestnut tree?

A pity. Close your eyes, my dear, and imagine.

In the Western city where I lived as a child grew hundreds of
chestnut trees. Whole alleys of them, whole gardens, whole parks
even. They were beautiful trees, tall and strong, some of them centuries old. For one week in the spring, the city would light up with
thousands upon thousands of soft candles of chestnut blossoms, and
in the fall, when pavements whispered with dead leaves, there would
be thousands of chestnuts, hard and glossy, hidden among them.
Their color was bright—not quite brown, not quite red, much like
the lustrous, heaving sides of horses I would sometimes see pranc-
ing along the paths in the chestnut parks.

Our second autumn in the city, my mother told me that chestnuts contained new chestnut trees inside them. She was always
teaching me the names of plants, the calls of birds, the wayward secrets of seeds. I was eight years old. The next day in the park, I
stomped on a chestnut until it split open. It had a wrinkled kernel
inside. I tried another, and another, and another—they were all the
same. But I could not forget my mother's words. I began to believe
that some chestnuts were different, rare and precious like four-leaf
clovers. The special chestnuts concealed inside them the gift of a real
tree, half the size of my little finger, yet grown to miniature perfec-
tion, with hair-thin branches and droplets of pink and yellow blossoms. I started spending hours in parks and gardens, turning over
damp, sweetly rotting leaves. Gathering handfuls of chestnuts, I
broke them open, hoping that after two or three or four hundred
attempts I would at last be rewarded with a tiny enchantment complete with gnarled roots and the smell of spring flowering.

The leaves yielded other secrets now and then; one day I uncovered a golden pendant shaped like a dainty slipper, and another

time, a mildewed silk glove of a lovely turquoise tint. These small offerings only left me wistful. As twilight claimed the city, I would hurriedly cram more chestnuts into my pockets, into my dance bag, and bring them home, and, spilling them on the floor of my room, smash them open with a bronze paperweight in the form of a boot. Later I would secretly dispose of the dusty remains. They lost their velvety sheen when broken.

After a while I stopped prying the chestnuts apart. I let them accumulate instead, lined them along the walls, arranged them in curves and circles. I thought that perhaps, without my knowing, a hidden chestnut grove rustled and blossomed in my bedroom, and that was enough.

Eventually my mother noticed.

Our concierge knew a great number of chestnut recipes. Chestnut croquettes were her favorite. You mixed hot mashed chestnuts with egg yolks, thick cream, and sugar, then added essence of vanilla. My mother let me shape the paste into little balls. I became quite skilled at it.

Of course, you'll ask whether I stopped believing, or whether I still thought that, perhaps—oh, pardon the—

On the other side of the wall, her mother coughed, and with a start, Anna opened her eyes. The place was absolutely still, but she suddenly had the same sense of marvelous, secret things ripening stealthily within the bud of the night—except that now she too was a part of it, she too was slowly growing, cresting within the darkness. Then, as she was, barefoot, in her nightgown, she rushed out to the landing, and down the steps, her feet burning on the icy concrete. Mercifully, the bag was still there, behind some empty bottles. She took it inside, and for a long, long time rinsed the fruit in warm water, trying not to notice the two or three small insects with whitish, bloated, segmented bellies that swam up and drowned and twirled away.

In the morning she almost cried as she remembered her dream—

the translucent green glow under the closed door, the pocket-sized chestnut forest, the dates miraculously restored to the windowsill— but when she entered the kitchen, the dates were there, the dates were there!

She hummed under her breath while cooking her family breakfast.

She continued to hum for the next two weeks as she went about her stealthy errands, making inquiries of her acquaintances, standing in other lines, assembling little by little the impossible, precious ingredients. At last, just in time, all was ready; for surely, sugared water with a lemon squeezed into it would be just as good as orange flower water, whatever that might be, while strawberry jam (a gift from her downstairs neighbor) was much, much tastier than apricot— and almonds, well, never mind the almonds; all the saleswomen had laughed in her face at the mere question.

On a bright, windy afternoon in early April, just after five o'clock, she met Sergei at the corner to take his tuba from him and to hand over their number and a *buterbrod* wrapped in a napkin, as she did every day. "I'll see you at the usual time, then," she said, struggling to keep her excitement from breaking into her voice with an expectant, girlish giggle. Her fingers briefly lingered in his.

Withdrawing his hand, he slid the number into his pocket and his eyes past her face.

"Yes, yes," he said. As he walked away, she stood gazing for a moment at his retreating gray jacket, smiling to herself. Then she ran home, the tuba impatiently nudging her in the back.

She was eager to begin their evening.

When he joined the line, Pavel, the tanned man at number 136, was there already, having just replaced a woman in a vulgar flowery hat; Sergei saw her motley scarf stream around the corner. The young woman with the pale eyelids appeared at the end of the street a half-hour later, as always, crossing the boundary between the clear dusk and the uncertain street illumination. In the last few days, a new sonorousness had spread through the air, as it did for a short time every April; her steps rang with a small crystal sound as if she were walking on a sheet of glass. He imagined the glass to be deep blue in color, vibrating lightly just beneath the veneer of the city.

"I've given your arguments some thought," he was saying as he pretended not to watch her, "and I fear I can't agree. Folk songs . . . Oh, hello, Sofia Mikhailovna, nice evening, isn't it? . . . Folk songs do not come from the depths of the 'national spirit,' as you call it. On the contrary, they lie on the surface—simple music, wholly devoid of individuality or inspiration, field rhythms, chanted by peasant masses to avoid dozing off while planting potatoes and whatnot."

"You do not, then, believe in the national spirit?" Pavel asked.

"There you go again," Sofia Mikhailovna said without smiling.

"I do, I do wholeheartedly! But to my mind, it's to be found elsewhere—namely, in the unique creations of our brightest composers, and the more original, the better. Like Selinsky. It's precisely in these flashes of genius, born every generation or two—"

"Pardon me, I didn't mean to eavesdrop," interrupted a balding middle-aged man with a shoe brush for a mustache, two places behind, "but did I just hear you say that Selinsky embodies our national spirit? Because, and you must pardon me for the intrusion, that is nonsense." Taking a step off the sidewalk, he bent down, scraped his fingers against the still-hardened ground; the bald spot on his head flushed red with the effort, and in the opening of his shirt Sergei glimpsed the swinging of a small pewter cross on a thread. "This," the man said, holding up his hand smudged with dirt, "this is our national spirit. No more, no less. Selinsky chose to leave his country, and by doing so, betrayed his gift. He may well be a genius—and I for one will gladly sacrifice my time for the pleasure of listening to his music—but as he no longer stands on his native soil, his art can't possibly have roots. An artist creates true art for his people only so long as he lives, and suffers, among them."

"But surely you're following the letter, not the spirit, of the matter!" Sergei objected. "Take our greatest writers of the past century—did most of them not spend years and years abroad, in the West? Yet no one questions their place in our culture . . . What do *you* think?"

"I believe one can carry one's country within," she said with her usual soft-spoken conviction. "It's the depth of—of one's affinity that matters, not one's address . . . But I think you're wrong about our folk songs. Maybe you've just never listened to them properly."

"Perhaps," he said, "but don't you think—"

The evening was deepening, floating on a wave of cool, radiant dusk. He searched for, and failed to find, that initial disappointment that had gripped him some days earlier, when he had first realized he was in for a longer wait. With a clean, young, forgotten kind of pleasure, he filled his lungs with the small nighttime breezes as he drifted in and out of conversations, listened to Pavel sing in a reedy yet oddly stirring voice, watched the thin chill of darkness slowly transform Sofia Mikhailovna's pallid features until, once again, they acquired that fragile, feathery purity of an old painting. Later, at ten o'clock, just as he was about to take his reluctant leave, the bearded organizer moved down the line, marking off names and informing everyone that the neighboring Nightingales kiosk had received an unexpected delivery of tickets at two in the morning and that it might make sense to stick around longer tonight. Sergei's heart leapt with a surprising, fierce gladness; and he was suddenly grateful to the selfless man with the list, to the people in line around him, these strangers who held dear the very things that were dear to him.

"Two in the morning?" he said loudly. "That's outrageous, what next!"

"An alphabet game?" inquired Pavel. "I give you a letter, you give me a composer. Vladimir Semyonovich, are you in?"

"You bet," said the man with the shoe-brush mustache.

When he came home that night, pale squares of windows swam through the darkness; the sky was already holding its frosted breath in anticipation of a new day. Leaving the place unlit, he walked to the kitchen. On the threshold he halted. There was a chaos of indistinguishable shapes on the table, on the chairs, on the counter— small, discrete, mysterious gaps in the fabric of shadows. For an instant he felt a peculiar sensation in his nose, in the cavity of his mouth, as if something viscous and sweet were pushing its way through some invisible barrier; but before he quite made up his mind to investigate, the deepest accumulation of shadow resolved itself unmistakably into the curved spine of his wife collapsed asleep at the table, her cheek on her outstretched arms.

A heady rush of unease swept him off into the bedroom, and kept him in a state of sleepless, tense immobility all through the early-morning hours, even while she softly called his name as she readied herself for work. After her departure, he drifted off to some frozen terrain, the gliding ice field of a dream dipping unsteadily through cold black waters. Waking up with a start an hour later, he was so hurried to get to the theater on time that he cast only the most cursory glance into the kitchen, and saw, through the spiraling of his tuba, a pattern of plates he did not recognize, of candles melded into saucers with careful spillages of wax, of glasses neatly arranged, as though in readiness for something. But as he chased an errant trolley down the street, another windy day got tangled up in what was left of his hair and wiped his puzzlement out; and by the time he met her on their usual corner, he had forgotten all about it, overwhelmed as he always was by a weak-kneed surge of guilty relief—another afternoon passed, and the tickets hadn't gone on sale yet, not on her watch, not on her watch—

She seemed about to speak, was peering at him with some timid yet urgent purpose.

"I'll see you at the usual time," he said quickly, already moving away to prevent her words from being born; but later that evening, the bearded organizer announced that he thought it prudent to extend their waiting for another night or two, just in case. When darkness crept in, the line began to twitch with unrest. People came and went; old characters, their faces worn thin by the weeks of vigil like profiles on coins long in circulation, slunk off in search of un-damaged telephone booths, new characters stepped into the fray, and the organizer swore with passion as he struggled to keep up with the rapidly metamorphosing list. At ten, Pavel made his exit, announcing that his replacement would be by in a bit, and in an-other half-hour, Sofia Mikhailovna turned upon Sergei her bruised gaze of a medieval angel and, thanking him quietly for his kind offer, gave him her number, her fingers brushing his palm in passing—unintentionally, he was sure—and left in turn.

He spent the rest of his time in a trance of exhaustion, his eyes closed, his wife's number folded in his right hand, Sofia Mikhail-ovna's in his left, the enormity of the wait beginning to bear down on his spirit at last. At two o'clock he staggered away, feeling as if the tips of his curled fingers had dissolved in chilly numbness. A bearded old man sat smoking on the curb, flipping a matchbox up into the air, catching it, tossing it up again. As Sergei stumbled into a drift-ing cloud of smoke, the dark street beyond shimmered and vanished. The old man looked up.

"Patience," he said thoughtfully. "It will be worth it."

"What?" Sergei paused involuntarily.

When the old man smiled, his features became impossible to dis-cern, obliterated by a cobweb of minute lines. "The music," he said. "The most beautiful music you've ever heard."

Sergei's eyes followed the flips of the matchbox—up and down, up and down, up and down in the wide strip of lavender streetlight went the sky-blue box with the golden script on one side . . . In the end he said nothing, only nodded, and walked home, his head ringing with hollow lightness from lack of sleep; and in the morning, after waiting, with his eyelids pressed tightly shut, for the front door to close behind his wife, he threw the blanket aside and, leaping barefoot into the hallway, cornered his son on his way out.

"All right," the boy said morosely. "It will cost you a fiver, though."

Sergei considered him in disgusted silence, thought of launching into a speech about their lost savings, went to retrieve his pants instead (a glance cast into the kitchen revealed the two small armies of glasses and candlesticks still confronting each other across the table in a perplexing battle formation), turned his pockets inside out.

"Two now," he conceded. "Three more later, if you actually show up."

To his surprise, Alexander did, not precisely at ten, to be sure, but soon enough after. Sofia Mikhailovna had left a few minutes before; she too had arranged for a substitute, someone in the family, he gathered, to join the line shortly. He walked off, careless of the direction, thinking vaguely that he did not wish to go home just yet; it was, after all, a perfect night for a stroll. A street away, he chanced to glimpse her, and quickened his steps—then realized that she was talking to someone, a man; he could see the man's back curving like a tall question mark inside a light coat. He slowed down, fell back, his mood abruptly, inexplicably, soured; but in another minute, the man turned and shuffled forth with a laborious, aged tread, looking through Sergei with the pale bespectacled eyes of another injured angel. Her father, a voice shouted in his mind, and, exhaling, he ran down the street, heedless of the muddy stains from the rain that had trudged through the city earlier that day.

"Oh," she said. "It's you. You gave me a bit of a start."

"A pleasant evening," he said, out of breath. "Strange to be awake, yet not in line."

"Thank you again for last night. For keeping my place, I mean. I was very tired."

"Of course. Anytime."

They stood looking at each other in silence, then spoke at once.

He said, "If you like, I could walk you home, it's getting quite—"

She said, "It's late, but if you like, we could stop by my work, I'll play you some—"

Their words, colliding, intercepted each other in mid-flight.

She said, "Oh, thank you, I'd like—"

He said, "Sure, that would be—"

They laughed then, a short, embarrassed laugh, but a laugh all the same, and somehow the moment filled with lightness, and as they walked to the Museum of Musical History, a half-hour away, he thought that if he tilted his head up, he could watch the moment turn airborne and float away, small and carefree, through streaks of smoking streetlamps, through pockets of night, up over the roofs and the churches of the old city, growing nebulous and pearly until it became just another wisp of an April cloud.

In the old mansion where the museum was housed, he followed her from room to room. The corners were full of theatrical, dusty moonlight and indifferent late-shift caretakers and old instruments with lovely curves and stretched, sinuous necks. Standing so close to her that their shoulders almost touched—almost, but not quite—he marveled at the light azure lacquer of harpsichords with garlands of ivory cupids cavorting along their sides, and brittle violins with delicate landscapes blossoming inside their cases; and as she pointed out her favorite pieces, which she had known and tended for years, for which she had made up little affectionate nicknames, he imagined these rooms not bleak and dusty but brilliant with lights, adorned with silk, pastel-colored trifles, and her in a long, narrow dress,

seated at one of the azure harpsichords, playing melancholy, lingering music, or absently caressing a gold-throated harp with her pale
hands—but as he glanced at her hands, he caught the glint of a ring
on her finger, and his vision dimmed.

"Shall we go listen to your songs, then?" he asked brusquely.

"Of course," she said after the slightest pause. "This way. Could
you please turn off the light on the way out?"

She led him along a corridor with many closed doors, into a small
place crowded with a herd of gramophones. She appeared to hesitate briefly among their yawning black-tongued maws, then walked
over to one with an air of daring. "The earliest model we have. A bit
cranky, but so nice. Special. Here, you'll like this, I'm certain—"

She sat across from him, her eyes closed; he now discovered that
the thin blue veins on her eyelids had not been a trick of the evening
light after all. He forced himself to look away, to listen as the creaky
gramophone whined about fates crossing and stars falling and grasses
swaying, the whole world setting off on a treacherous, intoxicating
ride toward distant horizons where horses galloped and winds whis-
tled and lovers died young and doomed and maddeningly happy.
Then his thoughts wandered. He remembered meeting Anna, two
decades ago now, in the neighborhood doctor's dingy vestibule; neither of them had been ill, but both needed the doctor's signature on
a document required by their place of employment; both had been
bored and distracted, wedged next to each other in a restless crowd
of coughing supplicants. He had incurred some crone's wrath for allowing Anna to go in before him, out of turn, and later, leaving the
office, had been touched to find her there still, waiting for him in
the windowless trap of the room before the forbidding blind door.
He thought too of all the many closed doors he had glimpsed in the
secret reaches of this place, opening, he imagined, onto polished
vistas of grand pianos and mysterious little gardens of impercepti-
bly vibrating violins and deep moonlit pools of symphonies and

sonatas flitting about with the shimmer of chance reflections, with
the grace of rare butterflies—

"So what did you think?" she asked.

The song had ended. She was looking at him.

"You were right," he said, rising. "It was special."

An hour later, having seen her to her building, he slowly walked
home. His way took him past the kiosk. The line had dispersed, but
a few characters still clustered in the moist darkness, their lit cigarettes circling about their heads like a flock of dull red moths. He saw
his son talking to some man whose face was invisible, whose shadow
made wild leaps across the pavement; the streetlamp blinked erratically, for the bulb needed replacing. He called out across the street,
watched one burning moth dive to the ground, become hastily
squashed.

He thought of speaking sharply to the boy, then said nothing.

Their steps kept falling out of rhythm as they crossed what was
left of the night.

"Mother came by the line looking for you," the boy said. "She
had a pie with her."

"A pie?"

"A pie or a cake. Something she baked. She wanted you to
have it."

"How silly," Sergei said absently. "Why not wait till I get
home."

He wondered whether she wore perfume. He would never
know, he supposed; it was not the kind of thing one could casually
ask—though perhaps he would ask, on the evening of the concert.
For the first time openly, without willing himself to suppress the
indulgent thought, he dared to picture the unrolling staircase, Sofia's
small hand trembling lightly in the crook of his arm, a row of soft
velvet chairs, the girlish angularity of her pale cheek inclining gently to his shoulder, a hush so perfect, so palpable, it would rise like
a cloud to the immensity of the ceiling, and then the communal in-

take of breath, Selinsky, Selinsky, it's really him, the flying steps, the flying tuxedo coattails, the flying white hair—and then the first, dizzying twirl of a baton flying through the awed air—and then . . . But here his fantasy grew vague, then stalled altogether. The draining necessity of daily evasions, the stress of worrying about the ticket falling into his wife's oblivious possession, the harrowing prospect, in the event of his success, of having to concoct some explanation for his empty-handed return from the line, of then finding a safe place to hide his treasure, of erecting another precarious scaffolding of lies to obscure his absence on the night of the concert—the constant, unclean exertion of it all oppressed him again, and again he assured himself it was only right that he should be the one to hear Selinsky, he was not a dishonest man, he was entitled, yes, entitled—for had his whole life, with all its missed chances, its unrealized longings, its reversals of fortune, not guaranteed him this music, this gift, this—

"They told everyone to hang around till two again tomorrow," his son said with a sideways glance, and, when Sergei did not respond, offered, "I can replace you at ten like today, if you want. For another fiver."

"Math isn't your strongest point, is it? Do you know what my salary is?"

"Three, then, I'll do it for three," Alexander said quickly.

They stopped before their building. Sergei looked at him for a moment. It would be madness, he knew, to try to explain; the boy could never understand what it meant to desire something with such ache, such fierceness . . .

"You can't stay out till two on a regular basis," he said at last. "You have school."

"It's not regular. It's only two days, today and tomorrow. I just want to help."

Sergei hesitated.

"Well, all right," he said then. "Just one thing. If the tickets go on sale on your watch, bring the ticket to me. I want to give it to your grandmother myself. Agreed?"

"Sure, whatever," Alexander said, though he wouldn't quite meet his father's eyes.

Struggling to disregard the bitter taste in his mouth, Sergei hunted for his wallet.

3

YOU MUST BE NEW, I haven't seen you here before."

"Yeah, just helping out with the late shift."

"Ah yes, the late shift! Some people are complaining, you know, what are the chances, they say, that the tickets will go on sale at one in the morning. But I say to them, you never know, these things can't be predicted, and in any case, a little extra hope never hurt anyone . . . Have one to spare, perhaps? And a light? . . . Thank you, thank you kindly. And then, let's face it, it's not like we'd rather be somewhere else. I suffer from insomnia, you know—used to sit in the dark for hours, talking to myself. Now I come here, meet people, shoot the breeze, it's something to do. Folks trade jokes, there's a fellow who sings over there . . . Ah, I see another new face, a boy, must have come to help out his father. See the man walking away? A great expert on music, that one, he and that other fellow, the one with the mustache there—"

"Hey, I know that boy. Well, I better get to my place. See you around, then . . . Why, hello, looks like we're neighbors, you're number one thirty-seven? What, don't you recognize me? Nikolai, remember?"

Alexander did not reply. He had spotted the bastard only a

minute earlier, a hulking shadow in the misty blur of the streetlamp, sharing a smoke with some other crook, both of them turning to stare at him, and laughing, laughing . . . His breath still had not returned.

"So whatever happened to you?" the scoundrel asked cheerfully. "I waited at the station for three hours, but you never showed up."

Alexander stood seething, directing his gaze above the man's head.

"Ah, I get it. I get it. You think—you must think I cheated you out of your money or something. Well, I'm offended. I'm actually offended. I should make you eat that stupid ticket I bought you— had to wait in line for it, too—only I misplaced it somewhere."

"Misplaced it. That's rich," Alexander said between his teeth.

"Believe me, don't believe me, it's all the same to me. It's no good now, anyway. In any case, you shouldn't care, you're about to strike gold, why should you care?"

"Oh, yeah? And how am I about to do that, exactly?"

The thief seemed surprised. "You're here for the Selinsky concert, yes?"

"So?" Alexander said, refusing to look at him.

"So just think." He pushed his face so close that Alexander could smell his stale odor of drink and sweat. "A fancy composer returning home for one single concert! Hordes of folks will be dying to see him, but not everyone can spend their days hanging around this sidewalk. Get my meaning? Your time here is money, my friend. You buy at a low State price, pay a little visit to a certain little place you and I know, I introduce you to some good people, you walk away with your pockets stuffed."

Against his will, Alexander's thoughts flared out to let in the chilled church air that had seemed cut from a slab unlike the air outside, the rolling of flashlight beams over the half-glimpsed manifestations of his most secret, inarticulate desires, the expansive, generous feeling that for a few heartbeats had swelled his chest with an exhilarating foretaste of adulthood, the sense of something happening, happening at last, in his life . . .

"How much, do you think?" he blurted.

The man leaned in to whisper, his lips almost touching Alexander's ear.

"Get lost," Alexander gasped, staring.

The man nodded solemnly. "Maybe more. Enough to take your train three or four times over."

And immediately Alexander's thoughts shrank to a bright, glaring pinpoint of anger. The station, the slobbery confidences he had drunkenly drooled to the bastard, the humiliation of watching the trains together . . . His insides twisted hotly. He took a step back.

"This ticket isn't mine," he said in a voice strained with renewed fury.

The man shrugged good-naturedly. "Whatever, I'm only trying to help. You'd be doing your family a favor. I mean, if I were your mother, I'd rather buy something nice with the extra cash than spend two hours sitting in a stuffy room listening to creaky violins. But I guess she really loves music. I always say, there's no accounting for people's tastes—"

"Don't waste your breath," Alexander spat, and turned away.

The night slithered past, leaving everything moist and glistening in its wake. Just before midnight, his mother shuffled by, mortifying him with some smelly cake wrapped in a bundle. As it grew later, the last dim windows in the apartment buildings lining the street were extinguished one by one, and the city was erased until morning, sunk like a dull, heavy stone to the nightly bottom of its dreamless sleep. He stood staring into the spring vastness of the sky, which floated so high above that it seemed to belong to an entirely different city, and his thoughts floated after it, unsettlingly adrift. He was here for one night only, though, so there was no need to worry about what the man had said, he wouldn't trust him anyway, nor would he be around when the tickets went on sale, there was no need at all . . .

In another hour, a fellow with a brigand's beard, from the front of the line, announced that they should expect to stay late the next day as well, and possibly the day after that, perhaps through the end of the week; a late-night delivery, said the fellow, was quite likely. He could not help thinking about it then, at least in passing. Little by little he fell into an uneasy conversation with Nikolai. Nikolai told him stories. His stories transpired on the far edges of the land, where the trees came so close together that the sun could not reach the ground, and fierce animals roamed the shores of blinding lakes, and men with chins rough as sandpaper and arms the width of his thighs drove trucks along dangerous roads, across twisting canyons, through small, wild villages where almond-eyed women wore their hair long and loose, and barefoot boys rode unsaddled horses, and lives had the timeless inevitability of legends . . .

When he stopped to catch his breath, Alexander swallowed and said, "But what would I tell them?"

Nikolai grinned at him. "Have a cigarette. Let's see, you were already mugged once, right? . . . Well, how about—it fell out on the way home because you have a hole in your pocket."

"I don't," Alexander said. His throat felt burnt.

"Do you happen to have that knife on you still? I thought you might. Here, don't move for a second . . . and there you go, you do now. What do they teach you in school, anyway?"

Alexander pushed his fingers through the rip, wiggled them a little.

"Hey, I think that man there is calling you."

Alexander wheeled around and abruptly dropped his cigarette at the sight of his father.

"Oh, yeah, him," he said. "A fellow I drink with now and then. Well, better be off."

"See you tomorrow?"

"Yeah, maybe, if I'm not too busy."

Anna woke up when her husband and son stomped past the kitchen. She did not lift her head, only opened her eyes and watched them from the darkness. Her neck was sore; for the third night, she had fallen asleep at the table. The lived-in space around her was dense with the odors of sugar and the barely present suggestion of a roach spray used some weeks before.

She felt invisible.

The next morning, Sergei was still asleep; he always was these days. She paused in the bedroom doorway, looked at the side of his face squashed against the pillow. For one instant she thought she saw his eye dart tensely beneath his lid, and held her breath, but there was no other movement; she tiptoed out. In the kitchen, she packed the date tart into her school bag.

She had stopped by the floor below on the previous evening, to return the glasses and candlesticks she had borrowed. Elizaveta Nikitishna, her voice simpering, had asked about the anniversary supper. "Your twentieth, wasn't it?" she had exclaimed. "How did it go?"

"It was lovely," Anna had replied, and the neighbor, who was not married, had pressed her hands together and breathed out, "Oh Annushka, you're so lucky."

"Yes," Anna had agreed sadly, gazing over Elizaveta Nikitishna's shoulder at the stretch of her shining parquet corridor, a broom resting discreetly in a corner, ready to be banged against the ceiling at the first sounds of the tuba.

In school, Anna stashed the tart in her desk drawer and closed it with care, to trap the scent of musky fermentation. She taught three classes that day. She had decided she would call her first class to attention just before the bell rang, extract the treat with a modest flourish, smile as the children clapped; but when the time came, it was only ten in the morning, and amidst the bright confusion of sunbeams crossing on the ceiling she did not yet feel ready to part with the image she had carried within herself for almost a month—her husband in the luminous, intimate shadows of the candles, leaning toward her as he asked for another piece—though she did not blame him for her disappointment, of course; she knew it was only the line, scraping their days empty of meaning and warmth, taking them away from each other, making their lives so much smaller. She let the second class go as well. The third period seemed to last longer than its allotted hour. A boy stood up to read a story he had written, about a man who lost an arm in a factory incident under the old regime and later led his fellow workers in a righteous rebellion, shooting the factory director with his one good arm in the triumphant final scene. The boy's exultant diction disturbed her; she gave him the highest mark. A girl asked for permission to take a bathroom break, and crept back almost half an hour later, crying. Anna tried not to look in her direction, but she felt an odd touch of fear—not fear of these children, exactly, but of some presence she sensed in the room, vicious and strident. When the bell sounded, she watched them leave without moving.

She knew a little park near her building that was always full of pigeons; as she stood in line that afternoon, she considered walking over as soon as she was free, tossing crumbs on the ground, letting the feathery waves lap and flap and scramble at her feet. Then she thought of something else. Turning, she looked at the boy behind her.

He did not resemble the children in school.

"Do you like sweets?" she asked.

He said nothing, only nodded. He had been silent of late; the sky in his eyes had grown overcast. "I have something for you, then," she said with an odd sense of relief, and added in a low voice, so as not to be overheard by the bright-mouthed woman before her (they had avoided speaking to each other since the dates incident), "I'll give it to you once we leave here."

The boy nodded again.

At five, she asked him to wait while she met with her husband. The afternoon was gray and quiet; as she hurried toward Sergei, she could hear his footsteps at the other end of the street falling in with hers, as though she were being approached by her own echo.

"Any news?" he said, stopping. It was his day off, but he looked tired, his eyes washed out, deeper shadows beneath them; within his absent, preoccupied face, the animated, handsome face of a man she had once known lay obscured as if by a layer of thin, translucent wax. It's the line, she thought again, and looked away, pained, saying with a small, insincere smile, "Everyone says it will be soon now," holding out their number. He exhaled—dismayed, she knew, that another afternoon passed and it wasn't yet over—then moved beyond her; and immediately her chest felt hollowed out by a gust of panic, a sense of something precious escaping her, perhaps forever—

"Wait!" she cried, catching his sleeve.

He paused. "What is it?"

Hesitating, the bag with the tart heavy in her hand, she glanced back. The boy was where she had left him, standing on the corner, his eyes cast down, dragging his foot back and forth along the pavement, drawing some figure in the dust. Her heart twisted inside her.

"Nothing," she said, releasing him.

"Well, don't stay up for me tonight. I might be late. The line, you know."

"I know," she replied after a pause, and turned away slowly.

They walked, she and the boy, until the kiosk was out of sight; then she halted.

"I baked it myself," she told him, taking out the wrapped tart and offering it to him. "You could invite some friends over for a party. Is your birthday anytime soon?"

"It was last month," he said without moving.

"Well, then, just have a nice cup of tea with your parents."

"Mama won't be home for a few hours."

She waited, but he did not add anything about his father, and she was conscious of standing before him like a supplicant, her hands outstretched, the hush closing in on her.

"You could come with me," the boy said, staring at his shoes.

She thought of the meal she was expected to start preparing in another half-hour, as the spring's transparent wings beat wildly against the kitchen's steamed-up windowpanes—and was surprised to hear herself reply: "Thank you. I'd like that."

They did not talk on the way. Beyond the sour depths of an alley with its plaster gouged out by vandals, the robust aromas of other families' suppers reached her with efficient clicks of utensils through windows opened to the first warm evening of the year. At the end of the next street, the boy showed her inside a gray building lowered like a gloomy brow, and on, through the dim confinement of a foyer lined with darkened rows of mailboxes, to the elevator, which seemed only slightly larger than a mailbox and into which they squeezed like two letters through a narrow mail slot. He pressed a button with a tentative air, then waited, his head tilted; after a long pause, ancient cogs jerked moaning into reluctant motion somewhere beneath them, and the box shook upward, going dark, then light, then dark again as they passed the floors. Released onto the landing of the fourth floor, Anna inhaled a whiff of sour milk, glimpsed a blue-rimmed saucer, the darting streak of a homeless cat; then the door squealed inward.

"This way," said the boy, gesturing, though there was only one way to go.

The living space beyond was small, badly kempt, driven into tight corners by the advance of heavy brown furniture, bulky tables, deep armchairs, all much too large for it. "I sleep on the sofa here," he said as he switched on a lamp. In the blotchy light, she was startled to see photographs gleaming under glass amidst the faded floral garlands of the ancient wallpaper, each frame now containing a small, blinding image of the squat orange lampshade. Hesitantly she approached, found herself looking at two stiffly attired lanky youths, the older one smiling, the younger serious, their arms around each other's shoulders.

"That's grandfather with a cousin," the boy explained, intercepting her glance. "They both studied music, a long time ago."

She saw the elaborate, old-fashioned scroll designs in the margins of the picture, a child's fingerprints glistening darkly along the edges of the dusty frame, and moved away in discomfort. She had been taught, though in such circumspect ways she was not even sure when or by whom, that old photographs possessed a vague air of menace, holding as they did a troublesome invitation to peer into thumb-sized, out-of-focus faces lined up in solemn tribute to forgotten occasions, family anniversaries, diminutive triumphs better left to lie concealed in the decaying obscurity of albums, nibbled by silverfish that scurried past.

"And who's this?" she asked, pointing.

The boy considered the laughing thin-faced man for some moments, as if seeing him for the first time.

"My father," he said then. "This was seven years ago, we don't have any recent pictures. And that's Mama . . . Here, I'll show you the way."

Anna followed him into the kitchen, which did not smell of food. He watched her with an odd look, shy yet avid, as she filled the teakettle with water, found two cups, got the tart out of her bag. "Only we don't have a plate big enough," he said. "Just some saucers."

"We'll cut it into small bits, then," she announced. "Where do you keep your knives?"

She felt awkward opening and shutting cupboards in someone else's house. Their insides breathed staleness; she caught a glitter of tarnished silver hidden behind a stack of mismatched dishes. The kettle would not boil for the longest time, minutes and minutes of waiting (she recognized the clock on the wall, big and round, its black-and-white face awash with excess blankness); when it did so at last, it whined like a forlorn provincial train, and the kitchen departed with a rickety, unsteady wobble for the nightly shadows.

"Can we just drink water?" the boy said, holding the open tea caddy. "Mama has only a couple spoonfuls of tea left."

She watched him as he gingerly tasted the cake.

"It's nice," he said, and set it down on his saucer.

She tried it in turn, found her tongue glued to her gums with the cloying sweetness of rot.

"I'm glad you like it," she said, setting her piece down as well. Must have kept the dates out on the windowsill for too long, she chided herself. For a while after that, they sat in silence, sipping hot water, inhaling the dim, stale, quiet smells of the kitchen filled with things unused, things not needed. "When I was little," she said at last, looking past him, "we had a big family and many friends. On my father's side. We had wonderful suppers together. My parents owned the most beautiful china, with thin golden rims, so delicate you could see candlelight right through it. Only one cup is left now, but once, there was enough for twenty-four people, and not one plate remained in the cupboards during our suppers, that's how many guests we'd have." As she talked, she felt the vague sketch of her childhood expanding around her, flooding with color, ringing with noisy children, warming with flames in glowing fireplaces— becoming real. "I remember soup smoking in the tureens. After we had our dessert, my mother would play the piano . . . Then my father died crossing the street. Automobiles were rare in those days, so people forgot to look. Before the Change."

"My father isn't dead," said the boy. "He's just away. He'll be back someday."

"Of course he will," she said with a teacher's bright intonation.

He looked at her mutely, and the clouds moved fast in his aged eyes.

She grew flustered then, and wanted to say something else, something meaningful, something he would remember, perhaps, years from now. For an instant she thought she sensed the right words: they were already crowding her mouth, powerful and wise, rolling like heavy, primordial boulders along her tongue—but as she was about to speak, a loud, leathery sound exploded in the next room, as if a demented bat had smashed into the wall.

The boy, who had been staring at her without blinking, waiting for something, quickly looked down at his hands. "Grandfather has a cough. It's not contagious or anything," he said.

The boulders rolled back down her tongue, smaller, smaller yet—mere rocks, then pebbles, then only sand, scratching, hurting her throat—until she no longer knew what they were, what they had been. "I thought you were alone," she said, whispering for some reason.

"Grandfather always naps in the evenings."

"I should go now."

"You could stay to meet him. He's awake."

She shook her head, rising.

"They'll be waiting for me at home," she lied. "I—I'll leave the cake for you."

She walked uneasily past the black-and-white strangers on the walls, feeling as if she had peeked uninvited through a keyhole and seen the intimate, raw underbellies of lives she had no right to invade—the dead man with a radiant smile, his mousy widow-wife, her eyes under invisible eyelashes stretched thin with sorrow, the two gangly, overdressed youths from the previous century who might have once, amidst the gilt, the stateliness, the tranquillity of the past, dreamed courageous dreams of becoming great musicians, of escaping the ordinariness of their lots—of not ending their days in shabby apartments of dreary buildings, cherishing no hopes but to live long enough to attend someone else's concert . . .

She walked slowly, but her heart beat as though she were fleeing.

Once outside, she ran, ran through the luminous April evening fresh with green twilight, through the light, clear smells that tugged at her hair, her clothes, her heart with fierce, wordless summons. When she got home, she hurried to the bedroom, and, consumed by urgency, plowed through a drawer, throwing clothes about in rising frustration, at last pulling out, from under a flattened layer of winter stockings, a brown-tinted snapshot, which fit inside her palm. She closed her hand over it, feeling the thickness of the paper under her fingertips.

"A big family and many friends on my father's side," she repeated aloud, indecisively, as if testing the truth of her words.

That night she did not sleep, groping for the contours of her past in the well of her memory the color of a winter night, encountering only the underside of strange, insubstantial feelings that scurried away from her touch like the cockroaches that ran off when the light came on in the kitchen. She had been only five at the time of the Change; she had forgotten more than she remembered. Sometime before dawn, she tiptoed down the corridor, and stopped, and listened; but of course, there was no voice, there had never been any voice, all was quiet. She wanted to burst inside, shake her mother awake, demand answers to all the things she did not know, all the things she had not thought to ask before. Tell me why you need a ticket to this concert. Do you miss your youth, your years in the ballet, before you had me, before everything changed? Tell me about your dancing. And my father, tell me about my father. Did he want you to keep dancing, or was he glad of me? Were you? And where did we live before that drafty communal apartment I remember from later? Did I have many friends? Did I dream up the fireplace, the piano, the suppers? And where were you on that day when my father stepped into the road without looking?

Did you cry for him?

Did you love him?

Were you happy?

She rested her hand briefly on the door handle, held its cold concealed in her palm, then returned to her bed, to her husband's unnaturally measured snores. She spent the next week or two combing the neighborhood, and in the end, slightly queasy, bought a small framed portrait of a somber-eyed woman, someone's aunt or godmother, perhaps, from a breezy character in a torn jacket who accosted her in a deserted alley, his breath vile, his pockets spilling with all sorts of pathetic, expiring knickknacks. At home, having mauled the corners of her father's square photograph with the dull scissors she used for splaying open her special-occasion chickens, she crammed it into the oval frame. She had not discarded the unknown woman; a bit of the woman's white dress still showed in a jagged rip produced by a nervous dip of her hand. When she was done, she studied her father's stolid middle-aged face, his nearsighted, kindly eyes, the shadowy presence of the second chin; then, not finding what she sought, she carefully placed the newly framed picture on her nightstand.

Still, that recent feeling of urgency did not release her, and one evening in May, with her husband waiting in line, her son eating a solitary supper, and her mother drawing a bath, she slipped into the room that was not hers, and hastily, her movements ugly, violated a dresser, making it yield its long-preserved scents of dried flowers and aged frailty and graceful turn-of-the-century transgressions. Flushed, she fumbled through the neatly folded strata of decaying lace, of silk worn thin and brittle as old paper. At last, lifting the edge of a musty green shawl, she found what she wanted, and stealthily carried the bundle off to her bedroom.

There, some hours later, Sergei happened upon her, sitting on the edge of the bed with her arms wound around her knees, her knuckles white.

"Has something . . . Are you all right?" he asked.

She nodded, but would not meet his eyes. Her eyelashes were spiky with dampness.

"I know my mother is difficult, but she's a sad woman, Serezha," she said in a whisper. "Thank you for—well, you know."

Shame rose in his throat like bile.

"It's nothing," he said, but after she fell asleep, he got up and left the room and hid in the blindness of the kitchen. He thought of the anticipation that held him, tight like clenched hands, all through his blurry days, and the evenings unfolding at last, resonant and deep, their blue spirals full of Pavel's singing, and passionate arguments with Vladimir Semyonovich about music and courage and destiny and many other things he had never put into words before, and later, Sofia's light heels etching a map of the mysterious city, the city in which he lived, had lived all his life, but which he no longer recognized through the gentle rain of falling white petals, through the mist of his near-happiness; and every evening, as he walked her to her building, talking about the concert, or their favorite composers, or the books they had read as children, or nothing at all, his happiness would expand until he would feel again that stab of pain, that tormented gasping for air, just as, after a soft good-bye, she would run up the stairs to her door, her ascending steps—one, two, three, the fourth cut off by the door bang—inscribing themselves on the black sheet of quiet as the notes of some elusive score he strove to decipher, and retain in his memory, so that he could keep at least a small part of it with him while he waited impatiently for the next evening, for the next walk . . .

_____

The hour crossed over the threshold of midnight. Globes of lamp-lights floated above the pavements, smoking with dense, foggy illumination; dogs held involved conversations in the distance, and, just down the street, a drunken brawl scratched the surface of the darkness with a flash of broken bottle, a flourish of headlights sliding down a blade—and still he sat without moving, seemingly without breathing, until he grew inseparable from the fabric of the spring night alive with pained, joyful, heady longings, with some vast, inarticulate promise; so much so that when, well after two o'clock in the morning, Alexander stumbled inside and made for the pantry without turning on the light, he confused his father's legs for a shadowy extension of a chair and went sprawling, and cursing, on the floor.

4

"MY FOLKS ARE BECOMING UNHINGED," Alexander said the next night, cupping glowing fingers around a flickering match. "The line's getting to them."

"Lucky for you you'll be making your escape any day now." Nikolai's teeth flashed briskly. "You'd better start packing, my friend."

"Yeah, sure," Alexander muttered. For a while they smoked in silence, two specks of light in the softly chilled darkness diluted by pale squares of windows above (the streetlamp had burned out the night before), the smell of cheap cigarettes mixing with the chemical smell of gasoline and something he could not immediately identify—something sharp and clean and not altogether unpleasant. "You know, I've been thinking," he said at last, "all these people waiting here for so long, just to get these tickets? Ever wonder about this man, what's his name? I guess he must be pretty special."

Nikolai's jacket rustled; Alexander guessed at a shrug.

"I'm just here for the money," Nikolai said. "A coward isn't worth my time. Ran off when things got tough, didn't he? Probably hangs around with the wrong kind of crowd Over There, too, I wouldn't be surprised—lots of fairies abroad, makes you sick!"

Alexander frowned at him. There might have been a new gathering of stormy color around Nikolai's left eye, but in the absence of light Alexander could not be sure. Nikolai shrugged again, shook his pack of cigarettes, poked inside it, turned it upside down and shook it with more violence, then spat, and tossed the pack away. "Damn it. All right, I won't be long. And if these louts try to start without me again, tell them I'll come back and wring their necks. You in?"

"I lost everything I had yesterday," Alexander said with reluctance.

"I'll lend you some."

"I won't be able to return it. My father has stopped paying me."

"No worries, we'll work something out!" Nikolai shouted from across the street.

Alexander was still looking after him when a laborious shuffle began at his back; he caught a straining movement out of the corner of his eye. The shadow straightened.

"Would you be so kind as to hold my place a minute, please," said an elderly voice.

Alexander grunted noncommittally. The old geezer in line next to him kept to himself; they had not spoken. The retreating taps of the cane scraped along the line's vertebrae, carrying away, he knew without turning, the crumpled cigarette pack that Nikolai had thrown to the ground. The geezer was long in finding a trash can; when he returned at last, Alexander sensed his tall, threadbare darkness leaning forward, and thought with exasperation, Going to lecture me on the uncivilized practice of littering, or else the harm of smoking . . . He glanced back all the same, irked by some vague, uncomfortable impulse—not quite curiosity, not quite belligerence. In the twilight that eclipsed the old man's small, neat, clean-shaven face, two round, gleaming holes flashed white and liquid in the light of a passing car before going dull again.

"It's not true, you know," the old man said mildly, righting his glasses.

"What's not true?"

"The things your friend said about Igor Selinsky. They aren't true."

"What, he's not a fairy?"

"He is not a coward," said the old man after a short silence.

"Ah, so he *is* a fairy, then," Alexander shot back, and instantly wished he had not; but just then there was a jolting up ahead, an uproar of voices spilling over, and as the line started to stumble, to trip over itself, Nikolai appeared out of nowhere to break up the fight—or perhaps he had been in the fight to begin with—and everyone shouted and ran here and there; and soon, trading jovial insults, they were already setting up empty crates on the sidewalk, preparing for their nightly game of cards.

And Alexander played that night, and lost some more money, this time not even his own, and lost again the next night, and the night after that, and after a week, Nikolai, in his usual cheerful manner, relieved Alexander of his knife, telling him that he could win it back anytime he wanted, of course, and in any case he could always borrow it for a day or two; and though Alexander was very sorry to see the knife go, he made no protest, because he had lost it fair and square, but also, mainly, because as he was handing it over, scowling to save face, he suddenly understood just how much he loved these nights—loved the brightening chill in the air past midnight, the freedom of going nowhere, doing nothing, existing in some secret, timeless pocket of invisibility, some private allotment of night, alongside these gruff, dangerous men; staying awake, alert, alive, while in identical, ugly buildings all through the city, nighttime windows quickened with identical, ugly lives moving like cutout puppets on dozens of lit stages in dozens of predictable plays, until one after another the windows, overripe, fell to the ground and were swallowed by darkness, and the hated city crawled into a torpor of communal slumber—and still they were there, gathered under the broken street-lamp, at one, at two in the morning, the men in their close, noisy circle pungent with the smells of nicotine and sweat and exotic fruit (dates, someone said, a limited shipment, once transported in the crates they used for tables and chairs), their faces a wild jigsaw of obscurity and light as the hours leapt by and emptied bottles clanked and rolled at their feet and the beams of their flashlights swung in increasingly erratic zigzags, sideways, and up, and down, illuminating a chin made doubly massive by its square deposit of shadow, a nose grotesque with nostrils that appeared to smoke with a thicket of bright yellow hairs, a hand of cards, a hand sliding a bill into a pocket, a hand landing a blow, a nose swelling with nostrils that ran black and dense down another unshaven chin—and above it all flowed that smell, crisp and clean and exuberant, which, he now knew, was simply the smell of the dying spring mixed with a trace of possible happiness.

He found himself hoping that the tickets would not go on sale, not just yet.

In the mornings, he would drag himself out of bed and into his school uniform, then leave with his book bag conspicuously slung over his shoulder. The bag had no books in it, only clothes. He would change in the stairwell, stuff the uniform into the bag, then limp to the neighborhood park and sleep off his hangover in the undergrowth behind an out-of-the-way bench. In the afternoons, he roamed the streets. The daytime city was just as drab as ever, but things felt different now, for the air tingled with possibilities, small chinks through which his other, secret life leaked in occasional, thrilling flashes. Often he would receive casual nods from men unloading trucks or disappearing into doorways—big, surly men whose faces seemed only half familiar in the daylight. Once, in the evening, a bejeweled woman in the window of a kiosk a few blocks from theirs beckoned to him as he passed, and, squinting at him through heavily caked eyelashes, gave him a meat pie and a miniature tube of foreign toothpaste, and would not take his money. "My husband owes you, anyway," she said inexplicably, before dismissing him with a royal toss of her earrings.

On another occasion, when he had a particularly vicious headache and only the haziest recollection of the previous night, he had run into a schoolmate on a street corner, and they had just fallen into step when a youth with a fading scar under his eye ambled up to them. "Shit," the schoolmate said under his breath. Alexander too shrank away, recognizing the character who that past winter had sold him the bottle of cognac in the abandoned church. He expected to be insulted or even hurt, but the youth thrust a couple of small bills into his hand instead, and, sauntering away, threw over his shoulder, "Thanks for yesterday, brother."

"Sure thing," Alexander called after him loudly. "Anytime." After that, he was accorded so much respect at school that he even went once or twice, but it quickly lost its appeal.

Sometimes, when the pounding in his temples was not too fierce, he wondered whether his mother knew: she herself taught younger classes, but other teachers must have complained about his absences. Every morning, as she ironed his uniform, she sighed and said, "Sashenka, just what do you do to get it so wrinkled?" She never offered to accompany him, though (they had been leaving home separately since he was eight or nine), and never asked anything else—not until that Monday three weeks before his final exams, when she followed him to the door and, in the dimness of the foyer, placed her hands on his shoulders.

"Is everything all right with you, Sasha?" she said quietly.

Next to them, in the brown, sad depths of an old mirror, a dumpy middle-aged woman moved her lips without a sound, imploring, imploring a reedy young fellow for something important. As Alexander strained to read the words on the woman's lips, his eyes met the fellow's bleary, cagey eyes, and held them, and sneaked away.

"I'm fine," he said to his mother, "just a bit tired. It's, well—it's the line, you know."

She bowed her head. Her hair was thinning a little, he saw; he had really shot up in the last few months, was taller than she was now, taller than anyone in the family, in fact—they all wondered whom he had taken after. She seemed about to say something, then did not; but as he was stepping over the threshold, he cast an uneasy glance back, and the dumpy woman in the dark, abandoned cave of the mirror was speaking, speaking with passion, as if apologizing, as if thanking him for something . . .

He felt an odd wince of pity and guilt, an almost physical sensation of a hot hand reaching out to squeeze his throat, then letting go.

"Bye, Mama," he muttered, and shut the door louder than he had meant to.

Left alone, Anna slowly walked back to her bedroom; she had called in sick at school, for the second time that month. She drew the curtains tight against the light, then sat down on the bed, reached under the mattress, and pulled out the bundle of postcards. She held them in her hands for a quiet minute before untying the balding velvet ribbon that bound them together and spreading them along the edge of the blanket in the amber dimness of the exiled morning. There were a few landscapes—a full moon over a lake, a night sea at the foot of some cliffs, a whitewashed village in the mountains. Most, though, were views of a city—foggy boulevards with rows of gas lamps shining through honey-edged mists; cobblestone streets, dark and ancient like dragon hide, winding up steep hills, small tables set out on the sidewalks; a mansion abloom with stone curlicues and nymphs, one of its windows marked with a green-ink cross; a chestnut alley, a river embankment, a cathedral, an arch. Men populating these places strolled along at a leisurely pace, carrying bouquets and walking sticks, pale gloves slung over one arm; women glided under lacy parasols and enormous hats, their faces in deep shadow.

She found it heartbreakingly beautiful.

She ran her hand over the postcards, tenderly touching the sepia-tinted paper, then flipped them over, one by one. She had hoped, had expected, to find among them her father's letters, but in that she had been disappointed. Again she studied the delicate pastel-colored stamps, the foreign names of churches and squares printed along the edges in exaggerated gothic scripts; again she skimmed this postcard or that, picking out random sentences she now knew by heart.

Bought a bent candleholder at that little market you showed me, and thought of you, how your pirouettes would look in its decrepit light. Vaslav ran off with the new choreographer. Don't forget you promised to return by the end of the summer. My cat died last night, and now I can't sleep, so I'm writing again. Please come back soon. It's been raining for two whole weeks, the ceiling in our dressing room leaks, and my lipstick is a pink lake—even the music has begun to sound as if spilled. At a book stall by the river I chanced upon this postcard—do you recognize it, do you remember, I marked the window. Is it snowing there yet? Tamara and I tried to mail you a bottle of your favorite champagne, but the postal clerks mocked us, so we drank it instead and then laughed and cried like two fools. Do you still wear those earrings, they used to sparkle so when you danced. Do you still dance? Little Anya is probably walking, no, running by now. Thank you for the photograph. I saw the sun come up over the roofs, and I tried to recite that poem you liked, the one about waiting, but I can no longer remember

the words. Today I thought that you might never come back. It has
now been three years.

Dearest Maya. Maya, my heart. Maya, Maya, Maya . . .

She had fallen silent by degrees, small increments of shared joys
and sorrows bleeding out through invisible cuts. By the time Anna
had finished school, her mother often had what Anna thought of as
quiet days, until there was a quiet week, and then—then silence, soft
and comforting at first, a wise, forgiving presence presiding over the
household, it seemed to Anna, then hardening into a crust of ice
with the passing of years. But she had talked when Anna was young,
not much, hardly ever about the past, yet enough for Anna to re-
construct her life's simple geography. As a child she had studied
dancing abroad, in a dazzling city of light at the heart of the cultured world, to which she returned much later with a touring ballet troupe, and where she gained fame, and stayed, and lived for
years, a celebrated dancer in a legendary company, until she met a
man from her native city, almost two decades her senior, and, having
married him, departed with him on a brief visit to his family; and
her daughter was born, and her husband died, and the revolution
happened, and she never went back. These, then, were the postcards:
the echoes from the life she had left behind, her dancing, her friends,
her city.

There were different names, different handwritings. Vaslav's was
the girlish calligraphy on the backs of the impossibly romantic
moonlit landscapes; Tamara, the one with the dead cat, wrote in unsteady lavender ink, the tails of her words flickering in wet smudges.
There were nicknames, inside jokes, a couple of postcards signed
"The Bow," a few more from someone who called herself "Powder
Puff" and scented her lines with a dramatic perfume whose ghost
still floated nearly half a century later over her dips and curls. Hardly
any were dated, but it was easy enough to trace their chronology.

The early ones echoed with triumphant performances, sleepless nights, frequent heartbreaks—an unfamiliar, brilliant, intoxicating world of music by candlelight, glittering glances, sweet, heavy aromas of broken-stemmed lilies in champagne buckets, youth, exuberance, chaos, joy, pain, life. The later ones, fewer, contained guarded mentions of a small child, congratulations on her first, second birthdays.

After that, there was nothing.

When skinny parings of sunlight squeezed through the cleft in the curtains, Anna checked the clock and began to gather the postcards. Some minutes later, she entered the dusty twilight of her mother's room, the bundle in her hand. She crossed to the dresser, opened its top drawer, and only then looked around. The room was empty; her mother was not there. She had wanted to be discovered, she realized now—had, indeed, held on to the postcards for so long in a vague hope of forcing her mother to speak. Disappointed, she listened to the sound of water running in the bathroom, then slid the postcards back into the drawer, between a small jar full of dung-colored beads and a box of dark green velvet. For another minute, she lingered, long enough to pull out the box, open it idly. In the perpetual rose-hued shadows of the place, the diamond earrings lay dull on their fraying cushion, their darkened facets empty of sparkle.

The water was still running.

Anna shut the box, shut the drawer, shut the door to the room.

But later that afternoon, waiting in line behind the woman who was there to further her husband's career, in front of the boy who was hoping to make his grandfather happy, she thought that perhaps she had misunderstood, misunderstood everything. Perhaps it was not, as she had presumed, a record of loss. Perhaps, though none of the postcards was from her father, they were the only tangible, the only possible, evidence of a love he and her mother had shared, of a full, fulfilled life he had given her, if only briefly—a life, a family worth the sacrifice she had made.

She thought, then, about Alexander, who lied to her about school yet gave up his studies and his rest only to please her, to atone, she had guessed, for his long-forgiven lapse. She thought too about Sergei, who hardly talked to her, who had feigned sleep for weeks, yet who spent all his free time, day after day, standing in this soul-numbing line on her behalf, renouncing his own hope of attending the concert.

And then, growing quiet inside, she thought of something else—something she could do, something that, thrillingly, was in her power to do; and her early expectation of a surprise, of a present, of a change at the end of the line, which she had laid aside with such bitterness, flared up anew within her breast, this time vivid and certain.

That night she waited for her son to come home from his shift. He returned after two in the morning. She met him in the corridor; the smell sickened her, but she did not reprove him.

"Sasha, I need to ask you a favor," she whispered, and shivered, and drew her robe closer about her. "If they sell the tickets on your watch, please bring the ticket to me."

He stared at her with drowsy, bloodshot eyes, swaying slightly; she could not discern his expression in the dim yellow spill of the foyer lamp at his back.

"Not to your grandmother. To me," she repeated. She was suddenly aware of the absolute stillness in the place, which seemed to surround her words, magnify them, lift them, clear and treacherous, into the air, for anyone to hear. "Will you—do you understand?"

His gaze shifted away, restlessly moved up and down the wall, as if caged by the stripes of the wallpaper. "Sure," he murmured, and, veering wildly, stumbled off to his room.

Lying awake in the graying predawn light, nursing within herself the small, hopeful, newborn warmth of her private excitement, Anna felt sure, almost sure, that her mother, who had turned her back on her whole world for the man she loved, would understand, and forgive.

5

TWO WEEKS BEFORE HIS EXAMS, Alexander was dozing in the bushes behind his usual bench when it creaked under someone's weight. Lifting his head, he peered, half asleep, between the bench's legs, saw a beat-up pair of shoes and the pointed end of a cane, and, sinking once again to the ground, promptly tumbled back down a dark tunnel rushing with swift, whistling trains. When he woke up next, the shadows had moved from his left to his right, but the ancient shoes were there still. He brushed away the weave of sickly grass that had embedded itself into his knees and elbows, scrambled through the undergrowth, and strolled past the bench.

Sitting in the afternoon glare, reading a book, was the old geezer from the line.

"Hello," the geezer said pleasantly. "Nice day to be out enjoying nature."

Alexander considered him with suspicion. "It's . . . you know . . . one of those May holidays," he said, not certain what date it was. "School's out."

The old man did not appear to have heard him, busy fishing for something in the voluminous folds of his cardigan, producing at last an oily package.

"Bread and jam. Are you hungry?"

"I have homework to do," Alexander said, moving off.

That night they nodded to each other in line, but did not talk. It rained for the next three days, so, to avoid getting soaked, Alexander idled the mornings away at school; but on Friday, passing through the park, he found the old man seated on the same bench.

"Another holiday?" the old man inquired, not lifting his eyes from his book.

"I'm skipping school," Alexander said shortly. The exams were drawing closer and closer, and he was in a vile mood. The old man seemed unperturbed.

"Have you had breakfast yet?" he asked. "Fancy a boiled egg?"

Alexander looked at the shrunken egg laid out on a napkin in the old man's lap.

"No," he said. "And this is *my* bench."

"This," said the old man, "is a communal bench. Incidentally, shall we make our acquaintance? I'm Viktor Pyetrovich."

Alexander glared at him. "Your glasses are cracked, did you know that?" he said, turning to go, and that night ignored the old man resolutely; but the next day, the old man was in the park again, feeding pigeons with bits of some dark, dense mass that stuck to his fingers.

"Trying to poison them?" Alexander inquired. "Commendable."

"Gives me something to do," the old man replied mildly. "Finding things to do is a problem at my age. You've read all the good old books by now, and discovered that there aren't any good new ones. Though hopefully, things will be different in another sixty years."

"My mother tells me not to say things like that."

"And she is very wise, I'm sure. Old age has its advantages too. One is no longer afraid."

"I'm not afraid." Alexander fell silent, feeling the question push against his teeth, yet hesitating to ask. The old man glanced up at him; thrust into the light, his tidy little face flashed with two eyeless white suns, the left one split in the middle. Alexander squinted. "That one time, in the line—you said something about Selinsky. I just wondered what . . . what you know about him."

"Quite a bit, as it happens."

"Like—what?"

When the old man leaned back into shadow, the eyes abruptly emerged in his face, light and distant behind the old-fashioned silver-rimmed glasses. "Well, did you know, for instance, that when he found himself in the East—"

"The West, you mean." Alexander sat down on the edge of the bench; the pigeons pressed against his feet with deep, throaty burrs.

"No, no, Selinsky went East first. During the civil war, he escaped to the southern sea. The war was spreading, and people were trying to flee across the sea, but boats were few, and the army was fast approaching. So with the last of his mother's jewels, which he had smuggled out most ingeniously—but that's another story—he purchased a small boat and started transporting refugees across the water. Of course, he never accepted payment for it, even though he himself had nothing left. Then one time, after his seventh crossing . . . But I shouldn't be telling you things like this."

"I won't tell anyone," Alexander said quickly. "I swear."

"Well, I don't know. Maybe just this one, then."

The old man talked with his eyes half closed, sitting hunched forward and absolutely still, save for his long, bony fingers, which moved with a constant, nervous motion in his lap, tangling and untangling an invisible knot. Alexander listened, watching a solitary spot of light beneath his bench shift slowly across the gravel as the morning crept toward noon, watching the crazed pigeons with bloodied beaks chase one another away from the last sweet-smelling black crumbs. After a while, the warm, sunny air carried toward them the chiming of the hour from several radios set up before open windows in the buildings surrounding the park; having just begun, the chiming stopped, and, with a small exclamation, the old man consulted his watch, then hastily stood up and shuffled away, leaning heavily on his cane. Later, in the line, his bleached eyes were once again swimming in the bleak pools of quicksilver dusk lit up now and then by headlights, so Alexander could not be entirely sure; but it seemed to him that a look of fleeting understanding passed between them just before he joined the fellows for another spell of card-playing.

That night, as he lay awake, staring at the arrivals and departures of shadows on the ceiling, he imagined his room rocking slightly from side to side, imagined a man with proud eyebrows and the profile of an eagle bearing down on the oars of a small boat as it pulled away from shore, two families crowded inside its listing belly. The shore stood out black against the black sky; it was so quiet he could hear, beyond the lashing of the waves against the planks, the frantic hooves of invisible horses striking the pavement of the seaside promenade in the darkness beyond, and gunfire, and cries. The guide, a swarthy, gap-toothed youth on a second set of oars, allowed no light on board until the land was out of sight, but even when the danger was well past, no one rose to light the lantern in the prow, and no one spoke; only the guide muttered to himself the names of the constellations overhead.

The man with the eagle profile was a powerful rower. His shoulder blades were sore, but they did not slow down. Hours later, a point of light appeared dipping and rising in the shadowy swell before them and, nearing, resolved into the gray shape of a fishing boat, the lone fisherman holding up a lamp by its ring, the water lapping at the boat in brilliant flashes of many-splintered reflections. After a while there was another light in the distant fog, and another, and yet another, until he found himself straining to push his way through a floating mist of pale white stars, above and below and all around him. Then the sky grew warm, peach-tinted, the stars and the lamps faded, and the slender silhouettes of minarets pierced the musk-scented horizon.

"If you have any valuables on you," the guide said through the gap in his teeth, "hide them now."

That night, as always, he and the guide stayed at the house of a woman he knew, had known in another life. A long time before, when he was barely past twenty, in an elegant, pearl-colored city under remote pearl-colored skies, she had come to one of his concerts and tossed a bouquet at him from her velvet-padded box. Later, there had been the silky closeness of her carriage and a strand of pearls breaking in the dark, and later still, a secret exchange of letters, and that gray, chilly dawn when he had stepped outside his hotel, carrying his violin case and a small suitcase. A boy had run up to him all out of breath, and, inquiring after his name, thrust a note into his hand. As he stood reading it, the wind ripped it from his gloved fingers, but not before he had seen the words "returning unexpectedly today" and "mustn't do anything rash"—

"Will there be a reply?" the boy had asked.

"No reply," he had said, and dropped some coins in the boy's proffered palm, and gone inside, and unpacked the suitcase, and let his life flow in a different direction, until, a decade later, after their second run across the sea, he and Marat were walking along the awakening bay in the rosy light of the eastern morning, and peacocks cried hoarsely in hidden gardens, and a middle-aged woman passed them, then stopped, and turned, and said slowly, "My God."

"You're here with your husband?" he had asked.

"My husband's been dead eight years," she had replied. "I have a place nearby, if you and your friend need somewhere to stay."

And they had stayed at her place that night, and had returned, again and again, every time they had come into the city. On this night, the night of their seventh crossing, the youth fell asleep on a pile of rugs, in a first-floor room she had begun to rent out to a carpet shop next door; her money was running short. The two of them sat upstairs, by an open window, drinking the cool mint tea she had brewed, watching a large pale moth draw circles around the lamp.

"It's over, you know," she said after a while. "You can't go back. Not this time."

"I've made promises," he said. "People need me."

"You'll be shot," she said.

He was silent.

"I need you," she said.

He thought of telling her that his music had remained behind, the dark symphony he had written in feverish bursts, to drown out the ugly staccato of gunfire in his ears; he had left the notes in a neat stack on his desk, a guarantee against a sudden attack of cowardice—

"You don't need me," he said.

She sighed—a small sigh, as if she had briefly forgotten how to breathe—then set down her cup, and took his cup out of his hand, and blew out the lamp; but after he had drifted off to sleep, she rose, and felt for a small sandalwood box in a secret drawer of her nightstand, and tiptoed downstairs, and shook the youth awake.

In the morning, he was untroubled to find his friend gone.

"Marat must be waiting for me at the bay," he said. "I must go now."

She kissed him as she always had, in the doorway, repeating, "Careful, not across the threshold," standing on tiptoe to reach him.

"I'll see you soon, I promise," he said to her, also as always—and, surprised, searched her face; for her lips had not trembled.

She believed he would be returning before the sun turned white in the midday sky. She waited all through the evening, and at night stood by the window, staring into the street, enormous brown moths beating softly against her face. He never came back. He spent the night wandering by the harbor, looking across the dark roll of the waters toward the land to which he had not been allowed to bid farewell. When the sun rose, he turned and vanished into a maze of ancient streets; but as he passed watermelons glistening in the limpid early light and girls beating carpets, Alexander fell to wondering whether eastern girls left their faces draped or uncovered, and what musk and rose oil smelled like, and as his thoughts grew more and more muddled by sleep, he had somehow retraced his steps and found himself back in the woman's house, drinking cool tea, only the woman was much younger this time, entwining soft, naked arms around his neck, and the pearls went bouncing off the luxurious rugs once again.

"So what happened to that music he left in his room?" he asked Viktor Pyetrovich when they met in the park the next morning.

"Gone," the old man said. "The house burned down when the army set fire to the town."

Alexander thought for a minute. "How do you know about it, anyway? Not the kind of thing they'd put in history books or whatever."

"Oh, he'll be in the next editions for sure," the old man said with a smile. "Times are changing. All the same, I doubt I'll live to see in print the story of his being mistaken for a spy in an opium den in the Far East, where he traveled collecting songs after leaving the minaret city."

"How does that one go?" Alexander asked—and it was only much later, when the old man had departed, that he realized his other question had been left unanswered.

It drizzled for the next few days, and Viktor Pyetrovich did not come to the park. Alexander hesitated to address him while in line, and the puzzlement grew in his mind—how did the old man know, how could he possibly know such things? He often drifted into thinking about it, especially late at night when the city grew so quiet he imagined he could hear birds rubbing feathers in their sleep outside his window, and the rustle of cockroaches in the kitchen trash can, and that disembodied voice that some faulty conjunction of pipes carried from somewhere deep in the building—the ancient singsong voice that he had first heard in the early spring, and that now frequently rose in the predawn hours, talking of outlandish, theatrical things. Crisscrossing his sleep again and again, like a swift silver needle pulling a thread back and forth across the fabric of darkness, the voice would stitch the hours together, seamlessly merging its stories with his own dreams, his own thoughts, so he would often awaken with his head inhabited by a swarm of buzzing visions, half believing he had invented all of them himself—mermaids sipping frothy drinks from dainty little cups in terraced cafés, hiding their tails under elaborately ruffled skirts; songs extracted with special curved spoons from the rosy spirals of seashells sold in hidden street markets; goldfish languidly swimming inside the limbs of glass mannequins in the fashionable shops of some city—the faraway, fantastical, nonexistent city that the voice always haunted as it leaked through the tiny cracks in his slumber.

The voice did not sound every night, but as he fell into anxious sleep on the Saturday before his exams, he thought he heard it begin a story about a curtain rising over a stage in the heart of the fairy-tale city. Yes, the curtain rose at last; the musicians leapt into their melodies like swimmers into pools of startlingly cold, clear water; the dancers flew out from behind paper trees. The music was unlike anything ever heard before—the ballet had been written by a young composer of brilliant promise. They said he was living in the city at that time, but no one had seen him at the rehearsals. We were all curious, of course, but for me, it went beyond curiosity. As weeks of grueling practices went by and he did not appear, I began to feel restless.

I wanted him to watch me dance, you see.

"Geniuses are peculiar," Vaslav said to me on opening night, and stroked my hand as one strokes a cat, tenderly and with caution. "You should know, my heart."

The stage was a soft velvet void aglow with flickering lights: the floors and the walls had been draped in black, and hundreds, maybe thousands, of candles had been lit in tiny holders of gleaming black crystal—so many, indeed, that they had brought in two or three boys from the street an hour before the performance, to assist in lighting the wicks. I watched them from the wings, entranced by darkness coming alive, by the manifold eyes of light opening one after another.

I was nervous.

It was the hardest thing I had ever done, that solo dance, and also the most beautiful. There was one moment, toward the end, when the beauty became so terrible that I felt I was dying. But then, that was as intended: the candles, you see, were the stars, and I the moon, and I waxed, and I waned, and I died. On that first night, I danced, and danced, and danced, until my eyes grew blind, and my feet grew wings, until the world around me was waxing and cresting and fading with me, the lights dancing deep beneath my skin, the music an elusive trickle, then a roaring waterfall, then a drip-drop of falling stars in my ears, then a long, delirious moan. When the heartbreak of it all had whittled my soul down to nothing and my last silver veil had glided to the floor, I took that final, breathless leap through a black rip in the black sky. The next morning, they wrote about it in all their newspapers. Impossible, impossible, they exclaimed in their birdlike voices—"Oh, it looked just as if she was flying!"—and they crowded into the theater the next night, and the night after that, and for many more nights, to see me suspended in flight for that one extra heartbeat they claimed was unnatural. "She who doesn't come down with the music," they called me. And in truth, the leap was wrenchingly difficult. At rehearsals, the backup dancers would stand in the wings, waiting to catch me as I descended from my velvet heavens, and I would slip through their well-meaning, oblivious fingers, and crumple to the ground.

On that first night, though, there were no backup dancers in the wings—someone else arrested my flight, someone I did not know. And when my breath returned at last, there he was still, gazing at me from the shadows, and I recognized one of the boys who had helped light the candles. As I looked at him, I saw he was not a boy but a young man of twenty-three or twenty-four. He had a sad face, an expressive mouth, surprising green eyes. Then he spoke, and he seemed older still. "Thank you," he said—and just like that, I knew who he was. Thank *you*, I wanted to say, but I could not, because suddenly I felt like weeping. But at this point, as often happened, the voice must have begun to slip away, diluted by Alexander's dreams, for the mysterious candle boy turned out to be the reclusive composer Igor Selinsky, and, gaining courage, Alexander was soon asking him the question that was bothering him still, how did the old man know, how did he know all these things about you, and Selinsky, whose face was no longer a face, whose face was a candle flame guttering and waving, replied in a voice that was like a breeze through Alexander's head, "He knows because he is me, because you are me, because I do not exist," and then the moon waned and died, and at last Alexander slept fully.

The next morning, the last Sunday in May, his father intercepted him in the hallway.

"Your exams start in just a few days, don't they?" he said. "I guess I'll take over the night shift for a week or two, so you'll have nothing to distract you for the duration. You've wasted too much time in that line as it is."

"Sure, but I might as well go one last time tonight," Alexander said offhandedly. "I have to—that is—"

He was racking his brains for some excuse to add when his father nodded and walked off; he seemed to be thinking about something else.

That night, it continued to rain. Viktor Pyetrovich fought a gigantic umbrella with a flapping edge; the cough from which he had suffered for a while had gotten worse. Alexander waited for a chance to speak. Sometime past midnight, his friends clustered in the bushes around a flashlight, shining it on small, faintly glittering things in their hands, discussing something incoherently but with passion; he could hear Nikolai's voice raised among them. He turned back, ducking the umbrella's bare spokes, which the wind was tossing above Viktor Pyetrovich's head.

"You've stopped coming to the park," he burst out, and immediately winced at how childish he sounded.

"I'm sorry," said the old man. "I haven't been feeling well lately. In fact, I'll have to miss a few nights here. They want me to rest, this weather isn't good for my bones. You can always stop by my place, though, if you want to talk. Here, I'll jot the address down for you."

Alexander held the umbrella, which kept trying to fly off into the glistening darkness, over Viktor Pyetrovich while the old man struggled to write. Receiving the scrap of paper, Alexander turned it over in his fingers, slippery with the rain. It was a corner of some score. He saw a treble clef, the only symbol he had ever learned to recognize after all of his father's efforts to teach him musical notation; its tail ran thick and wet, smudged by a chance drop of water.

"Visit me anytime," Viktor Pyetrovich had scrawled on the other side, above the address.

Nikolai was now returning from the shadows, calling out to Alexander across the road.

He shoved the note into his bag and, taking a step back, asked in a hasty undertone: "So then, how do you know about Selinsky?"

He had already looked away when the old man bent forward and whispered: "Selinsky writes to me."

6

SO WHAT DID YOU FIND OUT?"

"Nothing whatsoever. She wouldn't talk to me. Said she was busy."

"What's she busy with? There are no tickets to sell anyway, she just sits there."

"Well, maybe she has accounting to do, or ticket schedules to go over. She looks so cross she must be doing *something*. Though she could be knitting, I suppose . . . Oh, and by the way, I saw that relic of a man again, he never seems to leave, morning or night. Doesn't he have any family to take over for him?"

"You mean the ancient fellow at number seven? He looks happy enough, always smiling at people. Perhaps he's touched. I doubt he has anything better to do with himself, in any case. Waiting passes the time."

"Very true, very true. Indeed, I sometimes worry that's what it's all about."

"What do you mean?"

"Well, what if there aren't actually any tickets to any concert?"

"Are you mad?"

"What's he saying? I'm hard of hearing."

"He's saying there won't be any tickets."

"What?!"

"Has the concert sold out already?"

"How is that possible, is there another kiosk somewhere that—"

"No, no, you misunderstand. All I'm saying is, there are hundreds of kiosks all over the city, and they are all selling something, and there are lines to all of them, you know?"

"Where is he going with this?"

"He's gone daft, don't pay any attention!"

"All I'm saying is, it's a very efficient way of disposing of people's time, don't you see? Thousands of us, some waiting for stockings, others for symphonies. But what if there aren't any stockings, what if there aren't any symphonies, so to speak? What if all of this is just a means to keep the masses occupied and hopeful—a cheap solution to the problem of time?"

"Wait, does this idiot seriously believe that the State is maintaining a system of phony kiosks just so we waste our time waiting for things that don't exist?"

"No, no, I'm not claiming that's how it is, I'm only saying it philosophically. Like a metaphor, a metaphor of life, do you understand?"

"Well, metaphor or not, this smells of subversion to me. You'd do well to keep your voice down—"

"I'm not listening. I'm not listening. If anyone asks, I heard nothing!"

"Oh God, this is absurd. I'm going to march up to that woman right now and demand an answer. Surely she knows when the bloody tickets will be in."

PART THREE

SUMMER

I

THE EVENINGS OF EARLY SUMMER were filled with lucid light, the day's soft lingering. "Days in June have double bottoms," Sofia said to him during their first night shift together, "have you noticed? Just when you think it's over, another, secret drawer full of light slides open."

Shortly after ten o'clock, the day's second drawer would shut with a noiseless click and darkness would move in abruptly.

"As if someone careless has broken a bottle of ink in the sky," she said that first night, glancing up. Sergei saw the hollow palpitating like a pale bruise at the base of her neck, just where a delicate, pearly button of her blouse had come undone, and looked away quickly. The evening crowd was now leaving; he watched Pavel and Vladimir Semyonovich depart together, deep in conversation. The line was already losing its well-defined contours, shifting into a shapeless, shifty mass, disintegrating into islands of indistinct figures seated along curbs or gathering under trees, dribbling unsteady flashlight beams onto shadowy preoccupations. Glasses clinked, cigarettes flared; he heard a fight erupt somewhere ahead. The street-lamp, he realized suddenly, was burnt out, probably had been burnt out for a while; and as the familiar surroundings of his evening vigils—the fence, the low buildings along the street, the cutout of the church against the pale sky—stepped back into the night's expanding darkness, he witnessed a different, unrecognizable city come into being before him, one that was foreign, perhaps even vaguely dangerous, yet somehow larger than the earlier city, its great obscure stretches sheltering unpredictable, mysterious happenings and emotions.

He felt unmoored.

"Sergei Vasilievich, are you hungry?" Sofia called out.

She had walked over to a patch of wilted grass by the sidewalk and sat down on the ground. He hesitated. It had rained the day before, and the dampness lingered; briefly he worried about the grass stains likely to imprint themselves on his pants. Yet when he saw her gazing up at him expectantly, an unbearable thought took hold of him—What if she thinks of me as an affable, staid, prudent fellow, a type of uncle, soon to be fifty? He crossed over to her, and, throwing himself down, stretched out on his back and stared upward, at the vague white cloud hovering at the top of the dead streetlamp's pole, at the trees, which in the daytime were stunted and scarred with graffiti, but now were only a black rustle of invisible leaves in the sky. "Isn't it wonderful to lie in the grass in the early days of summer, looking at the stars?" he exclaimed; and oddly, though his words had sounded stiff and affected, a caricature of themselves, some part of him had meant some part of them.

She glanced at him with a slight frown, hunted for something in her handbag.

"I fear it's not much," she said, unwrapping a parcel.

Embarrassed, he sat up, murmured his thanks—but as he clumsily relieved her of a slice of bread, their hands touched in passing, and the unseen city behind them grew darker and larger, more thrilling.

In the morning he discovered that both his pants and his jacket had nasty green stains in their folds, but he no longer cared. They shared late suppers for the next two weeks. After the evening shift left, she would take out a loaf of rye bread, a container of butter, some parsley she had bought from a woman at the tram stop. "I'm sorry I don't cook," she kept apologizing; and he could not bring himself to tell her how much he loved the simplicity of their meals, how many times he wished he could preserve some small, random moment just as it was, unchanging, unmoving—the slow tide of nighttime conversations drifting in, distant cigarette sparks flickering in the shadows, the taste of butter and herbs in his mouth, the pensive incline of her neck, her thin, graceful hands slicing the bread, spreading the napkins . . .

The ring was on her finger, as before, but it upset him less now.

They talked as they ate, continued to talk after she had packed away the leftovers. As days went by, he felt they had more to say to each other, not less. One night in mid-June, they were talking still when, at two in the morning, characters wandering around the kiosk began to fade away and he helped her up and guided her past the drunks splattered over the sidewalk dealing cards, spitting on the ground, cursing some Sashka who had skipped out on them for the second week running. As always, he walked her to her building. They never discussed their daily lives. He had alluded to his family enough for her to understand that he was married to a schoolteacher, had a nearly grown son, and found contentment in neither. He, in turn, had gathered that there had been some entanglement with an unlucky outcome in her past, but that she was alone now; as for her ring, she probably wore it because at her age—she was thirty-three, she had told him—spinsters were pitied. He felt certain that all the blank, reticent spots would be filled in time, but these nights, they talked about music. He told her about his childhood, his love for the violin, his parents who had believed in his talent, his teachers who had spoken of his promising future. Selinsky, by the way, had started out as a violin player himself, did she know?

"I didn't know," she replied. "I've never even heard any of his music."

"You just need to be patient for a little while longer," he said.

Her steps quickened. She seemed to force herself to slow down, to walk beside him.

"But you play the tuba now," she said.

"Yes, well, my music school—" He caught himself deliberating, choosing his words, and felt instantly ashamed of his caution. "My parents were paying for the best musical education, but after the Change, the State enforced open admission to my school. 'Bringing Art to the Masses,' they called it. Of course, most of the newly enrolled were not interested in music. And those of us who were considered privileged were expelled or, if lucky, assigned to instruments regarded as sufficiently revolutionary. I was among the lucky ones, I got the tuba. My best friend got the drums. He could have been a true virtuoso. A pianist."

She halted, touched his arm.

"Perhaps we were born at the wrong time," she said softly, "but it will be different for our children." She was looking up at him now, her hand still resting, warm and light, in the crook of his arm. His breath caught. He felt the night leaning closer against them, wrapping them in their own private darkness, the few glowing balloons of surrounding streetlamps drifting upward into the sky, where someone celestially indifferent had spilled ink anew—and already he was taking a step forward, so near her now, and already he was— but though there had never been another moment as perfect, as quiet, as self-contained, he saw something still and pained in her face, not quite as obvious as a bitten lip or a frown, rather a subtle, paling withdrawal . . .

He took a step back, small and endless. She exhaled.

"Well, here we are, then," she said. "Thank you as always."

He hadn't realized they had stopped in front of her building.

"Of course," he said, exhaling also. The pressure of her hand was gone. "Anytime."

One click—two clicks—three clicks—four . . . On the top step, she turned, nothing but a smudged, wispy silhouette in the dark— a purse, a skirt, a hint of a glinting button—yet he imagined he could see the faint glow of her mournful eyes in her thin, shadowy face. "I meant to tell you, I won't be doing late nights any longer, just evenings," she said. She had never explained, but he had surmised that there was an illness in her family, her elderly father, perhaps. "And your son, is he still taking his exams?"

"Today was his last one," he said, not knowing whether it was true. "In fact, I'm done with the night shift myself."

"Ah. Well, thank you again. I'll see you tomorrow evening."

"Yes," he said. "Good night."

After the front door closed, he stood still for a while, willing himself not to give in to the dismal sense of finality that had threatened to overwhelm him, looking at the blind windows of the building, waiting for one of them to come alive. The windows stayed dark. He did not know what floor she lived on; she had never asked him to come up. He turned away.

The balloons of the streetlamps had returned to their perches by the time he reached home. Everyone was asleep. In the kitchen, he poured himself a cup of cold tea, to postpone his entombment in his wife's bed, and sat at the table, Sofia's words circling in his mind like a moth around the lamp lit on the veranda of his childhood summer house, where he used to while away evening after evening ensconced within the lamp's soft green circle, a nine-year-old boy deciphering a score. It will be different for our children, it will be different for our children, it will be different . . . A neighbor's radio muttered on the other side of the wall, and the lump of sugar

refused to dissolve in the cold water, and he swirled his spoon in
the cup, round and round, in the dull rhythm of her words, of the
moth bumping against the lamp—"Serezhenka, sunshine, come inside, Katya has served the pastries and your tea's getting cold!"—
and still the radio program droned on and on, the elderly voice of
an announcer tossed up and down on static waves, until, tuning in
involuntarily, he realized it was the same odd program they had
recently begun to broadcast late at night, which he heard through
the wall now and then while he sat in the kitchen during his spells
of insomnia.

He did not listen as he sipped the pale, tasteless liquid, because
his thoughts were elsewhere, but also because the stories that the
voice had read on those other occasions had always been drivel—
something about a confectionery shop that sold enchanted chocolates with the power to bring to memory the most perfect day of
one's life; or the ghost of a cat named Cloud that haunted the wings
of some theater in a distant city; or a girl spending all her wages on
an extravagant, hideous hat in the shape of a violin on the day she
had fallen in love with a boy whose job, if he had heard it right, was
to light candles—yes, shockingly frivolous drivel, which had absolutely no place on the radio, and which, if he was to be honest
with himself, made him sad for some unfathomable reason.

He did not listen, then, as he sat sipping tea in his wife's dark
kitchen at three in the morning, but the voice still rode the waves,
and single words or phrases or at times whole passages surfaced on
their crests—"a movement of piercing beauty . . . the sensation of
the season . . . my costume was sewn with sharp spangles, and Vaslav
cut his hands lifting me. When I took my bows, my dress was
smeared with blood. An ill omen, they exclaimed as they flocked
around me backstage, ah, such an ill omen . . ."

He set his cup down, spilling the tea, held his breath.

". . . And finally, the Waltz of the Fireflies," read the announcer.
"The first modern waltz ever written, they called it. Once in a

garden at night, just before a summer storm, he had seen hundreds
of fireflies blinking on and off, drawing a glowing figure in the sky.
That was when he conceived the theme—the gentle flickering, the
first sinister notes of distant thunder, the chaos of light and darkness
welling up just beneath the orderly movement, well, you've heard
it, I'm sure, I don't have to go on. Of course, the story of the fireflies was known to the music critics of the day, hence the name, but
I was one of the few, perhaps the only one, who knew what the
figure had been, the figure that the fireflies had drawn in the troubled sky—"

The voice grew muffled, as if the announcer had begun to speak
into a pillow. Sergei leapt up, turning the chair over with a crash,
rushed to the window, flung the pane open, and stuck his head out,
and listened, hoping that the unknown neighbor might have her
window open as well, hoping that the sound would reach him better here. The night outside hung enormous and warm and still, like
a taut black sheet clipped to the heavens by some celestial housewife
going about her chores. All was silent. Not giving up, he dashed to
the bedroom, found his own radio in the dark, and for some minutes
furiously mauled the dials. On one station a shrill-voiced choir jab-
bered patriotic songs; on the rest, there was only dead crackling.
His wife stirred, sighing some indistinct word in her slumber; he
switched the radio off. But as he was falling asleep, just before
dawn, he thought again of her words, and he knew she was right,
and nothing was over, and as he waded into a shallow dream, stream,
dream, fireflies flickering above its water, his feeling of despair lifted
at last, for she did not mean *her* children, of course, it was only a figure of speech—and soon, very soon, he would tell her.

When he awoke the next morning, the other side of the bed was
deserted; bright birdsong and noisy sunlight filled the window. He
lay still, measuring the silence in the apartment, then rose, slapped

his barefoot way into the dim corridor, where the telephone, a large cranky animal prone to grunts and squeaks, resided in a nest of cords.

Sviatoslav had been asleep. "What?" he said hoarsely.

"Do you have any music by Selinsky?"

"Sergei? Is that you? What time is it?"

"It's late, you should get up anyway. Selinsky, do you have anything by him? There must be some old records still around. It's only a matter of time before they start performing his music everywhere, of course, but in the meantime—"

"Listen, I told you, I don't want to get involved in this. And you, of all people—"

"How often do I have to tell you, it's all right. It's not just the concert anymore, either, there was a program about him on the radio last night, fascinating, did you know—"

"I'm going back to sleep," Sviatoslav announced.

"Wait, you know the Firefly Waltz in his second ballet? Well, apparently . . . Hello? Hello?"

A door opened, and immediately a thin tongue of light darted across the corridor, licking his bare toes; his son walked out yawning. "Who are you talking to?" he asked.

"Nobody," Sergei said, replacing the receiver. "So, how are your exams coming along?"

"Fine," the boy mumbled with another yawn. "Just two left. Chemistry this afternoon, music tomorrow. Want me to go back to the line tonight?"

"What about tomorrow's exam?"

"Oh, music's a joke, really—we sing a couple of songs, our country this, our country that, eternal friendship of the peoples, I don't have to be awake for it."

Sergei thoughtfully watched his son's retreating back, then caught up with him in the kitchen. Dusty yellow sunlight was everywhere here—in diamonds on the walls, in stripes on the floor, falling in big hazy chunks out of the open cupboard through which the boy was now rummaging—and still he knew it to be the same hushed, dark place where, the night before, he had received yet another sign that his life was building up toward a certain fulfillment.

"Fine, go tonight," he said, "but can you do something for me?"

Alexander emerged with an aged bagel and, squinting, studied it gloomily.

"Could you ask Zoya Vladimirovna if, by chance, she has any records by Selinsky? Tell her I'd like to borrow some, she knows me. Do you think you could do that?"

"Yeah, whatever," Alexander said, and dove back into the cupboard.

The next afternoon, Alexander rushed roaring through the school hallways with a few classmates at his heels, waving his blazer like a flag over his head, and, hoarse with yelling, flew down the steps into the courtyard. There the others stopped and, huffing like a herd of middle-aged walruses, began to discuss the admission policies of various institutes and the schedules of university entrance exams. "So what are your plans, Sasha?" one of them asked. Without warning, Alexander found himself staring into the rapidly telescoping depths of an empty summer followed by an empty year followed by an empty decade followed by—but here the telescope jammed, and he felt a blinding pain between his eyes quite as if he had been gazing into the white glare of the sun for too long. His classmates were silent, waiting for his answer.

"I've forgotten something inside," he muttered, and turned and went back in.

Aimlessly he wandered through poorly lit, deserted spaces that smelled of starch and stale socks and wasted time, until he stood, without quite meaning to, before the music room. The corridor was empty save for two junior teachers who were shouting angry instructions at each other as they struggled to put up a poster unrolled crookedly between them. WELL DONE, GRADUATES! read its enormous letters, which appeared gray to him but were probably red.

"You there, how about some help?" one of the teachers called out.

"I have an appointment," Alexander said, and pushed the door open.

Zoya Vladimirovna was sitting by the window, next to the silent bulk of the record player she used during lessons, a plate of powder-sprinkled *pastila* at her elbow. She looked up, her plump fingers, white with the sugar, splayed in midair, her eyes magnified and alarmed behind her thick glasses. "Ah, Sasha, come in, please come in!" she exclaimed. "Free at last, it must be a wonderful feeling! Oh, but if you're wondering about your grade, it's excellent as always . . . No surprise there, of course, what with your father being a musician—"

"A tuba player," Alexander said, not moving from the doorway.

"Yes, yes, I remember." Squeezed into the tight, oily dress she always wore during exams, her voice fluttering like nervous wings, she resembled a fat, aging dragonfly. "Oh, but please, help yourself to these, I always buy them for the finals, in case, well, in case someone stops by afterward, to, you know, to say good-bye—"

She laughed unexpectedly, an awkward, high-pitched laugh. He wanted to leave, but something about this moment—the unappetizing display of sweets, the hopeful dawning on the woman's puffy face, the dazzle of the summer leaking pale and sickly through the grimy windows, the long, long life stretching before him—something about it, he did not know what, trapped him into taking a step inside, into saying, "Sure, I'll have one."

Her features sagged into a smile. "Lovely, lovely!" she breathed, heaving herself up. "Oh, and would you like to hear some music? Here, you'll love this, a composer from the last century, unjustly forgotten, they—I mean, we—no longer teach him in schools . . .

Oh, but he's not banned or anything, of course—it's marvelous, marvelous, just wait till you hear—"

He sank behind one of the desks, his lips stale with sugar dust. The music started with a quiet groaning of traction, with small creaks of rotation. Why the hell did I do this to myself, he thought. The tune, or whatever it was, seemed familiar in a vague, dreamy sort of way; it reminded him, he realized, of those times, long past, when his father used to burst out of the bedroom, his hair wild, his face "like a beet," his mother would say, and cry about this or that masterpiece on the radio, spraying spittle in his excitement, asking them to please come, to join him, to listen . . . His mother would always beg off, claiming a need to attend to something burning on the stove, but Alexander, who was not yet Alexander to his father—at first Sashenka, later Sasha—not knowing how to refuse from the disadvantage of his eight, nine, ten years, would tread after him and collapse miserably onto the bed and, bored, watch the striped curtains strangling a stray sunbeam for unbearable stretches of time, while his father paced about, gesticulating with passion, humming "tahm-pahm-pahm," moaning, "Sashenka, listen here, here, ah, isn't that beautiful!"

Of course, his father no longer invited him to listen to anything, had not done so in years—not since that time, he remembered unhappily, when, aged twelve, he had shouted that only old fogies and dotards could like such depressing, pompous, toothache-inducing noise, that he, Alexander, was nothing like them, nothing like *him*, that he would never, no, not ever—

The music ended. In the abrupt lull he heard the two teachers still screaming at each other in the corridor outside; their voices' panicking echoes tossed from wall to wall, frantic to escape the suffocating entrails of the school, and failing, failing . . .

He stood up, anxious to go.

"Oh, but it's not over yet, that was just the first movement," Zoya Vladimirovna gasped, rising also. The laborious sound of the music starting again scratched painfully at his hearing.

"I must run, I have to buy bread for supper," he lied quickly. "Oh, yeah, I almost forgot, my father wanted me to ask if you have any Selinsky records, you know, the guy whose concert—"

"Yes," she said. "Please tell your father I'm sorry, but the ban on Selinsky's music hasn't officially been lifted, he must not be aware . . . No one has anything."

"Sure, whatever, I'll tell him. You don't like the guy's stuff?"

In the white-walled, gray-windowed silence of the classroom, one note lingered, piercing, relentless. She glanced back at the closed door, stepped closer to him.

"Igor Fyodorovich Selinsky is the greatest composer of this century," she said, quietly and sternly. Her voice had ceased fluttering.

"So why aren't you waiting in that line? Everyone else is," he said with sudden hostility.

The woman's eyes swam inside their plastic frames in perfect, un-blinking stillness; she was so near he could see the faint mustache darkening her upper lip.

"I don't believe the concert will ever take place," she said at last.

The high solitary note still trembled in his ears, refusing to go away. His dislike of her grew, fed perhaps by some darker, subter-ranean emotion. "Yeah? And why's that?"

She looked at the door again, seemed to hesitate for a moment. "Tell your father I'll try," she said then. "I have a friend who . . . I'll see if I can find a record or two. My mother used to teach at a music school before the . . . before the educational reforms, so I know something of your father's story. I'd like to do something for him."

Alexander moved to open the door.

"Father doesn't have a story," he said from the threshold.

The school courtyard was empty now, its asphalt sweating with the afternoon warmth. He stood still for some time, staring into the pale immensity of the sky. That night, he wanted to talk to Viktor

Pyetrovich, but he was never alone; his friends were celebrating his return to the line and the beginning of his adult life. When the line dispersed at last, he walked home, through streets that oddly ran in many directions at once, veering off sharply, treacherously, bouncing him into walls with no warning, and across parks that were not parks at all but close, black, sinister forests filled with murderous benches leaping at him like tigers striped with planks of shadow, and a disconcerting signaling of bandits' flashlights, which at closer quarters turned into glowing bugs and flew away, and along sidewalks that rose underneath him like rearing horses, so he had to straddle them firmly with his knees, repeating in a voice harsh with affection as he ran his fingers through their manes, "There, there, steady now!" Then someone laughed a nasty laugh above him, and the horses were gone. Picking himself off the ground, he continued to stumble through woods and fields, along train tracks, inside spirals of darkness, thinking vaguely that, maybe, taking the train east would solve nothing after all, until somehow, hours later it seemed to him, he made his tentative way into his kitchen, and turned on the light, and his father was blinded.

And as Alexander looked through the wavering haze at the man squinting before him, the middle-aged man going wide in the waist and loose in the face, he thought again—or perhaps he had never stopped thinking—of the tormenting creaking of music in the classroom, and those times when his father, younger, thinner, had pleaded with him to listen to something he loved; and the endless lectures he had endured, about time and choices and wisdom, which had seemed to him so tedious, so insincere—and somehow, before he knew it, he was saying things, heated things, surprising things, and his words were rushed, and wet, and heavy in his mouth.

Listen, I'm sorry, if you ever want me to hear some tunes you like, I won't mind, and the ticket, you can have it, I won't sell it, I'll work hard, I'll return what I owe you, I didn't mean to, I'm sorry about your money, can't we, can't we just, can't we just be—

❧

Sergei considered his son with distaste. This was the third if not the fourth time he had seen him drunk. The boy stood before him blubbering, mumbling something incomprehensible about money, probably asking for more.

"Go to sleep, Alexander," he said sharply.

The boy fell silent. Sergei was unsettled by a strangely naked, hurt look on his face. Then the boy turned and went away without saying another word. This is what he needs, Sergei thought uneasily, discipline's good for him; but for some minutes after the door to his son's room had closed, he sat blinking after him.

Eventually he moved to switch off the lights—he imagined he could hear better in the dark—and for another hour intermittently coaxed the dials on his radio and muted it to lie in wait for the neighbors'. There was nothing about Selinsky that night, or the next, or, in fact, for a week or two, though on one occasion the same announcer's voice drifted to him through the wall, or possibly seeped in through the open window, to talk about an admirer taking a girl to a shop and, too poor to enter, standing on the sidewalk, gazing with her at a display window full of jeweled splendor, saddened by a pair of earrings that she liked but would never have. Finally, on one of the last June nights, the Selinsky series was resumed. He caught only a snippet. "The set was simple," read the voice behind the wall. "The stage was the sea, a blue cloth piled up in undulating waves. We stood straight and quiet, everyone alone, evenly spaced, solitary islands submerged in silk up to our knees. It was his own idea. The choreographer was outraged. 'How will they dance?' he cried. 'You can't wrap the stage in fabric, they'll trip, they'll fall!' But Igor Fyodorovich said, 'They can dance with their hands. They can dance with their eyes.' 'There will be a scandal,' the choreographer warned. 'So be it,' he said, 'this is not about dancing. I want them to hear my music, I want them to . . .'"

The voice tapered off, but that night Sergei went to bed nearly happy, and for a long time lay awake, thinking of her as yet unseen home, and the antique gramophone, or was it a phonograph, from the museum, and the record he would gently slide out of a sleeve under her bright, misting eyes. And the record, black and shiny, would begin its measured circling, round and round, like a spoon in a cup of tea, like a moth round the lamp on his childhood veranda, and the night, black and shiny, would spin round and round too, and the night's giant tonearm would draw closer, closer—and at last it would touch the black, circling surface, and, together, they would hear it at last.

2

CAN YOU BELIEVE IT'S ALMOST JULY?"
"Don't rub salt in my wounds! We had to cancel our vacation this year. My daughter spends her days playing in the dust."

"My in-laws tell me, If you want to hear music so much, why not turn on the radio. They aren't cultured people, my in-laws."

No one says anything for some time after that. It is almost too hot to talk, the sun glossing their noses and melting the ice cream cones they take turns buying at a nearby ice cream kiosk.

"Do you know what's peculiar?" someone ventures at last. "After all these months of standing in line, you'd think some people would have gotten sick of waiting and dropped out."

"Sure, or died."

"Or moved somewhere."

Another small silence, this one concealing a chill at its heart—or maybe, Anna thinks uneasily, it's only the ice cream running down the inside of her throat.

"Well, anyway, if people are leaving, how come the line isn't getting any shorter?"

"Maybe they give their places to friends when they go. And

those who die probably write it into their wills. Like an inheritance, right?"

"Or maybe it's not them. You know that fellow with the black beard, the one who checks the lists and organizes everything? Why, do you suppose, has he taken all that work upon himself? I bet he's running some underhanded scheme, pushing the available spots on the side."

"Ooh, I've just had a terrible thought . . . Come closer, come closer . . . What if people who vanish from the line are being transferred somewhere, somewhere far away, and the man with the beard is in charge of the cover-up? Didn't he get everyone to write their names and addresses down?"

The numbers system has long been abolished; they now mark their names directly on the list. This time the chill has nothing to do with the ice cream, Anna knows. They shouldn't be discussing such things out in the open, or at all; and in any case, whenever people are transferred to remote places, she is sure they deserve it. She casts a worried glance at the boy—the two of them have had tea without tea leaves a few times this summer—but he does not look up from his book. A light breeze comes out of nowhere, tosses sun spots back and forth under their feet, shadows merging with the polka dots on their dresses, trees rustling pleasantly above. The girl two spaces in front exclaims, "This is ridiculous, people aren't vanishing anywhere, I'll just go and count everyone!"—and no one tries to silence her, they just watch as she waddles off. She often has impetuous moments of recklessness, this girl, but ever since the line shed its winter clothing, people have understood, and been forgiving; some women have even taken up knitting tiny socks and hats—it will be soon now.

"Well, did it add up?" they ask when she returns. She shakes her head. It's hopeless, just as they knew it would be. Since the beginning of summer, the daytime line has become unruly, overflowing

with children out of school whiling their time away jumping rope
and drawing with chalk on the sidewalk, and old women sunning
themselves on the fold-out chairs some enterprising man is rent-
ing out by the hour, and housewives wandering in and out of the
sewing circle that congregates daily at noon, and pecking couples
leaning on sunbeams, and no one seems to stand for long in one place,
and there are pink and white rivulets of ice cream everywhere, so the
ground itself has grown sticky; and gradually the light glinting off
the leaves that have not yet dulled with a coating of grime, and the
sweet, gummy smell of lindens, and the oily, hot smell of meat pies,
which a harsh-voiced woman carries by the line a few times a day,
and the evenly spaced rhythm of a rope hitting the pavement and
small shoes coming down with a thump, and a thump, and a thump,
the children shrieking giddily—gradually, then, another warm
afternoon dissolves their wary hush in its green, bright, aromatic
passage, and they start talking a little, then laughing, about recipes,
and men, and books, and the day moves on.

Later, laden with vegetables from a nearby stall, Anna walks
home through the evening. Streetlamps are beginning to come on,
mild and hazy like dozens of moons, but there is no need for them,
for it is still light, will stay light for hours. She is almost happy—and
hers is not a calm, contented kind of happiness, but a young, leaping happiness with an undercurrent of excitement that feels much
like rebellion, and a just rebellion at that; for after all the time she has
spent swallowing her resentment, allowing that imperious, self-
absorbed woman to silently rule her life, she has earned the right to
do something for herself, has she not—to do something she herself
wants to do . . .

She walks down the street, smiling a small, hidden smile, nursing her thought: I have a secret now, a purpose to my daily waiting.
And as soon as I have the ticket in my hand, my life will change, my
life will change.

LATE ONE MORNING in the second week of July, Alexander was lying dressed on his unmade bed, letting his gaze wander over the ceiling, imagining wisps of evil-smelling smoke drifting through a low, dark dive. On its dirty floor, men sprawled, their expressionless faces tough as hide, their jaundiced eyes watching the jagged flights of a shadow cast by a tall, pale stranger with an eagle profile. The stranger sat cross-legged in the yellow circle of a solitary kerosene lamp in a corner, scribbling in a notebook; and when the proprietor of the establishment bent over the man's shoulder to ask his desire, he glimpsed a page covered in symbols that belonged to no language he knew—birdlike, teardroplike, dragonlike signs, with fast-flying tails and fantastic curls like the curls of the sinister smoke rising now toward the ceiling—but just then the ceiling was sliced by a blade of sunlight as the door opened with a cursory knock.

Alexander sat up.

"I wanted," his father said, "to discuss your plans for the summer, and beyond. It seems we haven't spoken in a while. Would you like me to go to the university with you?"

"What for?"

"To register for the admission exams. They start next month, do they not?"

"I've registered already," said Alexander coldly. "And I can't talk right now, I'm late for this study group I go to, I was just looking for my bag . . . Ah, here it is. See you later."

Once outside, he stood undecided for a minute, then headed to the park; but the park had been empty for days, even the birds had fled its baked brown lawns. Halting, he rummaged in his bag, jerking his hand away as a discarded star-shaped school pin pricked his finger with its green point; then, diving back in, he dug out at last, from beneath abandoned compositions, dull pencil stubs, and an apple-core fossil from the previous fall, a crumpled ball of paper marked with a treble clef. He smoothed it out. The address was still legible.

Ever since Viktor Pyetrovich had answered his question, he had avoided discussing Selinsky with the old man, knowing that the explanation was likely to be some kind of a joke on Viktor Pyetrovich's part, or else his hearing betraying him in the rustling rain, in the whistling wind—knowing it, of course, yet for some reason unwilling to part with the mystery. He looked at the note, hesitating again; then, irritated with himself, firmly strode down the street.

The city lay bleached by the sun; in its white, unkind glare, the building before which he stopped looked old, sullen, unkempt; the kind of building, he thought with a sinking heart, in which nothing out of the ordinary ever transpired. He pushed the front door open, stumbled in from the light, was immediately blinded by the dimness of the foyer. The ancient elevator gaped at him with its black toothless maw; he swerved around, groped his way up the stairs instead, the banisters slowly swimming up from the gloom as he ascended, skipping steps to escape the sharp stench of cat urine that lingered in the stairwell. For a long while after he rang the bell nothing happened. He checked the note again before dropping it into his bag, waited another minute. He was just turning to go, feeling an odd mixture of disappointment and relief, when a shuffle of slippers sounded inside, punctuated by the tapping of the cane. The door yawned.

"What a nice surprise," Viktor Pyetrovich said from the shadows. "Please, please."

Wiping sweat off his neck, Alexander followed the tapping inside, past a dark stretch of bookcases along the wall of one room, and into another room, so small it could have been a closet, or was a closet perhaps. "Do sit," the old man said, patting the bed. "I'm sorry I've stopped coming to the park—my legs, you know. The line is all I can manage, and one can never have a decent talk there, funny how that is . . . Make yourself comfortable, I'll be right back."

The room too was disappointing, its sole furnishings a chair, a square of sunlight on the bare floor, a narrow bed under a drab checkered blanket, and a standard-issue world map on the wall, like the one they had used in school. Alexander was all at once certain that Selinsky would never bother with a man who lived in such a room. Dispirited, he walked over to the window with no curtains, looked out at the back wall of an apartment building across the yard, saw, in other windows, pots of wilting plants, dozing cats, leaping splashes of sun, a motley patchwork of drying laundry. He was about to move away when, on the sill of a particularly grimy window on the top floor, he caught a glimpse of a peculiar hat, tall and dark; he remembered seeing its like in an old photograph of a crowd strolling up a wide staircase of some columned building with white horses on its triangular roof, printed in their history textbook above the caption: "Idle ballet-goers: Decadent pastimes of the rich." The incongruous hat made him strangely hopeful. He was still squinting, trying to see better past the smeared windowpane, when the tap-tap-tapping, the slapping of the slippers, rose behind him, along with a clanging of metal, a clinking of glass.

Bounding away from the window, he accepted the loaded tray from the old man's hands.

"That was lucky, I nearly dropped it," Viktor Pyetrovich observed mildly. "I would hate to have damaged these."

The two glasses were set in silver glass holders; the silver was blackened, but the scrollwork was magnificent.

"I saw holders like these on a train once," Alexander said. They felt cold and a bit clammy to his touch, as if kept in damp obscurity for a long while. "Except yours are a lot nicer."

"They were in my family," Viktor Pyetrovich said; and only now Alexander noticed the initials snaking amidst the tangle of fruit and leaves, and felt another tiny jolt of hope. Maybe, he thought. "I don't use them much, special occasions only . . . There's nothing sweet, my apologies. If you had come in the spring, I would have given you a cake. Though it wasn't very good."

"I don't like sweets anyway," Alexander said untruthfully.

Perched next to each other on the edge of the bed, they sipped their tea. It tasted slightly metallic, as if the silver had seeped into the water, and there was now a bitterness lingering in Alexander's mouth. The old man held his glass with a gentleness that was almost a caress.

"So, you live here with your children?" Alexander asked.

"I have one son. He used to live here. He lives elsewhere now. You remind me of him, a little, when he was your age. He too shot up early . . . I've never asked you, by the way, why do you want the ticket? Do you like music so much?"

"It's not for me," Alexander said, and looked away. "It's for my grandmother."

"Ah. That's kind of you. My grandson helps with the line, too. You'd like him if he were older."

"Do you . . . Are you a musician?"

"I studied, but I never became one. I dreamed of traveling the world, but I kept putting it off, and then, well, you know . . . After the Change, I taught geography. I'm retired now, of course."

The air in the room was stuffy, yet he was wearing a woolen

cardigan, as if chilled; his buttoning was askew, Alexander noticed. Through the open window, he could hear a child in the yard shrilly calling his mother, the sudden gunshot of a tire blowing out some streets away, a sharp crackling of wings as a pigeon plunged off a roof. A small silence stretched in the patch of dusty sunlight before him. He did not want to ask; he wanted to ask; he opened his mouth, preparing to receive some pedestrian truth like a cold stone sinking into his chest.

"Is that how—I mean, did you meet Selinsky when you were a music student, then?"

Viktor Pyetrovich studied his empty glass; his eyes were invisible, only two silver glass holders hung gleaming darkly in the round blankness of his spectacles.

"I knew him from childhood," he said, looking up at last. "Our fathers were related."

"You—Selinsky is your relative?"

"A cousin. A distant one. We had a large family."

Alexander gaped at him.

"It's not something I tell people, ordinarily, so I hope you won't—"

"I won't tell anyone." His heart was thumping, slow, hard, joyful, in the light, liberated hollow of his rib cage. "Is it possible . . . Could I maybe see some of his letters? The ones where he describes all those things, you know, his escape, the East, everything?"

"They're a bit difficult to get to right now," Viktor Pyetrovich said. "I keep them in a safe place, you see. Maybe next time . . . Would you like some more? No, no, leave it, then, I'll wash it later . . . I do have something I can show you, though, hold on."

Dazed, Alexander tried to decipher the sounds of fumbling and scraping against the wall of the next room. When the old man returned, he was carrying a framed photograph.

"Igor's on the right," he said, knocking on the glass with a yellowed nail. "I'm twenty-four, he's seventeen." I just turned seventeen five days ago, Alexander wanted to shout, but did not. July sun glared off the glass, making it hard to see, turning the two faces into blurs of light. "This was taken at a party at my parents' country estate. You can't tell here, but Igor is wearing a bright red cravat. He often wore red. Ironic, that. I asked him once, why red, but he pretended not to know what I was talking about. 'Red?' he said to me. 'I never wear red.' It got him in trouble, too. One time— but that was much later, of course—he was staying in a southern town. I have a postcard, I'll show you someday . . . Anyway, he was walking to his hotel from a concert he'd given, and he happened to be dressed in a red blazer."

"And?"

"And, well," said Viktor Pyetrovich, his glasses twinkling, "it also happened to be the week of a town festival when they let all their bulls run free in their narrow streets, and by some coincidence, you see—"

Alexander felt the room widening, quite as if its walls had dissolved into new windows through which another, astonishing world was entering in large, luminous pieces. It was a world he had sensed before in the old man's presence—a world he had fully expected to give up only an hour earlier—a place where no object was meaningless, no action inconsequential, where every word, every turn, every note led to some adventure resonating deep within one's soul; but this time, he felt that he himself had been admitted to the story. And so urgent, so bright was his sense of inclusion that he did not for a moment begrudge Selinsky his rather unremarkable black-and-white face with no trace of an eagle profile; nor was he upset when, upon leaving in the early afternoon, he cast another glance outside, and saw that the window on the top floor of the opposite building was standing wide open and that the tall black hat on the windowsill, now sharply outlined by the sun, was nothing but an ordinary cooking pot.

It did not matter, for everything seemed possible—was possible—

in that other world, and he knew with an absolute, invigorating certainty just how he was meant to gain his entrance to it.

"Stop by anytime," Viktor Pyetrovich said from the doorway.

"Could I come tomorrow?" Alexander said quickly.

He nearly skipped as he ran home, past the line, past a short black-bearded man fuming over some list, past an ancient man with deep eyes smiling tranquilly into the sky, past the physics teacher who had given him a grade he had not earned, past an enormous girl who made him glance away in embarrassment, past his mother talking to that painted woman who had pressed a meat pie upon him some months before. He did not stop, only waved from across the street, for underneath his excitement, he did feel a bit troubled; but his father did not deserve the truth, he told himself as he rounded the corner, because the man understood nothing beyond his blinkered, self-righteous pigeonhole of accomplishments, clocks, and rules, and his grandmother was crazy, and as for his mother—as for her, he would take care of her once he was traveling the world with Selinsky, yes, he would send her many beautiful things, like those leather gloves he had once seen her admiring in a magazine, or a pair of high-heeled boots, if, of course, they weren't too bulky to cross the border.

Anna followed him to the corner with her eyes.

"Liubov Dmitriyevna, look, that's my son," she said proudly.

"I've seen him around," the woman replied with a shrug, and turned away.

Stifling a sigh, Anna resigned herself to more hours of patient boredom.

The day, the week, the month were dragging on slowly, so slowly. The sun beat down without cease, children shrieked in the dust, and the expecting girl in front complained of the sun, of the dust, of the children's loud voices, day after day after day, until one day—"The

twenty-second of July, mark your calendars!" someone exclaimed—
the girl doubled up, then straightened and gazed about, slack-jawed
and puzzled. Instantly there was a tumult, women shouting, urging
the girl to breathe, fanning her with newspapers, the air smelling of
ink and perspiration, someone running to telephone the girl's husband, someone else to telephone a friend who had a friend who had a
car. When the chugging automobile had finally taken her away, seated
in the back between two women delegated by the line, Anna exhaled
with relief. She had a distinct sensation that the summer had broken
at last, that the waiting was over.

"I wonder if it's a boy or a girl," she said. "Liubov Dmitriyevna,
what's your guess? A fellow back there is taking bets, I heard."

The woman's eyeliner had grown sloppier over the past few
weeks, and her lipstick often strayed onto her teeth. She stared at
Anna without speaking, as if she hadn't understood; then her eyes
started to glisten.

"Are you all right?" Anna asked, astonished.

"Fine," the woman snapped, and would not look at Anna for the
rest of the afternoon.

The next morning, when the girl's friends had rejoined the line,
fresh from the hospital, delivering the word (it was a boy), Anna noticed the woman blowing her nose into a handkerchief, and went to
buy two ice creams. "I just wanted to get rid of some change in my
pocket," she said offhandedly, ready to discard the extra one; but to
her surprise Liubov Dmitriyevna took it, and ate it greedily, licking
her fingers with large, ungraceful, pink-tongued licks. The day after
that, a rain shower washed the heat away for a few hours, and, confined to shafts of dampness under their dangerously bony umbrellas, they exchanged some remarks about the weather; and the day
after that, Liubov Dmitriyevna offered Anna a lipstick in a lovely
golden case. "My husband's given me three just like it," she said
breezily.

Anna accepted it with gratitude all the same.

That night she changed into a dress he used to love, and sat before the mirror in their bedroom, gazing at her face, at the round lines that used to be straight, at the straight lines that used to be round. Then, tenderly, she slid the lipstick out and began to draw the contours of her mouth. The lipstick was pale pink, shimmering with barely discernible particles of gold—a young, hopeful color, the color of a sunrise over warm pebbles somewhere by the sea, the color of satin petals in a happy bride's hair. When she was done, she gave her lips one final pat with a square of toilet paper, then lay down on the bed, leafed through a volume of poems she had borrowed from her mother's room. Her clock said it was nine. All at once exhaustion moved in her bones, subterranean and pervasive. As she read first this verse, then that, she felt time slowing around her, becoming denser, thicker, brighter, until it acquired the consistency of amber, and she herself was now a mote of dust, or perhaps a fly, yes, a fly suspended for a small, private eternity in this hour, this day, this never-ending year, time's full, rich, golden luminescence enveloping her like a soft, gentle promise—If you want to live forever, she thought drowsily, spend your life waiting for some great future happiness—the light shining through her closed eyelids; or perhaps not a fly but a bird, a cuckoo, I live like a cuckoo in a clock, the clock saying it was now eight-thirty, which was impossible unless time was moving backward, backward, through all the concrete-walled corridors into a sunlit childhood room in a past so deep that its very air was scented with joy.

When, in another half-hour, Sergei came in, the lamp was lit, and his wife asleep on top of the bedspread, a book with a liver-spotted cover in her limp hand. She wore an unbecoming dress, which cut ugly red grooves under her arms and made the buttons on the front seem dangerously close to popping off; her chin was smeared in pink glitter. As he looked at her, his heart stilled, and a horrifying thought

burst within him: What if my inability to be happy here, to feel love
for this kind, selfless woman, has nothing to do with her failure to
grasp my oh-so-lofty thoughts, to share my passion for music—
what if it is, in truth, nobody's fault but my own, some visceral
flaw within myself, some deep-seated failure, some lack, some
tragic lack—

He killed the light.

The next evening, standing before the kiosk, he felt restless and
unsettled, worn-out, cut off from the mass of humanity, from the
small agitations around him. When is it going to end, people were
asking one another up and down the line, enough is enough. As
she had done every day for the past month, just before six o'clock—
the summer kiosk hours had been extended—the kiosk seller packed
away her knitting, drew down the shutter, stepped outside to lock
the door, then clicked away, wobbling a little on her needle-thin
heels, watched by many hostile eyes. "We should follow her home
one day," someone muttered under his breath, "and put the question
to her clearly, once and for all." A few men laughed uneasily.

In a while the hot July dusk lengthened along the ground like a
glossy-skinned animal stretching, and shadows yawned, lazy pink
tongues of the first streetlamps flickering within their jaws. Later
still, a band of unpleasant characters strolled by, from the Northern
Nightingales line. Their concert had taken place back in April, to
everyone's great satisfaction; rumor had it that there would soon be
tickets for a performance by the legendary folk ensemble the Little
Fir Trees, but the kiosk was currently closed for restocking, and they
had time on their hands.

"Enjoying yourselves?" a man shouted from across the street.
"Overeducated idiots!"

A girl on his arm giggled.

"I bet there isn't even any concert, they just like one another's
company!"

The line around Sergei shifted uncomfortably.

"Idiots yourselves," someone suggested in a timid undertone, but no one else said anything. The Nightingales sauntered off, cat-calling and whistling.

"I do wish they'd hurry up already," grumbled Pavel.

"How about a song?"

"No, not tonight."

"Oh, come on!"

"Listen, I'm not in the mood, all right?"

"Fine, I was just saying . . . Hey, did you hear the latest? Word is, the man up front, the organizer, you know, he isn't . . . Well, but it's probably nothing. Just a rumor."

"What are you talking about?"

"I'm not sure I should tell you, but if you really must know—"

The elderly man a few spaces ahead was whispering to a circle of people, their heads close together; Sergei could hear only the frequently echoed word—"provocation"—and, amidst the whispers, the indignant exclamation of Vladimir Semyonovich, who strode away, fiercely kneading his mustache, spitting out: "What vile nonsense!" Sergei glanced after him, frowning, then shook his watch out of his shirtsleeve. It was nearly ten; Sofia, he saw, was already sliding her novel into her bag.

"May I walk you home tonight?" he said, though without any hope.

She had been quiet the past few weeks, ever since the end of their night shift, reading rather a lot, only rarely lifting her transparent eyes from the page. He still asked every night, even if she had declined his every offer.

"It's very kind of you," she said, not looking at him, clicking her bag shut with a crisp, precise snap, "but I'll be fine, there's still some light left—"

"You should take him up on it, you know," Pavel interjected. "Lots of shady types out and about tonight. The Nightingales can get rowdy."

"Well—" she said, hesitating.

"I'll get your bag," Sergei said quickly.

After a block or two, his meager attempts to start a conversation lapsed. They walked in silence, which seemed to him to grow more tense and awkward with every step; and as the habitual sequence of fences, apartment buildings, tram stops, benches, rows of dusty saplings unfolded before his eyes, the day's accumulation of disturbing little incidents, its lingering malaise, grew huge within him and, welling over at last, resolved into a sharp, simple, terrible feeling. He was seized with the horror of old age creeping closer, of his life irrevocably hardening into a fixed, unchangeable shape of many bleak years to come—and against this nearing horror, the concert, he knew with unfamiliar anguish, was no longer enough.

He stopped abruptly. She stopped too. There was no one around; it was another anonymous street corner, another lukewarm streetlamp drooling light and shadow onto their faces. The nighttime city crouched behind them; he could sense its warm, expectant, animal breath on his neck. "What is it?" she asked.

He had not planned it—had not wanted it like this, on some random street, with the muggy blot of municipal light staining the skies above them, with shadowy, silent dogs swiftly pursuing some invisible prey along the pavements—but the almost physical sensation of his time running out was already squeezing the words, uncertain, enormous, out of his throat.

"Sofia Mikhailovna, there is something I must tell you. I—"

He faltered. She was searching his face with a gaze light and gray as a feather; he could see two tiny question marks of streetlamp reflections frozen in her eyes.

"What is it?" she repeated, and in her voice he heard an urgency that was oddly like fear.

One heartbeat, two heartbeats, three heartbeats, four . . .

"I have a surprise for you," he blurted out. "A record of Selinsky's music. I thought—since you wanted to hear—so you won't have to wait until—"

"Oh," she said, and he did not know what filled the small hollow in her exhalation, relief or disappointment. "A record of Selinsky? But how did you, where did you—I looked myself, it's not—and have you heard it, what is it? That's—oh, but that's wonderful!"

The hollow was joy, he realized now, and he wanted to weep.

"I—I don't have the right kind of player at home," he said, not meeting her eyes.

"Oh, of course." She began walking again, airy, happy steps, almost running; he followed, the pavement clutching at the soles of his shoes like mud. "Bring it to the line tomorrow, we'll go to the museum afterward—"

"I'm afraid it can't be tomorrow, I don't have the record myself, it's at a friend's right now, so it will be a couple of days. A few. Maybe a week, the friend's out of town." Her building loomed at the end of the street, blocking the sky. He was talking very fast now. "And I'm not sure the museum is a proper place. You may not realize, but officially, his music is still banned. It might put you in an awkward position if someone were to come upon you at work—listening to banned records on State property, you know—"

"Yes, you're right, home would be better," she said, stopping again. "I do have a player that should work. Well, as soon as your friend comes back, we'll figure it out. Oh, but this really is the most wonderful gift, thank you, thank you, Sergei Vasilievich—"

Then, unexpectedly, it happened—a swift, birdlike dash, the darkness leaping toward him, a single excited curl escaping the tight bun of her hair, brushing his cheek, her dress so soft in the cup of his hand, what fabric was that, her lips so close to his, yet not, not quite, only grazing his chin, her shoulders already slipping from under his arm, Good night, thank you again, one, two, three, four, the bang—and as he gazed at the closed door, he remembered the scene he had imagined so many times, the black luster of the record circling, the shadows moving on the ceiling of her room, the music rippling like liquid sunshine on their closed eyelids—and was deeply disgusted with himself.

The next morning he managed to catch his son just as he was about to run out the door.

"I've told you already, she doesn't have it," the boy said impatiently, shifting some books under his arm.

"Not her. I thought you might know some other people," Sergei said in a lowered voice. "From the night shift. People who can get things, I mean."

The boy appeared taken aback. "Well, I don't know," he said after a moment. "Maybe. I guess some of them might have, you know, contacts."

"Please," Sergei repeated. "Please ask around. Any record will do, any price, I don't care."

"Well, all right," the boy said from the threshold. "Can't promise anything, though."

"Thank you, Sasha," Sergei said quietly as the door closed.

He did not think his son had heard, but Alexander had, and, surprised, paused at the top of the stairs. That night he pulled Nikolai away from the kiosk.

"I'll see what I can do," Nikolai said, shrugging. "Stepan might know where to find it, I'll talk to him. A pointless pursuit, but whatever, not my money. Let's get back now, they've just opened a fresh one."

He drank less than the others that night, and though it was so late when he got home as to be early, he stayed up reading for some time, one of the books Viktor Pyetrovich had lent him. The book was from another century, with miraculously preserved brittle pages and the quaint pre-revolutionary alphabet, which Viktor Pyetrovich had taught him; it was not that difficult, only a matter of a few odd-looking letters. There were stories of travels—not the galloping, tough adventures he had been spinning out of the fabric of his nights for some time now, but slow, meandering incidents with seemingly no beginnings and no ends, hushed conversations with strangers in narrow streets of somnolent towns, afternoons by some river, evenings spent drinking tea, chants of unfamiliar names and places— all of it filled with such quiet, ordinary beauty that he kept turning the pages even though he drifted off to a doze now and then, turn-ing the pages, turning the hours, turning the corners of sleepy boule-vards in cities red and golden and full like fairy-tale apples, drifting in a boat down a river through an infinite perspective of weeping willows, green and tranquil like monastery cloisters, and that old voice from behind the wall slipping in and out between the lines, the pages, the hours, telling him about a river, a boulevard, yes, walking down a boulevard with my beloved, hand in hand, happy as the full bloom of summer, and a mansion on the boulevard, and the cool of the stairwell, and the cool of our kisses in the stairwell, a friend's apartment, a confusion with the keys, we were a bit tipsy that day, all that champagne, we had been celebrating another triumph, you re-member, and then the sunny cool of that airy, breezy room, like a piece of the sky, our sky, the cool of the linens, do you remember, the small balcony where we stood afterward, looking at the river, and two years later, when I was already living somewhere else, with the man I had married, no longer dancing, you found a postcard at one of the book stalls lining the river, and there it was, in a brown photograph, our mansion, the stone nymphs gazing down at us with heartbroken forgiveness, the small curly clouds like sighs in the skies, and you marked the window with a cross, and you sent it to me across the continent, asking, Do you recognize it, do you remember?

I remember.

4

By MID-AUGUST, the bright, green, delightful summer spell was long over, the heat unbearable, the city exhausted. Trees feebly stirred their sooty leaves, rare automobiles spat out clouds of scorching dust, and the air hung so thick with the smell of burning that it seemed to leave dirty, hot smudges on everything it touched. In the sullen line, feet swelled, pages of books turned gray and sticky, conversations dried out. The formerly pregnant girl now brought along her infant in a knitting basket, and his raisin of a face gaped in a constant pink-gummed scream.

"I've been very patient," Anna said, "we all have, but surely it'll end by autumn?"

"I know the kiosk seller, and she has no idea," Liubov Dmitriyevna replied.

"You *know* the kiosk seller?"

The woman was weakly fanning herself with a glossy magazine; through the blur of radiantly smiling beauties riding well-shined horses along the foreign shores of cool, tranquil lakes, Anna glimpsed her cheeks running with pink and blue rivulets of makeup. "All of us in the area know one another," the woman said, sighing. "Though this one's new."

"All of who?"

Liubov Dmitriyevna hesitated, a suede high-heeled boot flickering back and forth across her melting face, then said, cryptically and briefly, "Come with me later." They did not talk much for the rest of the day, but at five o'clock, just as the evening shift was scheduled to replace them, she led Anna down an alley, across two streets, through the park, to another kiosk. DRY GOODS, announced the square black letters above; Anna remembered having bought some buttons here two or three summers earlier. The line before it was short, eight or nine women only, waiting in silence. Ignoring them, Liubov Dmitriyevna walked around, rapped on the door at the rear. The door gave in, revealing a tight, dim corner where a man, his back to them, was busy shrugging out of a kiosk seller's smock, his elbows bumping against the cramped walls. He glanced around, grinning; as his eyes skidded like olives in the brown oil of his face, Anna recalled seeing him in the line on a few occasions. Divested of his uniform, he tossed it at Liubov Dmitriyevna, stepped outside, pecked her on a cheek, waved at the puzzled Anna, and walked off swiftly, calling behind him, "Keys in the door," closely chased by a sharp smell of cologne. "Pashka, my younger brother," Liubov Dmitriyevna said, pushing her arms through the smock's grayish sleeves. "He works days here, I work evenings. We don't close until nine."

"Oh," said Anna lamely. "I see."

The waiting women stared at them with dull, glazed eyes the color of slush, their faces like unwashed laundry, not moving, not speaking.

"Can't breathe in here, why must he always pour whole bottles of the stuff on himself? Of course it's imported, but still . . . Well, come in, come in." Grumbling, Liubov Dmitriyevna prodded Anna inside, then bolted the door behind them. It was, Anna thought looking around, a lot like finding oneself confined to a slovenly scented drawer. The air was overpoweringly sweet; dust swarmed in a wedge of stuffy, tired light that oozed through the square of the small window; there was barely space for the two of them to turn among all the boxes crammed into the place, some on the shelves at their backs, others, rather more mysterious, below the counter. Having nowhere to sit, Anna pressed herself against the far wall, and, awed, bent her head to gaze at a perky battalion of golden lipsticks, a cascade of stockings in gleaming crimson packages that made them look like candy bars or in shining oval containers that resembled painted eggs, a few tantalizingly opaque plump bottles, some tangled lengths of silky gauze, which may or may not have been an assortment of scarves, some of which she quite possibly recognized . . .

Liubov Dmitriyevna had just finished dismissing the last woman in the line. Pivoting on her stool, she leafed through the scrawled cardboard signs stacked on the counter—Anna glimpsed *Closed for accounting* and *Seller sick until further notice*—then pulled out one that read *Back in 15 minutes* and propped it up, blocking the window. Immediately, brown, claustrophobic dusk fell within their drawer; the only illumination was a narrow thread of late, pale sunlight that squeezed in from outside to hazily outline the sign. In the dimness, Anna heard the sounds of opening, fumbling, rustling, shutting; then she became aware of another smell, round, rich, soft, flowing in a dark, slow stream through the sharp sweetness of the cologne, and held her breath.

A bare lightbulb creaked into life on the ceiling. A small pink box, she saw, sat on the counter between them; within its ruffled rosy depths nested a flock of chocolate swans, black and white, each in its own glinting pool of silver foil.

"From Over There. I have a sweet tooth. Here, have one." Liubov Dmitriyevna crammed a swan whole into her mouth, smearing dark chocolate and red lipstick over her chin, and spoke indistinctly: "Anyway, about the other kiosk. As soon as I heard of it, back in

November, I went over to welcome the new arrival on the scene, we sellers have our little arrangements . . . Also, I'd been looking for a pair of boots, none of my contacts had them. But the new woman turned out to be useless. She's from another bureau, I think. I couldn't come to any agreement with her, had to wait in line like everyone else. She had no idea what her kiosk would stock, either. Didn't know the first thing about kiosks, in fact. Then—then my husband heard about the concert."

She fell silent. On the other side of the thin corrugated wall, Anna could hear a new line starting to form, steps shuffling, people lying in wait. She tried to think of something to say, but her head was beginning to swim in the perfumed, cramped, stuffy glare. Liubov Dmitriyevna fingered the crinkling pink tissues in the box, picked out and ate another chocolate.

"All those things I told you, about being a housewife, you know?" she said, not lifting her eyes. In the close confinement of the kiosk, under the unforgiving light of the bulb, below makeup glossy as an oil slick, her face lay exposed; and as Anna looked at her closely, she thought in surprise, Why, she's not in her thirties, she's no younger than me, older perhaps—and glanced away quickly, uncomfortably, as if she had just uncovered someone's shameful secret. Liubov Dmitriyevna pushed the box toward Anna. "You haven't had one yet, take it, take it . . . I just thought you'd turn up your nose at me if you knew. You were always going on about how your husband is an important musician, and your son is about to enroll in the university, and you with your fine education, reading poetry and all that—"

Anna gently wrapped the foil around a white swan and tucked it into her pocket. "Oh, no," she said. "Not at all. I thought . . . Not at all. Liubov Dmitriyevna, would you—if you want, we could have tea at my place sometime. Maybe tomorrow?"

"I would like that," Liubov Dmitriyevna said. "And it's just Liuba."

꙳

A few days later, she in turn invited Anna over. Her apartment proved to be exactly like Anna's, in an identical building just two streets down; and though it overflowed with a great many desirable things, scattered on the surfaces, stacked darkly in the yawning wardrobes, glittering in the cupboards, they seemed to Anna, as she waded her careful way through the place, like pieces that did not form a whole, the chaotic back room of a secondhand shop. Following Liubov Dmitriyevna—Liuba, she reminded herself—into the kitchen, she glimpsed a silk blouse, its tag still attached, hanging in a doorway, a gathering of three bronze lamps without lampshades on a corridor counter, an open suitcase spilling its contents onto a crisp rug that smelled new and clashed with the wallpaper.

"Your place is nice," she said insincerely. "Can I help?"

Liuba was clearing a patch off the kitchen table, brushing to the floor two or three pairs of stockings in unopened packages, an unused eastbound train ticket, a delicately painted Oriental fan. Falling, the fan flickered open in a momentary, heartbreaking vision of a different, clear, simple life—a tiny village, the shore of a blue lake, horses running in a meadow beyond—then shut abruptly. Liuba silently set the cups and the plates before Anna, flopped onto a chair, dropped her head in her hands, and started to cry, her shoulders shaking with big, sloppy, uncontrollable sobs.

Anna stood horrified before her, excruciatingly aware of her empty hands hanging by her sides. Then, sitting down so hurriedly that the chair legs scraped the floor with a jarring metallic moan, she put her arm around the woman's shoulders as if trying to hold them down, to make them stop jerking in that awful, defenseless, rag-doll way. After a minute, the shoulders subsided. Anna removed her arm. "Try the cakes," Liubov Dmitriyevna said, wiping her face roughly with the back of her hand, the last small sob caught in her throat like a hiccup, her mouth running with blood-red lipstick. "I got them through a special connection."

"Thank you," Anna said, picking up a pastry. "They're wonderful," she added after a pause, but Liubov Dmitriyevna—Liuba, just Liuba, she told herself again—did not respond. Humbled in the presence of someone else's unfathomable grief, ashamed to be its witness, Anna looked out the window. The city was being rubbed out by dusk, and the dusk had a new quality to it: light around the edges, it now concealed at its heart a darker, chillier, autumnal kernel, like a cool pebble buried in damp sand; and there was her reflection again, stripped of the years, evenly meeting her gaze in the sky.

She was still staring outside when Liuba spoke. "My husband has a daughter who lives with us," she said in a voice so quiet that Anna had to lean forward to hear. "You saw the closed door in the hallway? . . . The girl is ill, she never leaves her bed, and refuses chocolates. What kind of a child refuses chocolates? Her lips are so transparent you can almost see her teeth through them . . . And I, I don't have any children, I've spent years and years hoping, but I'm forty-six, it's too late now . . . And my husband, he drinks, and has no steady job, and risks his skin selling stuff in those places—well, you know—and lifts my things too. Two of my rings, my mother's picture, and six spoons went missing not long ago, though he denies it, of course—"

"But does he love you?" Anna asked softly.

Liuba thought for a moment. "You know how it is," she said with a shrug. "One day he'll come home stewed and smack me a good one, then he'll be all contrite, kisses, presents—stolen, mostly, but even so . . . Yeah, he loves me."

Anna looked back at the window, watched her reflection's eyes grow dark and still. "I think my husband doesn't love me," she said.

Liuba briskly blew her nose into a napkin, poured out more tea, pressed another pastry upon Anna, listened to her talk.

"What he needs is not pies in the kitchen, he's sick of the kitchen," she then said, nodding with authority. "You should meet him somewhere outside your home, somewhere romantic."

"There's the cafeteria," Anna said uncertainly.

"No, honey, not the cafeteria, what's romantic about the cafeteria?"

"I had an éclair pastry there once. With cream."

"No, no. Somewhere in nature, I think. You lie on the grass, you listen to birds, you drink some wine. I saw that in a film once."

"The park, maybe?" Anna said. "There are pigeons in the park. But they don't sing, they just make those coughing noises like they're choking—"

Liuba frowned. "The park might work," she conceded at last. "You won't see the trash cans and the dog shit once it gets dark. I'll find you some wine that won't give you a stomachache—don't forget to open it beforehand, though, nothing worse than grunting over a cork when you're trying to be romantic. And you said you're preparing some surprise for him—well, don't wait, surprise him now. Oh, and you'll need to wear something he's never seen, something tight and plunging, you know, and some makeup. You have a beautiful face but you don't take care of yourself. I'll lend you things, I have plenty, a pretty necklace, a pair of earrings—"

"Thank you," Anna said, a bit stiffly. "I don't need earrings, I have a pair already."

"Listen," Liuba said. "You have a husband who doesn't drink, chase skirts, or squander away all your money, and a son, a handsome, healthy son who is about to become a student at the university. You are lucky." As she spoke, she wouldn't quite look at Anna.

Anna grew warm with pity and shame. "I'm so sorry," she said, squeezing Liuba's hand.

Liuba turned away, blew her nose again, turned back. "Hell," she said, smiling a bright, devastated smile. "Let's go look in my closet."

~ঙ~

A week later, her bag sagging in an oblong shape suggestive of a
bottle, Anna watched Sergei turn the corner. He walked slowly,
stooping a little in the thin gray jacket he had worn for years. He did
not notice her until he was almost upon her, then looked up in surprise; but underneath the surprise she glimpsed another look, one of
defeat, and her heart turned hot and tight in her chest. "When you're
done tonight," she said, "could you come by the park?"

"Why?" he asked without interest.

Liuba had counseled her to turn the evening into an adventure,
something new.

"Oh, Sasha asked me to tell you if I ran into you," she said non-
chalantly. "I guess he wants to see you before his shift. He'll be
waiting for you."

After a short pause, he spoke. "I'll be there, thanks."

She followed him with her eyes, wondering whether she had
imagined the unexpected brightening in his face, then ran home. She
would have liked to take a bath, but there was no hot water—they
shut it off for a month or two every summer, for maintenance, the
notice on her building always read—so she put on a teakettle, then
poured its steaming stream into a large pot filled with cold water,
and ladled diluted lukewarm cupfuls over herself while she crouched
in the tub. As a week's worth of summer grime left her skin, she
began to feel small whirls and lulls in the air, tiny pocket-sized
breezes, dips and rises in temperature, the evening, the world, stirring
alive in barely perceptible, hopeful ways.

She dashed from the bathroom as she was, unembarrassed by her
nakedness, the linoleum cold against her feet, and in the bedroom
pushed the window wide open, her full breasts grazing the sill.
Breathing deeply, suddenly exhilarated, she looked at the flat roofs,
the lamps starting to come on in other homes, the moistly gleaming
fish scale of the crescent moon.

Liuba's blue satin dress was carefully spread out on the bed; she touched its pearly softness to assure herself that it was real.

A little past nine o'clock, as she was applying a layer of matching blue paint to her eyelids, she heard the front door open and close. Throwing on a robe, she walked out of the bedroom. Her son was striding down the corridor toward his room, carrying a load of books in his arms. Studying so hard for his entrance exams, she thought, and stopped, seized with a desire to say something to him, something warm, something that would include him in her nearing happiness; but just then, the telephone jumped into shrill existence behind her back.

She answered. A boy's voice asked politely for Sasha.

"It's for you," she said. He picked up the receiver.

"Yeah?" he said. "Oh, Stepka, hey! . . . Right now? Actually, I'm just . . . Oh, I see . . . Where? . . . Not a problem, I'll be right there."

She gazed after him a bit regretfully, sorry to have been checked in her generous impulse; she wished the night could be special for everyone she loved.

The park was deserted, shadows dense underfoot, the air deep, cool, charged with approaching autumn; a few dead leaves rustled on the path as Alexander hurried along.

His friend sat sprawled on a bench, tossing rocks at the streetlamp.

"That was fast," he said, and waved his cigarette at his feet. "Here it is, then."

Alexander bent, picked up the flat square-shaped parcel bundled in newspapers.

"What's the damage?" he asked.

The youth threw another rock at the lamp as he replied. The metal post issued a hollow clang, swallowing Alexander's gasp.

"Took some doing," Stepan said with a shrug. "Almost impossible to find. Banned, right? This one's from Over There. Might be a scratch on it, but it shouldn't skip too much."

He searched the ground for a bigger rock, took aim.

"When do you need the money?"

Glass shattered, and darkness leaked out, as if autumn had arrived abruptly in the park. The scar under Stepan's eye vanished; his face dissolved into a vague, satisfied, smoke-wreathed blur. In the pale echo of light from the windows above them, Alexander watched him lean back, ease out a bottle from the crook of his arm.

"For you, no rush," Stepan said. "I can wait till next week. Want some?"

"No, I should go, my shift's coming up."

"You and that line of yours—such dedication . . . Well, I'll be here for a while if you feel like stopping by later. Been running around like crazy the last few days, I figure I deserve to sit back for a few hours, smell the roses."

"Yeah, sure," Alexander said. "Thanks, brother. See you around."

Not willing to risk standing in line with the black-market merchandise in his possession, he walked back home. In the shaky dimness of the elevator, he ripped off the newspaper skin, a few stray phrases dangling in thin shreds under his fingers—"under the auspices of," "repeatedly with a heated iron," "to the glorious end" . . . He slid the record out of its sleeve and held it locked between his palms, the black brilliance of its concentric circles moving round and round between his hands like grooves of a tree trunk, the edges brittle and sharp, the label reading *Igor Selinsky, Violin Concerto in*— The doors jerked open, and, his eyes still on the label, he stepped out, and smashed headfirst into a woman in a horrid shiny dress.

He felt his hands go limp, heard the sickening crack of something hard hitting the concrete of the landing, her high, incongruously girlish giggle, "Ah, Sasha, it's you, I just thought I'd go for a little walk, there are cold cutlets if you're—" But already the doors were groaning, closing by fits and starts like creaking old jaws taking small bites out of the terrible vision of his mother, her face motley and glossy, her eyelashes twitching with mascara like the hairy legs of some squashed insect, her skin showing white and thick through the silky stockings, her smeared lips smiling, smiling at him for one instant from inside the elevator's painfully, pitilessly illuminated box, in another instant nothing but a fissure of light going down, down . . .

Frantically he fumbled for his keys, let himself in, and, bursting into his room, thrust the record under his lamp, gave it a rapid once-over. There was a nasty slash running through it; he did not think it had been there before, but he could not be sure. He pushed it back into its sleeve, his hands trembling so much that he made another awkward movement, felt another creak-crack of plastic under his fingers. Leaving the record on his desk, he switched the light off and rushed out.

There was no trace of his mother on the street. He walked briskly, as if to flee his unease, and reached the kiosk before ten, just as the evening shift was departing. His father was there still; Alexander saw him wave, then turn to speak to someone behind him, and move toward him with broad, impatient strides. They met on a corner half a block away.

"You're early, were you waiting for me at the park?" his father asked in a hurried undertone. "Do you have it?"

Alexander glanced at him in surprise.

"How did you . . . I didn't know you knew . . . Never mind. Yeah, I have it. It's in my room, on the desk. There might be a . . . it may skip a little. They want the payment by—"

His words choked as his father embraced him.

"Thank you, Sasha," he said. "I'll have the money. And anything you want, just ask."

❧

Sofia was waiting for him in the next street.

"Oh, Sergei Vasilievich, I can't believe this," she said. "To tell you the truth, I started thinking there was no record—that I somehow dreamed our conversation—"

He laughed with relief, lightly touching her elbow. They walked quickly, though not by the shortest route; they circumvented the park because it looked too dark and a drunken hollering interspersed with abandoned shrieks was rising in the heart of its shadows. Someone having a bit too much fun in a public place, Sergei thought with embarrassment, making an effort to ignore it, careful not to glance at Sofia until the shrieks became sobs, then drowned in the silence behind them. When they reached his building, he left her in the foyer by the mailboxes and, anxious, tiptoed inside his apartment, readying some innocuous lie for his wife. His wife, however, did not emerge from the bedroom—she must have gone to sleep early again—and there was the record, in a nest of torn newspapers on Alexander's desk, just as the boy had promised.

He departed without anyone's having seen him.

They covered the distance to her home almost at a run, not talking. He felt the neighborhood streets stretching tediously like an accordion, his impatience a drawn-out note, his thoughts a feverish, excited, apprehensive whirl. At last they were there. One, two, three, four—but now the echoes of their footsteps merged together, the resistance of the front door yielding magically under his hand; and already they were leaving the blank outside darkness to enter the enchanted darkness inside.

She pressed the elevator button. He imagined the cramped cage sliding open before them, the cigarette butts and spittle on its rickety floor, and how close they would stand, and was all at once nervous and distracted; but after she had held her finger on the button for a long, frustrating moment, it became clear that the elevator was stuck somewhere above.

"It's only the fourth floor," she said. "I'm sorry. Please watch your step, the lights are out."

He followed her, blindly feeling his way along the banisters, her silhouette dissolved in the murkiness of the unlit flight of stairs, then outlined, briefly, tantalizingly, against the pale glow of a narrow window on the landing, and dissolved, and outlined again. With each ascending step, he sensed the nearing of so many nighttime mysteries, simple and inevitable as breathing—even if it was his own, somewhat labored, middle-aged breathing as he trudged up, and up, and up; but also, and no less compellingly as he climbed higher, pressing the precious parcel against his chest, glimpsing the increasingly distant floating of the streetlamp spheres in the city that was being left below, he began to anticipate at last the unwinding of the as yet unheard Selinsky melody—that ecstatic rising from note to note, that rare, exultant, vertiginous moment he loved most of all, when his very essence seemed drawn out of his body after a piercing surge of music, when all the inexpressible, mute feelings, all the neglected longings of his soul, found a language full and perfect and forgiving, flowing freely in some other place where beauty was as ever-present as air, where future was pure time, endless time, allowing space enough for anything and everything, all the hopes he had ever cherished, all the greatnesses he had ever wanted to accomplish, all the dreams from which he had ever woken up—

"I apologize for the smell," Sofia said, turning. "Cats, you know."

He started, stumbled, nearly laughed, and, slipping on something mushy—a potato skin, maybe—descended heavily to his knees, his bag tangled below him.

"Are you all right?" she asked quickly, reaching out to catch him, her eyes moving in the dimness, a hovering, concerned angel with a pale bluing of the temples.

"I'm fine, I'm fine," he said, rising with stiff dignity.

He tried not to dwell on the unmistakable sensation of something plastic snapping beneath him as his weight had come down to the floor.

In the doorway, she put her finger to her lips.

"It's late," she whispered, "people are sleeping."

He was not sure whether she was talking about neighbors whom she did not want alerted to a stranger's visit so close to midnight, or about someone living in her apartment. He stepped into the darkness after her, and then her hand was in his. He pressed her fingers, her ring pinching him painfully, and the darkness swirled around them, fast, faster, in breathless eddies that pulsated with the enormous pounding of his heart; but her hand resisted his pressure, pulling him forward instead. Obeying, he moved after her between the corners of unseen furniture, a straggling light from the street below fleshing out the many frames that glinted on the wall—no doubt paintings, soft, honey-rich paintings he would see in the daylight soon—and a hump of blankets on the sofa where, he supposed, her father lay slumbering, dreaming of plush slippers and small bowls of preserves and other simple comforts of uneventful old age—

I am not old, he thought with defiance, I am not old yet, I am only forty-seven, I will not be old for a long time . . . A door opened, shut behind them, her hand eluded him, the light went on. He closed his eyes for an instant as the sun exploded in his head, then saw a room emerging.

"Please, sit down," she said. "I'm sorry about the mess, I didn't expect—"

There was a chair; he sat. The curtains were powder-blue, and the small space seemed to undulate with a profusion of clothes, cloths, fabrics; the night wind blew the curtains, the shadows, the cooling of August, inside through an open window, and the sleeve of a discarded blue blouse moved ever so lightly, like a wing rising and falling, like the breath of someone peacefully asleep. He felt as if he had found himself at the heart of a cool blue jewel filled with faint, fluid breezes, brushing through him like the advent of happiness.

The room was so narrow that his knees touched the edge of her bed, but he did not look at the bed. He watched her back instead as she bent over the record player on her dresser, watched her hands as she carefully wiped the spindle with a square of cloth.

She straightened, picked up the record, gazed at him. "Do you know what I imagine?" she said. "Something so new I can't even imagine it. I was born three years after he left. Something I don't know, then. Something I can't suspect exists, do you understand?"

Their eyes fit together at last, and there it was—the dizziness, the night wind caressing her hair, his heart losing its mooring, falling somewhere, somewhere joyous, the music spiraling into the skies through the gash of the window, higher, higher, her clothes cascading to the floor as she took a barefoot step, leap, flight toward him, the violins sobbing over a life that was nearly wasted, but not quite, not quite . . .

Turning back to the player, she slid the record out of its sleeve.

He heard a pained intake of breath.

"What is it?" he asked.

"The record is badly cracked," she said in a near-whisper. "I don't know whether—I'll try, of course, but I don't think—see, it's almost broken in half—"

He stood from his chair, looked in turn. The wind died in the room.

As the record began to rotate, the tonearm shook and jumped and jerked, and there were horrible hiccups, and the noise of teeth grinding, and, most heartrending of all, a tiny snippet of a melody—three, four notes, which kept repeating themselves, reaching the edge of beauty again and again a mere heartbeat before going over into a crackling chasm.

He attempted to talk, but his lips only rustled like dried in-sect wings.

The tonearm shivered to a stop.

"I'm so sorry, but it won't work," she said, taking the record off.

"No, no, let me, I will, I might—" He tore the record out of her hands, and pressed it back on the turntable, and pushed, and pulled, and kneaded, his trembling fingers trying to cajole the sound into life, in vain, for things kept jamming, and some invisible machinery groaned in protest, until, gently wresting the record away from him, she said, "Please, Serezha, it's no use, you'll just break the player."

On the other side of the wall, sofa springs complained as some-one shifted.

"I should be going," he said, and stood motionless for another silent moment.

"I'll walk you out," she said.

In the hallway, they paused. She had left the door to her room open, and the low, blue-tinted light splashed about their shadowy reflections in the mirror.

"Sergei Vasilievich, really, it's all right," she said softly, "you'll hear the real thing in only three months, three or four, very soon now, don't be so upset."

"Of course," he said, forcing out a smile, then added, desperate to rescue something at least of his perfect evening, their first evening alone, "You know, maybe—maybe we could even go to-gether, you and I—"

"I would love that," she said, and looked away. "I would love that, but you see, the ticket's not for me, I'm doing this for—for someone else. I've been meaning to tell you—"

"Oh," he said, his voice deadened. "Oh, all right."

She embraced him, quickly, fleetingly, a brush of her hand on his shoulder; he barely felt it. "Thank you anyway, I know you tried." She was unlocking the front door now. "Here is the record, your friend must not have realized . . . Well, good night, see you tomorrow."

The elevator opened on her floor, swallowing him, then hung without going up or down for a long while, or not that long perhaps, he did not care, he did not notice, until, for no reason, the doors slid back open, regurgitating him on her threshold. He stared at the number of her apartment for a heavy minute, thinking of that seed of something small and dark and imploring he had imagined in her eyes the instant before she had averted them.

Then he turned, and trudged down the stairs. He stopped on the second-floor landing to stomp on the record, throw its pieces into the trash chute. He cut his palm on a jagged edge, and for another stretch of time stood still, pressing his forehead against the sweating concrete wall. It was past midnight when he finally stepped outside. He could not face the thought of going home. The park where he was supposed to meet his son two hours earlier was quiet now, and he stumbled along its unlit paths, scraping pebbles in his wake, smashed his knee on a bench, sat down. Someone had abandoned a nearly full bottle on the ground, next to the shed skins of what looked like silk stockings. At least somebody was having a good time, he thought, suppressing a sickened laugh. The unsteady boat of the crescent moon swayed in the pale waves inside the bottle; he picked it up, pulled out the cork, sniffed it mechanically, but, of course, smelled nothing. It was too dark to read the label. He wiped its neck with his sleeve, then carried it to his lips, and drank, and looked at the bottle again. It was wine—a strange thing to find unfinished in a public park in this city, he thought with indifference, and drank again, and again, deeper now, until, gradually, his eyes adjusted to the shadows, and his hand stopped bleeding, and he remembered that for the first time tonight she had called him Serezha, just Serezha, and found that everything was shifting into focus at last, becoming clear.

She wanted to hear Selinsky's music. He would make her a gift of it. He would wait in line, however long it took, and when he finally had the ticket, he would give it to her. He would give it to her, and this time, he would be worthy of her, he would expect nothing back, for she did not owe him any answers, did not owe him anything, he told himself sternly. But as the moon boat glimmered at the bottom of the bottle, rocking up and down in the sea breeze, smelling of all the wonderful things he had never smelled, the salt, the sand, a woman's damp hair, he could not help thinking of their hallway reflections embracing in a different world, a silvery mirror world where things were simple, where an embrace became a kiss, where a kiss deepened, natural as a bud opening, and a man's old-fashioned hat hanging on a nail transformed into a large shaggy bird and flew out the window, and a coat closet swung its doors wide, inviting them into its depths, and its depths were dark and soft, darker than the fur of a hundred fur coats, softer than the fluff of a hundred feather beds, and the softness, the darkness accepted them, two people who, in this simple mirror world, were not afraid to tell each other how they felt.

5

ANNA HAD BROUGHT her mother two full cups of tea, yet the old woman would not leave the room, and by half past nine Anna had grown restless. Liuba had advised her to wait until some minutes after ten ("You should be a bit late," she had said, "it's better to keep him in suspense"); but at nine-forty, unable to bear the insidious whisperings of the clock any longer, she stood up to go. Already at the threshold, she heard at last her mother's light steps in the corridor outside, the lavatory door swinging and closing, water gushing into existence. Relieved, she ran into the empty room, tore at the drawer. The box of dark green velvet was there still; as its lid flipped open with the softest of plops, the trapped diamond light, in escaping, scratched at her eye.

The water stopped with one last noisy eruption. Anna shut the box, pushed it back into its musty grave, and hurried out.

On the landing, she unclenched her hand, the sharpness of the clasps imprinted on her palm like a snakebite. The jabs through her earlobes were painful—she had not worn earrings in a long while—and she was still gasping, wondering whether she had drawn blood, when the elevator spilled her son straight into her. She saw in his face one instant of blankness, a perfect lack of recognition,

and felt a sudden thrill. Anya, is that really you? Sergei's amazed
voice said in the recesses of her mind. She stepped into the elevator
smiling.

Outside, the city closed around her, dark and cool; the last bits
of summer lay resting in buckets of roses sold at a night kiosk by
the tram stop. She teetered along the streets as quickly as she could,
though her ankles, unaccustomed to heels, kept betraying her. She
imagined her shoes tattooing a graceful rhythm across the velvet
underside of late August, carrying echoes to expectant girls who sat
dreaming about life by their cracked windows; imagined, too, the
shallow perspectives of the park already stretching deeper to admit
her. Drumming on the back of his bench, bored by the prospect of
a conversation with his son, he would see the silhouette of a lovely
(if somewhat full-hipped) woman at the end of the alley and, in-
trigued, watch her approach through the leafy shadows, until
slowly, slowly, his appreciation would deepen into astonishment
and an exclamation would escape his lips.

"My God," he would breathe out, "is that you? Oh Anya, you're
beautiful."

And then—then the faint scents of grass and flowers and the
golden bouquet of a wonderful wine, its grapes ripened by the
southern sunshine in some mythical land where storks flap their
weighty wings in nests made of cart wheels, and meadows sway in
the breeze, and donkeys tread up winding mountain tracks loaded
with jugs of the purest chilled water. A clinking of glasses coming
together, his whisper in her ear, the tender cooing of dreaming pigeons. I wanted to surprise you, Serezha, the ticket you've been
waiting for all this time—the ticket is for you, it's yours, my gift to
you, you can hear your music now, can't we be happy like we used
to be, or were we ever— Of course we were, we still are, thank you,
thank you, Anya, I love you.

The park's approaches yawned with blackness. She hurried along
a deserted alley, saw, at its end, the outline of a man sitting on a

bench. It was not yet ten; he had come early. Her heart licked at her breast with a few tentative, hopeful shudders.

The gravel crunched under her heels; the invisible pockets of intimate darkness on both sides of the path smelled damp and full, promising to disclose some soft, unbearably poignant secrets as soon as she stepped off it, dissolved in the night. The man rose, squinting at her across the late hour; the nearest streetlamp had gone out. Glad of the shadows, she took another wavering step, and another, and there was the bench, and the man lunged toward her, his fingers clamping down on her wrist.

"Well, well," he said. "Just as I was getting lonely."

His voice exhaled soured drink into her face. It was not Sergei. The darkness was packed tight around them, but accidental moonlight leaked through the trees, and his face skipped in and out like a voice nearing and fading. She glimpsed his youth, eighteen maybe, maybe twenty, and a vicious puckering under one eye, and an insolent, inebriated tilt to his mouth, and she wanted to scream, she screamed, she screamed louder, but no one was around, and already his face was shoving hers toward the bench, his hands groping at the seams of the dress that was not hers. She thought, as if from some other, safe, suspended place, It's a lovely dress, I can't damage it, she'd never lend me anything again. Then there were steps echoing along the boundary of the park, Sergei coming, she knew for one vast exhalation of relief, but the steps did not move closer, two sets of steps skirting the boundary of normal life, somewhere out there, and the brutality of it all swung at her like a fist, and she was screaming again, hoping someone would appear, someone would shake her awake. But the steps were retreating already, and the opened bottle of wine she had brought along tumbled out of her bag, rolled over her foot, and the darkness was blinding, thrusting toward her, and the man, the boy, was ripping, tugging, pulling at her edges, and she began to weep, "I'm a mother," she sobbed, "I have a son your age, about your age," and as the silk stockings Liuba had given her split open to let the night in, she collapsed onto the bench, crying, "Please, please, take these instead, they're worth a lot of money—"

His arms tensed along her sides. There welled a heartbeat of stillness.

"Take what?" the boy's voice said into her neck.

Her hands shook as she fought the clasps. The shadows leapt about, straining through the wetness in her eyelashes. "These," she said, her palm open. A sudden cold draft swept at her exposed knees. "These, see?"

His eyes glinted.

"They're real diamonds," she pleaded. "Please."

His hand swooped over hers, scooped hers out. As though from some vantage point above it all, she watched the moonlight fill hollow pockets of radiance between the boy's fingers. In the next moment, the fingers clenched, the radiance drowned, the weight lifted. For a breathless minute she was afraid to move. Then, incredulously, she sat up, pulled the dress down over her knees, stared into the darkness. The darkness contained nothing now but the receding friction of shoes on gravel, a splash of reflected light in the wine rocking at her feet, a rustle of feathers—a pigeon dreaming, she guessed dully.

After a while, she stood up. Her stockings were torn, and her right heel had snapped when he had first slammed her toward the bench, but she was otherwise unhurt. She loosened the straps of her shoes, peeled off and discarded the stockings, and, barefoot and barelegged, her shoes in her hands, the night freely lapping at her thighs, ran home, numbly sidestepping smashed shards of bottles glistening here and there on the sidewalks. The kiosk by the tram stop was now shuttered, the roses gone; in the half-hour since she had passed here, late August had finally forced the summer out, and autumn rang in the air, clear and sharp and bright like a piece of cold glass. A passerby gave her a shocked look, and a dark stretch of the city later, she saw, in the mirror of her hallway, what he had seen: a pale aging face with hair plastered damply over the forehead, drops of dried pain congealed in one earlobe, temples blue and shining with smeared paint, lips bleeding crimson onto the chin, eyes blank with desolation.

For a long while she gazed at herself, her hands pressed to her cheeks, then, turning away from the mirror, knocked on her mother's door, and walked in.

The light was on, the bed unruffled, the stuffy air tinted rosy brown, and darkly scented, and thick with silence, as it always was; time never moved here. She thought the room empty until the chair by the desk creaked around. Within its niche of shadow sat her mother, drowned in her ancient satin nightgown the color of moth wings, the color of fading memories, so small her feet barely touched the ground.

"I borrowed your earrings," Anna said in a still voice, "but I was mugged, and I lost them. I'm sorry, I know how much they—how much you—"

Her mother's eyes were dark and startled, a pair of beads. Anna's words felt powdery in her throat, insubstantial and meaningless, blown on her breath, scattering into silence. She stood without moving, then turned, and stumbled to her room, and fell onto the bed, as she was, in her beautiful borrowed dress, her legs splattered with mud and leaves, the soles of her feet black with the dirt of the entire summer in the city. Lying facedown on the bed, she felt her chest at last heaving open with sobs; but as she pressed herself into the tight, close darkness that smelled of warmth and sleep and loneliness, she sensed a presence hovering about her, a hand brushing her back, light as a bird's feather, a voice, which she scarcely recognized, her mother's voice, repeating into her hair, "Don't be upset, don't be upset, my dear, it's only things, and it serves me right, I haven't taught you properly—diamonds should never be worn in the summer—don't be upset, this isn't what matters . . ." And somehow, as the hand continued to stroke her back, she felt calmer, and heavier, and smaller, until there she was again, a little girl curled up under a comforter of down, cradled in the hollow of the night, weighty with dreams, absolved from the grown-up complexities of existence, free to close her eyes, and listen to her mother's fairy tales, and drift, weaving bright, magic fabrics from the patterns of words, from the texture of her mother's even voice, secure in the knowledge that things would be easier, better, happier, upon awakening.

And as Anna allowed herself to fall asleep, she could not tell whether the hand continuing to brush her back was real or part of the night, whether the voice was there or in a dream, whether, at some nebulous junction in time, she had truly opened her eyes to find Sergei kneeling by the bed, grief deepening the lines of his swiftly aging face, or whether his face too was sewn from the shimmering predawn essence, along with the grand boulevards she traveled in silver heels, and the rivers passing slowly under medieval gargoyles, and the dream voice reaching through her sleep, gently tiptoeing up some narrow steps, depositing her in a cool, stony, whispery place with stained-glass windows that stretched floor to ceiling. It was a church in the heart of a foreign city, that place, an ancient church whose windows shone with many solemn colors— the blue birth of the world, the purple procession of prophets who had guessed at some purpose in mankind's future, the proud red of martyrs who had taken that purpose on faith, the glowing green of the world's lucid, liquid end—all etched in beauty, all unearthly.

I came here often on summer afternoons, after rehearsals, the dream voice said, to let perspiration turn to chill on my shoulder blades, to hear my steps echo under the vaults, to pass, again and again, through the wedges of the luminous colors.

I came here that day in August, I remember.

I was not feeling well that day, had not felt well for some weeks, some months. I would often succumb to queasy spells in the midst of pirouettes, and my body had grown unfamiliar in varied ways, some subtle, some rather less so; yet still I continued to dance. I would not hear of visiting a physician.

We were preparing his third ballet. The second one had been a great success, the toast of the previous season; there had been evening gatherings in salons exquisite as gilded teacups, and leisurely carriage rides through falling leaves, and late-night bouquets of roses delivered to our dressing rooms, jeweled bracelets snaking artfully about the glossy thorns. He too had money now. One night in autumn, as I was leaving after a performance, he waited for me on the steps, a shadow against a wall. He refused to tell me where we were going, but I recognized the streets shivering in the gaslights through the curtains on the carriage windows. When we stopped, the hour was close to midnight, but the pavement outside the shop was bright with the squares of illumination. Inside, two elegant flutes of champagne stood bubbling, just for us, and two or three young men slid by noiselessly with velvet trays of glitter in their manicured gloves, and a plump little proprietor with a glass protuberance grotesquely attached to his eye swept his cuff-linked hand over the displays, gushing respectfully: "Mademoiselle, mademoiselle—"

I wanted nothing.

He chose for me: a pair of diamond earrings much like the ones we had admired in the window the year before, when we had owned nothing but the river below a balcony and a sunbeam across a friend's sheets and the exuberance of champagne drunk straight from the bottle after that first review had come out. I thanked him, and from then on I always wore them when I danced, but I often felt sad, as if, with the comforts of life advancing at us sleekly, softly, on velvet paws, something fierce and vital and young had been lost—though why that should be so, I did not know. We were still young then, even if we did not suspect it. Perhaps we believed that beauty or happiness had to be brief in order to live forever in one's memory, like a dancer's breathtaking leap, only one improbable second too long, lit, frozen, above the stage. Or it could have been simpler than that—perhaps he had merely fallen out of love. We had a new soloist that season; I saw him looking at her during rehearsals. I do not

mean to say that what we had shared was not strong, my dear, only
that geniuses are sometimes like that—they love their own fire, their
own brilliance reflected in those around them, and there will always
be someone whose mirror is brighter, or else newer and thus more
given to reflections, than your own. Or at least, that was what Vaslav
said, patting my hand as he consoled me, though he didn't put it
quite like that, of course. I hadn't yet learned to be silent, you see.

I cried all winter, and in the spring I met a man from the city of
my birth. He was old enough to be my father, his eyes were the light
blue color of melting snows, and he made everything around me
feel so solid and clear that I would sometimes forget the sadness I
carried within me, curled up in the dusty wings of my soul like a
once loved beast now eternally cold. Yet from time to time all
through that summer, the summer of my queasiness, I would grow
weary of my new, quiet contentment, and come to you in search of
something else—something secret, something that frightened me,
something that gave me joy. You stayed in hotels now, so we no
longer had to borrow friends' flats; the hotel rooms had scores of
scores scattered everywhere, and expensive linens that did not feel
cool against my skin, and, at times, silk things that did not belong to
me, crumpled in out-of-the-way corners.

Whatever it was I searched for that summer, I never found it.

I do not remember exactly when I began to guess, but on that
August day, after a particularly grueling practice, when I stood in the
ancient church I liked to visit and looked down at the floor and saw
my shoes filling with blood, I had known for a very long time. It
was a bright afternoon. I remember the fractured sun falling all purple and green and blue on the stones around me, and the hollow
drip-drip of blood on my sensible flat-heeled shoes, and a woman
screaming next to me, and on my chest, the trembling projection of
a vivid, sun-colored saint, and the knowledge, calm now, that I
would not dance again—not here, not for you.

They took me to the hospital. My child was saved, and the man

I had met in the spring got there fast, and, squeezing my hand so violently it hurt, kept repeating, "You should have told me, you should have told me—did you not know I would—did you think I wouldn't—"

We were married in that church in the early fall. It was hardly ever used for ceremonies of the sort, but I had fame and Andrei had means and a special permission was granted. A week later, we left for his city, the city of my birth, his family home. The night before our departure, our suitcases packed, I escaped my own farewell party, and hurried along the foggy streets to a familiar hotel. As I splashed through its grand golden letters quivering on the wet sidewalk under my feet, I was hoping, hoping against hope, that it was not too late—but of course it was, and you were still not back from your two months touring on the other side of the ocean, and the concierge, peering into my face, instantly shed his icy tone and, his snowy gloves fluttering, his stare darting, asked for an autograph, and, changing my mind, I crumpled the letter I had written.

I walked back slowly through my dark, autumnal, beloved city, the invisible river lapping beside me, the mansions along its banks asleep save for the garret windows that glowed softly, secretly, with someone else's happiness, and I thought, I will come back, I will come back soon, I will see you again; for, even though I understood it too late, I now knew it was possible, possible for the leaping dancer not to descend with the music every time. Back in my rooms, it was stuffy and merry, and Vaslav had become hysterical and Tamara's Cloud escaped and we chased it meowing and squealing with laughter all up and down the stairwell until I was all out of breath and my husband begged me to rest and corks smashed into ceilings and no one noticed the look in my eyes and everyone promised to write.

The things we remember longest are not necessarily the most permanent or even the most meaningful, but they are often the brightest, and maybe that is why in the end they matter most. Forty-four years is a long time, my dear. When I heard of the concert, I thought, I will wait for the winter, and put on my earrings, and go.

I will still go, of course.

I do worry that you will not recognize me without them.

Perhaps it's for the best, I do not know.

If only—if only I could forget my daughter's face as she walked barefoot into my room.

PART FOUR

FALL

1

SEPTEMBER WAS SOAKED THROUGH, and the damp, rustling days soon began to smell of mildew. Some people claimed to find it a relief after the hazy heat of the summer, boiling in the city's immense vat of concrete for weeks on end, but most complained. The man who had rented fold-out chairs for a handful of coins had not been seen since July, and the older women suffered; two or three even left the line for good, and one was taken away on a stretcher.

"Have you heard?" Emilia Khristianovna said one morning as Anna paused on the way to her place in line. It was raining again; when she lowered her voice to a whisper, Anna had to duck her head under the other woman's umbrella to discern her words amidst the wet rush of the street. "They're saying the man with the chairs was, you know, transferred. Someone saw him at dawn, getting into a car with tinted windows."

"But why?" Anna asked, shifting; her own umbrella was leaking under her collar.

"Running an unauthorized business, I'm sure." They were both silent for a moment, walled off by the rain from the rest of the glistening, shivering line. "Listen, Anna Andreyevna." As the physics teacher looked away, her umbrella nudged the top of Anna's head.

"I meant to tell you, my schedule has changed, it will be difficult for me to spot you in the mornings like before. And they're beginning to frown at our constant schedule-juggling, I'm worried that . . ."

Her voice trailed off. This close, Anna could see the pores in the woman's kindly, anxious round face, the mole on her cheek, the plump lips chewing the unfinished sentence. Discomfited, she took a step away, dove back under her umbrella, receiving as she did so another rivulet of cold water down her neck.

"That's all right," she said quietly. "I'll work something out, that's all right."

But when she crossed her name off the list the next afternoon, the organizer leafed through some notes, fiercely mauled his beard, and informed her that her early shift had not been covered and that they couldn't let everyone do this, it would throw the whole system into chaos.

"Life's catching up with people, I understand, I'm inconvenienced myself," he said defensively, "but these are the rules, you know how it is."

She nodded mutely.

The next day she called in sick at school, and again the day after that. On the third day Emilia Khristianovna, who had abandoned her wait earlier that week, came by to warn her. "I overheard the principal talking with her assistant, they were talking about you, they said—" When she leaned close to her ear, Anna could once again smell the peculiar mixture of damp wool and hot metal of classroom experiments.

"Thank you," Anna tried to say, but could barely hear her own words over the constant drip-drop of water from the black, gleaming branches of the trees above.

That evening, after Sasha had finished his supper and left to study, and her mother had drunk her cup of tea (as she had done every night since the incident in the park, though she still said little beyond "No sugar, please" and "Thank you" and "Good night"),

Anna remained in the kitchen. She sat by the window waiting, her hands listlessly crossed in her lap, the night breeze siphoning rain and gasoline from the outside world into the darkened mouse-hole of her home.

Sergei returned just past ten o'clock. He winced when he saw her.

"The leftovers are on the stove," she said.

"I'm not hungry."

"We need to talk," she said.

Lowering himself onto a chair, he stared grimly at the rows of radishes lining their plastic tablecloth. He knew what was coming, of course. She had never convincingly explained her presence in the park that night—she said she had needed fresh air—but he had no doubt that she had heard rumors about him and Sofia and had set out in borrowed finery to spy on them. He tried to summon a feeling of anger and, failing, attempted to gather himself for the inevitable, terrible question she would now ask—

"I can't cover mornings anymore," Anna said. "My school schedule is different this fall."

"What?" he said, glancing up with a start.

"My mother can't stand in line." She was looking at the floor, speaking in a flat, tired voice. "And Sasha's a university student now, I don't want to burden him more than he already is. We're going to lose our place."

He swallowed something like a sudden sob. "I—I can help," he said.

"You can?"

"Sure. I can ask the director to shift my hours back. I'll talk to him tomorrow."

In the momentary silence, he thought he could hear the rain gently flicking at the windowpane, the splashing of footfalls through the puddles on the street six floors below, the slow, effortful lifting of Anna's eyes in her pale, thinning face. Within her still irises, two tiny lightbulbs hung like deep, glowing scratches. "I wish I still could . . ." she began, and stopped, her voice wobbling with an excess of some emotion he could not identify. "That is, I had a gift for you, but I can't now—not after losing her earrings—"

"A gift," he repeated tonelessly. He did not want to feel any more gratitude, could not bear to feel any more gratitude. "What gift?"

She stood up, walked to the stove.

"It's nothing," she said with firmness, as though closing some door. "Just an idea for—for your birthday that didn't work out. If you're not going to eat, I'll put it away."

"No, wait," he said. "I'll have a bite after all. Go get some rest now, I'll clean up."

She left. He gazed after her for a long moment. Behind the wall, a neighbor's radio started to broadcast a program about motherhood; the announcer's familiar old voice talked of the somnolent delights of a child's first year, a baby girl with a gurgling laugh and surprising green eyes. He listened as he ate, trying to ignore the strange, piercing feeling of regret—and something else, something else entirely, that kept rising in his throat like a half-digested belch, burning his insides, filling him with an insidious, impossible knowledge, about his wife, and his wife's mother, and this radio program that, he had known all along, might not be a radio program at all—until the announcer drowned in static.

The next morning he knocked on Ivan Anatolievich's door. The director was pushing his belly back and forth across his vast office with an air of beleaguered importance, the telephone receiver embedded deeply in the red folds of his neck, the cord trailing behind him like a puppet string. "Tomorrow, tomorrow, can't you see I'm in the middle of something!" he bellowed, dismissing Sergei with an imperious wave.

Sergei barely prevented himself from slamming the door on his way out; and all through the day, a dull, heavy anger simmered inside him, so much so that later that evening, when shadows crept forth around the kiosk and a small crowd of Nightingales hoodlums gathered once again on the other side of the street, jeering and taunting, he shouted back at them: "Go home to your barns and haystacks where you belong!"

Someone from across the street threw a rock. It drew a violent arc through the twilight; the line watched it in an anxious hush. When a hurt gasp splashed a few backs ahead of Sergei, the Nightingales howled with laughter and scattered into the darkness.

"That," said Vladimir Semyonovich quietly, "was uncivilized. You shouldn't have provoked them. We aren't like them."

"Ah yes, turn the other cheek. That cross must be rubbing off on you," Sergei snapped, and looked away, ignoring the stricken expression on Sofia's face, and was silent for the rest of the shift. He felt furious still as he walked home—furious and helpless; and when some nondescript fellow of indeterminate age, whom he had glimpsed once or twice at the end of the line, fell into step with him and curiously asked what the spat was about and whether the mustachioed comrade back there had displayed religious leanings, Sergei brushed him off with an uncustomary rudeness.

At home, in the bedroom's dimness, Anna's face was expectant, her eyes drained of color above the soiled lace of her old peach-colored robe, his third-anniversary present. When he walked in and saw her standing in the middle of the room—not doing anything, just standing, her face turned toward the door, her arms by her sides, as if she had been standing like that the whole time he was gone, waiting for his return—he felt his fury seep out as abruptly as it had swelled inside him. "I—I haven't yet cleared up my situation," he mumbled.

She emitted a very faint "Oh," less than a sound, more like a shape of her lips imprinted in a barely audible, disappointed exhalation onto the air.

He took an impulsive step toward her, touched his hand to her cheek; then, taken aback by his unexpected gesture, shifted away, began to unbutton his shirt, humming tunelessly. He would not look at her, but he could sense her starting into skittish motion, flitting swiftly about the room, readjusting the blankets, drawing the curtains, pushing up the lampshade to broaden the cone of beige light that fell onto the bed; he heard his tuba ring out as she stumbled against it, heard her laugh a tiny, flustered laugh.

"Sorry. Would you like—" she began.

He glanced up, his chest constricted.

She was holding out a shapeless white lump on her palm.

"It's melted a bit, but it still smells wonderful," she whispered.

He felt unable to move, suspended by the expectation of what she might say next, of what he might say in reply; but she was silent now, watching him, her head tilted, her eyes damp and tender, deepened by shadow. Shaking off his stillness, he hastily took the deformed chocolate from her hand, put it in his mouth, swallowed without chewing, all the while smiling wretchedly, his teeth smeared with untasted sweetness.

"Well, good night, then," she said softly.

For a long time, his heart muttering, he lay awake in the muffled chill of their darkened bedroom. The clock ticked, measuring out the empty leakage of his existence, prodding the year toward a close he was no longer able to imagine. His thoughts rambled. He thought of meeting Sofia, of meeting Anna, of the parchment-colored lamp glowing on his parents' veranda through a moth-whipped procession of summers lined in deep velvet; thought, too, of a few weeks in his childhood that he had spent practicing a violin solo in preparation for a school competition. It was to be the event of the school year: it was rumored that the piece's famous composer himself would come to judge the performances. All his classmates hoped to win, of course—the ambitious ones, to add another medal to their collection of distinctions; the obedient ones, to please their parents; the more farsighted ones among them, to attract the composer's benevolent interest in their future careers. He did not care about any of those things. He saw the piece as a puzzle that he had to solve, a deceptively simple mechanism of a sad melody that, if unlocked, would spring open to reveal a hidden compartment full of magical meaning. He followed the prescribed notation in class, but in the evenings, ensconced in the autumnal sonorousness of the unfolding high-ceilinged rooms of his parents' winter mansion as if inside a giant reverberating bell, he secretly embellished the phrase until, continuing along invisible trajectories and modulations that seemed inevitable to him, he transformed it into something different—something his own.

He tore through the final week before the competition in a state of shaky, joyful anticipation, imagining first the astonishment, then the understanding, pleasure at last, dawning on the as yet unseen face. His excitement crested in leaps and jolts, a wild bright-eyed beast cavorting with glad abandon in his ten-year-old soul—but just days before the event, men ran down the city streets in muddy boots, and windows shattered and shuttered, and someone soft-voiced spoke with a slight burr on the radio, assuring the populace of the good of something that he himself, enveloped in the safe warmth of his childhood, did not understand—and he never got to stand onstage before the celebrated composer, a violin trembling beneath his chin.

Half asleep, he wondered whether that might not have been his happiest day ever, the last, perfect day swelling with the immensity of his secret intent, secret creation—the day before everything changed—the day before he realized, for the first time, yet with absolute finality, just how small his private immensity really was when measured against that other vast, dark, impersonal immensity, call it God, or history, or simply life.

Anna had already left when he awoke the next morning. His
head ached after a bumpy night filled with potholed dreams, though
for just one instant, before his headache had set in, he seemed to
sense a piercing vibration in the air, a lingering coda of a winding,
heartrending melody that swiftly faded out of his reach before he
could fully hear it in his daytime mind, its silver shadow diving
deeper into the murk of the night's oblivion. In the kitchen he discovered a cup of lukewarm tea, a slice of ossified toast, and a folded
note addressed to him in Anna's most elaborate script. He shoved
the toast into the trash can, and the note, unread, into his jacket
pocket, and left for work.

The rain had ended at last; the fall sky stretched pale and remote
over the city. In the sharp morning clarity, the theater was dingy as
a basement, its windows squares of imitation daylight hung in a
laundry line of unwashed sheets on the gloomy red walls. The unnatural dusk of the orchestra pit pressed on Sergei's eyelids; all
through the performance, he felt as if he was struggling, and failing, to open his already opened eyes. The brandishing of the banners, the barking of the brasses, finally, mercifully, over, he headed
up the stairs to the director's office. He was met halfway by Ivan
Anatolievich himself, just descending. Forced to halt two steps
below the man's bulging peacock-colored vest, Sergei had to tilt his
head far back, to address him from the undignified, humiliating
position of a beseecher.

"Ivan Anatolievich, I would like a favor," he said, a bit curtly,
fighting to control his irritation. "The matinee hours are no longer
convenient for me, you see, so I thought—"

As he talked, he could feel his neck growing stiff. The director
listened, stroking the iridescent swell of his satin stomach, visibly
amazed. "I don't think you quite comprehend your situation," he
said at last, squinting down at Sergei; seen from below, his lips

crawled between his jowls like two fat, glistening caterpillars. "It's
my duty as the head of this establishment to make sure each and every
citizen in my care will reach his fullest potential, and therefore—"
Sergei tried to sidestep him so they were level, but the director's belly
was in the way. His anger was returning, its blind, wild flames licking at his insides, spreading, spreading . . . The officious voice continued to drone. "—and since your political maturity at this juncture
is a matter of grave concern, I would not deem it possible, in view of
the event of which you are well aware—the black mark on your
record, so to speak—"

"How do you live with yourself, you sanctimonious pig!" Sergei
suddenly roared. "I urinated alongside a foreign national!"

They stared at each other.

"You," the director boomed, "are fired."

In the hallways, musicians scattered; out of the corner of his eye
Sergei saw Sviatoslav vanishing with great alacrity around the corner.
He looked directly into the fat man's shaking, reddened face, not
moving for the duration of one full, liberated inhalation.

Then he nodded and, in silence, turned and walked down the
stairs.

Outside, the day had deepened in color, was blue and cool and
crisp, threaded with gossamer flashes of cobwebs flying by in the
wind; the leafy chill in the air crinkled like the cellophane wrapper
of a candy mauled by an impatient child. People waited at tram
stops, rustling their newspapers with resignation; he glimpsed the
front-page headlines, damp with smudged red print, proclaiming
from benches and sidewalks: "No Place for Indecisiveness in Our
Race to the Finish Line!" The city was already starting to accumulate air in its lungs in preparation for the trumpet blast of yet another anniversary of the Change. He strolled past, his hands in his
pockets—a man in no hurry to be anywhere, a man who had fallen
wholly outside the bustle and fuss of history, a man with a tremendous weight, the weight of a century, lifted from him. As his hands

nested deeper in his pockets, he felt something flimsy catch between his fingers. He withdrew the note, paused to unfold it.

"Happy forty-eighth, Serezha!!" Anna had written. "May it be your best year yet."

For a minute he gazed at the two exclamation points, then opened his fingers; the note became a leaf in a whirl of leaves and spiraled away.

They met in the street with the abandoned church at one end and the kiosk at the other.

"All taken care of," he said brightly. "I can do the morning shifts now."

"Oh, good," she said, but her voice was restrained, as if some other intonation beat against it. "I'll be switching to evenings, I guess. When do you start your new schedule?"

Only now did he understand the full implications of their revised arrangement. He sucked in his breath, thought briefly, agonizingly, of saying, Listen, I'm happy to do mornings, but let me keep evenings as well, I don't mind, I don't actually have—that is, I've been temporarily—I mean, sooner or later, I'm sure, it will be—

He looked at the ground, his shoes, hers—and in the next instant remembered the broken silver heel he had found just inside the door upon his return home that night—that night . . .

"Monday," he said blankly. "I can start mornings on Monday."

2

"Ever think about the nature of time?"

(Time? The flowing river one can never enter unchanged. The snake swallowing its tail. A dainty watch on the wrist of a beautiful woman who, in walking through the city, fends off eternal queries called out from all sides: "What time is it, please, and if you have a minute to spare, would you like to go for a walk?" Time as a monster devouring its children, time as the breath of God, time as the chalk-crumbling formula of a physicist sanctified by a silver nimbus of hair. And, for most of us, our own small stretch, bleak and fast-rolling along its darkening bends, the happiest moments most likely spent hoping for something wondrous, something luminous—a brush, perhaps, with a tiny miracle of immortality, a sunbeam forever preserved in an amber tear, Faust's doomed plea: "Instant, freeze, you are perfect!" Oh, I could tell you plenty about time, but I will stay silent, I will merely listen.)

"Time?"

"Yes, time. Here's a question for you: Does waiting make time move faster, or slower?"

"Slower, of course. Everyone knows that time flies when you're happy, but when you're waiting, each moment crawls by."

(Each moment, they say. Ah, but moments are akin to snowflakes, no two alike. Some extend back like powerful microscopes, zeroing their light on some spot in the past, until the recollection, bright, enlarged, is spread for your contemplation as if under glass. Others remind you of that curiously unpleasant mathematical paradox, that hapless runner trying to reach point B from point A in eternal increments of half the remaining distance, doomed never to arrive at his destination, the units of time sliding one out of another like endless smaller compartments hidden in larger ones, again and again and again, suspending time in an agony of futile anticipation. Then, of course, there are others, light and enjoyable, fleet and indistinct like dreams, like delightful childhood whooshes down a slide in some forgotten park, like so many of their moments spent waiting, spent daydreaming, here—if they but knew it. Here, then, is a better question for you: If you're happy when you're waiting, what happens to time then?)

"Me, I just can't help wondering—we've given up almost a year of our lives for one or two hours of enjoyment. Is it worth it?"

"But what would you be doing with your year if you weren't here? Let's face it, most likely you'd just be wasting it. In fact, this year of waiting hasn't been all that different from any other year of your life, has it—a whole lot of doing nothing—except now you can look forward to an hour of happiness at the end."

(Oh, but your year *has* been different—you've felt awake, you've felt alive, you've merged your icy breath with snow, you've walked midnight streets dusted with petals, you've read poems etched by decaying leaves into the sidewalks, you've stepped inside other homes, other lives, you've been touched by a brighter world. Of course, I will not say it, I will keep silent, I will merely smile at you to give you hope.)

"An hour of happiness, eh? But what if the concert doesn't live up to its promise, what then? Won't we feel stupid!"

"Well, I don't think it matters how good it will be. After a year of waiting it will *seem* wonderful, anyway. Haven't you ever noticed, the longer you wait for something, the better it is?"

(There was a poem I read in an old book once, a beautiful poem about desire.

When you long for something intensely,
when you long for a long time,
the purity of your wait transforms
your very nature from within,
and . . . and . . .

But it was decades ago, I forget now, there is just that snippet at the end, how did it go . . . ?

And when the promise is near,
the promise of what you wanted,
your essence is not the same,
you are not the same any longer,
and . . . and . . .

Ah no, it's all gone, quite gone now.)

"I disagree. The longer you wait, the higher your expectations. I suspect that's why people are beginning to leave in droves. Afraid to be disappointed, that's what I think."

"Leaving in droves? Who's leaving in droves?"

"Why, lots of people! Look around you. Where is that old woman with the carved cane? Or that fellow with the birthmark on his forehead? Or that other guy—you know the one—"

"Wait, you don't suppose—you don't think they might have been—well, you know—"

"What are you muttering there, I can't hear you!"

"Nothing, nothing, I'm just . . . It's nothing."

"Well, if it's nothing, you should keep your mouth shut, people are nervous enough as it is."

Silence fell among them, but the knot would not loosen in Sergei's insides; and when, sometime later, he turned to Sofia to say good-bye, to explain that he would no longer be here in the evenings, he found her absent.

"But—where is she?" he exclaimed involuntarily.

Vladimir Semyonovich had not appeared for two days. An unfamiliar schoolgirl whose face shone like a polished door handle stared at him with curiosity. "If you mean the mousy woman who always looks like she has a toothache, she had to leave early today. I'm holding her place till the next shift arrives. Does she owe you money or something?"

He shook his head, looking away already, his heart gone, replaced by a cold, hard pebble.

The morning light was somber, clouds sagging almost to the ground with their dank bellies. The city seemed flat, a black-and-white snapshot of itself, and the line, in which he took his place morosely, appeared to have shrunk as well, to have lost the wide, light-filled spaces where he had dwelled between the hours of waiting all through the spring and summer. The people around him had faces closed with worry—a girl who stared vacantly at the sky, a screeching basket by her feet; a brightly painted middle-aged woman with eyes like silver coins, whom he had seen on a few occasions talking to Pavel and who turned away when he attempted to greet her; a pale little boy behind him, who looked at him levelly and asked, "And who are you?"

"I'm Sergei Vasilievich," Sergei said, "and what's your name?"— but as the boy continued to regard him with a quiet, reproachful, painfully familiar gaze, his heart was back without warning, and sliding somewhere sideways, and for one moment he thought—he thought . . . But of course it couldn't be, it wasn't, he hastened to tell himself as he dove into his bag, fumbling for his book, not daring to look at the boy another time.

"There was a lady here before you," the boy said, "she was kind and beautiful, she made cakes and told me many happy stories of her childhood—"

"Pleased to meet you, young man," Sergei said firmly, already opening the weighty compilation of musical biographies.

When the endless shift was over at last, he was startled to discover a block of uncut time on his hands. He went home to pick up his tuba, as he would in the normal course of things, then trudged through the city. The park filled him with an obscure sense of shame, but there was no better place in the neighborhood for wasting hours undisturbed. He found a secluded bench and sat there until nightfall, watching the city turn into a negative of its daytime self—windows bright, skies black, houses blurry—watching time drop grain by grain from the greedy beaks of the frenzied pigeons fighting for crumbs on the paths, while his tuba rusted at his feet. Shortly before ten, he meandered along the streets she might pass on her way home. He did not see her; nor did he see her the next day, or the day after that.

When the week had expired, he wrote her a note. He hesitated over the phrasing; though he had little knowledge of such matters, dimly he felt that certain sentiments, when written down, lost their souls—yes, certain sentiments, like music, existed only as sounds—sighs, laughter, whispers, gasps—or not at all. He did use an intimate form of address, remembering that unbidden "Serezha" she had bestowed upon him the night of the billowing curtains, the night in her room; but his wording was restrained, and out of some vague sense of discretion he avoided addressing or signing the note.

Unable to find any means of passing it in person, he finally left it with the girl of the door-handle face, who had switched to morning shifts as well; the line had been in a state of restless flux for some time now. "Well, all right," she said doubtfully, "I'll ask my father to hand it over. The woman with the toothache, right?"

"The woman with lovely eyes," Sergei said sternly. "Sofia Mikhailovna."

The girl made a lukewarm effort to suppress a titter. "I'll tell him," she said, sticking the envelope negligently into her bag alongside a bunch of withered leeks.

He waited a day, then three, then a full week, but there was no word; he wanted to ask, but the girl had now been replaced by a large, matronly woman trapped behind the bars of a faded striped dress, peering at Sergei with hostile glances. He felt time drifting away from him; he stopped counting the days that passed, gray, chilled, damp, swiftly shrinking toward winter. One darkening afternoon, as he walked away from the line, he was approached by a man wearing a homburg and carrying a briefcase; the man's face, hidden in the shadow of the hat, was indistinct.

"Do I have the pleasure of addressing Sergei Vasilievich?" the stranger inquired, amiably touching the hat's brim. "Well, and in that case, are you not aware of the vagrancy laws, which state most clearly that all able-bodied citizens must be gainfully employed or be confronted by the consequences of their parasitism?"

The light was fading fast in the deserted street, and the man's face too appeared to gray rapidly, his features becoming still harder to pin down; the black automobile that loitered at the next corner seemed merely a dark shape cut out of the nearing night and pasted onto the evening. Sergei felt as if he were being interrogated by a ghost—or else as if he were a ghost himself, insubstantial, invisible save to other ghosts, passing through the city, through life, through time as through dust, without leaving a trace. And as he stood staring into the obscure face of his interrogator, he remembered the pale, infinite sky he had seen the previous winter, in the early days of the line, and the clear crystal notes he had imagined ringing in its vastness, floating above the city, soaring higher and higher in imperceptible phrases of perfectly sustained beauty—and his heart sickened.

"I'm ill," he stammered out.

"Ill?" his ghostly tormentor repeated, shaking his head in sympathy. "You don't say. And where, then, is your certificate from a doctor?"

"At home," Sergei replied, almost inaudibly.

"You will be so good as to present it tomorrow at the district bureau," the man said gleefully. He touched his fingers to his ghostly hat again and strolled away toward his silhouette car.

Sergei spent the remaining hours of the day rushing along the corridors of a neighborhood clinic, pleading with cleaning women who irritably banged their filthy mops against his shoes, until at last, after dusting a few hallways with his jacket and having two or three doors slammed in his face, he found himself sitting across a scuffed desk from a fat, red-jowled man in a once white coat, who looked so much like the theater director that for a second, upon entering his office, Sergei had a vertiginous sensation of spaces and days slipping, colliding, overlapping, throwing him off his already precarious balance. The director's twin gazed musingly into the middle distance until Sergei thought to empty the sad contents of his wallet onto the desk's surface. His expression bored, the man counted the bills with an expert fluidity, wrote a few words on a scrap of paper, negligently stamped it with a round red stamp and a square blue stamp, and, still without looking at Sergei, reached for the telephone.

Sergei's ghost, confounded and invisible as ever, edged out of the office.

The next morning, as he stood in line, feeling his empty pockets, wondering how he would pay if the tickets happened to go on sale just then, he glimpsed his son striding across the street. "Hey there," he called out. "Lectures ended early?"

The boy approached, his face flickering with an odd expression, almost a cringe.

"Such a nuisance," Sergei muttered, busy removing a leaf from the crook of his sleeve, "I seem to have forgotten my wallet at home. Could you stop by the school if you're free, and ask your mother? I only need enough for the ticket—in case, well, you know—"

"Yeah, sure," Alexander said, moving off.

He was anxious to escape before his father asked further questions.

They would find out soon enough, he supposed—but not yet, not just yet.

The pavements were slippery with shallow burials of sodden leaves; the air hung thick with the smells of mushroom pies, rain, and decay. Alexander had an odd, displaced feeling as he walked through the streets. For a decade the road to school, with its shuffled pack of familiar landscapes—the row of kiosks by the tram stop, the short-cut through the little playground, the alley with ugly brown buildings wedged into the recesses of dark mornings, the movie theater raising its Neanderthal's brow over the sidewalk—had been the frame on which he had stretched his life, like predetermined lines connecting dots in an uninspired children's game; yet now the streets were beginning to assume a kind of vagueness, the smudged unreality of an uncertain memory, and soon even that tenuous quality would dissipate, for soon, very soon now, this threadbare, graying city would be no more, this life would be no more, and he—he would be walking other streets in other cities, cities not at all like this one, cities brightly colored and tangible, bestowing upon him the long-awaited gift of their immense, stage-lit presence.

His practical preparations were nearly finished. He had gathered his few belongings and stored them under his bed, ready to be thrown into a bag at a moment's notice; his shoes were too tight, but Stepan

had promised to find him a suitable pair of sneakers. He had already
written the letter (though he kept adding pages to it now and then);
he planned to hand it over after the concert, when Viktor Pyetrovich
took him backstage. "Here's my address," he would say in a measured, mature voice, as soon as the two cousins disengaged from their
tearful embrace—or no, as soon as they stopped grasping each other's
hands, that was better, more fitting. "Please read this, Igor Fyodorovich." Then he would run, no, walk, home, the snow crunching
under his new shoes for the first and last time, and sit waiting in the
dark, and hours would pass and the snow would fall and fall, and just
as I begin to despair, there is a knock on my door, and he is standing
in the shadows of the landing. I was so moved by your letter, young
man, he says, or no, "young man" sounds condescending, he would
just call me by name, Alexander, he will say, I see how alike we are,
our two roaming, thirsty, adventurous spirits, you're like the son I
never had, I went to the embassy this evening and obtained permission for you to come with me, when can you leave?

And I will say: I am ready.

He had not been back here since graduation—only a few
months, but in that stretch of time his world had careened so far off
its axis that it shocked him to find everything exactly as it had been:
the reek of sweat and cafeteria gruel in the corridors, the magnified
echoing of delinquent steps during the hush of classes, the forced
enthusiasm of contests and day trips announced along the walls, the
cavernous, unclean hopelessness of it all. He glanced at his wrist,
then remembered and swore—he had sold his watch, along with
some other trifles, to purchase a flashlight and a compass for his
travels—then remembered again and, marveling at having already
forgotten something that had seemed seared into his very bones by
thousands of fearful repetitions, lifted his head to the enormous
clock presiding over the entrance.

A class had started some fifteen minutes earlier.

He passed the dozing caretaker, took the stairs to the second

floor, and halted, his hand raised, before the familiar classroom. A
pupil's timorous recitation had just fallen silent, interrupted by a
woman's admonishing, officious voice. The voice was not his
mother's.

He lowered his hand, considered the door, doubting his memory
again, then, frowning, wandered over to the teachers' lounge. It was
deserted. The monthly schedule was posted on the wall. He studied
it, but could not make out anything; whole portions of the grid
were crossed out, "Substitute" slashing in a nasty red diagonal over
some of the classes, names overwritten with names—

"Sasha, you're here!" a high-pitched, fluttering voice exclaimed
behind his back. "Oh, but how lucky, I have a free hour."

He glanced over his shoulder, and was instantly dismayed. "I
don't have time to listen to music right now," he said brusquely.
"I'm looking for my mother."

She did not seem to notice his rudeness.

"Oh, but I didn't know your mother was here today," she said.

"Where else would she be," he snapped.

He expected a rebuke, but she only stared, her face unsettled,
unsettling, quivering like a plate of dough about to rise. "Sasha, will
you please come with me," she said then, turning before he could
refuse.

Feeling coerced and resentful, he followed her thick trotting back
down the stairs, along hallways, around corners. She said nothing
as they walked, and he too was silent, reluctant to ask a question, as
if he had something to fear. Once inside the classroom, she closed
the door behind them with care. "Please sit down," she said.

He remained standing, his head bent, stubbornly studying the
fraying laces of his aged shoes.

"I must warn you about something, Sasha." Not looking up, he
could hear her move to her desk with a nervous rapidity, jerk open
a drawer, tug at something inside; there rose a rustle of crumpling,

resisting paper. "Your mother doesn't work here anymore. Now, I'm certain that she had her reasons to . . . not to . . . that is . . ."

She sounded so ill at ease that a feeling of pity seeped through his numbness. He lifted his eyes. "Zoya Vladimirovna, it's all right," he said, not knowing what he meant, knowing, in fact, that nothing was all right, that things were tilting and slipping and falling all around him.

"Oh no, how clumsy of me," she mumbled as she dove to collect the cookies that had spilled out of the liberated paper bag and rolled crumbling under her chair. "I thought you might like them, they have jam inside . . . Still, if I just dust them off a bit, they'll be quite . . . No? . . . Well, I do hope I'm not interfering, but you have so much to lose now, a student at our finest university, your mother was so proud, so proud. A few were surprised, to be honest, but I always knew, you always had so much potential . . ."

"I don't understand," he said.

She stopped fussing, turned to face him. "The concert, Sasha," she said quietly. "There seems to be some sort of . . . It's as if everyone connected with that line is being . . . That is, there was a regional inspector at the school and your mother had been missing for a week, sick, she said, but when he asked for a medical certificate, she didn't have one. Then also the physics teacher, some pupils had complained about her past absences, the principal told us, but what kind of pupils complain about canceled lessons? . . . Do you understand what I'm saying? The chemistry assistant was let go as well, and some others, not just at our school either—"

The music room was flooded with cold white light, flattened lamps humming and muttering in the pockmarked ceiling. The few instruments arranged along the walls looked long dead, their dusty limbs stiff with graceless afterlife—instruments that had sinned perhaps, whether by playing mediocre music or by submitting to unclean fingers or lips, and were now being punished in the purgatory of a classroom. It occurred to him that if he were to run his hand up and down the piano keys, there would be nothing but a horrid wooden clacking.

"I don't know what this has to do with me," he said, his words viscous and slow, coming out with effort, as though he had to peel each one off the roof of his mouth.

"I feel it's my duty to warn you, Sasha . . . Are you sure you wouldn't like one, they're only a little stale . . ." She had finished gathering the escaped cookies off the floor and was dropping them into the bag now; noticing a hair hanging off one, she blew on it, studied the cookie pensively, then placed it whole in her mouth.

"The concert," she said indistinctly, "cannot take place, in any case."

He caught a glimpse of her pale thick tongue, her moist gums working, and shuddered.

"Look, Sasha—" She paused to swallow, stepped closer to him. Her whisper smelled of shortbread. "I have a friend who has a friend who knows someone who sometimes travels Over There on State business. As a favor, the man occasionally brings back magazines and books about music. Between my friend and me, we can decipher four languages."

An unpleasant urgency began to spread through him. He wanted to leave. "Congratulations," he said; he sounded nasty, though he had not meant to. "I'll be going now."

"Wait, please wait." Her tone had deepened into gravity, which somehow bothered him more than her chirping. "Some time ago I read an article about Selinsky's last symphony, his ninth. The symphony was left unfinished, but what there is must be amazing. He was at his desk, you see, just where he'd spent most of his life, working on it, when he died."

There was a silence then, and more silence, and silence still, even the lamps on the ceiling had ceased their low humming, until it seemed to him that the silence grew larger than the glaring white room crammed with dead sounds, muffling it, muffling them, in its fog—and he needed to say something, anything, to break free.

"It was in a foreign language, right?" His voice was harsh. "You misunderstood."

"I used a dictionary. Igor Selinsky isn't coming, Sasha. He died seven years ago. I like your mother very much, and I have every respect for your father, but this—this is dangerous. Please abandon the line."

He looked at the aging woman standing before him in her bunched-up dress, crumbs in the corners of her mouth, her watery eyes enormous behind her glasses. He would have liked to throw some insult at her, to call her a coward, a liar, a joke, but he was too angry to speak. He turned to go, and a host of his reflections, a look of condemnation frozen in their eyes, ran in elongated rivulets down the dim sides of the brass instruments at his feet. She was fluttering after him now, warbling something about the Selinsky record, how she had been trying, she had not forgotten, in fact, a friend of hers might have something after all, not just yet but soon enough, she had even attempted to reach their apartment a few times, but her mother must have accidentally left a wrong telephone number in the school files, it was answered by an old woman who told her no Anna Andreyevna lived there—

Not listening, he yanked the door open. As if on cue, the bell exploded with shrillness in the corridor. "Wait, please," she gasped, folding a piece of paper with nervous hands, "give this to your father, just a few words, I've written down my number so he can call about the record—"

He tossed the note into his bag's yawn without looking.

"Please remember what I told you, Sasha. I wish you well!" She had to shout now, as the hallways trembled with the thumping and roaring of the approaching stampede.

He met her fearful, pleading eyes. "There is a cookie all the way under the piano," he said through his teeth. "You'll have to crawl."

She began to say something in response, but a wave of children had already swept her back into her classroom.

For a long time Alexander mindlessly walked the streets. When his soles felt numb and his toes ached from the confinement of the shoes he had outgrown, he headed to the park, preceded by the noiseless glide of dusk, followed by the orbs of dim lights popping up one after another in hazy rows in the skies above. In the park, leaves were falling darkly along the damp paths; his solitary steps rustled and crackled. There was someone sitting hunched over on his bench; through the thinning trees, he saw a dejected slump of shoulders in a gray jacket.

At the sound of his approach, the man looked up listlessly.

"Oh, it's you," he said. "You never came by with the money."

"Maybe I spent it," Alexander said.

"Did you?" His father's voice was devoid of expression. "No tickets today anyway."

"Mother wasn't at school, if you really want to know." He hesitated. "Had a day off or something. Shouldn't you be at the theater?"

"I too have a day off," his father said, his gaze dipping back to the ground.

He looked unwell, Alexander noticed, unkempt and somehow lost, graying at the edges of his unshaven face, his hands hanging limply between his knees.

"You all right?" he asked after a moment filled with an odd, tormented uncertainty.

"I'm fine, I'm fine. Hey, want to sit and talk? You have a while before your shift."

Surprised at the small leap of gladness in his chest, Alexander sat down.

"I feel like we haven't spoken in months," his father went on.

"You can tell me all about your lectures, and I actually—that is, there is something I—"

Alexander had risen abruptly. "I've just remembered, I have this thing, I really must . . . Oh yeah, I have a note for you, where was it, it should be somewhere in here—"

His hands were blind with anxiety as he scooped along the bottom of the bag, closed his fingers at last on a piece of paper, threw it into his father's lap, and strode away.

"Thank you, Sasha," his father called out after him. He sounded peculiar, as if something harsh had squeezed his throat, but Alexander was too shaken to wonder about it.

That was close, I really must tell them, he thought, yes, I will sometime soon.

He crossed the street, briefly debating whether to stop by the line and confront his mother, then, deciding against it, hurried in the opposite direction. The building's elevator had finally given up its ghost at the end of the summer; he assailed the staircase in leaps and bounds, mentally sorting through the stack of old books awaiting him on Viktor Pyetrovich's desk, choosing the next few to borrow. A little boy he had seen in the line opened the door and wandered off without a word. In the dim, sad kitchen, where there clearly had been no cooking that day, Alexander brewed two cups of potent tea with exotic tea leaves he had procured on the black market some weeks before; by now he had necessarily grown adept at small domestic gestures, for Viktor Pyetrovich struggled with chores, awkwardly clutching his cane under his arm to free his hands, as often as not dropping it on the floor with a bonelike clatter and then striving painfully to pick it up, until Alexander rushed in from another room to relieve him. When the tea ceased its steaming, the two of them sat side by side on the checkered blanket spread over the old man's bed in a close amber circle of light, drinking out of the silver glass holders, which was part of their ritual; and as the window before them slowly grew deep and blue, welling with the soft fall evening, Viktor Pyetrovich told him a marvelous story about Selinsky's being accidentally locked up for the night in an ancient tomb, where bats' wings slashed through the darkness like whispers and rare starlight drizzled down mysterious shafts in the massive walls, bringing hot, gamy wafts of deserts and camels and strange, nameless fruits whose mush tasted of girls' kisses—and where Selinsky took a calm nap in the cold sarcophagus of some dusty pharaoh, and later, waking up to the same unending darkness, for hours sat testing the patterns of hollows and monoliths with the echoes of his singing, which some months hence became, of course, his celebrated *Chamber of Echoes*.

Every so often, glancing at the old man's painstakingly shaven cheeks, at the excitable sparkle of his round glasses, Alexander would remember the horrible music teacher and her lies, and his chest would yawn with an immediate, frightening emptiness. He forced the feeling away. Shortly before ten o'clock, he helped Viktor Pyetrovich to his feet, and they walked to the line together, Alexander's hand discreetly hovering just below the old man's elbow. A few blocks away, someone was running along the opposite sidewalk, his unbuttoned jacket the color of night. Alexander paused for an instant, peering at the receding back that streaked in and out of shadow, wondering whether he had only imagined the man to be his father, wondering whether to call out. Then the instant passed; moving on, they arrived at the kiosk—and stepped into chaos.

People were dashing everywhere, hovering in agitated groups, shouting to one another: "Did you come out all right?"—"I'm fine, and you?" Alexander's heart bolted. The tickets—the tickets must have finally gone on sale, it's my mother's shift, that means she's got it, he thought with a rush of misgiving and, at the same time, inexplicable relief. His hold on Viktor Pyetrovich's elbow tightening, he pushed through the throng, to where he could already see Nikolai towering over the crowd. He shoved his way closer. Nikolai was cursing in a frothy rage, spitting out, along with mouthfuls of saliva and blood, "Damn bastards, drunken thugs, they think we're all spineless professors and fairies here, that they can just waltz in and do whatever the—"

Not the tickets.

"What happened?" Alexander screamed over the noise.

Voices tossed about.

"The Nightingales. They came and insulted us and things got out of hand and—"

"And there was a scuffle, they threw stones, some people were hit—"

"A woman's badly hurt. They ran when they saw the ambulance—"

"A middle-aged woman with light hair?" Alexander said quickly.

"A thin woman in her thirties?" asked Viktor Pyetrovich, and touched the coat over his heart.

"No," Nikolai said, and spat again, revealing a freshly chipped tooth. "It's Vera, the girl who had the baby this summer. Bastards, I'll get them for this, who do they think they are—"

Gradually the turbulence died down, the shouting subsided. The bearded organizer walked along the line with his nightly list. Someone started a game of solitaire on the curb, and, in the brittle fall air, the slapping of cards against concrete mixed with the clapping of pigeons' wings in their abbreviated flights from windowsill to windowsill and the sharp shots of windowpanes slammed shut against the chill. After his outburst, Nikolai was unusually quiet. Their shift was halfway over when he spoke for the first time.

"How about a little stroll? To stretch our legs. Our friends will cover for us."

His voice was casual, but there was something unfamiliar, something heavy, in his eyes.

"All right," Alexander said after a moment's hesitation.

Nikolai moved through the night with a purposeful air; Alexander walked a step or two behind, hurrying to keep up. "Where are we going?" he asked a few blocks later—though he had guessed by then, of course.

Nikolai stopped, turned to face him, gripped his shoulders.

"I have a sixteen-year-old daughter," he said fiercely, "only a few years younger than that girl. This kind of thing—we can't allow it, it's a matter of honor, do you understand?"

He was off again, almost running now, before Alexander could reply.

When they arrived, the street was empty, the Nightingales' kiosk locked, its TICKETS sign glistening dark and wet, as if newly painted, under a streetlamp; the announcement in the window stated that the Little Fir Trees would play on December 27 and the tickets would go on sale a week in advance.

"Well," Nikolai said, lighting a cigarette, "what do you say to camping out here for a bit, in case anyone turns up? I happen to have some fuel with me, it will feel like the good old days."

"Sure," Alexander said, without much enthusiasm; but a while later, after the darkness had grown so obscure that he had to feel for the bottle's neck with his increasingly tentative fingers, he found himself settling into the night, leaning back into it as on one of those couches he remembered from his time in the sleeper car, and the night soon began to move off, rocking gently, just like a train departing for some remote destination from the station he had not visited in many months, and the full October moon bounced from roof to roof like one of the train's wheels. And after a stretch of distance, or perhaps a length of time, he saw that there was not one but two beautiful, hazily radiant wheels speeding off into unknown celestial regions, and marveled at them, openmouthed, glad that life held so many surprises for him still—and then, in a rush, remembered everything once again. The nauseating suspicion gnawed anew through his insides, slowing the night down, merging the two brilliant wheels into one small, flat moon, making the train within him come to a halt at last with a grinding sigh; and, stumbling over his words, he found himself telling Nikolai about the music teacher, and the concert that would not take place, and Selinsky's death at some desk in some place with a foreign name, some random point on the globe, seven years ago.

"That," Nikolai said thickly, "is nonsense. Three hundred people can't be wrong. Your teacher is a fool."

"You really think so?" Alexander cried—and instantly felt that something within him, something vast and bright, was giving way, being released. He pressed his face into Nikolai's shoulder, and the man's thick jacket smelled of smoke and, unexpectedly, good home cooking, and Alexander wept, and couldn't stop weeping, like the child he had been once—weeping for this life in which nothing ever happened, weeping for his mother, and his father, and Viktor Pyetrovich who had wasted so much time waiting for something to happen, waiting in vain, for nothing ever happened in anyone's life; and then, somehow, he knew, without looking up, that Nikolai was weeping too, heaving with huge, childish sobs, his voice wobbling between gulps somewhere above him: "Listen, Sashka, I never—I never meant to sell the ticket, it's for my daughter, my daughter's sick, very sick, so I thought maybe, if she could only hear someone famous, someone great, she would get up, she would go, perhaps she would even feel better, they say music can cure people . . . But the kiosk seller, that bitch, we made her a good offer, but she wouldn't listen, so now we all wait, my wife, my wife's brother, he is helping too, he's a good fellow even if he's a fairy, has a beautiful voice . . . But those bastards, nothing is sacred to those people, they'd trample on anyone's hopes, they—"

He fell silent, choking on wet gasps, and Alexander was overcome by a tremendous warmth, an urge to proclaim all the gratitude, all the affection he suddenly felt for this man. He yearned to find the words, but his thoughts kept scattering, so he wrested the bottle away, and, holding it up to the light of the streetlamp, blurted out, "Thank you, friend, that's good stuff, not like that poison I once had that wouldn't even burn."

Nikolai lifted his head. His wet face sloshed in the light.

"What did you say?"

"I said thank you for this, I think you're—that is, I'm glad that you and I—I mean—"

"That," Nikolai said, leaping to his feet, "is precisely what we need. Any paper in your bag?"

Alexander watched, stupidly but without protest, as Nikolai up-ended his bag. Two books flopped to the ground, followed by a couple of school notebooks Alexander kept meaning to toss out, and some crumpled odds and ends.

"These will do as kindling," Nikolai said, appropriating the note-books, kicking the rest aside. "Even sorry fellows like me know better than to damage books."

Together, they balled up the lined and checkered pages criss-crossed with teachers' markings; then Nikolai sloshed what was left in the bottle against the back of the kiosk. "There's no streetlamp on this side, so it's less risky here," he said grinning. "More private." After that, things grew a bit hazy in Alexander's mind. He remem-bered Nikolai swearing and blowing on his fingers as match after match hissed and wavered and went out, and the first, cautious lick of a flame shriveling a page, and another, and all at once a spreading blaze, a rush of light and heat, the rearing of something bright and great and angry, like the anger Alexander himself was now feeling, anger at the lies, at the lines, at the inability ever to know anything for sure, at the inability to break the hollow bonds of time, the painful bonds of place, that bound them all—but break out he would, he promised himself as he ran down the street laughing, Nikolai run-ning and laughing in the darkness somewhere ahead, break out he would, and his life would be different, one way or another it would be different, full and brilliant like—like the full, brilliant life of the mysterious genius Igor Selinsky, who was alive, of course, alive somewhere, and not bent over some desk, either, but having glorious, fantastical adventures—or the full, brilliant wheels rolling over the skies, drawing closer and closer to some faraway, brightly lit, wondrous place—or the fire he recalled seeing somewhere not that long ago, the full, brilliant fire that danced behind his closed eyelids as he was falling asleep in his small, drafty room.

Just before he drifted off completely, he remembered with a jolt that Viktor Pyetrovich's books, the books he had borrowed that evening, remained lying on the ground among the jumbled contents of his raided bag, and was touched by a chill of apprehension. But his apprehension flickered and died like another clumsy match, and he laughed softly into the pillow, seeing the frenzy of the flames before his eyes, their magnificent, dazzling red color.

3

For a very long time, possibly an hour, maybe longer, Sergei sat on the bench looking at the folded note in his lap, at the treble clef on its back. The note was crumpled, frayed, almost furred at the edges. She must have written it weeks earlier, and someone had neglected to pass it along; or else it had traveled for days up and down the line, gathering mold and crumbs from the insides of anonymous purses and pockets, ending up at last in Sasha's bag. He hesitated to read it, fearing that it might disintegrate in his grasp—or so he told himself.

After a while, he glanced at his watch. Five minutes had passed since Sasha had left him.

He tore the note open, and his world flushed hot and bright.

It was brief, no greeting, no signature. "Visit me anytime," it said, in large, shaky letters; she had scribbled it hurriedly, he saw, while standing in line, probably balancing the scrap of a score on her book. Underneath was the address. The lines were crucified by creases, nearly illegible, but enough to make out the apartment number—the number he had not been able to erase from his memory for weeks, the number at which he had stared for some tortured minutes at the end of the summer, lingering in the dimness of her landing, waiting, not daring to knock.

The hands of his watch continued to creep with tormenting slowness, as if the figures on its face were spread with glue; yet second by agonizing second, time squeaked along. Just before ten he rose and strode to her building, fast, faster now, until he found himself running, running through the shadows, through the chill of October, past some commotion exploding with cries a short distance away, then falling behind him, past some faceless passersby— a few men sprinting by, students perhaps, tossing jokes to one another with the high spirits of youth, a dutiful grandson leading his aged grandfather on a leisurely stroll—all of them sketched by the night in black ink on a black background, the city's small, quiet gestures brushing by him like an autumn wind.

He was out of breath when he reached her street. He counted, one, two, three, four; the windows on her floor alternated light with darkness, and he did not know which one was hers. He stood looking up, until his neck grew stiff, then, gathering himself, went inside.

He did not want to ring her bell for fear of waking the invisible someone who slept on the invisible sofa under the invisible paintings, so he knocked softly, and after a while knocked again. The door opened suddenly, and there she was, her coat still thrown over her shoulders, her shadow falling across the threshold at his feet. He was pierced by an instant disappointment: she was not as he remembered her, as he had imagined her all these weeks, but drawn and plain and blanched, her eyes flat. Then her gaze met his, and she was as before, her face sewn out of tiny particles of pure, transparent light.

She did not seem surprised to see him, but quickly, before he could say anything, pressed her finger to her lips and moved away. He followed her through the unlit places to her room, and the room appeared subtly different, as though it had obtained more angles since his first and only visit, but he did not have time to notice anything else, for she now closed the door and turned to him, and his heart was again sliding somewhere flushed and vivid and happy.

"So kind of you to check on me," she said in a low, urgent voice. "I'm all right, but poor Vera, oh, it was horrible, I've just been sitting here stunned ever since—"

He did not know what she was saying; he did not listen, could not listen. He took a step forward, and somehow so did she, and for a few heartbeats he felt her melting into his shoulder, his chest; but as he buried his fingers in her hair, so soft, so surprisingly soft, he sensed her stiffening, forcing him away, slipping back.

"I fear you've misunderstood, Sergei Vasilievich," she said repressively.

They looked at each other without moving; her face was as it had been in the doorway, drained of light. She seemed on the verge of saying something else. He waited, watching her lips, watching her eyes, wondering wildly, desperately, whether he might somehow die at this suspended moment, the hands of his watch forever frozen now. Then, wordlessly, she turned away, crossed over to the window; and as he followed her weary progress, her coat dragging behind her like some heavy-limbed, wounded creature, he finally saw what was different about the room: its surfaces were erupting with bulky masses of the ancient gramophones from her museum, the corners crowded with a dark geometry of shapes. His breath scratched painfully at his chest; he remembered the night when she had played him gypsy romances and sat listening to the music with her eyes closed, her face solemn yet also ecstatic, angelic, remembered the blue hollows of her temples, the shape of her mouth as it formed the word "special"—

When he spoke, his voice barely held together.

"You got my note" ("I never got a note from you," she whispered, still not facing him), "and you wrote me your note, inviting me here, and—"

"I never wrote you a note."

This time he heard her.

"You never—why are you—you must think I'm—"

The paper trembled in his hand as he stretched it toward her across the darkness, trembled more in hers. "It's not my handwriting," she said faintly.

"It's your address, whose handwriting can it possibly be?"

"My father-in-law."

"Your who? Your—"

"My father-in-law. The concert ticket is for him. He lives here. I thought you knew I was—"

There was a minute of perfect blindness—a bright blindness, white and cruel and harsh, and a rush, a swishing of blood in his ears, like a drum, a tribal drum, and someone was screaming, and swinging, and all around, things were crashing to the floor, crashing with metallic, screeching noises of disintegrating machinery, shiny black cogs leaping away from the light like insects, horrible, meaningless insects that should be squashed, like this, like this, yes, all of it meaningless, and cacophonous, and never-ending . . . And then the door was thrust open, and in a sudden square of stark, orange illumination he saw himself standing in the middle of her room, a gramophone bleeding at his feet, and in the doorway a pale barefoot boy in an oversized nightshirt, blinking at them with frightened eyes the color of broken glass.

Her hands were at her mouth. The room was absolutely still.

The boy said, "Why are you wearing your coat, what happened, Mama?"

Sergei sat down on the floor.

"Nothing, nothing," she was saying, "go to sleep, this is Sergei Vasilievich from the line, I accidentally dropped this and he's helping me fix it, go back to sleep."

The boy stared at them, then stumbled off, his face already vague with the next dream. The door remained open, but the orange light went out. Time slowly took off again.

The gramophone was quite dead now.

"Oh, God," he said dully.

She kneeled next to him. Tiny mysterious pieces lay all around them.

"We can't fix this," she said quietly, not looking at him.

"Oh, God. I didn't mean—I'll buy you a new one, I—"

"This was the oldest model we had. The one—you remember."

"I remember."

"I take them home once a year for special cleaning. You can't buy them, there are very few of them left—"

"I'll find one, I have connections, I know people who could . . . Please, let me help you."

They spoke as if their voices belonged to others, and they still would not look at each other as their hands efficiently crept across the floor, avoiding accidental touches, hunting out sad misshapen remains from under her chair, from under her bed. After a while she said, "What's that, is it smoke?" and, standing up, returned to the window, and opened it, and leaned out. "Something's burning out there, can you smell it?"

"No," he said, standing up also. "I should go. I must tell you I—"

"Please, don't," she said. She remained at the window. At the threshold of her room he dared to lift his eyes to her, but she was gazing out over the city, her face averted. With an ache that was unlike any he had ever known, small and hard and infinite, infinite, he thought, This is it, this is final, my last view of her—and he tried to gather her into his memory as she was, her shadowy back, her graceful fingers resting listless on the windowsill, the incline of her neck that seemed somehow hurt, as if her thoughts were too heavy for it to support them, the gentle curve of her pale cheekbone, her hair, so soft, so soft, he remembered without warning, remembered too her melting into his chest, only an hour, or was it a year, or a century ago . . .

"I'll show myself out," he said.

꧂

On the street, numbness descended upon him, and would not release him for days, for weeks. As October darkened into November, the line buzzed with agitation, but it was through a haze that he heard of the Nightingales attack, and the girl who had lost an eye and would not be returning, and the fire at the Nightingales kiosk, in which one of their own had been suspected until the authorities located a few illicit pieces of evidence at the crime scene (pre-revolutionary books glorifying life Over There, whispered two or three people in the know) implicating a certain music teacher at a local school, the leader of a conspiracy to seduce the youth away from patriotic music (a blackened scrap with her telephone number was recovered in the ashes, it was rumored). It was not all that surprising, people said in careful undertones, there was trouble at schools nowadays, did you hear about that physics teacher, fired for no reason, thankful to work as a janitor now, oh really, how unsettling, but you know what they say, where there's smoke, and so on, and at our school, they let go the literature teacher, my son's favorite, she read them things that were not part of the curriculum, but beautiful, beautiful, he brought home some poems last spring, something about a cuckoo, I seem to recall, well, maybe that's why, then, cuckoos aren't exactly patriotic, are they, they push their fledglings out of the nest or else foist them upon others, parasites, really, so this teacher of yours has only herself to blame, and please keep your voice down.

Sergei tuned the gossip out, preoccupied as he was. He had made inquiries; at his insistence, his son had taken him to a hidden courtyard with an old church, and introduced him to a couple of helpful acquaintances who eventually arranged a meeting with an expert, a taciturn man with a face the texture and color of seasoned leather. The man had listened politely, holding the tips of his leathery fingers at a joined incline under his chin, asked a few pointed questions in a leathery voice, then half closed his eyes and thought for a moment. "It's challenging, but I trust I can find the right model," he had announced at last. "It will take about a month. Perhaps sooner, perhaps later. I'll let you know through that clever boy of yours."

"And the price?"

The leathery lips exhaled an astronomical number.

"Pleasure doing business with you," Sergei had said flatly.

For the next few weeks he kept busy. He sold a pair of golden cuff links he had inherited from his father; he sold all his ties, which, true, were of shoddy local manufacture and brought very little money, but which he did not need in any case, now that he was no longer performing; he sold his one good suit. His efforts to find a steady job were unsuccessful, but his fake medical certificate would cover him through the end of the year, and his son, who proved to have an impressive breadth of resources at his disposal and who asked no questions, put him in touch with some burly fellows in need of occasional help unloading fruit from trucks.

He was still short of the necessary sum, however, so one chilly, sunless afternoon he walked to the ruined church with his tuba slung over his shoulder. A street away, he was stopped by a group of men with red ribbons on their sleeves, rushing in the opposite direction.

"Where are you going?" they cried. "The parade's over there!"

He gazed at them blankly.

"Ever heard of the Change?" a red-faced, heavy-chinned man asked, stepping forward, a burgeoning threat in his voice. With the same kind of blankness, Sergei stared at the man's hands, huge, raw, blunt-edged slabs stirring, seemingly on their own, by the man's sides.

"Nah, leave him alone," another man said, pulling at the red-faced man's sleeve. "He's feeble-minded, can't you see?"

The group fell silent, shifted uneasily, and, without addressing Sergei again, hurried off.

He stood watching their backs for a minute, then descended the stairs into the familiar basement, crossed the yard, and laid his tuba in front of the leathery man. The man's lips curled in disgust. "This so-called instrument," he said, prodding it carefully with the tip of his brilliant shoe, "has the air of an old bum. Has it been drinking heavily and sleeping under bridges? Appropriate, I daresay, for one of such revolutionary inclinations. Tubas are not in vogue nowadays, the thirty-eighth anniversary notwithstanding. This is all I can offer."

As Sergei walked away, he listened to other tubas booming in the celebration parade a city stretch away—ghostly sounds in a ghostly city, carried off on the cold November wind like dead leaves, crumpled newspapers, torn cobwebs—while somewhere above them, somewhere else, the celestial music continued to play, undimmed, untouched, still out of his hearing yet drawing closer perhaps . . . Freed from his habitual brass weight, he found himself straightening, forcing his shoulders apart, filling with a lighter heartbeat. He thought he should feel at least a twinge of sorrow for his companion of so many years, for someone he had kissed scores upon scores of times, but he felt nothing—or rather, he realized as he entered his bedroom that night and saw the emptiness in the corner where the tuba had rested its weary coils for two decades, he felt an odd sense of relief, as if his life had become simpler, clearer, stripped of at least one lie.

He told Anna he planned to keep it at the theater from now on. They needed the space.

4

⁓

ANNA DISLIKED CONCEALING the truth from her family, but she did not want them to worry.

"It's only temporary, of course," Liuba had told her. "My brother goes south every winter, to, well, let's just say, engage in some transactions. You can start right away. The pay isn't much, but there are fringe benefits, if you see what I mean."

"Thank you, I'll do it," she had said quickly.

She would leave home at the same early hour as before and walk to the nearby street. She had her own keys. She liked the flimsiness of the construction: on clear days, she had only to open the door to find herself framed in a rectangle of bright, blue crispness; on windy days, sudden vibrations of the walls made all the cans and jars perform little metal and glass jingles; on wet days, which were her favorite, raindrops pummeled the tin roof with such a hollow sonorousness that she felt herself a part of the soggy sky, separated from it by only the thinnest of membranes. The delivery van sneezed its way out of the morning fog shortly before eight; afterward, she enjoyed a quiet half-hour, allowing herself a luxuriant whiff or two from this or that bottle of perfume from under the counter. Once she pushed the window grate open at nine o'clock, she did not have many free moments, but she did not mind.

She had been waiting on the other side her whole life, and she liked having something that others might want to wait for.

In the afternoon, as soon as Liuba came to replace her, she hastened to the tickets line, bracing herself for another anxiety-ridden fading of daylight. The line had lost all traces of its summer tranquillity, had devolved into an unnerving shuffle of people who came and went, their schedules unpredictable, their errands murky, their tidings, bits and pieces overheard here and there in the city, increasingly disturbing. When they talked, they kept their voices low: a few uniformed men were now stationed at regular intervals along the street—for their own protection, they had been told, though the Nightingales had not returned since the night of the attack and the perpetrators had been apprehended. For some weeks the men did not address the line, merely patrolling up and down the pavements, pausing slightly when someone spoke with excessive agitation, until one evening in early November, Anna looked up from her volume of poems at a voice barking: "Everyone's papers out, now!"

A man was striding toward them, his face scrambled by shadows, a list of names in his gloved hand. People shuffled uneasily; a few timid voices rose among them, pale as steam: "What did he say?" "I beg your pardon?" "Did you hear him?"

"Your papers," repeated the uniformed man. "We'll be checking your papers during each shift, to weed out any undesirable confusion. Order must be maintained. Anyone without proper identification will be asked to leave."

"But this isn't how we normally do it," someone offered meekly. "There's a nice fellow here, you see, a sort of organizer, he takes care of—"

"The comrade in question will no longer be joining us," the official said impassively. "Your papers, please."

There fell a profound stillness, which lasted only one moment before dissolving in a rustling of pockets and bags hastily turned inside out. A confused elderly man who had no documents on him was forced out of the line; he hobbled down the darkened street without glancing back. A younger woman behind Anna, with whom over the previous weeks she had exchanged chance comments about the weather, started to cry soundlessly, not even trying to wipe her face; Anna offered the woman her handkerchief. Later, long after the official had departed into the gathering night, jotting something in the margins of his list, murmurs began to crawl. Some said the hapless organizer had been taken away, like the business-minded fellow with the chairs or Vladimir Semyonovich, that man with the mustache rumored to wear a cross under his shirt, you know the one I mean; but an ancient crone who claimed to live on the first floor of the organizer's nearby building dribbled some whispers through her toothless gums into a neighbor's ear, and by the end of the shift the word was that he had not been taken away after all but had been followed from the line late one night, whether by the Nightingales or by someone discontented with his methods of keeping track of the Selinsky tickets, no one could be sure, and had been brutally beaten just steps from his front door, behind some lilac bushes, causing a pack of stray dogs to howl two streets away.

"Here," said the woman behind Anna, holding out Anna's handkerchief. "Thank you."

Her cheeks were still streaming, but it was drizzling now anyway, the chilly mist turning into ice in midair; it would not have made any difference.

"Are you all right?" Anna asked, peering at her closely. "Do you have an umbrella?"

The woman's eyes were swimming in the blank of her face.

"Oh, I don't need one, I'll be fine," she said.

When she tried to smile, a sense of familiarity brushed Anna, as if she had seen her face, with that tormented smile and those pale

eyes under invisible eyelashes, somewhere before, somewhere outside the line; then the feeling passed. "It's wet," she said decisively,
taking hold of the woman's arm, lifting her own umbrella above
them. "Come, I'll walk you home. I'm in no hurry."

They trudged through the city in silence. After a few blocks, the
younger woman stopped.

"You're very kind," she said, "but I'll be all right from here, it's
no longer raining. I—I don't know what came over me earlier, I just
felt . . . I just suddenly forgot why we were there—like the concert
no longer existed, no longer mattered, you know, and we were
somehow condemned to wait forever, like—like being punished for
something . . ."

The street stretched black and glistening before them; the light
from the corner lamp drooled in a wan, exhausted trickle, drowning bleakly in the folds of the disheveled umbrella at Anna's feet,
splashing hollow and white in their faces.

"This ticket you're waiting for, is it for you?" Anna asked softly.

She had spoken unconsciously, voicing a thought, and immediately felt startled by her boldness; for while the question had been
a simple one in the early days in the line, it had become something
else in the past few months, a momentous, compelling inquiry into
one's nature almost—

"It's for my husband's father," the woman said.

"He loves music?"

The night drizzled around them, and in its limpid, cold, glinting
darkness, the woman's eyes were enormous and filled with light—
the feeble, flat light of the streetlamp above, and, beneath it, hidden
in a secret pocket, another light, dark and luminous, like a candle
flame briefly covered by a hand. "It's not about music for us." She
spoke quietly, yet her voice was all at once reckless, defiant. "It's
about my husband. He—they took him away seven years ago."

"Oh no, what did he do?" Anna exclaimed.

The woman looked down. As the streetlamp reflections fled her

eyes, her whole face seemed to have gone out, and Anna saw it as
she had seen it first, devoid of color, pinned behind glass to the wall
of the boy's apartment, next to the photograph of her laughing husband. She pressed her hand over her mouth. "I'm sorry, I didn't
mean—"

"You're lucky," the woman said, and in her eyes, when she raised
them, there was no anger, only sadness. "I used to think like that
too, until it happened to us. Sometimes—sometimes things just
happen, I think . . . They don't need to have a reason, you see. We've
tried everything to get my husband released, but we don't even
know where he is. Now my father-in-law thinks that going to the
concert might help. I'm not so sure. Still, we can only try—"

Anna touched the younger woman's hand.

"You must really love him," she said gently. "Your husband."

The woman was silent.

"Do you know, I turned thirty-four last month," she said at last
with a small, pinched smile. "When I was a girl, I read old-fashioned
novels and I believed in love and happiness. But life is not about happiness, nor is it about love, or at least not the kind of love they write
about in novels. My husband was—my husband is a good man
whom I haven't seen in nearly a decade, whom my son does not
remember, and who now, right now, is in some faraway place, suf-
fering horrors I can't even begin to imagine, and I—I met someone,
you see, someone else, but it doesn't matter, I would never . . . I'm
sorry, I have no idea why I'm telling you all this. I should be going,
thank you for everything."

Anna felt her chest expanding with pity.

"Of course," she said. "Good night. See you tomorrow."

She followed the woman with her eyes, until she was only a
blurry white haze moving from streetlamp to streetlamp through
the sleet and the darkness. Then, slowly, Anna turned and walked
home, feeling obscurely different, cleansed somehow; holding on
to that large, light feeling as she stood in line the next day, and the

day after that, and through another celebration of the Change, which carried the strained puffs of brass instruments and the dismal crashing of cymbals from streets far removed from their own solemn, expectant street, with its kiosk at one end and its neglected church at the other. The people of the line had grown silent, weary, casting furtive glances at the faceless officials who prowled the sidewalks, yet at the same time, Anna sensed, there had been, since the beginning of fall, since the fall of darkness, an imperceptible drawing closer, quite as if their communal, increasingly dangerous wait had rubbed their souls raw, had made their emotions transparent, had marked them all with an invisible sign of shared time, of shared expectation, so that every once in a while they could turn to one another with a kind of heedless, naked urgency and talk as they would talk only to their families, and perhaps not even to them, united by fear and hope and trust under black, pregnant skies.

In the final week of the month, the skies flooded at last, and it began to snow. Anna was talking with Viktor Pyetrovich, Sonechka's father-in-law, who had taken Sonechka's place in line in the past few days—she herself was home sick and Anna had brought her some soup that afternoon—when an elderly man approached them and peered into Anna's face. "The woman with lovely eyes, just as he said," he then pronounced smiling, and extended an envelope to her. "I hope it was nothing urgent, my daughter's memory is like a sieve."

Mechanically, Anna accepted the envelope, holding it stiffly with her gloved fingers.

"I'm sorry?" she said.

"My daughter was asked to pass this on well over a month ago, but forgot. She forgot your name too. My apologies."

"But who is it from?"

"A man in the morning shift. In his fifties, she said, wears a gray jacket. Had a tuba with him once or twice."

"Oh," Anna said, "thank you," and, tearing off the glove, hastily freed the sheet of paper from the envelope—and indeed it was Sergei's handwriting. She read it, once, twice, three times, the letters starting to slip into one another, melting under the snow that was coming down faster now, large white flakes gently erasing the words before her eyes—or perhaps it was the sudden moist wavering of the whole city through her eyelashes. She folded the paper and hid it under her coat, pressing her fingers against it as if against her heart, to check its pulse, and waited, waited for the hours to end, the longest hours ever. At last, there was Sasha coming toward her to take over; she squeezed his hand gratefully as she passed. She walked to the corner, then, rounding it, began to run, her recently acquired boots skidding on pavements that shone astonishingly white and clean in the rich, soft darkness of the nearing winter; and as she ran, the two lines of his apology moved through her mind, round and round, round and round, an apology, she understood now, that he had been too ashamed to offer in person—*I wanted the ticket for myself, but I'd like to give it to you now, I want nothing but to make you happy. I wanted the ticket for myself, but I'd like to give it to you now, I want nothing but to make you happy. I wanted the ticket for myself, but I'd like to give it to you now* . . . And as she rushed home, as the words rushed within her, she felt the layers of buried misunderstandings, unvoiced resentments, solitary grievances sweeping away, the entire world around her opening, flooding with brilliant clarity, as though shutters were being lifted all over, so she could finally, finally, see that stooping old man in a disheveled fur hat being dragged on a leash by his giant dog, and two whispering shadows kissing by the fence, and the misty spheres of light floating above her, and the snow, the white, sparkling, wonderful snow, gliding over the streets like furry eyelashes lowered in slow assent, falling over the city, over the world, falling within her now, leaving her clear and vast and bright—free to live at last.

She did not have the patience to wait for the elevator. She burst in, out of breath, snowflakes melting with tiny pinpricks on her lips and eyebrows, and flew to the bedroom, her coat streaming behind her. He was lying on his side of the bed, fully dressed, gazing at a wall with unseeing eyes. Throwing herself before him, she cried, "Oh, Serezha, Serezha, things will be so different now, everything will be so happy, you'll see! The ticket—I understand, it doesn't matter, I wanted to give it to you anyway, you know, that night I tried to meet you in the park—"

He sat up, looking dazed; she saw things swiftly sliding in his face, a slackness overcoming it, more shutters being raised, though she could not quite discern what was behind them. "That night you tried to meet me in the park," he repeated.

"Oh, it doesn't matter now," she whispered, hiding her face in his shoulder; his sweater smelled of sweet, decaying leaves, the change of seasons, the earth's steady, joyful rotation. "I wanted to surprise you with it, you see, like a gift—but the ticket's not important, let my mother have it, I already lost her most precious possession and she has so little else, while you and I—"

He shifted his shoulder away, cupped her cheeks in both hands, looked at her.

"Anya, I'm sorry," he said slowly, his voice hardened, unfamiliar. "I'm not a good man, you deserve better than this, I must tell you I—"

"Please, don't," she said, moving quickly; and in the instant before she switched off the light she thought she saw his face bled of all expression, thought she saw a horrifying blankness, bleakness, in his eyes, and her heart was tripping, falling, could it be that she had been mistaken, could it be—but the room had just tumbled into darkness, and the snow dancing outside the window was slowly filling it with a pale, luminous glow, like the expanding, pure glow she again discovered within her, and she was crying now, and his breath was on her neck, his hand on her shoulder, and of course she had forgiven him completely, and it was nothing, it was nothing . . .

◦❧◦

Later, he slept, his face pressed into the pillow. He looked at peace. She watched him for some time. As she in turn began to descend, slow and weightless as a feather, into a well of quiet, dark gladness, dreams met her at the bottom with a splash of warm, ancient waters on which there flickered fragmented reflections of the day, her husband promising to make her happy, the concert surging forth at last in a rising of white-shirted orchestral chests, her mother in the front row, everyone's guilt erased, washed away, and the old sleepless voice was once more lulling her into a deeper dream, the voice she had been hearing so often in the middle of the night when she slept with her ear to the wall, the dream voice that always sounded so much like her mother's, and the voice was telling her, I'm sorry too, I'm sorry for everything, my dear, in so many ways I am such a selfish old woman. You see, I did not stop talking all those years ago because I had nothing to say, or because I did not love you, or because I had grown muddled with age. I stopped talking because that was my way of preserving the past, of denying the pain that had torn my life in two unequal halves, of bottling what I so bitterly, so near-sightedly considered the better half inside me as if in a flask with a stopper that wouldn't budge—all my precious memories, all my untold stories, fermenting in my soul until I walked through my days eternally inebriated with the heady magic of my childhood, with the sweaty music of my youth—until the memories had begun to conceal, underneath their enchanted sweetness, a soured darkness of rot—until I no longer knew you, your husband, your son—until I was alone.

Perhaps, too, walling myself off from the long rest of my life was a way of atoning for the guilt I felt about your father, atoning for that November day Andrei had run out without a hat, without a coat, seething from an unfinished conversation. It was the anniversary of a certain encounter I treasured. Feeling sentimental, I had talked about my past, my dancing, other matters. I was careless in my choice of words. He grew upset.

He crossed the street before our house not looking left or right.

I remember hearing the squeal of tires, a dead hush before the screaming started.

For a long minute I did not dare come to the window.

Afterward, I punished myself with silence. And then I became old, without noticing when or how, one year flowing into the next—empty, empty. Age did not make me wise. I never asked, and I never gave, and when I did ask, I asked for myself alone. But the night came when, bare-legged and barefoot, you walked in from the street, and I saw your face, and I heard your voice, and my present began to haunt me the way other people are haunted by their pasts.

I understand now, my dear. My past is just that, past, and my silence is over. After so many years of wading through the mists of remembrance, I no longer need to spend two hours pinned to a straight-backed chair striving to catch a painful echo of my youth. So this, then, is what I would like. I would like you to put on your best shoes, your most beautiful dress—and oh, do not feel bad about my earrings, they were always yours, I only wish I had something else to give you. I would like you to cross the city whose ugliness will be concealed by New Year snow, soft and forgiving—your favorite time of the year when you were little, do you remember, all the sledding you did, laughing, your mouth full of snow? I would like you to enter the brilliant hall with the same excitement with which you entered the theater as a child to watch me dance when I still danced, in the brief years before the Change, though I'm sure you've forgotten that also, and walk down the velvet aisle, and immerse yourself in the plush of the night. I would like you to look at the man who will come striding across the stage, and I would like him to look at you.

And oh, you should hear his music, my dear, for it is truly not of this world, though it should belong to everyone in it. It will one day soon, that I know.

This is a small thing, you see, the beginning of my amends. I will not be going to the concert. This ticket, my child, is for you.

PART FIVE

DECEMBER

1

ALEXANDER VISITED THE PLACE with stubborn frequency in the early days of December, to check on Stepan's progress in obtaining a pair of shoes.

"I want padded soles," he repeated on the second Friday of the month, "also, if possible, silver arrows running along the sides, I've seen a picture in a magazine."

Ordinarily Stepan would nod with patience, but on that afternoon he appeared distracted, and anxious to be left alone. "Can't talk now, I'm unloading some merchandise I've been trying to get off my hands for a while," he said at last, glancing at the door to the yard, then at his watch. "Stop by in two days."

On his way out, in the cramped maze of the basement, Alexander met his father.

"Thanks for letting me know," his father said. "Is he there now?"

"Yeah, waiting for you with that pile of junk. How was this morning, any trouble?"

"No, all was calm today."

"They hauled two more off last night," Alexander said quietly.

"Who?"

"Some woman, she had no documents on her—claimed

someone had stolen them in a tram. And a really old fellow with a beard, he's been around forever. He spoke out for her, so they searched him and found some incriminating stuff in his pocket, I didn't see what it was—a napkin or a menu or something from a foreign restaurant, I heard."

Sergei was silent for a moment.

"Listen, Sasha," he said then, "I think you should stop coming here, our position is precarious enough as it is. You must think about your future, you're a university student now."

"Yeah, about that, I keep meaning to tell you," the boy said, "I actually—"

A door banged upstairs, and there were echoing steps above their heads.

"Let's talk at home," Sergei whispered. "Thanks again, and oh, button up, it's snowing."

At four in the afternoon, dusk had already congealed, and the courtyard lay patchily illuminated by the windows of the surrounding buildings, a giant chessboard of light and dark. As he strode toward the man he could see leaning against the church wall, toward the precious parcel resting by the man's impeccable footwear, a memory of other windows lighting up other snowdrifts on a street he had walked almost a year ago, clutching in his sweaty hand a matchbox the cloudless color of a foreign sky, anticipating some deep intimation of another, truer, life that would somehow transform his own—the memory of it, vivid and painful, rose and tangled in his mind with an unfolding vision of the future, making him slow his steps.

The man was so close now Sergei could discern the dry folds in his leathery cheeks. Ah, so you got my message, good, and the money? Right here, the agreed price. Yes, pleasure as always, be careful not to drop it, it's rather heavy. Then the rush across the city, the familiar building, the elevator eternally out of order, the breathless assault on the staircase, he is not old yet, not old, nothing is over, her face framed in the door, her eyes yet again filling with that tremulous light. I've kept my word, this is for you. Oh no, I can't accept it. Please, this is all I can give you, you see, I was hoping to give you my ticket, but things have changed, I owe it to—to someone else now . . . For a moment he is afraid that she will again stiffen, push him away, but she does not, and with a clunk his gift is abandoned in the dusk of her hallway to exchange rattling reminiscences of bygone days with its reflection in the dusty mirror, and there is that melting he remembers, and the softness of her hair, and the surprising, timid dryness of her lips, and here the shadows become deep and golden and draw over them like curtains, and when he pulls the curtains apart, he finds the world bright with brittle wintry joy and her room blowing with chilled breezes and light, blue-tinted scents he has never smelled before, and, half rising on her elbow from the swirling foam of sky-blue sheets, she whispers, "Serezha, I've managed to get extra tickets, would you like to come with me?"

Two weeks later the tickets go on sale during his shift, he hands the ticket over to his wife, to his mother-in-law, and, with this simple discharge of duty, he is freed from all future duty, his life wiped like a slate, and, clean, free, he waits until the last evening of the year, until the entrance he has rehearsed so many times that it now slides past hardly invading his imagination—the rapid, well-practiced succession of stairs, chandeliers, seats, her cheek on his shoulder—and then the old gray-eyed man with the noble profile swiftly dances out onto the stage, and the lights dim, and the man's arm is raised.

It is curious, he realizes now, that in all this time, through all his manifold replays of the intricately constructed scenario—the glorious reward at the end of his tortured wait, which he could visualize down to the marble veining of the conservatory columns—his thoughts have invariably stopped just short of the actual music, never once daring to push past the lifting of the baton, never once daring to imagine the sound he is about to hear. This, then, is the

OLGA GRUSHIN

moment of unveiling, the ninth symphony of a genius—and though he has in his hand the concert program (printed with luxuriously raised lettering on beautiful cream paper), which he will take to his new home, her home, and treasure for decades as a keepsake of their beginnings, though he could easily look down, then, and skim the description of the symphony's conception, history, influences, he will not do so, he will close his eyes instead, and merely listen.

What was it that someone in the line said so long ago—an overview of the history of civilization, from tribal dances to the present day . . . And indeed, this is how it starts, with a solitary drum that emerges out of expectant silence, in the beginning only a low, arrhythmic pulse, the first rumblings of humanity lifting its still somewhat furry head, then growing louder, more assured, being joined by other drums, and cymbals, and more drums, cresting to a cacophonous, monstrous, exhilarating explosion of sound, of conscience, and gradually, out of chaos, acquiring a rhythm, a wild rhythm full of fires flickering in nights pitted with menacing stars and callused palms slapping the taut animal skins of primitive instruments. The beat becomes faster, faster, and then slower, more ritualistic, until it is dignified and almost stern, until the orgiastic splashes of cymbals fall away and trumpets enter in a celebratory fanfare, and the music transforms into a military march, sloe-eyed legions passing north in precise geometric formations, through jungles, along rivers, across deserts, carrying on their outstretched arms the building blocks of the first great civilizations, of pyramids and temples; yet somewhere deep below the marching, the earthy heartbeat remains, the faint but persistent throbbing of dark soil, of dark blood, of sacrifices to cruel gods of the southern sun. But as the parade across sands and ages thunders farther north, it becomes drier, lighter, cleanses itself of excess sound, and suddenly there is a hush, out of which a lone flute is born, a lucid, beautiful, seaborne melody, the classical harmony of antiquity, already swelling with other flutes into a pure, swanlike song, which, he knows, will soon turn languid, luxurious, Oriental, perversely wind itself around the militant theme, then be drowned in a newly erupting chaos of barbaric hordes, yet with the sole flute surviving like a slender silver thread beneath the noise, to stretch and surge out of the darkness with the unexpected strength of a human voice.

And as the orchestra falls silent, more voices soar in a heavenly chorus, and he thinks, Ah, I see, that's who these people were, standing about the stage in mute blue-and-silver ranks. Listening, he is astonished by how perfectly everything fits together, how one thing flows into another, how easily thousands of years translate into a seemingly uninterrupted musical phrase, how naturally the chorus of the eastern empire becomes tired and fades, yet not before passing its sound, moments before expiring, to an organ half the known world away, how gloriously the organ then carries it forth into the somber sonorousness of cresting medieval cathedrals, toward radiant devotions of sunlight splintered into a skyful of stained-glass rainbows, to be overcome, in turn, by a soft triumph of cellos unfolding and uniting in the fullness of humanity's rebirth. This unity is then dispersed by multiplying, thinner voices of violins, each thrusting its own increasingly shrill, diverging tune into the stream of time. He already senses what will happen to the music next, guesses, in a sort of visionary echo preceding the melody itself, the unraveling of beauty from its luminous peak, a mirrorlike unwinding, a repetition, in reverse, of the symphony's beginning; but the repetition is a little smudged and hurried, an imperfect, inferior reflection, as if mankind is now impatient and impoverished, merely going through the motions—the exotic eastern whine tamed for polite society, the classicism of flutes grown hollow and pompous in a strained imitation of ancient serenity, the marching warlike precision losing in strength what it gains in terror as it ushers in the present century—all of it disintegrating at last into a horrifying burst of noise, then silence, then the hoarse whisper of a lone, uncertain drum.

The curtains drew shut. He stood still, breathing.

Snowflakes were descending invisible ethereal ladders.

"By all means, take your time," the man with the leathery face said acidly from under the weather-stained, crumbling arches. "I've got all day, I'll be happy to wait some more."

"I'm sorry, I was somewhere else, I guess," Sergei said, and stepped forth into the shadows.

"I suppose you'd like to see for yourself," the dealer offered, beginning to remove the wrappings. Sergei gazed about. The doorway to the church gaped dark, empty of its secretive, erratically lit activity; the courtyard too was nearly deserted. Absently he watched a sharp-faced youth in a pink-and-orange scarf, whom he had seen with Sasha once or twice; the youth was sitting on the porch steps, fidgeting, checking his watch now and then, occasionally producing a small red box from his pocket, pushing it open to steal a glance inside as if to verify something, then hiding it back in his pocket, checking his watch once more.

"Almost done," the leathery man announced. "It requires a delicate approach."

As the box slid open again, Sergei caught the unmistakable flash of gemlike fire, and bent forward to see better.

The youth shoved the box shut.

"A beauty, isn't it," the man said fondly.

Sergei's heart was flailing. The future he had just rehearsed was retreating, back into the dreamlike, unconvincing realm from whose thin fog it had formed, and as it lost its substance he knew he would not see her again—unless, perhaps, he happened upon her by chance, as all of them constantly happened upon one another within the invisible boundaries of their small world, so confined that after some time even random encounters, even coincidences, began to appear predictable—yes, unless he happened upon her waiting in some neighborhood line, for milk for her father-in-law, maybe, or pencils for her boy, and tried to explain, in public, hurried, failed words, that he was unable to find the right model.

"But this isn't what I asked for," he said.

The dealer considered him without expression. Sergei's lips started to move mechanically around some explanation. The ensuing argument crisscrossed in the air, vague and abusive, until the man, losing his contemptuous calm, gathered the gramophone in its wrappings and departed, directing a final salvo at several generations of Sergei's family.

Exhaling, Sergei meandered over to where the youth was again consulting his watch.

"Hello," he said.

The youth frowned but did not reply.

"Sasha's father, remember? Nice scarf you've got there, unusual colors."

"Do you have anything to sell, or what?" the youth said reluctantly.

"Not today—but this item of yours, can I see it?"

"I already have someone lined up. She should be here any minute."

"Oh, I just want to look," Sergei said, sitting down on the step next to him.

The youth shrugged, reached into his pocket. For an instant Sergei was horrified at the thought that he had been mistaken, that he had just casually, without deliberating, committed yet another betrayal—and committed it in vain. But he had been right. Pushing their heads close together in the winter dusk, they gazed at the icy sparkling confined within filigree settings, the diamonds burning darkly in the dim light, and he thought, These are the trifles that summon thrilling visions of grace and delight, golden curlicues of theater boxes, waltzes across grand mirrored ballrooms, poems in some aromatic hour past midnight, music, laughter, champagne, the bright, delicate, swiftly whirling foam of life—but not for me. They will consign me to years of shared habits, rooms brown and low-ceilinged like lingering hibernation, an infinity of homemade meals, a bed quietly creaking; and perhaps one is worth the other, perhaps one has always been worth the other . . .

The youth, stifling a yawn, moved to close the cardboard box. It had a dark strip running along one side, Sergei noticed now—a matchbox, he realized, and laughed a short, silent laugh, and placed his hand on the youth's wrist. "These," he said evenly, "belong to my mother-in-law. They were taken from my wife just around the corner from here, on her walk through the park."

It was so quiet he imagined he heard the crunch of snow under the feet of a crow crossing the dusky yard, the small collapse of dampened plaster in the church at their backs.

"I don't know about any parks," the youth hissed, trying to jerk his hand away. "I got them from a man at the train station."

His face was half obscured, illuminated in streaks and blotches, but Sergei could see a rash of tiny, loathsome pimples on his fore-head, a base fear stealing like fog over his eyes.

"I'm not asking where you got them," Sergei said, "I don't want to know. I want the earrings. I will pay." Releasing his grip, he glanced behind him; they were alone. He began to pull out handfuls of bills, which probably smelled of rotten fruit, unloved musical instruments, lost familial keepsakes, furtive, unclean transactions—the sum of his life's worth. Two or three notes fell in the slush by his feet; he did not stoop to pick them up. "That's all I have. If it's not enough, I can send the rest with my son later, just name your price."

"That's fine," the youth said thickly, and for one moment Sergei saw him as a little boy, freckled, his lower lip trembling at some transgression, not that long past, before his face had been marked with a scar in some alleyway brawl. "That's fine."

The youth's hands shook as he crammed the money into his jacket.

Back on the street, Sergei turned left instead of right, narrowly avoiding a collision with a passerby who flashed past him, slapping his nose with a damp end of her scarf. Three blocks away he stopped, and stood in a pool of darkness, gazing at the people beneath the falling snow, gray, hunched over, faceless in the shadows, indistinguishable save for an occasional sleeve or boot thrust into a pocket of spilled, sickly light; but he thought he could see a place in the line where two women leaned toward each other, talking, their heads, their hats—one light, one dark—drawn close together.

He wondered briefly what would happen to his life if he approached them. Then he turned and walked away, and the music of the symphony he had imagined moved through his mind, softly at first, then gaining in volume, and he let it linger this time, running this or that phrase over his lips, humming this or that fragment, as he wandered the city and the night.

2

ONLY ONE MORE WEEK! I won't know what to do with my time once this is over."

"Me, I can't wait to get out of here. My cousin's brother-in-law has a car, he's agreed to lend it to me, so I'm going on a trip . . . Of course, there's a waiting list for driving lessons, but I've put my name down already, they say it won't be long, no later than next fall."

"I'm thinking of taking up sports, but my doctor says I should lose some weight first."

"And you?"

"I guess I might do some painting. An artist lives in my building, he's always having pretty girls over. Or maybe I'll learn to play the piano. Or write a book. I haven't decided yet."

There was a somewhat deflated silence. The snow was coming down faster now.

Anna turned behind her.

"It's a year to the day today," she said, "since I first joined this line. December twenty-third. I remember I was hoping for a cake. A cake would have been simpler, but I'm glad. Of course, I've lost my job as a result, but apart from that . . ."

Sonechka breathed on her fingers; she looked almost transparent with cold. "I dropped a glove somewhere," she said, glancing up with a pale smile. "Are you interested in working at the Museum of Musical History?"

"You have an opening?"

"We will soon. They're letting me go. They think I've stolen a valuable piece from the museum. It accidentally got broken, you see . . . But it was inevitable in any case, times are changing, and with my husband where he is, I'm a liability."

"But Sonechka, what will you do?" Anna exclaimed.

"I don't know. Stay home and learn to cook, maybe. Spend more time with my son . . . I still have friends at the museum, though, I'd be glad to put in a word for you if you like—"

Snow groaned under three or four pairs of boots; the uniformed men were striding down the sidewalk for the evening inspection. Anna turned away hurriedly, searching for the documents in her bag. After all this time, the line's really nearing its end, she thought, strangely affected by the realization; and even though she knew that in the coming year all of them would still be shopping in the same bakeries, sitting on the same benches, and seeing the same films at the local theater, she had a vertiginous sensation of breaking away, quite as if they were taking leave of one another before each setting sail on a mysterious expedition to different, unknown shores.

The feeling was as sad as any farewell, yet exciting at the same time.

That night, when she walked home, the air was soft, filled with the gentle movement of descending snow; apartment windows glowed through the snowfall in hazy patterns that seemed to form the letters of some heavenly alphabet, spelling out a word she could almost decipher. Wrapping the winter around her in the folds of her coat, she moved farther into the darkness; and as the air grew colder, she felt the year rushing along on its ice-bound, sparkling way toward its certain conclusion. She had always known that the tickets would go on sale during her shift—the line contracting in thrilled little spasms toward the kiosk, the seller beaming at her, a ticket stub in her naked, freezing hand. A cursory knock on the door, Mama, you won't believe this, Mama, look! Thank you, my dear, you don't know how happy you've made me. Her mother's scent as they embrace—not the sour whiff of old age, but a faint flowery scent of the past century kept like a dried blossom between the pages of some much-treasured book. Then the next few days, spent in busy, glad preparation as she bustles about the kitchen during evenings that are suddenly brimming over with time that is hers, hers alone—and at last New Year's Eve, the night of the concert, her mother returning just before midnight, looking younger by decades; and as the four of them raise their glasses in a toast, she thinks to herself, Yes, this year will be truly new, everything about it will be new, her family, her job, her life; and now, in her kitchen, with the clock striking twelve and champagne foaming over and everyone laughing, she can already feel her life deepening, can feel herself sailing off on the slow, tranquil journey of her future years—Sergei's hand on the small of her back, the taste of a perfectly baked date tart on the lips she is kissing, the candles nodding in glowing unison, Sasha's excited university stories, her mother thanking her again with shining eyes, It was wonderful, wonderful, my dear—and oh, turn it up, listen, they are playing the symphony on the radio right now, Sergei can hear it too—and the music, yes, the music, just like—here her thoughts stumbled a little—just like that melody from her childhood, the only melody she could ever hum.

When she unlocked the door, winter scampered inside the apartment like a frozen little creature at her heels. Divesting herself of her coat, she walked into the kitchen, and stopped short: Sergei and her mother were sitting at the table, their faces turned toward her as if in expectation. "Ah, there she is," her mother said, smiling.

"Mama, is that a new dress?" she asked, startled—and in the next moment saw the large white box presiding over the table, and some-how missed her mother's answer. Smiling also, Sergei reached over and lifted the box's lid; and immediately the kitchen filled with the bittersweet smells of chocolate and cream. She stared at the pink rose in the middle of the cake, two or three petals squashed.

"No candles, sorry," Sergei said. "And it's too bad Sasha's stuck in the line."

"I too have something for you," her mother said. "I'm afraid it's not wrapped."

Flushed, she accepted a small rectangular box from her mother's hands. Something hard rolled inside it as she pushed it open. She grew still.

"Happy birthday, my dear," her mother said softly.

"But—how—where—"

"A girl in the line was selling them. An amazing coincidence, she said she got them from someone at the train station," Sergei ex-plained, was explaining still; but her mother had already risen from the table and was guiding Anna to the foyer mirror, urging, "Well, try them on, try them on!" Stunned, she blinked at her blinding reflection, while her mother bobbed behind her, almost too small to be reflected herself.

Later, after they had eaten the cake, she stood alone by the sink, pretending to wash the dishes, letting hot water run over her hands until her fingers became white and puckered, thinking about all the things she had recently learned to let go—her youth, the wild transports of girlish happiness, the vulgar bouquet of romantic commonplaces—so she could keep other things, quiet things, sim-ple things, secret things, things that, she believed, would ripen with the passage of time into a warm, rich, mature contentment. After a while, she turned off the water, and, resolved, went to her mother's room, forcing the earrings open as she walked, though her swollen fingers would barely obey her.

The door was cracked; she opened it and stopped just past the threshold, talking already, having started to talk in the hallway, saying the words she had run through her mind in preparation: "Mama, I can't have these. I'm so relieved you found them, but they're yours, and they remind me of . . . Oh sorry, I didn't realize—"

Her mother, she saw, was undressing. Becoming aware of the sheen of the faded black silk carefully laid out on the chair—not a new dress, just one she had not seen in some twenty-five years—of the old woman's milky-white legs exposed, as she bent forward, between the folds of the last-century robe, Anna hastily averted her gaze.

"Come in, come in, it's all right . . ." Anna heard the bed creak lightly, heard the rustle of the robe being drawn. She entered the room, closed the door behind her, then stepped over to the dresser and gently placed the earrings on its scratched surface, where they lay glittering and sinister, a pair of brightly carapaced bugs from some exotic, unimaginable land.

"I would really like you to have them, Anya," her mother said slowly behind her back. "I want you to wear them to—on a special occasion."

"What special occasion?"

"When I was dancing in the West," her mother said, "I met Selinsky."

Anna turned. Her mother was now sitting on the edge of the bed, her small body hidden within her regally voluminous robe.

"You did? You never told me."

"It was not safe to mention his name, my dear. Then too, you might have noticed, I was not a talkative sort. But times are changing now. I knew Igor Fyodorovich well. I danced in his first two ballets. I rehearsed the third one as well, but I had to leave the city before it opened. The new soloist was magnificent. He married her later, I heard, but it didn't last."

"Oh," Anna said. "I didn't know he wrote ballets."

A short silence stole between them, then deepened; and as her mother's moist dark eyes rested quietly on her face, Anna felt all at once overwhelmed—overwhelmed by an irrational and terrible certainty that something momentous was about to be said in this stuffy, faintly perfumed box of a room forever trapped in the wrong century—something that would change her life in some enormous new way she could not possibly foresee or expect; and, unable to move, unable to breathe, she looked away, the cold blue fire of the diamond earrings nipping at the corner of her eye, and still the silence continued, and she thought she could not possibly stand another instant of—of—

"I'm not going to go to the concert," her mother said.

Her breath released, Anna stared at her. The old woman's face was serene, her back straight, her bare ankles unsettlingly brittle and sharp, lost in the dust-colored slippers two sizes too large that Anna had given her on some birthday long past.

Sitting down next to her, Anna touched her hand gently, as if she were a bird that might fly away. "But Mama—" she said in a near-whisper.

Her mother smiled, a surprising smile, warm and quick; and unexpectedly Anna thought of her dutiful childhood visits to vast, cavernous studios that reeked of State-sanctioned effort, with pale winter drafts whistling through white windowpanes, and mirrors along sloping floors reflecting her mother's tight-lipped struggles to impart grace to the thick limbs of clumsy peasant girls in sweaty tights, which little Anya had found faintly disgusting, and the following years of injuries, illnesses, and exhaustion, and an early retirement rewarded, in negligent fashion, with a medal engraved "For Unwavering Devotion to the Future of Our Ballet"—a medal, she recalled with a quick flush of shame, that she had not seen among the treasured keepsakes in her mother's dresser—and, dimly, she understood, the protests dying in her throat.

"And the ticket?" she asked softly.

"The ticket," said her mother, "is yours. Put on the earrings, my

dear, and go to the concert, the music will be beautiful, you remember that summer I—"

Anna felt her eyes beginning to well up but fought her desire to
cry, tightening her hold on her mother's hand instead, bending to
press her cheek to her mother's palm, then rising, speaking fever-
ishly, not noticing whether her mother was talking still, the words
of gratitude leaping off her lips—"Serezha will be so happy, so
happy!"—and somehow, in the next moment, finding herself already running down the corridor to the bedroom, pursued by the
staccato of her rushed steps; pursued, too, by a darkening look,
oddly like disappointment, or else resignation, in her mother's
eyes—or perhaps it was only the wavering of light in the room, the
trembling of the world through her tears, the shifting of things as
they found their rightful places at last.

Sergei was sitting in the armchair in the corner, writing in a thick
notebook, the shadow of his swiftly moving hand flying across the
wall behind him; as she lowered herself to the floor by his feet, she
glimpsed a page scribbled over with a hurried procession of many-
legged insects, clusters of berries, curling eyelashes.

She pressed her head to his knee.

"Mama has given us the ticket," she said in a muffled, laughing
murmur.

He was frozen for a long moment, one second, two, three,
four . . . When she lifted her face, yellow lamplight fell squarely
upon her; her gaze shone. He looked at her blankly.

"Do you hear, the ticket is ours now," she cried.

It was not the lamplight, he realized then; everything about her
was bright—her eyes, her teeth, her disheveled hair . . . His chest
received a painful nudge; he could see her former beauty rising in
her worn-out face. He glanced away, spoke with an effort.

"Your mother doesn't want the ticket?"

She shook her head, laughing again.

"It's ours now," she said, "I mean, it's yours. You can go to the concert!"

All was quiet within him—quiet, and dark, and still, devoid of thoughts.

He moved his lips, tried to say it, but the words had no sound.

"What was that, I didn't hear—"

She was smiling, smiling up at him—radiant, and gentle, and young, so young, as if she had somehow moved backward in time, merging with an early memory he had of her . . .

He tried again, and this time heard his voice, or what sounded like his voice.

"I think you should go instead."

"What?" she said, smiling still.

"I think *you* should go to the concert."

And as the words escaped him, what had seemed only a nonsensical dream an instant before—the harsh yellow light, the difficult melody he had been trying to pin down to the page, the happy, dancing, golden-green gaze of the beautiful woman he had known in some other, better, time, the astonishing gift falling into his lap, which he longed to accept with every particle of his being, and which, with the cruel logic of dreams, he was powerless not to refuse—all of it suddenly became a fact, and lay before him, cold and small, and unchangeable, forever unchangeable now.

The smile slowly ran off her face. "It won't be worth a year of waiting," she said, rising from her knees. "I won't be able to appreciate the music."

"Let's give it back to your mother, then, she's the one who should have it."

"She won't take it. Can you—" Her voice buckled. "Serezha, I understand why my mother doesn't want it. This—this I don't understand. I thought you'd be so glad . . . Can you just tell me why?"

Because it is impossible, he thought, because it is too late. If only this had happened earlier—before you put on a silk dress and waited for me on that park bench, before another woman stood without moving in the window and said, "Please, don't," before I broke something precious, and lied, and plotted, before I crossed the line—before a concert ticket changing hands stopped being a matter of concert attendance, became instead my only means of proving to myself that I'm not completely unworthy of everything I hold dear, be it music or love or—or simple human decency.

Because, you see, I will not be rewarded for my doings of the past year, of many past years.

He pulled her next to himself, carefully stroked her hair.

"Because I've learned a lot about Selinsky's music," he said, "and I doubt that his new symphony would be to my liking. His recent stuff is disappointing, too formalistic. I'd rather remember him for his early pieces, you know. There was this one thing I played when I was a boy—beautiful, beautiful . . ."

A moment tiptoed by. She sighed. He felt her settling into his shoulder.

"How did it go?" she asked.

Some hours before sunrise, as he lay awake in the dark, the ticket being passed in his tired mind from his mother-in-law to his wife to him, then back to his mother-in-law, and again to his wife and again to him, in an infinite, tedious, hopeless exchange, he heard a key turning in the lock, and was struck by an idea. He climbed out of bed and stumbled barefoot into the foyer to intercept the boy, but found only a damp coat tossed on the counter, saw only a thin sliver of muted light seeping out into the corridor as the door to the old woman's room drew shut.

Having closed the door behind him, Alexander faced his grandmother.

"You wanted to talk to me?" he asked, puzzled.

"I wonder if you could do me a favor, my dear," the old woman said briskly. She reached out her hand, her bony wrist adrift in the heavy velvet of the cuff; he squinted across the shadows at something dazzling on her childlike palm. "Can you get rid of these for a good price?"

His surprise deepened.

"Are you sure? Aren't these like souvenirs or something—"

"Oh, I'm absolutely sure. An admirer once bought them for me in a foreign city, but I find I no longer want to keep them around. Now, where was that silly matchbox?"

Frowning, he watched her fuss about her dresser, opening drawers, energetically shifting bundles of ancient, mysterious things; he could see dust rising into the air in pale, scented puffs.

"I didn't know you lived in a foreign city," he said. "Mother never told me. When was it? And where? And what was it like?"

She glanced over her shoulder, studied him for a moment, then extracted something from a drawer, shut it with another explosion of aromatic dust, and nodded at the chair. "Sit, and I'll tell you a story," she said. "It's rather late, of course, but then, you're a late bird like me . . . Just throw this over the light, be a dear, it's too bright for my eyes."

Obediently he tossed the old shawl over the lamp, and immediately the night trapped in the small, hot room grew flushed with a peculiar deep glow, the color of fire, he thought, gleaming darkly on the walls of some ancient cave. He felt disoriented and a little uneasy, yet also secretly thrilled, as if he had found himself in some unfamiliar, outlandish place. In bed now, his grandmother regarded him with alert black eyes from under the blanket; and when she spoke, he knew that her voice sounded just like a voice he had been hearing for a very long time.

"My parents first took me there when I was eight, you see. It was early spring when we arrived. The sky was like translucent silk, the roofs were like wet glass, the trees like hieroglyphics carved upon

the air. My father rented an apartment just off the boulevards. I studied ballet in the afternoons, but I spent my mornings at home. One
morning our bell rang, and three small liveried men came in carrying an enormous carpet on their shoulders. They set it down in the
dining room and began to unroll it. Its inside was soft and blue, rich
with golden birds, and I got down on my knees to see it better. And
it was then that I noticed the first one."

She fell silent abruptly.

Alexander leaned forward in the red glow.

"The first what?" he asked.

ALEXANDER WOKE UP tired and vaguely unsettled. He moved through the day yawning, his hand tightened around the matchbox in his pocket, his head muffled with insomniac visions of chimney sweeps dancing on tiptoes across tiled roofs, and bright petals swimming in buckets of flowers sold by mysterious girls on the corners of foreign boulevards. When the dreary afternoon had bled its shadows into the black evening, he walked to the familiar courtyard. The place was nearly empty, as it often was this winter; people were being more careful. On the porch steps, a drunk with a reedy, goatlike beard swayed above a fence of warped, worm-nibbled icons; a frightened-looking boy crouched beside him, his skinny arms protectively encircling something that glittered weakly in the dusk—a pair of tarnished silver candlesticks, Alexander saw as he came closer. Four or five fellows in enormous fur hats stumbled past him through the poorly lit snowdrifts, excitedly jabbering to one another in what, he registered with a start, was foreign speech; behind them trailed a fat man with no neck who mumbled in native undertone, nervously glancing around: "You can't find these in the official, State-run, stores—unique pre-revolutionary relics here, pieces of history, bargain prices—"

The group rounded the corner, but one man lingered behind, craning his neck at the peeling church domes that were quickly merging with the night. Alexander strode up to him and casually slipped the matchbox open. Just then a window lit up on the first floor of a nearby building, casting a pale rectangle at their feet; the diamonds flared up.

"Over two hundred years old," Alexander said under his breath.

The tall, elderly foreigner bent to examine the offering with shrewd gray eyes.

"A celebrated jeweler of the tsar," Alexander added hastily. "Museum quality. My grandmother was a countess, priceless gems, do you understand?" More windows were softly emerging in the deepening dusk around them, and with each new flash, it seemed more and more as though he held a small piece of fire on his palm.

The man was nodding, smiling down his long, distinguished nose.

Back in the basement, Alexander counted the money again, and thought in disbelief, People are such fools. He walked to the line, now and then touching the bulge in his back pocket, continuing to run his hand over it, to reassure himself, all through the night.

It grew increasingly cold; the unfortunates in the last, midnight, shift were still, all in their own muffled worlds of jealously guarded heat, clouding their raised collars with effluvia of onion stews and weak teas. Rare voices arrived in explosions of steam.

"He picked the wrong time to come back," someone said with grim satisfaction. "Let's hope he hasn't grown too tender among his orange groves and seaside resorts."

"Oh, he'll be all right in his foreign furs. Better to worry about yourself!"

"That's what I keep saying, we'll all get sick, this is inhumane!

The kiosk closes at five o'clock, so what's the use of our hanging about till—"

"What, I can't hear you, that van is so noisy—"

"A van, what van?"

"There, look, it's coming to a stop at the corner."

Alexander glanced up. The headlights chug-chugged to a halt, damp slush mixing with the limp snow that tossed back and forth beneath the recently repaired streetlamp. The van's door was kicked open from within; the driver emerged and, looking neither left nor right, proceeded to the kiosk. The line squirmed with cautious excitement. The man dug into a pocket; keys jingled. The line gasped and compressed forward, holding its three-hundred-headed breath. Alexander was watching closely now. The man disposed of the lock with astonishing efficiency and vanished inside. A woman squealed.

The grate over the kiosk window was being pushed up.

"Bet you your ticket," whispered Nikolai, "it'll be another notice—'Seller out till the Second Coming,' or 'We ran out of trees to print tickets,' or—"

The window now glowed from within, an egg of desirable light and warmth, from which hatched the van driver's head. A uniformed official approached, and the two conversed briefly. Alexander craned his neck until it ached. The official was already walking back, switching on his flashlight, unfolding some papers. "Straighten up, straighten up!" he shouted. "The tickets will be distributed in strict accordance with the list, only one per person. When you hear your name read, produce your documents and step forward."

The wildfire of voices ran up and down.

"The tickets, did you hear, did he really say—"

"Well, I'll be damned!" Nikolai cried, slapping Alexander on the back.

Behind them, the line gave in like collapsed dough.

"Ah!" Viktor Pyetrovich sighed softly, sorrowfully, and Alexander half turned to catch his heavily settling body against his shoulder.

"Are you all right?" he asked, his eyes glued to the kiosk window. Viktor Pyetrovich did not reply, his weight crushing Alexander's collarbone. Alexander glanced back.

The old man's face was the shade of yesterday's ash, his lips shaking in a pitiful attempt to assemble themselves in a smile; his gloved hands crawled unseeingly over his coat as if trying to ascertain the presence of something very important underneath its cheap fabric.

"Are you all right?" Alexander repeated, more urgently, gazing into Viktor Pyetrovich's face through the increasingly frantic shadows; the line was trembling, jerking, leaping now, and the darkness darted here and there like a flock of maddened bats, trying to escape the agitated slicing of flashlights.

"I—" the old man mouthed. "I—"

The voice would not squeeze out of his throat, and Alexander had the sudden unpleasant image of old toothpaste congealed in a tube. With rising alarm, he pulled on Nikolai's sleeve.

"He's sick or something," he said fiercely.

It was impossible to see what was happening at the kiosk window now; the backs had multiplied and grown violent, huffing, shoving, pressing.

Nikolai gathered the old man like a rag doll. "Damn it," he spat out. "Might be a heart attack, he needs an ambulance. I'll hold him, run!"

Alexander ran.

He ran slipping on snow, tripping over pavements, the icy wind stinging his face. Alleys crept out of the night with the drunken leers of unsteady, decaying streetlamps; the solitary silence of winter rang in his ears like the beating of blood, the rasping of breath, the tolling of bells long since fallen mute in the skies. Oh, the hateful city, where time is communal and worthless, where seasons follow one another like obedient comrades shuffling forward in line, where age erases identical, meaningless lives before they are even written . . .

His chest was tight with frenzied tears.

Two streets away, the phone booth shone dimly through the snow, a glass full of hazy, chilled milk. He dashed to it. A large man was inside, his back plastered against the door. The door was cracked, and out leaked the lived-in, soured warmth of a big body and the monotonous rumble of a low voice dictating to someone on the other end of the line. "And also one kilo of sausage," Alexander heard, "and half a dozen eggs, and dried fish, not the kind you got last time, but the kind he likes, you know the kind—" Alexander knocked, then tore off his glove and knocked again. Slowly the man rotated, until his stomach was squashed flat against the side of the booth, and he peered from the milky light into the outside darkness with small eyes that glistened like fish scales. His voice continued to drone. "And half a kilo of cheese if you can get it, give her fifteen for it, and also—" Still talking, his face enormous and bare, he jerked the door toward himself, and the crack vanished, and the voice became a wordless hum.

Alexander started to pound the heel of his hand against the glass, shouting, "A man's life, life and death, do you understand?"—but the fish scales only glimmered coldly; and suddenly lives no longer seemed to Alexander identical and meaningless, nor was time communal and worthless.

It was very particular, and very precious.

He flew farther, his toes numb in his inadequate shoes, and the park dragged at him with an oblivion of branches and benches and bottles, and there was that other phone booth he remembered across the road, but it was dark, and the light would not come on even when he pulled the door open. The receiver dangled heavy and dead, icy to the touch, and still he tried to push his coin into the slot, with shaking, treacherous hands, pleading with the silence for a whole minute, then, nearly crying, ran back to the first booth, and found the large man gone and the wires viciously torn out of the wall, a tangle of multicolored metallic bits and pieces spilling out like entrails.

He stared for a heartbeat, then stumbled back to the kiosk, sobbing under his breath, "I'm sorry, I'm so sorry . . ." The line had not moved much—it was maybe ten or fifteen people shorter; the window was dripping with shrill sounds of indignation, but he had no time to stop and listen. Viktor Pyetrovich's cheeks were flushed, yet his lips were deathly white, as though smudged with winter. "I'm fine, fine now," he breathed, "but I fear I must leave, it might be better for me to lie down, I—"

Nikolai released him, and he collapsed against Alexander.

"You're in no condition to walk by yourself," Alexander snapped. "I'll take you home."

"Sasha, what are you doing, the tickets!" Nikolai protested hotly in his ear.

"I'll be back in a few minutes, his place is nearby. And if my turn comes before I'm back . . . But I'll be back, just—just hold them off somehow if you can."

Viktor Pyetrovich had seemed skinny, insubstantial, but his weight was hard and unwieldy against Alexander, sharp angles bruising him—knees, shoulders. The old man's feet kept catching each other, and Alexander weaved from left to right under his burden, leaving an unsteady braid of tripped, tipsy footsteps in the snow. His struggling heart would not stop, jumping from his chest to his throat and back. I have to, I can't just leave him, I'll manage, there will be time, plenty of time . . . His arms ached. On a corner he paused to rest, propping Viktor Pyetrovich against a lamppost, and at last clearly saw the old man's face, deadened in the poisonous electric glare, glistening with two sleek ruts.

He's crying, Alexander thought, and, frightened, averted his eyes.

"Only a little way now," he said brightly.

They set off again. He tried to walk faster, time pushing him in the back, tick-tock, tick-tock, must be fewer than a hundred people left before him in the line, faster, faster . . . Viktor Pyetrovich's head was bobbing up and down as if tied to a string, and his lukewarm breath brushed Alexander's neck in wheezing exhalations, but he could discern little more than "Selinsky" and "concert." "Everything is all right, you'll be all right, don't worry," Alexander was repeating mechanically. "They'll hold our tickets, don't worry." Just as he felt unable to walk any farther, there was the building, the familiar oily smells of the foyer. The elevator was broken, of course, so, gritting his teeth, Alexander half carried Viktor Pyetrovich up the endless flights of stairs, terrified at the soft, apologetic moans issuing from somewhere in the old man's throat, maneuvering his body past overflowing trash chutes and blind little windows through which winter gleamed bleak and white and unclean, like shut, swollen eyes ripening with disease; and with each laborious step his hope of ever escaping it all lessened, lessened, until at last, sweaty and breathless, he fell against the door, groping for the bell in the dark.

The protracted ringing, the scrape of steps, the middle-aged woman with eyes like pockets stretched out with their habitual load of misery, the fearful stumbling through unlit rooms, that little boy wandering lost in the sudden forest of clumsy adult legs, the water splashing onto the floor out of a cup pressed to lips that did not obey by a hand that could not stop shaking, the confetti of pills spilling out of a bottle, the spectacles clanking on the nightstand—everything seemed in slow motion now. Alexander pushed Viktor Pyetrovich onto the bed, battled blankets and pillows, the boulders of wet shoes, can't be more than eighty or seventy people now, no matter how slow the line, faster, faster, please . . .

Viktor Pyetrovich was mumbling, imploring someone named Sonechka to leave him, run, get to the line in time for their turn, didn't she know how important, how very, very important—

"I will do no such thing," the woman said firmly. "Lie still, I think I hear the medics."

And then the room was empty.

"I should get back," Alexander muttered, "but it's all right, you mustn't worry, even if you can't come to the concert, Igor Fyodorovich will certainly pay you a visit here—"

The old man's fingers closed over Alexander's hand with a shockingly strong, cold grip.

"I can't die without seeing him again," he whispered in a horrible torrent of thick, misshapen words, "my only son, taken away because of nothing, because of his being related to Selinsky, but times are changing, if Igor Fyodorovich could only get the foreign press behind him, something could be done, I must go, do you understand, he would never come here, he probably doesn't even remember me, he has so many distant relatives, he—"

"But of course he remembers!" Alexander cried. "All the letters, all the postcards he's sent you! . . ."

Viktor Pyetrovich closed his eyes. For a few heartbeats it was horrifyingly quiet, a deep chasm opening between the sounds, time falling away—and then Alexander knew with an absolute certainty that there never had been any letters. In the next moment the room erupted with people, coats, smells of snow and medicine, the stomping of boots, a bright-voiced heaving, moving, shifting. Liberated at last, Alexander walked out, carrying away Viktor Pyetrovich's pained white gaze, unfocused without his spectacles, the final dry scratch of the old man's whisper against his ear, "Do you understand?" Slowly, as if asleep, he drifted past the shadowy accumulations of bulky furniture meant for some other existence, herded into this shabby place by a violent contraction of history, past a gilded clock on the wall, which either had stopped on some dull, dead, dusty afternoon when nothing much had happened or was telling him that it was now past one in the morning, reminding him to climb out of this hushed pocket of timelessness into which he had somehow fallen and run,

run, couldn't be more than fifty people left now—but just then the
darkness of the hallway parted, bearing the woman with those
strange eyes. She touched his sleeve shyly, then began to talk, quickly,
disjointedly. "I know who you are, he's so proud of you, please tell
him I'm not angry with him—or no, don't tell him that, tell him
instead that I will always—or better yet, don't say anything, just—"

"It will be all right," he said, gently moving her hand away, and
stepped over the threshold. Falling silent, she stood in the doorway,
watching him. All at once he was seized by sadness at not knowing
the right words with which to tell her how enormously sorry he
was. Pausing on the landing, he shook his head at the elevator grate.
"Doesn't work," he said loudly. "They should fix it someday."
Then, without looking back, he descended the stairs, gathering
speed from floor to floor, bursting at last into the stinging night.

The city flew past him—hazy streaks of streetlamps spreading out
like the tails of bleary comets; infrequent passersby hurtling like disoriented meteors from one nonbeing into another; lighted windows
coming to pale, glowing life like remote, clouded stars, dissipating
no warmth, then falling back; black holes of courtyard entrances
reeking of smoke and trash, of some deep, invisible processes of cos-
mic rotting—and as he ran, light and night, night and light, passed
through him again and again, time accelerating in rhythm with his
accelerating heart, and he felt its substance changing, changing with
the roaring of the chill in his ears, until his universe, which before
last year had stood completely still, his entire universe accelerated
too, became a spinning, vertiginous blur of colors and winds, then
rested, hard and brilliant, on one sharp, well-defined moment, the
pinhead of time, a crystal on the head of a needle, balancing precariously as he ran, chanting silently, I will be on time, I will be on
time, on time, on time, on time—

He was only two streets away now. There were voices ahead. He cut through a yard. Trees clinked with ice as he passed. Two men stepped out of the darkness.

"Hey, you there, have a light?" one called out.

Not slowing down, Alexander thrust his hand in his pocket, tossed out a matchbox, just like the one he had sold to that foreigner in the shadow of the church, so long ago . . . It was very quiet; his steps crunched in the snow and the trees sang a tinkling ditty.

"Always prepared for arson, isn't he?" the first man said.

The second joined hoarsely, "It's him, I just saw his face."

The crunching of the snow came to a halt. The men were standing in his path.

"Hey, what—" he said, and tried to sidestep them. The first blow bent him in half.

"Hey," he said again, hopelessly now, and put up his hands to protect his face. An overhead branch shook, and there was more melodious tinkling; icy powder descended on his head, dusting his eyelids with delicate, sprinkling touches. The men were working wordlessly, with satisfied grunts. Trying to ward off their blows, through the pounding and the sparkling and the ice, he thought he heard a remote tread of heavy boots, drawing close, closer, a voice crying, "Sashka, what the hell are you doing there, our turn is coming, what—!"

The voice, near now, cut off with an expletive.

As the flashing ceased in Alexander's temples, he saw Nikolai rocking back and forth on the balls of his feet, his thumbs hooked in his torn jacket.

"Take a walk," the first man suggested. "This is between the three of us."

"Yeah, we're reeducating a young criminal here," said the other man. "He set our kiosk on fire, I saw him running away laughing. He isn't laughing now, though, is he?"

The square of the yard was white and still, the snow slow, theatrical; the night had deposited an unreal, metallic taste in Alexander's mouth—or perhaps it was the taste of blood. He felt unreal himself, as if everyone were an actor reciting poorly written, forced lines, going through stiff, predictable motions. The light of the streetlamp flaring along the blade of a knife—his friend's knife, formerly his own, he realized with an internal half-chuckle, half-sob— seemed to belong to the same unlikely, artificial play, as did another explosion of pain somewhere and the cascade of dazzling white stars in the blackness of his head and the muddled sight of the two men falling upon the third, the man with the knife, his friend, he reminded himself through the pain that would not stop but was spreading with slowly widening concentric circles. Then there was the cold against his cheek, snow, he guessed dimly, and cries and steps above him, something smashing into his side, a shoe maybe, a beautiful athletic shoe with silver arrows along the sides, he saw through his closing eyelids, through the steady rotation of the world, through the fading, the fading, the fading of things. And then there was nothing—only the darkness, the crystal of the universe glinting on its pin black and small, shrunken, and the old man sitting in the kitchen, sipping hot tea, with cautious lips puckered in an attitude of gentle blowing, from a glass set in a lovely silver glass holder, talking as he did one autumn day, during one of Alexander's last visits.

"So, then, Viktor Pyetrovich," Alexander asks, "what do you suppose happens to us when we die? After, I mean?"

"I read something once in a clever book," the old man says between sips. "Maybe each of us gets whatever he believed in. A dead Hindu spends his eternity among a pantheon of blue-faced gods squirming with hundreds of arms and trumpeting through elephant trunks. A dead Muslim strolls in a rose garden fondling almond-eyed maidens and reciting poetry. A dead Christian floats amidst clouds filled with angels making music as Saint Peter strides past shaking his keys. And whoever believes there will be nothing after death gets precisely that—nothing. A small room full of spiders."

"But what do *you* believe, Viktor Pyetrovich?"

Viktor Pyetrovich smiles. "I'm hoping to arrange a fulfilling afterlife for myself. Another cup?" And as Alexander watches a stream of hot, steaming liquid splash into his glass, he suddenly thinks, What if my afterlife is only more of the same, this city I can never escape, the shoddy apartment blocks, the sharing of bottles in the dismal little parks, the lines, the winter, the dreary snow, the nausea in the mornings, the trains always departing without me, the eternal wait for something, anything, to happen—and then, horrified, sends a silent plea to whatever heavenly scribe might be up there in pearly-curly paradise jotting down prayers with a swan's feather in some gigantic compendium of life, No, no, please don't write that down, I don't really believe that, it was only a stray thought—but already Viktor Pyetrovich begins to thin out, to turn transparent, the glass, the tea growing darker, merging with the darkness all around him, and as he opens his eyes, he sees a square of black sky, the spilled sugar of stars, naked branches moving above him, stirring the air like spoons in a cup, the round coin of the moon, the kind one needs to make a call from a booth, unless the telephone's broken, and the snow, and the yard—and he sits up with a moaning, frightened whisper, "Oh, no."

His body aches, and his hand comes away wet from his face. His nose is quite possibly broken, and maybe a rib or two. His fear abates a little; he feels too sore to be dead. There is an old man crouching before him, but he is not Viktor Pyetrovich. Alexander frowns at him, then recognizes the uncombed beard, the grieving eyes, the ancient man from the line.

"I thought you were arrested," he says, and tries to stand up, and sits back down.

"So I was," says the ancient man kindly. "Not the first time, nor the last, I reckon. They can never hold me for long."

"Am I dead?" Alexander asks, just in case.

"Nothing wrong with you except a few scratches," the man

replies. "They ran away when I came upon them. Your friend's badly hurt, though. A knife wound. Help should be here soon."

And only now Alexander notices the man, his friend, Nikolai, lying on the snow, and he manages to pull himself together, and crawl toward him, and touch his forehead, which feels clammy, cold; and there is the knife, his old knife, which he picks up and holds for a moment, its familiar weight in his hand, then tosses it away into a snowdrift; and the snow around him, he sees, is red, bright red, a vivid, beautiful red, the color of fire, the color of a sunrise over the eastern sea. Other men appear then, and help Alexander up, and take Nikolai away, and Alexander comes with them, his head is humming, he too must be checked out, he can ride with the stretcher, they tell him. The ambulance is waiting on the corner, and as he limps toward it, he remembers something, and feels the back pocket of his pants. It is as he expected.

When they drive along the familiar street, he looks out through a small, dim window in the back door.

The kiosk is boarded shut, the pavement empty.

PART SIX

CHRISTMAS

1

ONCE ANNA HAD GONE TO BED, Sergei paced the unlit hallway, up and down, up and down, lying in wait for Sasha's return, determined to speak with him about the ticket. When his vigil
began to tire him, he went to the boy's room, switched on the bleak
overhead light. A clock on the desk shifted shadowy hands over an
indiscernible face; he had to bend closely to read it. It was just past
two; Sasha was running later than usual. He waited a little longer,
then turned off the lamp, lowered himself heavily onto his son's bed,
and closed his eyes briefly, opening them minutes later to a stretched
sheet of graying light—a window, he realized in another moment,
a predawn window in his son's room, to which his son still had not
returned.

He rose. His back was sore. Crows were rending the air apart with
hoarse cries. The clock, brighter now, as if time during the day were
different in color from time at night, announced seven-thirty in the
morning. He looked at it in consternation, with an undercurrent of
worry, then sat in the chair, drummed his fingers against the edge of
the desk. A thin stack of pages was lying on its surface, covered with
Sasha's sloppy handwriting—some lecture notes, no doubt, he
thought absently as he let his eyes drift over the words.

People will remember you, of course, because you've attained immor-
tality. It must feel strange, knowing you will live forever. For myself,
I don't care about being remembered as much as I care about my own
memories. My biggest fear is living to be my parents' age and discov-
ering that I have none.

Startled, Sergei hesitated for a moment, then flipped to the
beginning, read the opening lines.

Igor Fyodorovich, you may think I'm a regular concertgoer come to
admire your music. I am not. I don't know anything about music.

His hands unsteady now, he riffled through the stack, a sentence
here, a paragraph there, then shoved the pages away, and for a long,
long time sat staring into space, at the city rising from the murkiness
outside the window like a photograph in the process of being devel-
oped, morning lifting it by its corner with a pair of gigantic pin-
cers, shaking the shadows off. And as the light slowly ripened in the
sky, there welled inside him a tightness, a knot, and he thought, here,
in this city, which he once, not long ago, believed so entirely devoid
of surprises, on the city's dim outskirts, where centuries before
wolves had roamed through snowed-in villages and where now grim
apartment buildings grew along meandering, ill-lit streets, in an
apartment in one of these buildings, in the three rooms of the apartment, three people lived alongside him, had lived alongside him for
decades—his wife, his son, and his mother-in-law, whom he once,
not long ago, believed he knew so well he was bored by them—and
yet he now felt a terrible, heartbreaking certainty that he had somehow missed them completely, overlooked something vital about
them, and by doing so, wasted years of possible happiness.

The slamming of the front door, when it sounded at last, untied
the knot at once, and he wept, a silent, dry, relieved weeping. He
heard Alexander's shoes drop onto the floor, heard Anna's voice

clucking along the corridor; she had probably been up most of the night herself, listening to every noise, waiting.

He ran his hand over his face; it was not wet. He walked out of the room.

Alexander stood without moving on the doormat.

An unfamiliar youth briefly met his eyes in the mirror—a jacket with its pockets torn out, a crumpled face, black in places, with a thick bandage on the bridge of his nose and an ugly cut clotted on his left cheek, and something dark, something vast, in his gaze . . . Alexander turned away hastily, facing his parents instead, his father in a wrinkled shirt and a pair of pants that he appeared to have slept in, his mother, whose eyelids were swollen with recent fear. He heard her gasp as she came closer. He cleared his throat.

"The tickets went on sale last night," he said.

Another door thrust into the hallway, and he was blinded by the solid rectangle of sunlight that fell crashing onto the floor. It was, he realized, a bright morning outside; he had not noticed.

"Oh, my dear," his grandmother said, "what . . ."

Her words wandered off into silence.

"The tickets went on sale last night," he repeated.

He was not sure how to say the rest.

His mother began to speak then, quickly, quickly; he was reminded of the woman in Viktor Pyetrovich's apartment, the one with the eyes like dark holes torn by someone's thumb in the white sheet of her face, and his thoughts swam anxiously, and only after some minutes did he realize what his mother was saying in her rushed, panicked voice. The ticket is yours, Sashenka, do you hear, we've all decided, it's the best thing, you deserve it after all the time you've spent helping us, your grandmother no longer wants to go, and your father and I, we talked it over and we thought, such a unique event, you'll tell your grandchildren someday—

He filled his lungs with air, then let it out.

"I lost our place," he said.

All was still. He could see minute particles of dust swarming in the rectangle of light, obeying some radiant, airborne laws, shimmering constellations forming and dissolving, small and orderly planetary systems floating around brighter suns of larger dust motes, then dancing away along invisible orbits of their own; and he thought, None of this matters, everything is pointless and random. Then, abruptly, the light dimmed—the sun must have been swallowed by a cloud—and as the dust vanished, there emerged once again the shadowy hallway, and the mirror, and in it, the youth with something new, something pained, in his eyes, in his broken face; and Alexander knew that it was not true, that things mattered to him quite a bit after all. He looked at his family crowding in the corridor around him, found all three of them looking back at him—and, since the silence continued, realized he must have only imagined saying the words aloud, and tried again.

"I lost our place in the line," he said.

Their suspended expressions did not change. They must have heard him already.

"What happened to you, Sasha?" his mother asked.

"Someone was sick, I had to get him home, that's when the tickets—"

"No, what happened to *you*?"

"Oh, that. I was mugged on the way back. They took me to a clinic. I'm all right, honest. My nose may look a bit different." He added after a short pause, "Sorry about the ticket."

She breathed out audibly, then stepped toward him, as if finally granted permission; in the brown gold of the mirror's depths, he glimpsed her—made somehow unfamiliar, younger and brighter, by worry—touch a hesitant hand to the bruised cheek of that unfamiliar, older and darker, youth.

His father moved forward too, bent to extract his shoes from behind an umbrella stand. "I think," he said, crouching to untie the shoelaces, "I'll go over to the kiosk, just to check."

The hallway flashed and vanished in a dusty haze; the sun had come out again.

"Let's all go," said his grandmother briskly. "I daresay I could use a walk."

Some minutes later, they squeezed into the elevator—bulky coats, scarves, elbows, smells of winter soaked into collars and shoes, along with some light, flowery scent Alexander found surprising. The elevator groaned with the unaccustomed weight, dipped, then stalled for an instant between floors. His mother laughed unexpectedly. "Do you realize," she said, "this is the first time in something like a year, since we began with the line, I mean, that all four of us have been together . . . Imagine getting stuck right now."

They landed with a heavy thud. She laughed again.

Outside, the pavements were slippery, searingly white in the sun; his grandmother held on to his elbow with a hand as small and hard as a bird's claw. The old woman was wearing a peculiar little hat with a moth-eaten feather bobbing in its velvet band, and a pair of funny sharp-edged boots with pencil-thin heels; the feather tickled his chin. It baffled him that no one seemed concerned about the ticket; indeed, his mother appeared almost giddy now, and his father's eyes ran away from his own with a limping, oddly apologetic gait. When his parents walked on ahead talking, he felt a strange certainty that they were not discussing the concert.

He glanced at his grandmother, coughed uneasily.

"About your earrings," he said. "I sold them, for lots of money, but the money was in my pocket, and those men—I guess it was a bad night all around, I'm really, really—"

"What did you get for them, anyway?" she interrupted. "Ah. Well. You've been had twice, my dear, they're worth ten times that.

A pity. I have to say, our nighttime streets are in a shocking state. But perhaps it's for the best—easy come, easy go . . . Is the snow always this color? I remember it differently. And what, pray, did they do to that church?"

There were more people in the street now, groups of them hastening in the same direction, some silent, others burbling with agitation. Alexander saw familiar faces from the line, and found himself walking faster. A block away, the crowd grew denser still, spilling off the sidewalks into the road; an automobile was fuming on a corner, unable to squeeze through, its driver vainly leaning on the horn. As they circumvented the heaving car, he thought he spotted a dark-haired boy weaving through the throng on the other side of the street, and pulled on his father's sleeve. "Go ahead without me," he said. "I'll catch up."

The boy was crossing the street now, trudging toward him; Alexander had already seen a stack of books in his hands.

"Aren't you cold without a hat?" he called out.

"No," the boy said, stopping. "Maybe. I don't know. I've been looking for you all morning. I brought you these, I know you liked them."

"So then, which hospital is Viktor Pyetrovich in?" Alexander asked, hurriedly, loudly, as he freed the books from the boy's hands. "Is he allowed visitors today? I'll come by later, I have something to tell him, he shouldn't worry, everything will be fine, maybe the tickets haven't sold out yet, and, see, I have my own ticket now, which I don't need, I'm not really into music all that much, so your grandpa can have it, he can go to the concert, do you understand"—but as he talked, the boy stood quite still, and, looking at his painfully reddened ears, at his coat buttoned wrong, at the boy's eyes that appeared almost white in the glaring sun, sliding past his bruises and cuts without expression, Alexander felt himself letting go of his bright words, one after another, little exhalations of sounds leaking out, until he was silent at last.

"Grandfather had another heart attack last night," the boy said. "In the stairwell on the way to the hospital. Our elevator's broken. He died just before dawn."

"I—I didn't know," Alexander said. But of course he knew, had known from the moment he had seen the boy walking unsteadily through the crowd with the precious volumes clutched in his bare hands, their spines crumbling with gilded leathery dust over his numbed fingers. He knew too that he should drop the books, and put his hands on the child's shoulders, and tell him what he himself so wanted to believe, that Viktor Pyetrovich had left a sad, colorless place and gone to a place full of color, full of wonder, where he had only to arrest the world in its motley rotation by a finger planted on the convexity of a globe to be instantly transported to wherever his heart desired—ancient streets braiding hills into high-walled, fruit-scented towns, narrow boats gliding under white misty bridges, the shrill crying of peacocks in secret gardens at sunrise, chilled stars over desert temples, fierce, bright-eyed beasts prowling through vine-entwined jungles—all the places, all the things, all the adventures that did not exist here, in this life, in this place . . . But the boy's gaze was clear and old, and the terrible, white, sunny silence continued, and people pushed past them, swearing, slipping on ice, and the automobile driver kept blaring his horn—and suddenly Alexander was unsure whether that would have been the afterlife Viktor Pyetrovich would have chosen—whether he would not have preferred to sit in his small kitchen instead, with his wife, who must have died long before, with his son, returned safe and well, with his grandson, his many grandchildren who could have been born and were not, drinking tea from their familial silver glass holders, talking about the apple harvest, the rain last night, the symphony of their famous relative on the radio, and the mirage of the heavenly city would sway beyond the curtains, its rooflines soft and peaceful, woven out of clouds, and they would have all the time in the world, the whole of eternity, his, theirs, always—

"I never asked, what's your name?" he said.

"Igor," said the boy. "And you're Alexander. Grandfather talked about you all the time."

The world rushed past them, dazzling and cold.

"Good-bye," the boy said, still without moving.

"I'll see you around," said Alexander, and, wrapping the books in the fold of his jacket, let the stream of passersby carry him off.

At the kiosk, all was confusion. People were wandering around in hesitating little herds; a man was spitting out curses; a well-dressed woman sobbed, gathering her dissolved face into an elegant glove. Alexander found his family.

"So, it seems," his father said flatly, "the tickets that went on sale last night weren't the Selinsky tickets at all. They were for the Little Fir Trees show. Their kiosk burned down or something, I guess . . . And the Selinsky concert has been canceled. No tickets. Look, even the sign's gone."

Indeed, the CONCERT TICKETS sign, which for months had been baked by sun and washed by rain, was no longer nailed to the front of the kiosk. A new notice was posted in the window. A grim, mute crowd had gathered before it. Alexander came closer.

CONCERT CANCELED, read the fat block letters. KIOSK CLOSED FOR RESTOCKING. WILL REOPEN ON MONDAY.

It was astonishing how deeply he felt about so many things— unfamiliar, slow, wordless feelings that made him heavy and aching and full, almost as if he sensed, for the first time in his life, the presence of something real inside him, a soul perhaps—and yet how little he felt about this ticket, this ticket that no one he loved appeared to need after all.

Shoulder to shoulder with the others, Alexander stood and looked at the sign in the shuttered window.

꧑

By mid-morning, the day had turned brittle; clouds sliced through the pale sky like shards of ice, leaving white tears in the blue, and the waving black branches of naked trees swept the sky clean. Anna had taken her mother along on a shopping errand; Sergei and Alexander walked toward home together. They took their time, rambling aimlessly through the streets, pausing to dig out an icy bench from under a snowdrift, revealing in the process a few sparkling slashes of graffiti ("Oh, look," Sergei said, "you have a namesake who likes to vandalize benches"), then sitting in the park until their faces grew numb and their fingers cold and stiff.

The park was deserted, but filled with the frozen breaths of recent passersby, filled too with the transparent gliding of its resident ghosts—an old man feeding pigeons, his spectacles blazing in the sun; a beautiful woman, no longer young, her face smeared with tears, peeling off her torn stockings; a man huddled over a mute tuba, listening to the music soaring in his head; a boy lying on his back in the sickly grass, staring up at the sky, imagining ships and caravans gliding across it . . . Sergei and Alexander were silent at first, then, slowly, began to talk—of light, irrelevant matters, it seemed; Alexander was explaining how much he liked winter because he never had to guess what any of the colors were. Gradually, though, they talked of other things; or did not talk so much as allude to them, passing them by quickly, as if having tacitly agreed that there would be time, time enough to discuss everything later, that the only thing needed now was a silent, forgiving acknowledgment of a few facts—such as the fact that Alexander had never tried for the university after all, or that one of his two best friends had died the night before and the other had been so badly wounded he might not recover, or that both his father and his mother had been fired months earlier—or that all of them had not been entirely honest when it came to the concert ticket.

And as they talked, Sergei nodded gravely, breathing on his fingers, and thought that they had arrived at the end of this strange, long year with seemingly nothing to show for it, with, if anything, things lost, things both tangible and intangible—money, jobs, friends, unrealized loves, alternative futures closed off forever—and yet he felt his world to be so much larger now, and, too, felt so much larger himself, as though in the course of this year of hoping, of waiting, this year of doing nothing, he had, without noticing, stepped across an invisible line and been taken apart, piece by piece, then put together again; but the order of the pieces was subtly different, or else they fit together in a different, looser way, with spaces left between them for air, or light, or music, or perhaps something else altogether, something ineffable that made him feel more alive.

When, an hour or two later, they entered the apartment, they found the women already home. The kitchen was full of smoke and banging; their frozen faces began to sting in the heat.

"What's all the commotion?" Sergei asked.

"Oh, Mama has remembered some old recipes," Anna said, dashing from the stove to the table. "I thought I'd try them out."

"No chestnuts, though," the old woman said wistfully.

"Chestnuts, grandmother?"

"It's a long story, my dear. I'll tell you tonight if you like."

On the table were pots and pans and a tub of flour and a sack of dried fruits of an unfamiliar kind and something wrapped in foil and a pair of candlesticks Sergei had not seen before; and as he stood gazing at all the abundance, he felt an odd, sweet, powdery tingling in his nose, at the roof of his mouth. "When I was a child," he said, "my mother used to put up these big glass ornaments around the house during the holiday season. There were some red ones, I think, and also blue ones. They reflected candlelight beautifully."

"Well, maybe we too could get some," Anna said. "Now, could

everyone please leave, I need the space. Oh, and Serezha, bring over the radio, would you?"

After she was left alone, she stood still for a long minute, inhaling the delightful scent of cinnamon. It was a bit like sliding down a hill on a sled, which she suddenly remembered doing as a little girl—faster, faster, a marvelous sensation of freedom ripping through her hair, through her chest, the snow winking in the air like tiny crystals of pure light. The radio announcer crisply informed the city that it was now two o'clock in the afternoon; then music began to play. At once aware of the time—Two already, and I have so much to do—Anna flew about the kitchen, mixing, and stirring, and sifting, and the music burbled along, quiet and light as a stream, until she found herself listening, singing a little under her breath as she worked.

2

HE ENTERED THE CITY in the first-class compartment of a luxury train. He liked the smooth efficiency of trains—the compact sparkle of the built-in ashtrays, the even processions of lamps along the ceilings, the soft window shades that kept out the light and the noise, allowing him to fall asleep among dismal eastern plains with bumps of graying villages and stretches of forbidding forests and wake up on a distant horizon dotted with pretty castles on gentle hills, soon to be ushered to a front-row seat in a smoothly choreographed dance of dignified train conductors and baggage handlers with round golden buttons on their starched uniforms, and limousine drivers vying with one another for the honor of delivering him to his hotel—all the easy trappings of civilization, which fit him like a well-tailored tuxedo and which he had rather missed during his year in that barbaric, if curious, country.

His wife would already be waiting for him at their suite. They had agreed to rendezvous in the city of their not-so-distant honeymoon for a pleasant holiday spell. It was drizzling when he arrived. From the limousine window he watched the elaborate shop displays splash onto the wet pavements of the boulevards with shimmering red and golden spills of light, the ornaments of the Christmas season, just over, still arranged in glittering symmetrical designs behind glass—pyramids and roses and garlands made of gilded fir cones and lacquered toy beasts and pink angels whose white wings were lavishly sprinkled with fake sugar.

These trite symbols of a happy childhood bored him.

A fine jeweler's window attracted his waning attention, and, remembering, he asked his chauffeur to stop for a minute. Inside, he produced from his inner pocket the cheap red matchbox, which he had kept as a souvenir in its own right, a reminder of his fascinating little sojourn in the illicit bowels of that other city, kindly arranged by a local acquaintance who supplied the embassy with musicians. He watched in wry amusement the hesitating eyebrows of the jeweler, then pushed the matchbox open.

The jeweler's face altered, his eyebrows returned to their places. "Ah," he breathed, "magnificent, magnificent! And unmistakable, of course, but let me just check to make sure . . . Ah yes, here it is, the master's trademark, see this filigree detail, he alone in this city could—"

"They are from here, then?" he said, surprised and a little disappointed. "I was led to believe they were of Eastern provenance."

"Oh no, monsieur, they were made here, no doubt about it. If you like, you could visit the place itself, it's very near. Of course, he passed away two decades ago—a whole generation of secrets and skills vanished, a real tragedy! His son runs the business now."

"Thank you," he said, closing the matchbox.

He gave the new address to the chauffeur. The second shop was even more splendid than the first. A respectful clerk asked him to wait and disappeared into the opulent velvet depths, emerging a moment later with the elderly proprietor. The man allowed himself a few well-contained raptures. "Ah yes, I remember these well, he made only seven pairs," he gushed softly. "See the hint of the lyre shape, so unique, so enchanting? Where did you happen upon these, monsieur, if I may be so bold as to . . . Oh, is that so? How interesting. Yes, I daresay my father's creations were always popular among their nobility. In fact, one of these pairs was sold to a celebrated composer from over there—Igor Selinsky, one of my father's most loyal customers, you've heard of him, perhaps—"

"Indeed," he said politely.

He declined an offer to take a look around the shop, thanked the proprietor, and left. Back in the shadows of the limousine, he mused about the mysterious paths traveled by objects and men, the invisible threads linking lives over and over. He knew, of course, that the earrings could not have been the Selinsky pair—some destitute countess's most likely, as that fool of a boy had told him—but the tentative connection struck him all the same. Stretched out on the plush backseat, absently watching the brightly lit boulevards give way to the soft, exclusive darkness of quieter streets in the fashionable embassy district, he thought about the Selinsky performance he had attended many decades ago, and the odd, tearful, raw feeling that would not release him for some time after, as if he, an established young diplomat with brilliant prospects ahead of him, had gotten something wrong, had missed something important—

Even now, the recollection struck him as uncomfortable, and ever so slightly he prodded his thoughts along. In the smoothly gliding glow of the holiday illumination, he imagined his third wife, younger by twenty-three years, shrieking with excitement as she turned her head this way and that, gazing at her dazzling reflection in the mirror. He imagined telling her that the earrings were two, no, three hundred years old, estate jewels held by the illustrious Selinsky family for many generations and worn in turn by both wives of the genius—or no, better yet, by some dark and secret passion of his life—and smiled at last, and asked the chauffeur to hurry.

Afterward, they would go out to a nice dinner, of course.

He had not had any decent champagne in a while.

PART SEVEN

NEW YEAR

W ELL, AND THERE YOU HAVE IT: a year wasted. Might as well not have lived through it at all. By the way, did you hear why he isn't coming?"

"Afraid of being arrested, someone told me. Word is he was— come closer, come closer—he was at the head of a plot to overthrow the government. Funded by the West, you understand. But the authorities got wind of it, and canceled the concert."

"Nonsense, I heard he caught a cold on the border. The cold became pneumonia, so he had to go back. They say he took one breath of his native air and cried like a child."

"Of course he cried, ours is a mystical land, one feels a special, soulful purity here—no other place like it, saints still walk among us . . . He probably kissed the ground, too—"

"Oh, stop with that sentimental tripe already! The truth is, our Ministry of Culture didn't offer him enough money. Couldn't match his fees, you know, so he weaseled out of it at the last minute. I hear his new lady friend is quite young."

"He doesn't have a lady friend. I have a friend who has it from a reliable source that he has given up music entirely and is busy writing his memoirs now."

"None of that is true. There was never going to *be* any concert. The authorities just used the line to weed out the undesirable elements. A friend of mine has a sister who read in a foreign book that seven or eight years ago Selinsky—"

"Wait a moment, wait a moment, I don't understand . . . If all of you are so sure there won't be a concert, what are you still doing here, waiting in this line? What's this line for?"

"Oh, there's a rumor going around about a retrospective of Filatov's paintings, strictly ticketed access, so I thought, Might as well wait a bit, see what happens, maybe they'll sell the tickets here."

"Filatov, Filatov—yes, I remember, aren't his works banned?"

"Sure they are. Times are changing, though."

"Who told you about him?"

"That woman over there, see?"

"And who told her?"

"Some bearded old fellow in a funny coat. She said he seemed to know what he was talking about."

"But what does Nadezhda Alekseyevna say?"

"Oh, she's no use, you know how she is, she says the same thing no matter what you ask her: 'Will arrive soon, delivery pending, check back tomorrow.' Like a parrot."

"Now, don't be unfair, she's had a hard life, our Nadenka, four children to take care of, and no husband, and running a kiosk is not easy . . . Well, I suppose I could spare a bit of time. Who's last in line?"

They were quiet after that; it was too cold to talk. Many left. At midnight, the fifteen or twenty people who remained waiting before the kiosk, just in case, were surprised to hear a ringing of bells in the abandoned church at the other end of the street, the rising sound playing up and down the transparent silver keyboards of the sonorous skies. When the bells fell silent, the remaining men and women checked their watches, turned down the flaps of their hats, turned up their collars, and went off their separate ways, along darkened alleys, across snow-covered courtyards, calling out to one another: "Happy New Year!" and "See you tomorrow!"

HISTORICAL NOTE

IN 1962, the celebrated Russian composer Igor Fyodorovich Stravinsky accepted a Soviet invitation to visit his former country—his first trip to his native land after half a century of absence. He was eighty years old. A historic concert, with Stravinsky himself conducting, was given at the Great Hall of the Philharmonia in Leningrad. The line for tickets began a year before the performance and evolved into a unique and complex social system, with people working together and taking turns standing in line. After a year of waiting, an eighty-four-year-old cousin of Stravinsky was unable to attend, as the tickets had sold out; her number in the line was 5,001.

Although *The Concert Ticket* is set in a fictionalized version of Soviet Russia, its central premise is inspired by this historical episode. Likewise, while the characters in the book are invented, there are certain parallels with actual persons and events. Most notably, Maya's ballet world in the Western "city of light" is loosely based on the famous Ballets Russes, a company that was a sensation in Paris in the years before the Revolution and that included the incomparable Vaslav Nijinsky (once described as "the little devil [who] never comes down with the music") and the beautiful Tamara

Karsavina. Among the company's most groundbreaking productions were ballets written by the then unknown Stravinsky, including *The Firebird* (*L'oiseau de feu*, 1910), *Petrushka* (1911), and *The Rite of Spring* (*Le sacre du printemps*, 1913).

Finally, a word about chronology. The year in which the novel takes place is identified as the thirty-seventh anniversary of the "Change," which, of course, mirrors the October Revolution of 1917. This is not, however, intended to imply a temporal setting of 1954. Rather, I have borrowed freely from three different periods of Soviet history: the repression of Stalin's 1930s, the hopefulness of Khrushchev's Thaw (late 1950s–early 1960s), and the stagnation of Brezhnev's 1970s.

The verse about the cuckoo is taken from a 1911 poem by Anna Akhmatova, "I live like a cuckoo in a clock"; the translation is my own.

ACKNOWLEDGMENTS

I WOULD LIKE TO OFFER my thanks to Kate Davis, Lance Fitzgerald, Leigh Butler, and everyone else at the Penguin Group who worked to make this book a reality; my copy editor, Anna Jardine, for her unerring eye; and my wonderful UK editor, Mary Mount, for her astute reading. As ever, I am deeply grateful to Warren Frazier, my agent, for so many things, not least of them honesty, and Marian Wood, my publisher and editor, for her perfect understanding and her friendship. Finally, I would like to thank my family—my brother, Aleksei Kartsev, and my mother, Natalia Kartseva, for always being there during the saddest time in my life, and my husband, Michael Klyce, my first reader and greatest help. Most of all, I want to thank my father, Boris Grushin. Thank you, papa, for everything.

He just wanted a decent book to read ...

Not too much to ask, is it? It was in 1935 when Allen Lane, Managing Director of Bodley Head Publishers, stood on a platform at Exeter railway station looking for something good to read on his journey back to London. His choice was limited to popular magazines and poor-quality paperbacks – the same choice faced every day by the vast majority of readers, few of whom could afford hardbacks. Lane's disappointment and subsequent anger at the range of books generally available led him to found a company – and change the world.

'We believed in the existence in this country of a vast reading public for intelligent books at a low price, and staked everything on it'
Sir Allen Lane, 1902–1970, founder of Penguin Books

The quality paperback had arrived – and not just in bookshops. Lane was adamant that his Penguins should appear in chain stores and tobacconists, and should cost no more than a packet of cigarettes.

Reading habits (and cigarette prices) have changed since 1935, but Penguin still believes in publishing the best books for everybody to enjoy. We still believe that good design costs no more than bad design, and we still believe that quality books published passionately and responsibly make the world a better place.

So wherever you see the little bird – whether it's on a piece of prize-winning literary fiction or a celebrity autobiography, political tour de force or historical masterpiece, a serial-killer thriller, reference book, world classic or a piece of pure escapism – you can bet that it represents the very best that the genre has to offer.

Whatever you like to read – trust Penguin.